DEATH AT THE DOLPHIN

Dame Ngaio Marsh, one of the world's most popular detective novelists, has written twenty-two of her classical whodunnits since she published *A Man Lay Dead* in 1934.

Now in her seventies, she is New Zealand born and bred. Her first name (pronounced 'Nye-oh') is a Maori word which can mean a tree, a bug that lives on it, a light on the water – or simply 'clever'.

Many of her stories have theatrical settings, for Ngaio Marsh's real passion is Shakespeare. Almost single-handedly she revived the New Zealand public's interest in live theatre, and it was for this work that she received what she calls her 'damery' in 1966.

Her most recent detective story is *Black as He's Painted.*

Available in Fontana by the same author

NGAIO MARSH

Death at the Dolphin

FONTANA / Collins

First published in 1967 by William Collins Sons & Co Ltd
First issued in Fontana Books 1969
Fifth Impression December 1976

© Ngaio Marsh Ltd., 1967

Made and printed in Great Britain by
William Collins Sons & Co Ltd Glasgow

For Edmund Cork
in gratitude and with affection

CONTENTS

CAST OF CHARACTERS

A clerk
PEREGRINE JAY, *Playwright and Theatre Director*
HENRY JOBBINS, *Caretaker*
MR. VASSILY CONDUCIS
His Chauffeur
MAWSON, *His manservant*
JEREMY JONES, *Designer*
MR. GREENSLADE, *Solicitor to Mr. Conducis*
An Expert on Historic Costume
WINTER MORRIS, *Manager, Dolphin Theatre*
MARCUS KNIGHT —*'Shakespeare' in Peregrine's play*
DESTINY MEADE —*'The Dark Lady' in Peregrine's play*
W. HARTLY GROVE —*'The Rival' in Peregrine's play*
GERTRUDE BRACEY —*'Ann Hathaway' in Peregrine's play*
EMILY DUNNE —*'Joan Hart' in Peregrine's play*
CHARLES RANDOM —*'Dr. Hall' in Peregrine's play*
TREVOR VERE —*'Hamnet' in Peregrine's play*
MRS. BLEWITT, *Trevor's mother*
HAWKINS, *A Security Officer*
A Police Sergeant
DIVISIONAL-SUPERINTENDENT GIBSON
P. C. GRANTLEY
A Divisional Surgeon
SUPERINTENDENT RODERICK ALLEYN, C.I.D.
INSPECTOR FOX, C.I.D.
DETECTIVE SERGEANT THOMPSON, C.I.D.
DETECTIVE SERGEANT BAILEY, C.I.D.
MRS. GUZMAN, *An American millionairess*

1. MR. CONDUCIS

'Dolphin?' the clerk repeated. 'Dolphin. Well, yerse. We hold the keys. Were you wanting to view?'

'If I might, I was.' Peregrine Jay mumbled, wondering why such conversations should always be conducted in the past tense. 'I mean,' he added boldly, 'I did and I still do. I want to view, if you please.'

The clerk made a little face that might have been a sneer or an occupational tic He glanced at Peregrine, who supposed his appearance was not glossy enough to make him a likely prospect.

'It *is* for sale, I believe?' Peregrine said.

'Oh, it's for *sale*, all right.' The clerk agreed contemptuously. He re-examined some document that he had on his desk.

'May I view?'

'*Now?*'

'If it's possible.'

'Well—I don't know, really, if we've anybody free at the moment,' said the clerk and frowned at the rain streaming dirtily down the windows of his office.

Peregrine said, 'Look. The Dolphin is an old theatre. I am a man of the theatre. Here is my card. If you care to telephone my agents or the management of my current production at The Unicorn they will tell you that I am honest, sober and industrious, a bloody good director and playwright and possessed of whatever further attributes may move you to lend me the keys of The Dolphin for an hour. I would like,' he said, 'to view it.'

The clerk's face became inscrutable. 'Oh, quite,' he muttered and edged Peregrine's card across his desk, looking sideways at it as if it might scuttle. He retired within himself and seemed to arrive at a guarded conclusion.

'Yerse. Well, O.K., Mr. er. It's not usually done but we try to oblige.' He turned to a dirty-white board where keys hung like black tufts on a piece of disreputable ermine.

'Dolphin,' said the clerk, 'Aeo, yerse. Here we are.' He unhooked a bunch of keys and pushed them across the desk. 'You may find them a bit hard to turn,' he said. 'We don't keep *on* oiling the locks. There aren't all that many inquiries.' He made what seemed to be a kind of joke. 'It's quite a time since the blitz,' he said.

'Quarter of a century,' said Peregrine, taking the keys.

'That's right. What a spectacle! I was a kid. Know your way I suppose, Mr.—er—Jay?'

'Thank you, yes.'

'Thank *you*, sir,' said the clerk suddenly plumping for deference, but establishing at the same time his utter disbelief in Peregrine as a client. 'Terrible weather. You *will* return the keys?'

'Indubitably,' said Peregrine, aping, he knew not why, Mr. Robertson Hare.

He had got as far as the door when the clerk said: 'Oh, be-the-way, Mr.—er—Jay. You *will* watch how you go. Underfoot. On stage particularly. There was considerable damage.'

'Thank you. I'll be careful.'

'The hole *was* covered over but that was some time ago. Like a well,' the clerk added, worrying his first finger. 'Something of the sort. Just watch it.'

'I will.'

'I—er—I don't answer for what you'll find,' the clerk said. 'Tramps get in, you know. They *will* do it. One died a year or so back.'

'Oh.'

'Not that it's likely to happen twice.'

'I hope not.'

'Well, *we* couldn't help it,' the clerk said crossly. 'I don't know how they effect an entrance, really. Broken window or something. You can't be expected to attend to everything.'

'No,' Peregrine agreed and let himself out.

Rain drove up Wharfingers Lane in a slanting wall. It shot off the pavement, pattering against doors and windows and hit

Peregrine's umbrella so hard that he thought it would split. He lowered it in front of him and below its scalloped and beaded margin saw, as if at rise of curtain in a cinema, the Thames, rain-pocked and choppy on its ebb-tide.

There were not a great many people about. Vans passed him grinding uphill in low gear. The buildings were ambiguous: warehouses? Wharfingers offices? Farther down he saw the blue lamp of a River Police Station. He passed a doorway with a neat legend: 'Port of London Authority' and another with old-fashioned lettering 'Camperdown and Carboys Rivercraft Company. Demurrage. Wharfage. Inquiries.'

The lane turned sharply to the left; it now ran parallel with the river. He lifted his umbrella. Up it went, like a curtain, on The Dolphin. At that moment, abruptly, there was no more rain.

There was even sunshine. It washed thinly across the stage-house of The Dolphin and picked it out for Peregrine's avid attention. There it stood: high, square and unbecoming, the object of his greed and deep desire. Intervening buildings hid the rest of the theatre except for the wrought-iron ornament at the top of a tower. He hurried on until, on his left, he came to a pub called The Wharfinger's Friend and then the bomb-site and then, fully displayed, the wounded Dolphin itself.

On a fine day, Peregrine thought, a hundred years ago, watermen and bargees, ship's chandlers, business gents, deep-water sailors from foreign parts and riverside riff-raff looked up and saw The Dolphin. They saw its flag snapping and admired its caryatids touched up on the ringlets and nipples with tasteful gilt. Mr. Adolphus Ruby, your very own Mr. Ruby, stood here in Wharfingers Lane with his thumbs in his arm-holes, his cigar at one angle and his hat at the other and feasted his pop eyes on his very own palace of refined and original entertainment. 'Oh, Oh!' thought Peregrine, 'and here I stand but not, alas, in Mr. Ruby's lacquered high-lows. And the caryatids have the emptiest look in their blank eyes for me.'

They were still there, though, two on each side of the portico. They finished at their waists, petering out with grimy discretion in pastrycook's scrolls. They supported with their sooty heads and arms a lovely wrought-iron balcony and although there

were occasional gaps in their plaster foliations they were still
in pretty good trim. Peregrine's doting fancy cleaned the soot
from upper surfaces. It restored, too, the elegant sign: supported above the portico by two prancing cetaceous mammals,
and regilded its lettering: 'The Dolphin Theatre.'

For a minute or two he looked at it from the far side of the
lane. The sun shone brightly now. River, shipping and wet
roofs reflected it and the cobblestones in front of the theatre
began to send up a thin vapour. A sweep of seagulls broke into
atmospheric background noises and a barge honked.

Peregrine crossed the wet little street and entered the portico.

It was stuck over with old bills including the agents' notice
which had evidently been there for a very long time and was
torn and discoloured. 'This Valuable Commercial Site' it said.

'In that case,' Peregrine wondered, 'why hasn't it been sold?
Why had no forward-looking commercial enterprise snapped
up the Valuable Site and sent The Dolphin Theatre crashing
about its own ears?'

There were other moribund bills. 'Sensational!' one of them
proclaimed but the remainder was gone and it was anybody's
guess what sensation it had once recommended. 'Go home——'
was chalked across one of the doors but somebody had rubbed
out the rest of the legend and substituted graffiti of a more or
less predictable kind. It was all very dismal.

But as Peregrine approached the doors he found, on the
frontage itself high up and well protected, the tatter of a playbill. It was the kind of thing that patrons of the Players
Theatre cherish and Kensington Art shops turn into lamp-
shades.

THE BEGGAR GIRL'S WEDDING
In response to
Overwhelming Solicitation!!——
Mr. Adolphus Ruby
presents
A Return Performa——

The rest was gone.

When, Peregrine speculated, could this overwhelming solici-

tation have moved Mr Ruby? In the eighties? He knew that
Mr. Ruby had lived to within ten years of the turn of the
century and in his heyday had bought, altered, restored and em-
bellished The Dolphin, adding his plaster and jute caryatids,
his swags, his supporting marine mammals and cornucopia, his
touches of gilt and lollypink to the older and more modest
elegance of wrought iron and unmolested surfaces. When did
he make all these changes? Did he, upon his decline, sell The
Dolphin and, if so, to whom? It was reputed to have been in
use at the outbreak of the Second World War as a rag-dealer's
storehouse.

Who was the ground landlord now?

He confronted the main entrance and its great mortice lock
for which he had no trouble in selecting the appropriate key.
It was big enough to have hung at the girdle of one of Mr.
Ruby's very own stage-gaolers. The key went home and engaged but refused to turn. Why had Peregrine not asked the
clerk to lend him an oil-can? He struggled for some time and
a voice at his back said.

'Got it all on yer own, mate, aincher?'

Peregrine turned to discover a man wearing a peaked cap
like a waterman's and a shiny blue suit. He was a middle-
aged man with a high colour, blue eyes and a look of cheeky
equability.

'You want a touch of the old free-in-one,' he said. He
had a gritty hoarseness in his voice. Peregrine gaped at him.
'Oil, mate. Loobrication,' the man explained.

'Oh. Yes, indeed, I know I do.'

'What's the story, anyway? Casing the joint?'

'I want to look at it,' Peregrine grunted. 'Ah, damn, I'd
better try the stage-door.'

'Let's take a butcher's.'

Peregrine stood back and the man stooped. He tried the
key, delicately at first and then with force. 'Not a hope,' he
wheezed. "Alf a mo'.'

He walked away, crossed the street and disappeared between two low buildings and down a narrow passage-way that
seemed to lead to the river.

'Damnation!' Peregrine thought, 'he's taken the key!'

Two gigantic lorries with canvas-covered loads roared down Wharfingers Lane and past the theatre. The great locked doors shook and rattled and a flake of plaster fell on Peregrine's hand. 'It's dying slowly,' he thought in a panic. 'The Dolphin is being shaken to death.'

When the second lorry had gone by there was the man again with a tin and a feather in one hand and the key in the other. He re-crossed the street and came through the portico.

'I'm very much obliged to you.' Peregrine said.

'No trouble, yer Royal 'Ighness,' said the man. He oiled the lock and after a little manipulation turned the key. 'Kiss yer 'and,' he said. Then he pulled back the knob. The tongue inside the lock shifted with a loud clunk. He pushed the door and it moved a little 'Sweet as a nut,' said the man, and stepped away. 'Well, dooty calls as the bloke said on 'is way to the gallers.'

'Wait a bit—' Peregrine said, 'you must have a drink on me. Here.' He pushed three half-crowns into the man's hand.

'Never say no to that one, Mister. Fanks. Jolly good luck.'

Peregrine longed to open the door but thought the man, who was evidently a curious fellow, might attach himself. He wanted to be alone in The Dolphin.

'Your job's somewhere round about here?' he asked.

'Dahn Carboy Stairs. Phipps Bros. Drugs and that. Jobbins is the name. Caretaker, uster be a lighterman but it done no good to me chubes. Well, so long, sir. Hope you give yerself a treat among them spooks. Best of British luck.'

'Good-bye, and thank you.'

The door opened with a protracted groan and Peregrine entered The Dolphin.

II

The windows were unshuttered and though masked by dirt, let enough light into the foyer for him to see it quite distinctly. It was surprisingly big. Two flights of stairs with the prettiest wrought-iron balustrades curved up into darkness. At the back and deep in shadow, passages led off on either side giving entrance no doubt to boxes and orchestral stalls. The pit entrance must be from somewhere outside.

On Peregrine's right stood a very rococo box-office, introduced, he felt sure, by Mr. Ruby. A brace of consequential plaster putti hovered upside down with fat-faced insouciance above the grille and must have looked in their prime as if they were counting the doorsales. A fibre-plaster bust of Shakespeare on a tortuous pedestal lurked in the shadows. The filthy walls were elegantly panelled and he thought must have originally been painted pink and gilded.

There was nothing between Peregrine and the topmost ceiling. The circle landing, again with a wrought-iron balustrade, reached less than half-way across the well. He stared up into darkness and fancied he could distinguish a chandelier. The stench was frightful : rats, rot, general dirt and, he thought, an unspeakable aftermath of the hobos that the clerk had talked about. But how lovely it must have been in its early Victorian elegance and even with Mr. Ruby's preposterous additions. And how surprisingly undamaged it seemed to be.

He turned to the right-hand flight of stairs and found two notices. 'Dress Circle' and 'To the Paris Bar.' The sign-writer had added pointing hands with frills round their wrists. Upstairs first, or into the stalls? Up.

He passed by grimed and flaking panels, noticing the graceful airiness of plaster ornament that separated them. He trailed a finger on the iron balustrade but withdrew it quickly at the thick touch of occulted dust. Here was the circle foyer. The double flight of stairs actually came out on either side of a balcony landing that projected beyond the main landing and formed the roof of a portico over the lower foyer. Flights of three shallow steps led up from three sides of this 'half-landing' to the top level. The entire structure was supported by very elegant iron pillars.

It was much darker up there and he could only just make out the Paris Bar. The shelves were visible but the counter had gone. A nice piece of mahogany it may have been—something to sell or steal. Carpet lay underfoot in moth-eaten tatters and the remains of curtains hung before the windows. These must be unbroken because the sound of the world outside was so very faint. Boarded up, perhaps. It was extraordinary how quiet it was, how stale, how stifling, how dead.

'*Not a mouse stirring*' he thought and at that moment heard a rapid patter. Something scuttled across his foot. Peregrine was astonished to find himself jolted by a violent shudder. He stamped with both feet and was at once half-stifled by the frightful cloud of dust he raised.

He approached the Paris Bar. A man without a face came out of the shadows and moved towards him.

'Euh!' Peregrine said in his throat. He stopped and so did the man. He could not have told how many heart thuds passed before he saw it was himself.

The bar was backed by a sheet of looking-glass.

Peregrine had recently given up smoking. If he had now had access to a cigarette he would have devoured it. Instead, he whistled and the sound in that muffled place was so lacking in resonance, so dull, that he fell silent and crossed the foyer to the nearest door into the auditorium. There were two, one on each side of the sunken half-landing. He passed into the circle.

The first impression was dramatic. He had forgotten about the bomb damage. A long shaft of sunlight from a gap in the roof of the stagehouse took him by surprise. It produced the effect of a wartime blitz drawing in charcoal and, like a spotlight, found its mark on the empty stage. There, in a pool of mild sunlight stood a broken chair still waiting, Peregrine thought, for one of Mr. Ruby's very own actors. Behind the chair lay a black patch that looked as if a paint pot had been upset on the stage. It took Peregrine a moment or two to realise that this must be the hole the clerk had talked about. It was difficult to see it distinctly through the shaft of light.

Against this one note of brilliance the rest of the house looked black. It was in the classic horseshoe form and must have seated, Peregrine thought, about five hundred. He saw that the chairs had little iron trimmings above their plushy backs and that there were four boxes. A loop of fringe dangled from the top of the proscenium and this was all that could be seen of the curtain.

Peregrine moved round the circle and entered the O.P. box

which stank. He backed out of it, opened a door in the circle wall and found an iron stair leading to the stage.

He climbed down. Even these iron steps were muffled with dust but they gave out a half-choked clang as if he were soft-pedalling them.

Now, he was onstage, as a man of the theatre should be, and at once he felt much easier; exhilarated even, as if some kind of authority had passed to him by right of entry. He peered through the shaft of sunshine which he saw was dense with motes that floated, danced and veered in response to his own movement. He walked into it, stood by the broken chair and faced the auditorium. Quite dazzled and bemused by the strange tricks of light, he saw the front of the house as something insubstantial and could easily people it with Mr. Ruby's patrons. Beavers, bonnets, ulsters, shawls. A flutter of programmes. Rows of pale discs that were faces. 'O, wonderful!' Peregrine thought and in order to embrace it all took a pace backwards.

III

To fall without warning, even by the height of a single step is disturbing. To fall, as he did, now, by his height and the length of his arms into cold, stinking water is monstrous, nightmarish, like a small death. For a moment he only knew that he had been physically insulted. He stared into the shaft of light with its madly jerking molecules, felt wood slip under his gloved fingers and tightened his grip. At the same time he was disgustingly invaded, saturated up to the collarbone in icy stagnant water. He hung at arm's length.

'O God!' Peregrine thought, 'why aren't I a bloody Bond? Why can't I make my bloody arms hitch me up? O God, don't let me drown in this unspeakable muck. O God, let me keep my head.'

Well, of course, he thought, his hands and arms didn't have to support his entire weight. Eleven stone. He was buoyed up by whatever he had fallen into. What? A dressing-room turned into a well for surface water? Better not speculate.

Better explore. He moved his legs and dreadful ambiguous waves lapped up to his chin. He could find nothing firm with his feet. He thought: How long can I hang on like this? And a line of words floated in: 'How long will a man lie i' the earth ere he rot?'

What *should* he do? Perhaps a frog-like upward thing? Try it and at least gain a better finger hold? He tried it: he kicked at the water, pulled and clawed at the stage. For a moment he thought he had gained but his palms slid back, scraping on the edge and sucking at his soaked gloves. He was again suspended. The clerk? If he could hang on, would the clerk send someone to find out why he hadn't returned the keys? When? *When?* Why in God's name had he shaken off the man with the oil can from Phipps Bros.? Jobbins. Suppose he were to yell? Was there indeed a broken window where tramps crept in? He took a deep breath and being thus inflated, rose a little in the water. He yelled.

'Hallo! Hallo! Jobbins!'

His voice was silly and uncannily stifled. Deflated, he sank to his former disgusting level.

He had disturbed more than water when he tried his leap. An anonymous soft object bobbed against his chin. The stench was outrageous. I can't, he thought, I can't stay like this. Already his fingers had grown cold and his arms were racked. Presently—soon—he would no longer feel the edge, he would only feel pain and his fingers would slip away. And what then? Float on his back in this unspeakable water and gradually freeze? He concentrated on his hands, tipping his head back to look up the length of his stretched arms at them. The details of his predicament now declared themselves: the pull on his pectoral muscles, on his biceps and forearms and the terrible strain on his gloved fingers. The creeping obscenity of the water. He hung on for some incalculable age and realised that he was coming to a crisis when his body would no longer be controllable. Something must be done. Now. Another attempt? If there were anything solid to push against. Suppose, after all, his feet were only a few inches from the bottom? But what bottom? The floor of a dressing-room? An understage passage? A boxed-in trap? He stretched his

feet and touched nothing. The water rose to his mouth. He
flexed his legs, kicked, hauled on the edge and bobbed upwards. The auditorium appeared. If he could get his elbows
on the edge. No.

But at the moment when the confusion of circle and stalls
shot up before his eyes, he had heard a sound that he recognised, a protracted groan, and at the penultimate second, he
had seen—what? A splinter of light? And heard? Somebody
cough.

'Hi!' Peregrine shouted. 'Here! Quick! Help!'

He sank and hung again by his fingers. But someone was
coming through the house. Muffled steps on the rags of carpet.

'Here! Come here, will you? On stage.'

The steps halted.

'Look here! I say! Look, for God's sake come up. I've fallen
through the stage. I'll drown. Why don't you answer, whoever
you are?'

The footsteps started again. A door opened nearby. Pass-
door in the prompt side box, he thought. Steps up. Now: cros-
sing the stage. Now.

'Who are you?' Peregrine said. 'Look out. Look out for
the hole. *Look out for my hands. I've got gloves on. Don't
tread on my hands.* Help me out of this. But look out. And say
something.'

He flung his head back and stared into the shaft of light.
Hands covered his hands and then closed about his wrists. At
the same time heavy shoulders and a head wearing a hat came
as a black silhouette between him and the light. He stared into
a face he could not distinguish.

'It doesn't need much,' he chattered. 'If you could just give
me a heave I can do it.'

The head was withdrawn. The hands changed their grip.
At last the man spoke.

'Very well,' said a voice. 'Now.'

He gave his last frog leap, was heaved up, was sprawled
across the edge and had crawled back on the stage to the feet
of the man. He saw beautiful shoes, sharp trouser ends and
the edge of a fine overcoat. He was shivering from head to
foot.

'Thank you,' he said. 'I couldn't be more grateful. My God, how I stink.'

He got to his feet.

The man was, he thought, about sixty years old. Peregrine could see his face now. It was extremely pale. He wore a bowler hat and was impeccably dressed.

'You are Mr. Peregrine Jay, I think,' said the man. His voice was toneless, educated and negative.

'Yes—I—I?'

'The people at the estate agents told me. You should have a bath and change. My car is outside.'

'I can't get into anyone's car in this state. I'm very sorry, sir,' Peregrine said. His teeth were going like castanets. 'You're awfully kind but——'

'Wait a moment. Or no. Come to the front of the theatre.'

In answer to a gesture, Peregrine walked through the pass-door down into the house and was followed. Stagnant water poured off him. It ran out of his gloved finger tips and squelched and spurted in his shoes. They went through a box and along a passage and came into the foyer. 'Please stay here. I shall only be a moment,' said his rescuer.

He went into the portico leaving the door open. Out in Wharfingers Lane Peregrine saw a Daimler with a chauffeur. He began to jump and thrash his arms. Water splashed out of him and clouds of dust settled upon his drenched clothes. The man returned with the chauffeur who carried a fur rug and a heavy mackintosh.

'I suggest you strip and put this on and wrap the rug round you,' the man said. He stretched out his arms as if he were actually thinking of laying hands on Peregrine. He seemed to be suspended between attraction and repulsion. He looked, it struck Peregrine, as if he were making some kind of appeal. 'Let me——' he said.

'But, sir, you can't. I'm disgusting.'

'Please.'

'No, no—really.'

The man walked away. His hands were clasped behind him. Peregrine saw, with a kind of fuddled astonishment, that they were trembling. 'My God!' Peregrine thought, 'this is a morning and a half. I'd better get out of this one pretty smartly but how the hell——'

'Let me give you a hand, sir,' said the chauffeur to Peregrine. 'You're that cold, aren't you?'

'I can manage. If only I could wash.'

'Never mind, sir. That's the idea. Leave them there, sir. I'll attend to them. Better keep your shoes on, hadn't you? The coat'll be a bit of help and the rug's warm. Ready, sir?'

'If I could just have a taxi, I wouldn't be such an infernal nuisance.'

His rescuer turned and looked, not fully at him but at his shoulder. 'I beg you to come,' he said.

Greatly worried by the extravagance of the phrase Peregrine said no more.

The chauffeur went ahead quickly and opened the doors of the car, Peregrine saw that newspaper had been spread over the floor and back seat.

'Please go,' his rescuer said, 'I'll follow.'

Peregrine shambled across the portico and jumped in at the back. The lining of the mackintosh stuck to his body. He hitched the rug around him and tried to clench his chattering jaw.

A boy's voice in the street called 'Hey, Look! Look at that bloke!' The caretaker from Phipps Bros. had appeared at the top of his alley and stared into the car. One or two people stopped and pointed him out to each other.

As his master crossed the portico the chauffeur locked the theatre doors. Holding Peregrine's unspeakable clothes at arm's length he put them in the boot of the car and got into the driver's seat. In another moment they were moving up Wharfingers Lane.

His rescuer did not turn his head or speak. Peregrine waited for a moment or two and then, controlling his voice with some success, said:

'I'm giving you far too much trouble.'

'No.'

'If—if you would be so very kind as to drop me at The Unicorn Theatre I think I could——'

Still without turning his head the man said with extreme

formality, 'I really do beg that you will allow me to—' he stopped for an unaccountably long time and then said loudly 'to rescue you. I mean to take you to my house and set you right. I shall be most upset otherwise. Dreadfully upset.'

Now he turned and Peregrine had never seen an odder look in anyone's face. It was an expression almost, he thought, of despair.

'I am responsible,' said his extraordinary host. 'Unless you allow me to make amends I shall—I shall feel—very guilty.'

'Responsible? But——'

'It will not take very long I hope. Drury Place.'

'Oh lord!' Peregrine thought, 'what poshery.' He wondered, suddenly, if perhaps the all too obvious explanation was the wrong one and if his rescuer was a slightly demented gentleman and the chauffeur his keeper.

'I really don't see, sir—' he began but an inaudible conversation was taking place in the front seat.

'Certainly, sir,' said the chauffeur and drew up outside the estate agents. He pulled the keys out of his pocket as he entered. The clerk's face appeared looking anxiously and crossly over the painted lower pane of his window. He disappeared and in a moment came running out and round to the passenger's side.

'Well, sir,' he obsequiously gabbled, 'I'm sure I'm very sorry this has occurred. Very regrettable, I'm sure. But as I was saying to your driver, sir, I did warn the viewer.' He had not yet looked at Peregrine but he did so now, resentfully. 'I warned you,' he said.

'Yes, yes,' Peregrine said. 'You did.'

'Yes, well, thank you. But I'm sure——'

'That will do. There has been gross negligence. Good morning.' The voice was so changed, so brutally icy that Peregrine stared and the clerk drew back as if he'd been stung. They moved off.

The car's heating system built up. By the time they had crossed the river Peregrine was a little less cold and beginning to feel drowsy. His host offered no further remarks. Once when Peregrine happened to look at the rear-vision glass on the passenger's side he found he was being observed, appar-

ently with extreme distaste. Or no. Almost with fear. He
looked away quickly but out of the tail of his eye saw a gloved
hand change the angle of the glass.

'Oh well,' he thought bemusedly, 'I'm bigger and younger
than he is. I suppose I can look after myself but how tricky
it all is. Take away a man's clothes, after all, and you make
a monkey of him. What sort of public image will I present,
fleeing down Park Lane in a gent's mack and a fur rug, both
the property of my pursuer?'

They were in Park Lane now and soon turned off into a
side street and thence into the cul-de-sac called Drury Place.
The car pulled up. The chauffeur got out and rang the bell of
No. 7. As he returned to the car, the house door was opened
by a manservant.

Peregrine's host said in a comparatively cheerful voice: 'Not
far to go. Up the steps and straight in.'

The chauffeur opened the door. 'Now, sir,' he said, 'shan't
be long, shall we?'

There really was nothing else for it. Three impeccable men,
an errand boy and a tightly encased lady carrying a little dog,
walked down the footpath.

Peregrine got out and instead of bolting into the house,
made an entrance of it. He ascended the steps with deliberation leaving a trail of filthy footprints behind him and dragging his fur rug like a ceremonial train. The manservant stood
aside.

'Thank you,' Peregrine said grandly. 'I have fallen, as you
see, into dirty water.'

'Quite so, sir.'

'Up to my neck.'

'Very unfortunate, sir.'

'For all concerned,' said Peregrine.

His host had arrived.

'First of all, of course, a bath,' he was saying, 'and something to defeat that shivering, Mawson?'

'Certainly, sir.'

'And then come and see me.'

'Very good, sir.'

The man went upstairs. Peregrine's host was now behaving

in so normal a manner that he began to wonder if he himself had perhaps been bemused by his hideous experience. There was some talk of the efficacy of epsom salts in a hot bath and of coffee laced with rum. Peregrine listened in a trance.

'Do forgive me for bossing you about like this. You must be feeling ghastly and really, I *do* blame myself.'

'But *why?*'

'Yes, Mawson?'

'If the gentleman will walk up, sir.'

'Quite so. Quite so. Good.'

Peregrine walked up and was shown into a steaming and aromatic bathroom.

'I thought pine, sir, would be appropriate,' said Mawson. 'I hope the temperature is as you like it. May I suggest a long, hot soak, sir?'

'You may indeed,' said Peregrine warmly.

'Perhaps I may take your rug and coat. And shoes,' said Mawson with an involuntary change of voice. 'You will find a bath wrap on the rail and a hot rum and lemon within easy reach. If you would be good enough to ring, sir, when you are ready.'

'Ready for what?'

'To dress, sir.'

It seemed a waste of time to say: 'In what?' so Peregrine merely said 'Thank you' and Mawson said 'Thank you' and withdrew.

It was rapture beyond compare in the bath. Essence of pine. A lovely longhandled brush. Pine-smelling soap. And the hot rum and lemon. He left off shivering, soaped himself all over, including his head, scrubbed himself scarlet, submerged completely, rose, drank and tried to take a responsible view of the situation. In this he failed. Too much had occurred. He realised after a time that he was becoming light-headed and without at all fancying the idea took a hard-hitting cold shower. This restored him. Rough-dried and wrapped in a towelling bathrobe he rang the bell. He felt wonderful.

Mawson came and Peregrine said he would like to telephone for some clothes though when he thought about it he didn't quite know where he would ring. Jeremy Jones with whom he shared a flat would certainly be out and it wasn't the morning for their charlady. The Unicorn Theatre? *Somebody* would be there, of course, but who?

Mawson showed him to a bedroom where there was a telephone.

There were also clothes laid out on the bed. 'I think they are approximately your size, sir. It is hoped that you will have no objection to making use of them in the meantime,' said Mawson.

'Yes, but look here——'

'It will be much appreciated if you make use of them. Will there be anything else, sir?'

'I—honestly—I——'

'Mr. Conducis sends his compliments, sir, and hopes you will join him in the library.'

Peregrine's jaw dropped.

'Thank you, sir,' said Mawson neatly and withdrew.

Conducis? *Conducis!* It was as if Mawson had said 'Mr. Onassis.' Could this possibly be Mr. Vassily Conducis? The more Peregrine thought about it the more he decided that it could. But what in the wide world would Mr. Vassily Conducis be up to in a derelict theatre on the South Bank at half past ten in the morning when he ought to have been abominably lolling on his yacht in the Aegean? And what was *he*, Peregrine, up to in Mr. Conducis's house which (it now dawned upon him) was on a scale of insolently quiet grandeur such as he had never expected to encounter outside the sort of book which, in any case, he never read.

Peregrine looked round the room and felt he ought to curl his lip at it. After all he *did* read his *New Statesman.* He then looked at the clothes on the bed and found them to be on an equal footing with what, being a man of the theatre, he thought of as the décor. Absently, he picked up a gayish tie that was laid out beside a heavy silk shirt. 'Charvet' said the label. Where had he read of Charvet?

'I don't want any part of this,' he thought. He sat on the

bed and dialled several numbers without success. The theatre didn't answer. He put on the clothes and saw that though they were conservative in style he looked startlingly presentable in them. Even the shoes fitted.

He rehearsed a short speech and went downstairs where he found Mawson waiting for him.

He said : 'Did you say : Mr. Conducis?'

'Yes, sir, Mr. Vassily Conducis. Will you step this way, sir?'

Mr. Conducis stood in front of his library fire and Peregrine wondered how on earth he had failed to recognise a face that had been so widely publicised with, it was reported, such determined opposition from its owner. Mr. Conducis had an olive, indeed a swarthy complexion and unexpectedly pale eyes. These were merely facial adjuncts and might, Peregrine afterwards thought, have been mass produced for all the speculation they inspired. The mouth, however, was disturbing, being, or so Peregrine thought, both ruthless and vulnerable. The chin was heavy. Mr. Conducis had curly black hair going predictably grey at the temples. He looked, by and large, enormously expensive.

'Come in,' he said. 'Yes. Come in.' His voice was a light tenor. Was there a faintly foreign inflection? A slight lisp, perhaps.

As Peregrine approached, Mr. Conducis looked fixedly at his guest's hands.

'You are well?' he asked. 'Recovered?'

'Yes, indeed. I can't thank you enough, sir. As for—well, as for lending me these things—I really do feel——!'

'Do they fit?'

'Yes. Very well.'

'That is all that is necessary.'

'Except that after all they *are* yours,' Peregrine said and tried a light laugh in order not to sound pompous.

'I have told you. I am responsible. You might—' Mr. Conducis's voice faded but his lips soundlessly completed the sentence : '—have been drowned.'

'But honestly, sir!' Pregrine launched himself on his little speech. 'You've saved my life, you know. I would have just hung on by my fingers until they gave out and then—and then—well, finally and disgustingly drowned as you say.'

Almost soundlessly Mr. Conducis said: 'I should have blamed myself.'

'But why on earth! For a hole in The Dolphin stage?'

'It is my property.'

'Oh,' Peregrine ejaculated before he could stop himself, 'how splendid!'

'Why do you say that?'

'I mean: how splendid to own it. It's such an adorable little playhouse.'

Mr. Conducis looked at him without expression. 'Indeed?' he said. 'Splendid? Adorable? You make a study of theatres, perhaps?'

'Not really. I mean I'm not an expert. Good lord, no! But I earn my living in theatres and I am enormously attracted by old ones.'

'Yes. Will you join me in a drink?' Mr. Conducis said in his wooden manner. 'I am sure you will.' He moved to a tray on a sidetable.

'Your man has already given me a very strong and wonderfully restoring hot rum and lemon.'

'I am sure that you will have another. The ingredients are here.'

'A very small one, please,' Peregrine said. There was a singing sensation in his veins and a slight thrumming in his ears but he still felt wonderful. Mr. Conducis busied himself at the tray. He returned with a steaming and aromatic tumbler for Peregrine and something that he had poured out of a jug for himself. Could it be barley water?

'Shall we sit down,' he suggested. When they had done so he gave Peregrine a hurried, blank glance and said: 'You wonder why I was at the theatre, perhaps. There is some question of demolishing it and building on the site. An idea that I have been turning over for some time. I wanted to refresh my memory. The agents told my man you were there.' He put two fingers in a waistcoat pocket and Peregrine saw his own card had been withdrawn. It looked incredibly grubby.

'You—you're going to pull it down?' he said and heard a horribly false jauntiness in his own unsteady voice. He took a pull at his rum. It was extremely strong.

'You dislike the proposal,' Mr. Conducis observed, making it a statement rather than a question. 'Have you any reason other than a general interest in such buildings?'

If Peregrine had been absolutely sober and dressed in his own clothes it is probable that he would have mumbled something ineffectual and somehow or another made an exit from Mr. Conducis's house and from all further congress with its owner. He was a little removed however from his surroundings and the garments in which he found himself.

He began to talk excitedly. He talked about The Dolphin and about how it must have looked after Mr. Adolphus Ruby had gloriously tarted it up. He described how, before he fell into the well, he had imagined the house : clean, sparkling with lights from chandeliers, full, warm, buzzing and expectant. He said that it was the last of its kind and so well designed with such a surprisingly large stage that it would be possible to mount big productions there.

He forgot about Mr. Conducis and also about not drinking any more rum. He talked widely and distractedly.

'Think what a thing it would be,' Peregrine cried, 'to do a season of Shakespeare's comedies! Imagine *Love's Labour's* there. Perhaps one could have a barge—Yes. *The Grey Dolphin*—and people could take water to go to the play. When the play was about to begin we would run up a flag with a terribly intelligent dolphin on it. And we'd do them quickly and lightly and with elegance and O!' cried Peregrine, 'and with that little catch in the breath that never, *never* comes in the same way with any other playwright.'

He was now walking about Mr. Conducis's library. He saw, without seeing, the tooled spines of collected editions and a picture that he would remember afterwards with astonishment. He waved his arms. He shouted.

'There never was such a plan,' shouted Peregrine. 'Never in all London since Burbage moved the first theatre from Shore-ditch to Southwark.' He found himself near his drink and tossed it off. 'And not too fancy,' he said, 'mind you. Not twee.

God, no! Not a pastiche either. Just a good theatre doing the job it was meant to do. And doing the stuff that doesn't belong to any bloody Method or Movement or Trend or Period or what-have-you. Mind that.'

'You refer to Shakespeare again?' said Mr. Conducis's voice. 'If I follow you.'

'Of course I do!' Peregrine suddenly became fully aware of Mr. Conducis. 'Oh dear!' he said.

'Is something the matter?'

'I'm afraid I'm a bit tight, sir. Not *really* tight but a bit uninhibited. I'm awfully sorry. I think perhaps I'd better take myself off and I'll return all these things you've so kindly lent me. I'll return them as soon as possible, of course. So, if you'll forgive me——'

'What do you do in the theatre?'

'I direct plays and I've written two.'

'I know nothing of the theatre,' Mr. Conducis said heavily. 'You are reasonably successful?'

'Well, sir, yes. I think so. It's a jungle, of course. I'm not at all affluent but I make out. I've had as much work as I could cope with over the last three months and I think my mana's going up. I hope so. Good-bye, sir.'

He held out his hand. Mr. Conducis, with an expression that really might have been described as one of horror, backed away from it.

'Before you go,' he said. 'I have something that may be of interest to you. You can spare a moment?'

'Of course.'

'It is in this room,' Mr. Conducis muttered and went to a bureau that must, Peregrine thought, be of fabulous distinction. He followed his host and watched him pull out a silky, exquisitely inlaid, drawer.

'How lovely that is,' he said.

'Lovely?' Mr. Conducis echoed as he had echoed before. 'You mean the bureau? Yes? It was found for me. I understand nothing of such matters. That is not what I wished to show you. Will you look at this? Shall we move to a table?'

He had taken from the drawer a very small wooden Victorian hand-desk, extremely shabby, much stained, and Pere-

grine thought, of no particular distinction. A child's possession perhaps. He laid it on a table under a window and
motioned to a chair beside it. Peregrine now felt as if he was
playing a part in somebody else's dream. 'But I'm all right,' he
thought. 'I'm not really drunk. I'm in that pitiable but enviable
condition when all things seem to work together for good.'

He sat before the table and Mr. Conducis, standing well
away from him, opened the little desk, pressed inside with his
white, flat thumb and revealed a false bottom. It was a commonplace device and Peregrine wondered if he was meant to
exclaim at it. He saw that in the exposed cavity there was a
packet no bigger than a half-herring and much the same shape.
It was wrapped in discoloured yellow-brown silk and tied with
a morsel of tarnished ribbon. Mr. Conducis had a paper knife
in his hand. 'Everything he possesses,' Peregrine thought, 'is on
museum-piece level. It's stifling.' His host used the paper
knife as a sort of server, lifting the little silk packet out on its
blade and, as it were, helping Peregrine to it like a waiter.

It slid from the blade and with it, falling to one side, a
discoloured card upon which it had lain. Peregrine, whose
vision had turned swimmy, saw that this car was a menu
and bore a date some six years past. The heading : 'The Steam
Yacht Kalliope. Off Villefranche. Gala Dinner' floated tipsily
into view with a flamboyant and illegible signature that was
sprawled across it above a dozen others. A short white hand
swiftly covered and then removed the card.

'That is nothing,' Mr. Conducis said. 'It is of no conse-
quence.' He went to the fire. A bluish flame sprang up and
turned red. Mr. Conducis returned.

'It is the packet that may be of interest. Will you open it?'
he said.

Peregrine pulled gingerly at the ribbon ends and turned
back the silk wrapping.

He had exposed a glove.

A child's glove. Stained as if by water it was the colour of
old parchment and finely wrinkled like an old, old face. It had
been elegantly embroidered with tiny roses in gold and scarlet.
A gold tassel, now blackened and partly unravelled was

attached to the tapered gauntlet. It was the most heartrending object Peregrine had ever seen.

Underneath it lay two pieces of folded paper, very much discoloured.

'Will you read the papers?' Mr. Conducis invited. He had returned to the fireplace.

Peregrine felt an extraordinary delicacy in touching the glove. 'Cheverel,' he thought. 'It's a cheverel glove. Has it gone brittle with age?' No. To his finger-tip it was flaccid : uncannily so as if it had only just died. He slipped the papers out from beneath it. They had split along the folds and were foxed and faded. He opened the larger with great care and it lay broken before him. He pulled himself together and managed to read it.

This little glove and accompanying note were given to my Great-Great-Grandmother by her Beſt Friend : a Miſs Or Mrs. J. Hart. My dear Grandmother always in- ſifted that it had belonged to the poet. N.B. mark inſide gauntlet.

M.E. 23 April 1830

The accompanying note was no more than a slip of paper. The writing on it was much faded and so extraordinarily crabbed and tortuous that he thought at first it must be hiero- glyphic and that he therefore would never make it out. Then it seemed to him that there was something almost familiar about it. And then, gradually, words began to emerge. Every- thing was quiet. He heard the fire settle. Someone crossed the room above the library. He heard his own heart thud.

He read :

Mayde by my father for my sonne on his XI birthedy and never worne butte ync

Peregrine sat in a kind of trance and looked at the little glove and the documents. Mr. Conducis had left the paper- knife on the table. Peregrine slid the ivory tip into the gauntlet and very slowly lifted and turned it. There was the mark, in the same crabbed hand. HS.

'But where—' Peregrine heard his own voice saying, 'where did it come from? Whose is it?'

'It is mine,' Mr. Conducis said and his voice seemed to come from a great distance. 'Naturally.'

'But—where did you find it?'

A long silence.

'At sea.'

'At sea?'

'During a voyage six years ago. I bought it.'

Peregrine looked at his host. How pale Mr. Conducis was and how odd was his manner!

He said: 'The box—it is some kind of portable writing desk—was a family possession. The former owner did not discover the false bottom until——' He stopped.

'Until—?' Peregrine said.

'Until shortly before he died.'

Peregrine said: 'Has it been shown to an authority?'

'No. I should, no doubt, get an opinion from some museum or perhaps from Sotheby's.'

His manner was so completely negative, so toneless that Peregrine wondered if by any extraordinary chance he did not understand the full implication. He was wondering how, without offence, he could find out, when Mr. Conducis continued.

'I have not looked it all up but I understand the age of the boy at the time of his death is consistent with the evidence and that the grandfather was in fact a glover.'

'Yes.'

'And the initials inside the gauntlet do in fact correspond with the child's initials.'

'Yes. Hamnet Shakespeare.'

'Quite so,' said Mr. Conducis.

2. MR. GREENSLADE

'I know that,' Peregrine said. 'You don't need to keep on at it, Jer. I know there's always been a Bardic racket and that since the quarto-centenary it's probably been stepped up. I *know* about the tarting-up of old portraits with dome foreheads and the fake signatures and "stol'n and surreptitious copies" and phoney "discovered" documents and all that carry-on. I *know* the overwhelming odds are against this glove being anything but a fake. I merely ask you to accept that with the things lying there in front of me, I was knocked all of a heap.'

'Not only by them, I understand. You were half-drowned, half-drunk, dressed up in a millionaire's clobber and not knowing whether the owner was making a queer pass at you or not.'

'I'm almost certain, not.'

'His behaviour on your own account, seems to have been, to say the least of it, strange.'

'Bloody strange but not, I have decided, queer.'

'Well, you're the judge,' said Jeremy Jones. He bent over his work-table and made a delicate slit down a piece of thin cardboard. He was building a set to scale for a theatre-club production of *Venice Preserved*. After a moment he laid aside his razor-blade, and looked up at Peregrine. 'Could you make a drawing of it?' he said.

'I can try.'

Peregrine tried. He remembered the glove very clearly indeed and produced a reasonable sketch.

'It *looks* O.K.,' Jeremy said. 'Late sixteenth century. Elaborate in the right way. Tabbed. Embroidered. Tapering to the wrist. And the leather?'

'Oh, fine as fine. Yellow and soft and wrinkled and old, old, old.'

'It may be an Elizabethan or Jacobean glove but the letter could be a forgery.'

'But why? Nobody's tried to cash in on it.'

'You don't know. You don't know anything. Who was this chum Conducis bought it from?'

'He didn't say.'

'And who was M.E. whose dear grandma insisted it had belonged to the Poet?'

'Why ask me? You might remember that the great-*great*-grandmother was left it by a Mrs. J. Hart. And that Joan Hart——'

'Née Shakespeare, was left wearing-apparel by her brother. Yes. The sort of corroborative details any good faker would cook up. But, of course, the whole thing should be tackled by experts.'

'I told you : I said so. I said : wouldn't he take it to the V. and A. and he gave me one of his weird looks; furtive, scared, blank—I don't know how you'd describe them—and shut up like a clam.'

'Suspicious in itself!' Jeremy grinned at his friend and then said : '"*I would I had been there*".'

'Well, at that, "*it would have much amazed you*".'

'"*Very like. Very like.*" What do we know about Conducis?'

'I can't remember with any accuracy,' Peregrine said. 'He's an all-time-high for money, isn't he? There was a piece in one of the Sunday supplements some time back. About how he loathes publicity and does a Garbo and leaves Mr. Gulbenkian wondering what it was that passed him. And how he doesn't join in any of the joy and is thought to be a fabulous anonymous philanthropist. A Russian mum, I think it said, and an Anglo-Rumanian papa.'

'Where does he get his pelf?'

'I don't remember. Isn't it always oil? "Mystery Midas" it was headed and there was a photograph of him looking livid and trying to dodge the camera on the steps of his bank and a story about how the photographer made his kill. I read it at the dentist's.'

'Unmarried?'

'I think so.'

'How did you part company?'

'He just walked out of the room. Then his man came in and said the car was waiting to bring me home. He gave me back my revolting, stinking pocket book and said my clothes had gone to the cleaner and were thought to be beyond salvation. I said something about Mr. Conducis and the man said Mr. Conducis was taking a call from New York and would "quite understand." Upon which hint, off I slunk. I'd better write a sort of bread-and-butter, hadn't I?'

'I expect so. And he owns The Dolphin and is going to pull it down and put up, one supposes, another waffle-iron on the South Bank?'

'He's "turning over the idea" in his mind.'

'May it choke him,' said Jeremy Jones.

'Jer,' Peregrine said. 'You *must* go and look at it. It'll slay you. Wrought iron. Cherubs. Caryatids. A wonderful sort of potpourri of early and mid-Vic and designed by an angel. O God, God when I think of what could be done with it.'

'And this ghastly old Croesus——'

'I know. I know.'

And they stared at each other with the companionable indignation and despair of two young men whose unfulfilled enthusiasms coincide.

They had been at the same drama school together and had both decided that they were inclined by temperament, interest and ability to production rather than performance in the theatre. Jeremy finally settled for design and Peregrine for direction. They had worked together and apart in weekly and fortnightly repertory and had progressed to more distinguished provincial theatres and thence, precariously, to London. Each was now tolerably well-known as a coming man and both were occasionally subjected to nerve-racking *longeurs* of unemployment. At the present juncture Peregrine had just brought to an auspicious opening the current production at The Unicorn and had seen his own first play through a trial run out of London. Jeremy was contemplating a décor for a masque which he would submit to an international competition for theatrical design.

He had recently bought a partnership in a small shop in Walton Street where they sold what he described as : 'Very superior tatt. Jacobean purses, stomachers and the odd cod-piece.' He was a fanatic on authenticity and had begun to acquire a reputation as an expert.

Jeremy and Peregrine had spent most of what they had saved on leasing and furnishing their studio flat and had got closer than was comfortable to a financial crisis. Jeremy had recently become separated from a blonde lady of uncertain temper : a disentanglement that was rather a relief to Peregrine who had been obliged to adjust to her unpredictable descents upon their flat.

Peregrine himself had brought to uneventful dissolution an affair with an actress who had luckily discovered in herself the same degree of boredom that he, for his part, had hesitated to disclose. They had broken up with the minimum of ill-feeling on either part and he was, at the moment, heartfree and glad of it.

Peregrine was dark, tall and rather mischievous in appear-ance. Jeremy was of medium stature, reddish in complexion and fairly truculent. Behind a prim demeanour he concealed an amorous inclination. They were of the same age : twenty-seven. Their flat occupied the top story of a converted warehouse on Thames-side east of Blackfriars. It was from their studio window about a week ago, that Peregrine, idly exploring the South Bank through a pair of fieldglasses, had spotted the stage-house of The Dolphin, recognised it for what it was and hunted it down. He now walked over to the window.

'I can just see it,' he said. 'There it is. I spent the most hideous half-hour of my life, so far, inside that theatre. I ought to hate the sight of it but, by God, I yearn after it as I've never yearned after anything ever before. You know if Conducis does pull it down I honestly don't believe I'll be able to stay here and see it happen.'

'Shall we wait upon him and crash down on our knees before him crying, "Oh, sir, please sir, spare The Dolphin, pray do, sir".'

'I can tell you exactly what the reaction would be. He'd

back away as if we smelt and say in that deadpan voice of his that he knew nothing of such matters.'

'I wonder what it would cost.'

'To restore it? Hundreds of thousands no doubt,' Peregrine said gloomily. 'I wonder if National Theatre has so much as thought of it. Or *somebody*. Isn't there a society that preserves Ancient Monuments?'

'Yes. But "I know nothing of such matters",' mocked Jeremy. He turned back to his model. With a degree of regret to which wild horses wouldn't have persuaded him to confess, Peregrine began packing Mr. Conducis's suit. It was a dark charcoal tweed and had been made by a princely tailor. He had washed and ironed the socks, undergarments and shirt that he had worn for about forty minutes and had taken a box that Jeremy was hoarding to make up the parcel.

'I'll get a messenger to deliver it,' he said.

'Why on earth?'

'I don't know. Too bloody shy to go myself.'

'You'd only have to hand it over to the gilded lackey.'

'I'd feel an ass.'

'You're mad,' said Jeremy briefly.

'I don't want to go back there. It was all so rum. Rather wonderful, of course, but in a way rather sinister. Like some wish-fulfilment novel.'

'The wide-eyed young dramatist and the kindly recluse.'

'I don't think Conducis is kindly but I will allow and must admit I was wide-eyed over the glove. You know what?'

'What?'

'It's given me an idea.'

'Has it, now? Idea for what?'

'A play. I don't want to discuss it.'

'One must never discuss too soon, of course,' Jeremy agreed. 'That way abortion lies.'

'You have your points.'

In the silence that followed they both heard the metallic clap of the letter box downstairs.

'Post,' said Jeremy.

'Won't be anything for us.'

'Bills.'

'I don't count them. I daren't,' said Peregrine.

'There might be a letter from Mr. Conducis offering to adopt you.'

'Heh, heh, heh.'

'Do go and see,' Jeremy said. 'I find you rather oppressive when you're clucky. The run downstairs will do you good.'

Peregrine wandered twice round the room and absently out at the door. He went slowly down their decrepit staircase and fished in their letter box. There were three bills (two, he saw, for himself), a circular and a typed letter.

'Peregrine Jay, Esq. By Hand.'

For some reason that he could not have defined, he didn't open the letter. He went out-of-doors and walked along their uneventful street until he came to a gap through which one could look across the river to Southwark. He remembered afterwards that his bitch-muse as he liked to call her was winding her claws in his hair. He stared unseeing at a warehouse that from here partly obscured The Dolphin : Phipps Bros., per'aps, where the man with the oilcan—Jobbins—worked. A wind off the river whipped his hair back. Somewhere downstream a hooting set up. Why, he wondered idly, do river-craft set up gaggles of hooting all at once? His right hand was in his jacket pocket and his fingers played with the letter.

With an odd sensation of taking some prodigious step he suddenly pulled it out of his pocket and opened it.

Five minutes later Jeremy heard their front door slam and Peregrine come plunging up the stairs. He arrived, white-faced and apparently without the power of speech.

'What now, for pity's sake,' Jeremy asked. 'Has Conducis tried to kidnap you?'

Peregrine thrust a sheet of letter paper into his hand.

'Go on,' he said. 'Bloody read it, will you. Go on.'

Dear Sir, *Jeremy read*. I am directed by Mr. V. M. G. Conducis to inform you that he has given some consideration to the matter of The Dolphin Theatre, Wharfingers Lane, which he had occasion to discuss with you this morning. Mr. Conducis would be interested to have the matter examined in greater detail. He suggests, therefore,

that to this end you call at the offices of Consolidated Oils,
Pty. Ltd., and speak to Mr. S. Greenslade who has been
fully informed of the subject in question. I enclose for
your convenience a card with the address and a note of
introduction.

I have ventured to make an appointment for you with
Mr. Greenslade for 11.30 to-morrow (Wednesday). If
this is not a convenient time perhaps you will be good
enough to telephone Mr. Greenslade's secretary before
5.30 this evening.

Mr. Conducis asks me to beg that you will not trouble
yourself to return the things he was glad to be able to
offer after your most disagreeable accident for which, as
he no doubt explained, he feels a deep sense of responsibility. He understands that your own clothes have been
irretrievably spoilt and hopes that you will allow him to
make what he feels is a most inadequate gesture by way
of compensation. The clothes, by the way, have not been
worn. If, however, you would prefer it, he hopes that you
will allow him to replace your loss in a more conventional
manner.

Mr. Conducis will not himself take a direct part in any
developments that may arise in respect of The Dolphin
and does not wish at any juncture to be approached in the
matter. Mr. Greenslade has full authority to negotiate for
him at all levels.

                    With compliments,
                         I am,
                              Yours truly,
                                   M. SMYTHIMAN
                         (*Private Secretary to Mr. Conducis*)

'Not true,' Jeremy said, looking over the tops of his spectacles.

'True. Apparently. As far as it goes.'

Jeremy read it again. 'Well,' he said, 'at least he doesn't want
you to approach him. We've done him wrong, there.'

'He doesn't want to set eyes on me, thank God.'

'Were you passionately eloquent, my poor Peregrine?'

'It looks as if I must have been, doesn't it? I was plastered, of course.'

'I have a notion,' Jeremy said with inconsequence, 'that he was once wrecked at sea.'

'Who?'

'Conducis, you dolt. Who but? In his yacht.'

'Was his yacht called *Kalliope*?'

'I rather think so. I'm sure it went down.'

'Perhaps my predicament reminded him of the experience.'

'You know,' Jeremy said. 'I can't really imagine why we're making such a thing of this. After all, what's happened? You look at a derelict theatre. You fall into a fetid well from which you are extricated by the owner who is a multi-million-aire. You urge in your simple way the graces and excellence of the theatre. He wonders if, before he pulls it down, it might just be worth getting another opinion. He turns you over to one of his myrmidons. Where's the need for all the agitation?'

'I wonder if I should like M. Smythiman if I met him and if I shall take against S. Greenslade at first sight. Or he against me, of course.'

'What the hell does that matter? You place far too much importance upon personal relationships. Look at the fatuous way you go on about your women. And then suspecting poor Mr. Conducis of improper intentions when he never wants to look upon your like again!'

'Do you suggest that I accept his gorgeous apparel?' Peregrine asked on an incredulous note.

'Certainly, I do. It would be rude and ungenerous and rather vulgar to return it with a po-faced note. The old boy wants to give you his brand new clobber because you mucked up your own in his dirty great well. You should take it and not slap him back as if he'd tried to tip you.'

'If you had seen him you would not call him an old boy. He is the uncosiest human being I have ever encountered.'

'Be that as it may, you'd better posh yourself up and wait upon S. Greenslade on the stroke of 11.30.'

Peregrine said, after a pause, 'I shall do so, of course. He says nothing about the letter and glove, you observe.'

'Nothing.'

'I shall urge S. Greenslade to get it vetted at the V. and A.'

'You jolly well do.'

'Yes, I will. Well, Jer, as you say, why make a thing? If by some wild, rapturous falling-out of chance, I could do anything to save the life of The Dolphin I would count myself amply rewarded. But it will, of course, only be a rum little interlude and, in the meantime, here's the latest batch of bills.'

'At least,' Jeremy said, 'there won't be a new one from your tailors for some time to come.'

II

Mr. S. Greenslade was bald, pale, well-dressed and unremarkable. His office was quietly sumptuous and he was reached through a hinterland of equally conservative but impressive approaches. He now sat, with a file under his hand, a distinguished painting behind him, and before him, Peregrine, summoning all the techniques of the theatre in order to achieve relaxation.

'Mr. Jay,' Mr. Greenslade said, 'You appreciate, of course, the fact that your meeting yesterday with Mr. Conducis has led to this appointment.'

'I suppose so. Yes.'

'Quite. I have here a digest, as it were, of a—shall I say a suggestion you made to Mr. Conducis as he recollects it. Here it is.'

Mr. Greenslade put on his spectacles and read from the paper before him.

'Mr. Jay proposed that The Dolphin Theatre should be restored to its former condition and that a company should be established there performing Shakespeare and other plays of a high cultural quality. Mr. Jay suggested that The Dolphin is a building of some cultural worth and that, historically speaking, it is of considerable interest.'

Mr. Greenslade looked up at Peregrine. 'That was, in fact, your suggestion?'

'Yes. Yes. It was. Except that I hate the word culture.'

'Mr. Jay, I don't know if you are at all informed about Mr. Conducis's interests.'

'I—no—I only know he's—he's——'

'Extremely wealthy and something of a recluse?' Mr. Greenslade suggested with a slight, practised smile.

'Yes.'

'Yes.' Mr. Greenslade removed his spectacles and placed them delicately in the centre of his writing pad. Peregrine thought he must be going to make some profound revelation about his principal. Instead he merely said: 'Quite' again and after a dignified silence asked Peregrine if he would be good enough to tell him something about himself. His schooling, for example, and later career. He was extremely calm in making this request.

Peregrine said he had been born and educated in New Zealand, had come to England on a drama bursary and had remained there.

'I am aware, of course, of your success in the theatrical field,' said Mr. Greenslade and Peregrine supposed that he had been making some kind of confidential inquiries.

'Mr. Jay,' said Mr. Greenslade, 'I am instructed to make you an offer. It is, you may think, a little precipitant. Mr. Conducis is a man of quick decisions. It is this. Mr. Conducis is prepared to consider the rehabilitation of the theatre, subject, of course, to favourable opinions from an architect and from building authorities and to the granting of necessary permits. He will finance this undertaking. On one condition.' Mr. Greenslade paused.

'On one condition?' Peregrine repeated in a voice that cracked like an adolescent's.

'Exactly. It is this. That you yourself will undertake the working management of The Dolphin. Mr. Conducis offers you, upon terms to be arrived at, the post of organising the running of the theatre, planning its artistic policy, engaging the company and directing the productions. You would be given a free hand to do this within certain limits of expenditure which would be set down in this contract. I shall be glad to hear what your reactions are to this, at its present stage, necessarily tentative proposal.'

Peregrine suppressed a frightening inclination towards giving himself over to maniac laughter. He looked for a moment into Mr. Greenslade's shrewd and well-insulated face and he said:

'It would be ridiculous of me to pretend that I am anything but astonished and delighted.'

'Are you?' Mr. Greenslade rejoined. 'Good. In that case I shall proceed with the preliminary investigations. I, by the way, am the solicitor for a number of Mr. Conducis's interests. If and when it comes to drawing up contracts I presume I should negotiate with your agents?'

'Yes. They are——'

'Thank you,' said Mr. Greenslade, 'Messrs. Slade and Oppinger, I believe?'

'Yes,' said Peregrine, wondering if at any stage of his tipsy rhapsody he had mentioned them to Mr. Conducis and rather concluding that he hadn't.

'There is one other matter.' Mr. Greenslade opened a drawer in his desk and with an uncanny re-enacting of his principal's gestures on the previous morning, withdrew from it the small Victorian writing desk. 'You are already familiar with the contents, I understand, and expressed some anxiety about their authenticity.'

'I said I wished they could be shown to an expert.'

'Quite. Mr. Conducis has taken your point, Mr. Jay, and wonders if you yourself would be so obliging as to act for him in this respect.'

Peregrine, in a kind of trance, said: 'Are the glove and documents insured?'

'They are covered by a general policy but they have not been specifically insured since their value is unknown.'

'I feel the responsibility would be——'

'I appreciate your hesitation and I may say I put the point to Mr. Conducis. He still wishes me to ask you to undertake this mission.'

There was a short silence.

'Sir,' said Peregrine, 'Why is Mr. Conducis doing all this? Why is he giving me at least the chance of undertaking such fantastically responsible jobs? What possible motive can he

have? I hope,' Peregrine continued with a forthrightness that
became him very well, 'that I'm not such an ass as to suppose
I can have made an impression in the least degree commen-
surable with the proposals you've put before me and I—I——'
He felt himself reddening and ran out of words. Mr. Greenslade had watched him, he thought, with renewed attention.
He now lifted his spectacles with both hands, held them poised
daintily over his blotter and said, apparently to them:

'A reasonable query.'

'Well—I hope so.'

'And one which I am unable to answer.'

'Oh?'

'Yes. I will,' said Mr. Greenslade, evenly, 'be frank with
you, Mr. Jay. I am at a loss to know why Mr. Conducis is
taking this action. If, however, I have interpreted your mis-
givings correctly I can assure you they are misplaced.' Suddenly,
almost dramatically, Mr. Greenslade became human, good-
tempered and coarse. 'He's not that way inclined,' he said and
laid down his spectacles.

'I'm extremely glad to hear it.'

'You will undertake the commission?'

'Yes, I will.'

'Splendid.'

III

The expert folded his hands and leant back in his chair.

'Well,' he said, 'I think we may say with certainty this is a
glove of late sixteenth or early seventeenth-century workman-
ship. It has, at some time, been exposed to salt-water but not
extensively. One might surmise that it was protected. The little
desk is very much stained. Upon the letters H.S. inside the
gauntlet I am unable to give an authoritative opinion but
could, of course, obtain one. As for these two, really rather
startling documents: they can be examined and submitted to
a number of tests—infra red, spectography and so on—not in
my province, you know. If they've been concocted it will certainly be discovered.'

'Would you tell me how I can get the full treatment for them?'

'Oh, I think we could arrange that, you know. But we would want written permission from the owner, full insurance and so on. You've told me nothing, so far, of the history, have you?'

'No,' Peregrine said. 'But I will. With this proviso, if you don't mind : the owner, or rather his solicitor on his behalf, has given me permission to disclose his name to you on your undertaking to keep it to yourself until you have come to a conclusion about these things. He has a—an almost morbid dread of publicity which you'll understand, I think, when you learn who he is,'

The expert looked very steadily at Peregrine. After a considerable silence he said : 'Very well. I am prepared to treat the matter confidentially as far as your principal's name is concerned.'

'He is Mr. Vassily Conducis.'

'Good God.'

'Quite,' said Peregrine, doing a Greenslade. 'I shall now tell you as much as is known of the history. Here goes.'

And he did in considerable detail.

The expert listened in a startled manner.

'Really, very odd,' he said when Peregrine had finished.

'I assure you I'm not making it up.'

'No, no. I'm sure. I've heard of Conducis, of course. Who hasn't? You do realise what a—what a really flabbergasting thing this would be if it turned out to be genuine?'

'I can think of nothing else. I mean : there they lie—a child's glove and a letter asking one to suppose that on a summer's morning in the year 1596 a master-craftsman of Stratford made a pair of gloves and gave them to his grandson who wore them for a day and then——'

'Grief filled the room up of an absent child?'

'Yes. And a long time afterwards—twenty years—the father made his Will—I wonder he didn't chuck in a ghastly pun—Will's Will—don't you? And he left his apparel to his sister Joan Hart. And for her information wrote that note there. I mean—*his* hand moved across that bit of paper. If it's genuine.

And then two centuries go by and somebody called E.M. puts
the glove and paper in a Victorian desk with the information
that her great-great-grandmother had them from J. Hart and
her grandmother insisted they were the Poet's. It *could* have
been Joan Hart. She died in 1664.'

'I shouldn't build on it,' the expert said dryly.

'Of course not.'

'Has Mr. Conducis said anything about their value? I mean
—even if there's only a remote chance they will be worth—
well, I can't begin to say what their monetary value might be
but I know what *we'd* feel about it, here.'

Peregrine and the expert eyed each other for a moment or
two. 'I suppose,' Peregrine said, 'He's thought of that but I
must say he's behaved pretty casually over it.'

'Well, *we* shan't,' said the expert. 'I'll give you your receipt
and ask you to stay and see the things safely stowed.'

He stooped for a moment over the little, dead wrinkled
glove. 'If it were true!' He murmured.

'I know, I know,' Peregrine cried. 'It's frightening to think
what would happen. The avid attention, the passionate greed
for possession.'

'There's been murder done for less,' said the expert lightly.

IV

Five weeks later Peregrine, looking rather white about the
gills and brownish under the eyes, wrote the last word of his
play and underneath it: 'Curtain.' That night he read it to
Jeremy who thought well of it.

There had been no word from Mr. Greenslade. The stage-
house of The Dolphin could still be seen on Bankside.
Jeremy had asked at the estate agents for permission to view
and had been told that the theatre was no longer in their
hands and they believed had been withdrawn from the market.
Their manner was stuffy.

From time to time the two young men talked about The
Dolphin but a veil of unreality seemed to have fallen between

Peregrine and his strange interlude: so much so that he sometimes almost felt as if he had invented it.

In an interim report on the glove and documents, the
museum had said that preliminary tests had given no evidence of spurious inks or paper and so far nothing inconsistent
with their supposed antiquity had been discovered. An expert
on the handwriting of ancient documents, at present in
America, would be consulted on his return. If his report was
favourable, Peregrine gathered, a conference of authorities
would be called.

'Well,' Jeremy said, 'they haven't laughed it out of court,
evidently.'

'Evidently.'

'You'll send the report to the man Greenslade?'

'Yes, of course.'

Jeremy put his freckled hand on Peregrine's manuscript.

'What about opening at The Dolphin this time next year
with *The Glove*, a new play by Peregrine Jay?'

'Gatcha!'

'Well—why not? For the hell of it,' Jeremy said, 'let's do
a shadow casting. Come on.'

'I have.'

'Give us a look.'

Peregrine produced a battered sheet of paper covered in
his irregular handwriting.

'Listen,' he said. 'I know what would be said. That it's been
done before. Clemence Dane for one. And more than that:
it'd be a standing target for wonderful cracks at synthetic
Bardery. The very sight of the cast. Ann Hathaway and all that
lot. You know? It'd be held to stink. Sunk before it started.'

'I for one don't find any derry-down tatt in the dialogue.'

'Yes: but to cast "Shakespeare." What gall!'

'*He* did that sort of thing. You might as well say: "Oo-er!
To cast Henry VIII!" Come on: who *would* you cast for
Shakespeare?'

'It sticks out a mile, doesn't it?'

'Elizabethan Angry, really, isn't he? Lonely. Chancy. Tricky.
Bright as the sun. A Pegasus in the Hathaway stable? Enor-

mously over-sexed and looking like the Grafton portrait. In which I entirely believe.'

'And I. All right. Who looks and plays like that?'

'Oh God!' Jeremy said, reading the casting list.

'Yes,' Peregrine rejoined. 'What I said. It sticks out a mile.'

'Marcus Knight, my God.'

'Of course. He *is* the Grafton portrait and as for fire! Think of his Hotspur. And Harry Five. And Mercutio. And, by heaven, his Hamlet. Remember the Peer Gynt?'

'What's his age?'

'Whatever it is he doesn't show it. He can look like a stripling.'

'He'd cost the earth.'

'This is only mock-up, anyway.'

'Has he ever been known to get through a production without creating a procession of dirty big rows?'

'Never.'

'Custombuilt to wreck the morale of any given company?'

'That's Marco.'

'Remember the occasion when he broke off and told latecomers after the interval to sit down or get the hell out of it?'

'Vividly.'

'And when the rest of the cast threw in their parts as one man?'

'I directed the fiasco.'

'He's said to be more than usually explosive just now on account of no knighthood last batch.'

'He is, I understand, apoplectic, under that heading.'

'Well,' said Jeremy, 'it's your play. I see you've settled for rolling the lovely boy and the seduced fair friend and "Mr. W. H." all up in one character.'

'So I have.'

'How you dared!' Jeremy muttered.

'There have been madder notions over the centuries.'

'True enough. It adds up to a damn' good part. How do you see him?'

'Very blond. Very male. Very impertinent.'

'W. Hartly Grove?'

'Might be. Type casting.'

'Isn't he held to be a bad citizen?'

'Bit of a nuisance.'

'What about your Dark Lady? The Rosaline? Destiny Meade, I see you've got here.'

'I rather thought : Destiny. She's cement from the eyes up but she gives a great impression of smouldering depths and really inexhaustible sex. She can produce what's called for in any department as long as it's put to her in basic English and very very slowly. And she lives, by the way, with Marco.'

'That might or might not be handy. And Ann H.?'

'Oh, any sound unsympathetic actress with good attack,' Peregrine said.

'Like Gertie Bracey?'

'Yes.'

'Joan Hart's a nice bit. I tell you who'd be good as Joan. Emily Dunne. You know? She's been helping in our shop. You liked her in that TV show. She did some very nice Celias and Nerissas and Hermias at Stratford. Prick her down on your list.'

'I shall. See, with a blot I damn her.'

'The others seem to present no difficulty but the spirit sinks at an infant phenomenon.'

'He dies before the end of Act I.'

'Not a moment too soon. I am greatly perturbed by the vision of some stunted teenager acting its pants off?'

'It'll be called Gary, of course.'

'Or Trevor.'

'Never mind.'

'Would you give me the designing of the show?'

'Don't be a bloody ass.'

'It'd be fun,' Jeremy said grinning at him, 'face it : it *would* be fun.'

'Don't worry, it won't happen. I have an instinct and I know it won't. None of it : the glove, the theatre, the play. It's all a sort of miasma. It won't happen.'

Their post box slapped.

'There you are. Fate knocking at the door,' said Jeremy.

'I don't even wonder if it might be, now,' Peregrine said. 'However, out of sheer kindness I'll get the letters.'

He went downstairs, collected the mail and found nothing for himself. He climbed up again slowly. As he opened the door, he said: 'As I foretold you. No joy. All over. Like an insubstantial pageant faded. The mail is as dull as ditch-water and all for you. Oh, sorry!'

Jeremy was talking on the telephone.

He said: 'Here he is, now. Would you wait a second?'

He held out the receiver with one hand over the mouth-piece.

'Mr. Greenslade,' he said, 'wishes to speak to you. Ducky —this is it.'

3 . PARTY

'A year ago,' Peregrine thought. 'I stood in this very spot on a February morning. The sun came out and gilded the stage tower of the injured Dolphin and I lusted after it. I thought of Adolphus Ruby and wished I was like him possessed. And here I am again, as the Lord's my judge, a little jumped-up Cinderella-man in Mr. Ruby's varnished boots.'

He looked at the restored caryatids, the bouncing cetaceans and their golden legend, and the immaculate white frontage and elegance of ironwork and he adored them all.

He thought: 'Whatever happens, this is, so far, the best time of my life. Whatever happens I'll look back at to-day, for instance, and say: "Oh *that* was the morning when I knew what's meant by bliss".'

While he stood there the man from Phipps Bros. came out of Phipps Passage.

'Morning, guvnor,' he said.

'Good morning, Jobbins.'

'Looks a treat, dunnit?'

—

'Lovely.'

'Ah. Different. From what it was when you took the plunge.'

'Yes : indeed.'

'Yus. You wouldn't be looking for a watchman, I suppose? Now, she's near finished-like? Night or day. Any time?'

'I expect we *shall* want someone. Why? Do you know of a good man?'

'Self-praise, no recommendation's what they say, ainnit?'

'Do you mean you'd take it on?'

'Not to deceive yer, guvnor, that *was* the idea. Dahn the Passage in our place, it's too damp for me chubes, see? Something chronic. I got good references, guvnor. Plenty'd speak up for me. 'Ow's it strike yer? Wiv a sickening thud or favourable?'

'Why,' said Peregrine. 'Favourably, I believe.'

'Will you bear me in mind, then?'

'I'll do that thing,' said Peregrine.

'Gor' bless yer, guv,' said Jobbins and retired down Phipps Passage.

Peregrine crossed the lane and entered the portico of his theatre. He looked at the framed notice :

DOLPHIN THEATRE
REOPENING SHORTLY
UNDER NEW MANAGEMENT

It hung immediately under the tatter of a Victorian playbill that he had seen on his first remarkable visit.

THE BEGGAR GIRL'S WEDDING
In response to
Overwhelming Solicitation ! ! —
Mr. Adolphus Ruby ——

When the painters cleaned and resurfaced the façade, Peregrine had made them work all round that precarious fragment without touching it. 'It shall stay here,' he had said to Jeremy Jones, 'as long as I do.'

He opened the front doors. They had new locks and the doors themselves had been stripped and scraped and restored to their original dignity.

The foyer was alive. It was being painted, gilded, polished and furbished. There were men on scaffolds, on long ladders, on pendant platforms. A great chandelier lay in a sparkling heap on the floor. The two fat cherubim, washed and garnished, beamed upside-down into the resuscitated box-office.

Peregrine said good morning to the workmen and mounted the gently curving stairs.

There was still a flower-engraved looking-glass behind the bar but now he advanced towards himself across shining mahogany, framed by brass. The bar was all golden syrup and molasses in colour. 'Plain, serviceable, no tatt,' Peregrine muttered.

The renovations had been completed up here and soon a carpet would be laid. He and Jeremy and the young decorator had settled in the end for the classic crimson, white and gilt and the panelling blossomed, Peregrine thought, with the glorious vulgarity of a damask rose. He crossed the foyer to a door inscribed 'Management' and went in.

The Dolphin was under the control of 'Dolphin Theatres Incorporated.' This was a subsidiary of Consolidated Oils. It had been created, broadly speaking, by Mr. Greenslade, to encompass the development of the Dolphin project. Behind his new desk in the office sat Mr. Winter Morris, an extremely able theatrical business manager. He had been wooed into the service by Mr. Greenslade upon Peregrine's suggestion, after a number of interviews and, he felt sure, exhaustive inquiries. Throughout these preliminaries, Mr. Conducis had remained, as it were, the merest effluvium: far from noxious and so potent that a kind of plushy assurance seemed to permeate the last detail of renaissance in The Dolphin. Mr. Morris had now under his hand an entire scheme for promotion, presentation and maintenance embracing contracts with actors, designers, costumiers, front of house staff, stage crew and press agents and the delicate manipulation of such elements as might be propitious to the general mana of the enterprise.

He was a short, pale and restless man with rich curly hair,

who, in what little private life belonged to him, collected bric-à-brac.

'Good morning, Winty.'

'Perry,' said Mr. Morris as a definitive statement rather than a greeting.

'Any joy?'

Mr. Morris lolled his head from side to side.

'Before I forget. Do we want a caretaker, watchman, day or night, stage-door-keeper or any other lowly bod. about the house?'

'We shall in a couple of days.'

Peregrine told him about Mr. Jobbins.

'All right,' said Mr. Morris. 'If the references are good. Now, it's my turn. Are you fully cast?'

'Not quite. I'm hovering.'

'What do you think of Harry Grove?'

'As an actor?'

'Yes.'

'As an actor I think a lot of him.'

'Just as well. You've got him.'

'Winty, what the hell do you mean?'

'A directive, dear boy : or what amounts to it. From Head Office.'

'About *W. Hartly Grove*?'

'You'll probably find something in your mail.'

Peregrine went to his desk. He was now very familiar with the looks of Mr. Greenslade's communications and hurriedly extracted the latest from the pile.

Dear Peregrine Jay,

Your preliminaries seem to be going forward smoothly and according to plan. We are all very happy with the general shaping and development of the original project and are satisfied that the decision to open with your own play is a sound one, especially in view of your current success at The Unicorn. This is merely an informal note to bring to your notice Mr. W. Hartly Grove, an actor, as you will of course know, of repute and experience. Mr. Conducis personally will be very pleased if you give favourable attention to Mr. Grove when forming your company.

With kind regards,

Yours sincerely,

STANLEY GREENSLADE

When Peregrine read this note he was visited by a sense of misgiving so acute as to be quite disproportionate to its cause. In no profession are personal introductions and dear-boy-man-ship more busily exploited than in the theatre. For an actor to get the ear of the casting authority through an introduction to *régisseur* or management is a commonplace manoeuvre. For a second or two, Peregrine wondered with dismay if he could possibly be moved by jealousy and if the power so strangely, so inexplicably put into his hands had perhaps already sown a detestable seed of corruption. But no, he thought, on considera-tion, there were grounds more relative than that for his re-action and he turned to Morris to find the latter watching him with a half-smile.

'I don't like this,' Peregrine said.

'So I see, dear boy. May one know why?'

'Of course. I don't like W. Hartly Grove's reputation. I try to be madly impervious to gossip in the theatre and I don't know that I believe what they say about Harry Grove.'

'What do they say?'

'Vaguely shady behaviour. I've directed him once and knew him before that. He taught voice production at my drama school and disappeared over a week-end. Undefined scandal. Most women find him attractive, I believe. I can't say,' Pere-grine added, rumpling up his hair, 'that he did anything speci-fically objectionable in the later production and I must allow that personally I found him an amusing fellow. But apart from the two women in the company nobody liked him. *They* said *they* didn't but you could see them eyeing him and know-ing he eyed them.'

'This,' said Morris, raising a letter that lay on his desk, 'is practically an order. I suppose yours is, too.'

'Yes, blast it.'

'You've been given a fabulously free hand up to now,

Perry. No business of mine, of course, dear boy, but frankly
I've never seen anything like it. General management, director,
author—the lot. Staggering.'

'I hope,' Peregrine said with a very direct look at his manager, 'staggering though it may be, I got it on my reputation as
a director and playwright. I believe I did. There is no other
conceivable explanation, Winty.'

'No, no, old boy, of course not,' said Winter Morris in a
hurry.

'As for W. Hartly Grove, I suppose I can't jib. As a matter
of fact he would be well cast as Mr. W. H. It's his sort of
thing. But I don't like it. My God,' Peregrine said, 'haven't I
stuck my neck out far enough with Marcus Knight in the lead
and liable to throw an average of three dirty great temperaments per rehearsal? What have I done to deserve Harry
Grove as a bonus?'

'The Great Star's shaping up for trouble already. He's
calling me twice a day to make difficulties over his contract.'

'Who's winning?'

'I am,' said Winter Morris, 'So far.'

'Good for you.'

'I'm getting sick of it,' Morris said. 'Matter-of-fact it's on
my desk now.' He lifted a sheet of blotting paper and rifled
the pages of the typewritten document he exposed. 'Still,' he
said, 'he's signed and he can't get past that one. We almost had
to provide an extra page for it. Take a gander.'

The enormous and completely illegible signature did indeed
occupy a surprising area. Peregrine glanced at it and then
looked more closely.

'I've seen that before,' he said. 'It looks like a cyclone.'

'Once seen never forgotten.'

'I've seen it,' Peregrine said, 'recently. *Where*, I wonder.'

Winter Morris looked bored.

'Did he sign your autograph book?' he asked bitterly.

'It was somewhere unexpected. Ah, well. Never mind. The
fun will start with the first rehearsal. He'll want me to re-
write his part, of course, adding great hunks of ham and
corn and any amount of fat. It's tricky enough as it is. Strictly
speaking a playwright shouldn't direct his own stuff. He's too

tender with it. But it's been done before and by the Lord I mean to do it again. Marco or no Marco. He looks like the Grafton portrait of Shakespeare. He's got the voice of an angel and colossal prestige. He's a brilliant actor and this is a part he can play. It'll be a ding-dong go which of us wins but by heaven I'm game if he is.'

'Fair enough,' said Morris. 'Live for ever, dear boy. Live for ever.'

They settled at their respective desks. Presently Peregrine's buzzer rang and a young woman provided by the management and secreted in an auxiliary cubby-hole said: 'Victoria and Albert for you, Mr. Jay.'

Peregrine refrained from saying: 'Always available to Her Majesty and the Prince Consort.' He was too apprehensive. He said: 'Oh yes. Right. Thank you,' and was put into communication with the expert.

'Mr. Jay,' the expert said, 'is this a convenient time for you to speak?'

'Certainly.'

'I thought it best to have a word with you. We will, of course, write formally with full reports for you to hand to your principal but I felt—really,' said the expert and his voice, Peregrine noticed with mounting excitement, was trembling 'really, it is the most remarkable thing. I—well, to be brief with you, the writing in question has been exhaustively examined. It has been compared by three experts with the known signatures and they find enough coincidence to give the strongest presumption of identical authorship. They are perfectly satisfied as to the age of the cheverel and the writing materials and that apart from salt-water stains there has been no subsequent interference. In fact, my dear Mr. Jay, incredible as one might think it, the glove and the document actually seem to be what they purport to be.'

Peregrine said: 'I've always felt this would happen and now I can't believe it.'

'The question is: what is to be done with them?'

'You will keep them for the time being?'

'We are prepared to do so. We would very much like,' said

the expert and Peregrine caught the wraith of a chuckle in the receiver, 'to keep them altogether. However! I think my principals will, after consultation, make an approach to—er—the owner. Through you, of course and—I imagine this would be the correct proceeding—Mr. Greenslade.'

'Yes. And—no publicity?'

'Good God, no!' the expert ejaculated quite shrilly. 'I should hope not. Imagine!' There was a long pause. 'Have you any idea,' the expert said, 'whether he will contemplate selling?'

'No more than you have.'

'No. I see. Well : You will have the reports and a full statement from us within the next week. I—must confess—I—I have rung you up simply because I—in short—I am as you obviously are, a *dévoté*.'

'I've written a play about the glove.' Peregrine said impulsively. 'We're opening here with it.'

'Really? A play,' said the expert and his voice flattened.

'It isn't cheek!' Peregrine shouted into the telephone. 'In its way it's a tribute. A play! Yes, a play.'

'Oh, please! Of course. Of course.'

'Well, thank you for telling me.'

'No, no.'

'Good-bye.'

'What? Oh, yes. Of course. Good-bye.'

Peregrine put down the receiver and found Winter Morris staring at him.

'You'll have to know about this, Winty,' he said. 'But as you heard—no publicity. It concerns the Great Person so that's for sure. Further it must not go.'

'All right. If you say so : not an inch.'

'Top secret?'

'Top secret as you say. Word of honour.'

So Peregrine told him. When he had finished, Morris ran his white fingers through his black curls and lamented. 'But listen, but listen, listen, listen. What material! What a talking line! The play's *about* it. Listen : it's *called The Glove*. We've *got* it. Greatest Shakespeare relic of all time. The *Dolphin* Glove. American offers. Letters to the papers : "Keep the

Dolphin Glove in Shakespeare's England." "New fabulous
offer for Dolphin Glove!" Public subscriptions. The lot! Ah
Perry, cherub, dear *dear* Perry. All this lovely publicity and
we should keep it secret!'

'It's no good going on like that.'

'How do you expect me to go on? The Great Person must
be handled over this one. He must be seen. He must be made
to work. What makes him work? You've seen him. Look: he's
a financial wizard: he *knows*. He knows what's good business.
Listen: if this was handled right and we broke the whole story
at the psychological moment: you know, *with* the publicity:
the right kind of class publicity. . . . Look——'

'Do pipe down,' Peregrine said.

'Ah! Ah! Ah!'

'I'll tell you what my guess is, Winty. He'll take it all back
to his iron bosom and lock it away in his Louis-the-Some-
thingth bureau and that's the last any of us will ever see of
young Hamnet Shakespeare's cheverel glove.'

In this assumption, however, Peregrine was entirely mistaken.

II

'*But that's all one,*' Marcus Knight read in his beautiful voice.
'*Put it away somewhere. I shall not look at it again. Put it away.*'

He laid his copy of Peregrine's play down and the six remaining members of the company followed his example. A
little slap of typescripts ran round the table.

'Thank you,' Peregrine said. 'That was a great help to me.
It was well read.'

He looked round the table. Destiny Meade's enormous black
eyes were fixed upon him with the determined adulation of
some mixed-up and sexy medieval saint. This meant, as he
knew, nothing. Catching his eye, she raised her fingers to
her lips and then in slow motion, extended them to him.

'Darling Perry,' she murmured in her celebrated hoarse
voice, 'what can we say? It's all too much. Too much.' She

made an appealing helpless little gesture to the company at large. They responded with suitable if ambiguous noises.

'My dear Peregrine,' Marcus Knight said (and Peregrine thought : 'his voice is like no other actor's'). 'I like it I see great possibilities. I saw them as soon as I read the play. Naturally, that was why I accepted the role. My opinion, I promise you, is unchanged. I look forward with interest to creating this part.' Royalty could not have been more gracious.

'I'm so glad, Marco,' Peregrine said.

Trevor Vere whose age, professionally, was eleven, winked abominably across the table at Miss Emily Dunne who disregarded him. She did not try to catch Peregrine's eye and seemed to be disregardful of her companions. He thought that perhaps she really had been moved.

W. Hartly Grove leant back in his chair with some elegance. His fingers tapped the typescript. His knuckles, Peregrine absently noted, were like those of a Regency prizefighter His eyebrows were raised and a faint smile hung about his mouth He was a blond man, very comely, with light blue eyes, set far apart, and an indefinable expression of impertinence. 'I think it's fabulous,' he said. 'And I like my Mr W. H.'

Gertrude Bracey, patting her hair and settling her shoulders said : 'I *am* right, aren't I, Perry? Ann Hathaway *shouldn't* be played unsympathetically. I mean : definitely *not* a bitch?'

Peregrine thought : 'Trouble with this one : I foresee trouble.'

He said cautiously : 'She's had a raw deal, of course.'

Charles Random said : 'I wonder what Joan Hart did with the gloves?' and gave Peregrine a shock.

'But there weren't any gloves, *really*,' Destiny Meade said, 'were there, darling? Or were there? Is it historical?'

'No, no, love,' Charles Random said 'I was talking inside the play. Or out of wishful thinking. I'm sorry.'

Marcus Knight gave him a look that said it was not usual for secondary parts to offer gratuitous observations round the conference table. Random, who was a very pale young man, reddened. He was to play Dr. Hall in the first act.

'I see,' Destiny said. 'So I mean there weren't *really* any gloves? In Stratford or anywhere real?'

Peregrine looked at her and marvelled. She was lovely
beyond compare and as simple as a sheep. The planes of her
face might have been carved by an angel. Her eyes were wells
of beauty. Her mouth, when it broke into a smile, would turn
a man's heart over and although she was possessed of more
than her fair share of common-sense, professional cunning and
instinctive technique, her brain took one idea at a time and
reduced each to the comprehensive level of a baby. If she were
to walk out on any given stage and stand in the least advantageous place on it in a contemptible lack of light and with nothing to say, she would draw all eyes. At this very moment, fully
aware of her basic foolishness, Marcus Knight, W. Hartly
Grove and, Peregrine observed with dismay, Jeremy Jones, all
stared at her with the solemn awareness that was her habitual
tribute while Gertrude Bracey looked at her with something
very like impotent fury.

The moment had come when Peregrine must launch himself into one of those pre-production pep-talks upon which a
company sets a certain amount of store. More, however, was
expected of him, now, than the usual helping of : 'We're all
going to love this so let's get cracking' sort of thing. For once
he felt a full validity in his own words when he clasped his
hands over his play and said :

'This is a great occasion for me.' He waited for a second
and then, abandoning everything he had so carefully planned,
went on. 'It's a great occasion for me because it marks the re-
birth of an entrancing playhouse : something I'd longed for and
dreamed of and never, never thought to see. And then : to be
given the job I have been given of shaping the policy and
directing the productions and—as a final and incredible *bon-
bouche*—the invitation to open with my own play—I do hope
you'll believe me when I say all this makes me feel not only
immensely proud but extremely surprised and—although it's
not a common or even appropriate emotion in a director-play-
wright—very humble.

'It might have been more politic to behave as if I took it all
as a matter of course and no more than my due, but I'd rather,
at the outset, and probably for the last time, say that I can't
get over my good fortune. I'm not the first dramatist to have

a bash at the man from Warwickshire and I'm sure I won't be the last. In this piece I've—well you've seen, I hope, what I've tried to do. Show the sort of combustion that built up in that unique personality : the terrifying sensuality that lies beyond the utterly unsentimental lyricism : gilded flies under daisies pied and violets blue. His only release, his only *relief*, you might say, has been his love for the boy Hamnet. It's his son's death that brings about the frightful explosion in his own personality and the moment when Rosaline (I have always believed the Dark Lady was a Rosaline) pulls Hamnet's glove on her hand is the climax of the entire action. The physical intrusion and his consent to it brings him to the condition that spewed up Timon of Athens and was seared out of him by his own disgust. I've tried to suggest that for such a man the only possible release is through his work. He would like to be an Antony to Rosaline's Cleopatra, but between himself and that sort of surrender stands his genius. And—incidentally—the hardheaded bourgeois of Stratford which, also, he is.'

Peregrine hesitated. Had he said anything? Was it any good trying to take it further? No.

'I won't elaborate,' he said. 'I can only hope that we'll find out what it's all about as we work together.' He felt the abrupt upsurge of warmth that is peculiarly of the theatre.

'I hope, too, very much,' he said, 'that we're going to agree together. It's a great thing to be starting a playhouse on its way. They say dolphins are intelligent and gregarious creatures. Let us be good Dolphins and perform well together. Bless you all.'

They responded at once and all blessed him in return and for the occasion, at least, felt uplifted and stimulated and, in themselves, vaguely noble.

'And now,' he said, 'let's look at Jeremy Jones's sets and then it'll be almost time to drink a health to our enterprise. This is a great day.'

III

Following the reading there was a small party, thrown by the

Management and thrown with a good deal of quiet splendour. It was held in the circle foyer with the bar in full array. The barman wore a snowy white shirt, flamboyant waistcoat and gold albert. There was a pot-boy with his sleeves rolled up to his shoulders like the one in *Our Mutual Friend*. The waiters were conventionally dressed but with a slightly Victorian emphasis. Champagne in brassbound ice buckets stood along the mahogany bar and the flowers, exclusively, were crimson roses set in fern leaves.

Mr. Greenslade was the host. Apart from the Company, Jeremy, Winter Morris, the publicity agents and the stage director and his assistant, there were six personages of startling importance from the worlds of theatre finance, the Press and what Mr. Morris, wide-eyed, described as 'the sort you can't, socially speaking, look any higher than.' From a remark let fall by Mr. Greenslade, Peregrine was led to suppose that behind their presence could be discerned the figure of Mr. Conducis who, of course, did not attend. Indeed it was clear from the conversation of the most exalted of these guests that Mr. Conducis was perfectly well-known to be the presiding genius of The Dolphin.

'A new departure for V.M.C.' this personage said. 'We were all astonished,' (Who were 'we'?) 'Still, like the rest of us, one supposes, he must have his toys.'

Peregrine wondered if it would have been possible for him to have heard a more innocently offensive comment.

'It's a matter of life and death to us,' he said. The personage looked at him with amusement.

'Is it really?' he said. 'Well, yes. I can see that it is. I hope all goes well. But I am still surprised by the turn of V.M.C.'s fancy. I didn't think he had any fancies.'

'I don't really know him,' said Peregrine.

'Which of us does?' the personage rejoined. 'He's a legend in his own lifetime and the remarkable thing about *that* is: the legend is perfectly accurate.' Well-content with this aphorism he chuckled and passed superbly on leaving an aftermath of cigar, champagne and the very best unguents for the Man.

'If I were to become as fabulously rich as that,' Peregrine

wondered, 'would I turn into just such another? Can it be avoided?'

He found himself alongside Emily Dunne who helped in Jeremy's shop and was to play Joan Hart in *The Glove*. She had got the part by audition and on her own performance, which Peregrine had seen, of Hermia in *A Midsummer Night's Dream*.

She had a pale face with dark eyes and a welcoming mouth. He thought she looked very intelligent and liked her voice which was deepish.

'Have you got some champagne?' asked Peregrine, 'and would you like something to eat?'

'Yes and no, thank you,' said Emily. 'It's a wonderful play. I can't get over my luck, being in it. And I can't get over The Dolphin either.'

'I thought you looked as if you were quite enjoying it. You read Joan exactly right. One wants to feel it's a pity she's Will's sister because she's the only kind of woman who would ever suit him as a wife.'

'I think before they were both married she probably let him in by a side-window when he came home to Henley Street in the early hours after a night on the tiles.'

'Yes, of course she did. How right you are. Do you like cocktail parties?'

'Not really, but I always hope I will.'

'I've given that up, even.'

'Do you know, when I was playing at The Mermaid over a year ago, I used to look across the river to The Dolphin and then, one day, I walked over Blackfriars Bridge and stood in Wharfingers Lane and stared at it. And then an old, old stage-hand I knew told me his father had been on the curtain there in the days of Adolphus Ruby. I got a sort of thing about it. I found a book in a sixpenny rack called *The Buskin and the Boards*. It was published in 1860 and it's all about contemporary theatres and actors. *Terribly* badly written, you know, but there are some good pictures and The Dolphin's one of the best.'

'Do let me see it.'

'Of course.'

'I had a thing about The Dolphin, too. What a pity we didn't meet in Wharfingers Lane,' said Peregrine. 'Do you like Jeremy's models? Let's go and look at them.'

They were placed about the foyer and were tactfully lit. Jeremy had been very intelligent: the sets made single uncomplicated gestures and were light and strong-looking and beautifully balanced. Peregrine and Emily had examined them at some length when it came to him that he should be moving among the guests. Emily seemed to be visited by the same notion. She said : 'I think Marcus Knight is wanting to catch your eye. He looks a bit portentous to me.'

'Gosh! So he does. Thank you.'

As he edged through the party towards Marcus Knight, Peregrine thought : 'That's a pleasing girl.'

Knight received him with an air that seemed to be compounded of graciousness and overtones of huff. He was the centre of a group : Winter Morris, Mrs. Greenslade, who acted as hostess and was beautifully dressed and excessively poised, Destiny Meade and one of the personages who wore an expansive air of having acquired her.

'Ah, Perry, dear boy!' Marcus Knight said, raising his glass in salute. 'I wondered if I should manage to have a word with you. Do forgive me,' he said jollily to the group. 'If I don't fasten my hooks in him now he'll escape me altogether.' Somewhat, Peregrine thought, to her astonishment, Knight kissed Mrs. Greenslade's hand. 'Lovely, lovely party,' he said and moved away. Peregrine saw Mrs. Greenslade open her eyes very widely for a fraction of a second at the personage. 'We're amusing her,' he thought sourly.

'Perry,' Knight said, taking him by the elbow. 'May we have a long, long talk about your wonderful play? And I mean that, dear boy. Your *wonderful* play.'

'Thank you, Marco.'

'Not here, of course,' Knight said waving his disengaged hand, 'not now. But soon. And, in the meantime, a thought.'

'Oops!' Peregrine thought. 'Here we go.'

'Just a thought. I throw it out for what it's worth. Don't you feel—and I'm speaking absolutely disinterestedly—don't

you feel that in your Act Two, *dear* Perry, you keep Will
Shakespeare offstage for *rather* a long time? I mean, having
built up that tremendous tension——'

Peregrine listened to the celebrated voice and as he listened
he looked at the really beautiful face with its noble brow and
delicate bone structure. He watched the mouth and thought
how markedly an exaggerated dip in the bow of the upper
lip resembled that of the Droushout engraving and the so-
called Grafton portrait. 'I must put up with him,' Peregrine
thought. 'He's got the prestige, he's got the looks and his
voice is like no other voice. God give me strength.'

'I'll think very carefully about it, Marco,' he said and he
knew that Knight knew he was going to do nothing of the
sort. Knight, in a grand seignorial manner, clapped him on
the shoulder. 'We shall agree,' he cried, 'like birds in their
little nest.'

'I'm sure of it,' said Peregrine.

'One other thing, dear boy, and this in your private ear.'
He steered Peregrine by the elbow into a corridor leading off
to the boxes. 'I find with some surprise,' he said, muting the
exquisite voice, 'that we are to have W. Hartly Grove in our
company.'

'I thought he read Mr. W. H. quite well, didn't you?'

'I could scarcely bring myself to listen,' said Knight.

'Oh,' Peregrine said coolly. 'Why?'

'My dear man, do you know anything at all about Mr.
Harry Grove?'

'Only that he is a reasonably good actor. Marco,' Peregrine said. 'Don't let's start any anti-Grove thing. For your
information, and I'd be terribly grateful if you'd treat this as
strictly—very strictly, Marco—between ourselves, I've had no
hand in this piece of casting. It was done at the desire of the
Management. They have been generous to a degree in every
other aspect and even if I'd wanted to I couldn't have opposed
them.'

'You had this person *thrust* upon you?'

'If you like to put it that way.'

'You should have refused.'

'I had no valid reason for doing so. It is a good piece of

casting. I beg you, Marco, not to raise a rumpus at the outset. Time enough when anything happens to justify it.'

For a moment he wondered if Knight was going to produce a temperament then and there and throw in his part. But Peregrine felt sure Knight had a great desire to play Will Shakespeare and although, in the shadowy passage, he could see the danger signal of mounting purple in the oval face, the usual outburst did not follow this phenomenon.

Instead Knight said: 'Listen. You think I am unreasonable. Allow me to tell you, Perry——'

'I don't want to listen to gossip, Marco.'

'*Gossip!* My God! Anyone who accuses me of gossip does me an injury I won't stomach. *Gossip!* Let me tell you I know for a fact that Harry Grove——' The carpet was heavy and they had heard no sound of an approach. The worst would have happened if Peregrine had not seen a shadow move across the gilt panelling. He closed his hand round Knight's arm and stopped him.

'What are you two up to, may I ask?' said Harry Grove 'Scandalmongering?'

He had a light, bantering way with him and a boldish stare that was somehow very far from being offensive. 'Perry,' he said, 'this is an enchanting theatre. I want to explore, I want to see everything. Why don't we have a bacchanal and go in Doric procession through and about the house, tossing down great bumpers of champagne and chanting some madly improper hymn? Led, of course, by our great, *great* star. Or should it be by Mr. and Mrs. Greensleeves?'

He made his preposterous suggestion so quaintly that in spite of himself and out of sheer nerves, Peregrine burst out laughing. Knight said, 'Excuse me' with a good deal of ostentation and walked off.

' "It is offended," ' Grove said.. ' "See, it stalks away." It dislikes me, you know. Intensely.'

'In that case don't exasperate it, Harry.'

'Me? You think better not? Rather tempting though, I must say. Still, you're quite right, of course. Apart from everything else, I can't afford to. Mr. Greengage might give me the sack,' Grove said with one of his bold looks at Peregrine.

'If he didn't I might. Do behave prettily, Harry. And I must get back into the scrum.'

'I shall do everything that is expected of me, Perry dear. I nearly always do.'

Peregrine wondered if there was a menacing note behind this apparently frank undertaking.

When he returned to the foyer it was to find that the party had attained its apogee. Its component bodies had almost all reached points farthest removed from their normal behaviour. Everybody was now obliged to scream if he or she wished to be heard and almost everybody would have been glad to sit down. The Personages were clustered together in a flushed galaxy and the theatre people excitedly shouted shop. Mrs. Greenslade could be seen saying something to her husband and Peregrine was sure it was to the effect that she felt it was time their guests began to go away. It would be best, Peregrine thought, if Destiny Meade and Marcus Knight were to give a lead. They were together on the outskirts and Peregrine knew, as certainly as if he had been beside them, that Knight was angrily telling Destiny how he felt about W. Hartly Grove. She gazed at him with her look of hypersensitive and at the same time sexy understanding but every now and then her eyes swivelled a little and always in the same direction. There was a slightly furtive air about this manœuvre.

Peregrine turned to discover what could be thus attracting her attention and there, in the entrance to the passage, stood Harry Grove with wide open eyes and a cheerful smile, staring at her. '*Damn*,' thought Peregrine. 'Now what?'

Emily Dunne, Charles Random and Gertie Bracey were all talking to Jeremy Jones. Jeremy's crest of red hair bobbed up and down and he waved his glass recklessly. He threw back his head and his roar of laughter could be heard above the general din. As he always laughed a great deal when he was about to fall in love, Peregrine wondered if he was attracted by Emily and hoped he was not. It could hardly be Gertie. Perhaps he was merely plastered.

But no. Jeremy's green and rather prominent gaze was directed over the heads of his group and was undoubtedly fixed upon Destiny Meade.

D.A.T.D.   C

'He *couldn't* be such an ass,' Peregrine thought uneasily. 'Or could he?'

His awareness of undefined hazards was not at all abated when he turned his attention to Gertie Bracey. He began, in fact, to feel as if he stood in a field of fiercely concentrated shafts of criss-cross searchlights. Like searchlights, the glances of his company wandered, interlaced, selected and darted. There, for example, was Gertie with her rather hatchet-jawed intensity stabbing her beam at Harry Grove. Peregrine recollected with a jolt, that somebody had told him they had been lovers and were now breaking up. He had paid no attention to this rumour. Supposing it was true would this be one more personality problem on his plate?

'Or am I,' he wondered, 'getting some kind of director's neurosis? Do I merely imagine that Jeremy eyes Destiny and Destiny and Harry ogle each other and Gertie glares hell's fury at Harry and Marcus has his paw on Destiny and that's why he resents Harry? Or is it all an unexpected back-kick from the Conducis champagne?'

He edged round to Destiny and suggested that perhaps they ought to make a break and that people were waiting for a lead from her and Marcus. This pleased both of them. They collected themselves as they did offstage before a big entrance and with the expertise of rugby halfbacks took advantage of a gap and swept through it to Mrs. Greenslade.

Peregrine ran straight into their child actor, Master Trevor Vere and his mamma who was a dreadful lady called Mrs. Blewitt. She had to be asked and it was God's mercy that she seemed to be comparatively sober. She was dressed in a black satin shift with emerald fringe and she wore a very strange green toque on her pale corn hair. Trevor, in the classic tradition of infant phenomena, was youthfully got up in some sort of contemporary equivalent of a Fauntleroy suit. There were overtones of the Ted. His hair was waved back from his rather pretty face and he wore a flowing cravat. Peregrine knew that Trevor was not as old as his manner and his face suggested because he came under the legal restrictions imposed upon child performers. It was therefore lucky in more ways than one that he died early in the first act.

Mrs. Blewitt smiled and smiled at Peregrine with the deadly knowingness of the professional mum and Trevor linked his arm in hers and smiled too. There are many extremely nice children in the professional theatre. They have been well brought up by excellent parents. But none of these had been available to play Hamnet Shakespeare and Trevor, it had to be faced, was talented to an unusual degree. He had made a great hit on cinema in a biblical epic as the Infant Samuel.

'Mrs. Blewitt,' said Peregrine.

'I was just hoping for a chance to say how much we appreciate the compliment,' said Mrs. Blewitt with an air of conspiracy. 'It's not a big role, of course, not like Trev's accustomed to. Trev's accustomed to leading child-juves, Mr. Jay. We was offered——'

It went on predictably for some time. Trevor, it appeared, had developed a heart condition. Nothing, Mrs. Blewitt hurriedly assured Peregrine, to worry about really because Trev would never let a show down, never, but the doctor under whom Trev was and under whom she herself was—a monstrous picture presented itself—had advised against another big emotionally exhausting role——

'Why bring that up, Mummy?' Trevor piped with one of his atrocious winks at Peregrine. Peregrine excused himself, saying that they must all be getting along, mustn't they, and he wanted to catch Miss Dunne before she left.

This was true. He had thought it would be pleasant to take Emily back to their studio for supper with him and Jeremy. Before he could get to her he was trapped by Gertrude Bracey.

She said: 'Have you seen Harry anywhere?'

'I saw him a minute or two ago. I think perhaps he's gone.'

'I think perhaps you're right,' she said with such venom that Peregrine blinked. He saw that Gertrude's mouth was unsteady. Her eyes were not quite in focus and blurred with tears. 'Shall I see if I can find him?' he offered.

'God, no,' she said. 'I know better than that, I hope, thank you very much.' She seemed to make a painful effort to present a more conventional front. 'It doesn't matter two hoots, darling,' she said. 'It was nothing. Fabulous party. Can't wait to begin work. I see great things in poor Ann, you know.'

She walked over to the balustrade and looked down into
the lower foyer which was populous with departing guests.
She was not entirely steady on her pins, he thought. The
last pair of Personages was going downstairs and of the
Company only Charles Random and Gertrude remained. She
leant over the balustrade, holding to it with both hands. If
she was looking for Harry Grove, Peregrine thought, she
hadn't found him. With an unco-ordinated swing she turned,
flapped a long black glove at Peregrine and plunged downstairs. Almost certainly she had not said good-bye to her host
and hostess but, on the whole, perhaps that was just as well.
He wondered if he ought to put her in a taxi but heard Charles
Random shout : 'Hi, Gertie love. Give you a lift?'

Jeremy was waiting for him but Emily Dunne had gone.
Almost everybody had gone. His spirits plummeted abysmally.
Unpredictably, his heart was in his boots.

He went up to Mrs. Greenslade with extended hand.

"Wonderful,' he said. 'How can we thank you.'

4. REHEARSAL

'Who is this comes hopping up the lane?'

*'Hopping? Where? Oh I see. A lady dressed for riding.
She's lame, Master Will. She's hurt. She can't put her foot to
the ground.'*

*'She makes a grace of her ungainliness, Master Hall. There's
a stain across her face. And in her bosom. A raven's feather in
a valley of snow.'*

'Earth. Mire. On her habit, too. She must have fallen.'

'Often enough, I dare swear.'

'She's coming in at the gate.'

'Will! Where ARE *you.* WILL!'

'We'll have to stop again, I'm afraid.' Peregrine said.
'Gertie! Ask her to come on, will you, Charles?'

Charles Random opened the door on the prompt side. 'Gertie! On dear.'

Gertrude Bracey entered with her jaw set and the light of battle in her eye. Peregrine walked down the centre aisle and put his hands on the rail of the orchestral well.

'Gertie, love,' he said, 'it went back again, didn't it? It was all honey and sweet reasonableness and it wouldn't have risen one solitary hackle. She *must* grate. She *must* be bossy. Shakespeare's looking down the lane at that dark pale creature who comes hopping into his life with such deadly seduction. And while he's quivering, slap bang into this disturbance of—of his whole personality—comes your voice: his *wife's* voice, scolding, demanding, possessive, always too loud. It *must* be like that, Gertie. Don't you *see*? You must hurt. You must jangle.'

He waited. She said nothing.

'I can't have it any other way,' Peregrine said.

Nothing.

'Well. Let's build in again, shall we? Back to "*who is this*" please, Marco. You're off, please, Gertie.'

She walked off.

Marcus Knight cast up his eyes in elaborate resignation, raised his arms and let them flop.

'Very well, dear boy,' he said, 'as often as you like, of course. One grows a little jaded but never mind.'

Marco was not the only one, Peregrine thought, to feel jaded: Gertie was enough to reduce an author-director to despair. She had, after a short tour of the States, become wedded to 'Method' acting. This involved endless huddles with whoever would listen to her and a remorseless scavenging through her emotional past for fragments that could start her off on some astonishing association with her performance.

'It's like a bargain basement,' Harry Grove said to Peregrine. 'The things Gertie digs up and tries on are really *too* rococo. We get a new look every day.'

It was a slow process and the unplotted pauses she took in which to bring the truth to light were utterly destructive to concerted playing. 'If she goes on like this,' Peregrine thought, 'she'll tear herself to tatters and leave the audience merely wishing she wouldn't.'

As for Marcus Knight, the danger signals for a major temperament had already been flown. There was a certain thunderous quietude which Peregrine thought it best to disregard.

Really, for him, Peregrine thought, Marco was behaving rather well and he tried to ignore the little hammer that pounded away under Marco's oval cheek.

'*Who is this*——'

Again they built up to her line. When it came it was merely shouted offstage without meaning and apparently without intention.

'Great Christ in Heaven!' Marcus Knight suddenly bellowed, 'how long must this endure! What, in the name of all the suffering clans of martyrdom am I expected to *do*? Am I coupled with a harridan or a bloody dove? My author, my producer, my ART tell me that here is a great moment. I should be fed, by Heaven, fed: I should be led up to. I have my line to make. I must show what I am. My whole being should be lacerated. And so, God knows it is, but by what!' He strode to the door and flung it wide. Gertrude Bracey was exposed looking both terrified and determined. 'By a drivelling, piping pea-hen!' He roared, straight into her face. 'What sort of an actress are you, dear? Are you a woman, dear? Has nobody ever slighted you, trifled with you, deserted you? Have you no conception of the gnawing serpent that ravages a woman scorned?'

Somewhere in the front of the house Harry Grove laughed. Unmistakably, it was he. He had a light, mocking, derisive laugh, highly infectious to anybody who had not inspired it. Unhappily both Knight and Gertrude Bracey, for utterly opposed reasons, took it as a direct personal affront. Knight spun round on his heel, advanced to the edge of the stage and roared into the darkness of the auditorium. 'Who is that! Who is it! I demand an answer.'

The laughter ran up to a falsetto climax and somewhere in the shadows Harry Grove said delightedly: 'Oh dear me, dear me, how very entertaining. The King Dolphin in a rage.'

'Harry,' Peregrine said turning his back on the stage and vainly trying to discern the offender. 'You are a professional actor. You know perfectly well that you are behaving inexcusably. I must ask you to apologise to the company.'

'To the *whole* company, Perry dear? Or just to Gertie for laughing about her not being a woman scorned?'

Before Peregrine could reply, Gertrude re-entered, looking wildly about the house. Having at last distinguished Grove in the back stalls, she pointed to him and screamed out with a virtuosity that she had hitherto denied herself : 'This is a deliberate insult.' She then burst into tears.

There followed a phenomenon that would have been incomprehensible to anybody who was not intimately concerned with the professional theatre. Knight and Miss Bracey were suddenly allied. Insults of the immediate past were as if they had never been. They both began acting beautifully for each other : Gertrude making big eloquent piteous gestures and Marcus responding with massive understanding. She wept. He kissed her hand. They turned with the precision of variety artists to the auditorium and simultaneously shaded their eyes like comic sailors. Grove came gaily down the aisle saying : 'I apologise. Marcus and Gerts. Everybody. I really *do* apologise. In seventeen plastic and entirely different positions. I shall go and be devoured backstage by the worm of contrition. What more can I do? I cannot say with even marginal accuracy that it's all a mistake and you're not at all funny. But anything else. Anything else.'

'Be quiet,' Peregrine said, forcing a note of domineering authority which was entirely foreign to him. 'You will certainly go backstage since you are needed. I will see you after we break. In the meantime I wish neither to see nor hear from you until you make your entrance. Is that understood?'

'I'm sorry,' Grove said quietly. 'I really am,' And he went backstage by the pass-door that Mr. Conducis used when he pulled Peregrine out of the well.

'Marco and Gertie,' Peregrine said and they turned blackly upon him. 'I hope you'll be very generous and do something nobody has a right to ask you. I hope you'll dismiss this lamentable incident as if it had never happened.'

'It is either that person or me. Never in the entire course of my professional experience——'

The Knight temperament raged on. Gertrude listened with gloomy approval and repaired her face. The rest of the company were still as mice. At last Peregrine managed to bring about a truce and eventually they began again at : '*Who is this comes hopping up the lane?*'

The row had had one startling and most desirable effect. Gertrude, perhaps by some process of emotive transference, now gave out her offstage line with all the venom of a fish-wife.

'But *darling*,' reasoned Destiny Meade, a few minutes later, devouring Peregrine with her great black lamps. '*Hopping*. Me? On my first entrance? I mean—actually? I mean what an *entrance*! *Hopping!*'

'Destiny, love, it's like I said. He had a thing about it.'

'Who did?'

'Shakespeare, darling. About a breathless, panting, jigging, hopping woman with a white face and pitchball eyes and blue veins.'

'How peculiar of him.'

'The thing is, for him it was all an expression of sexual attraction.'

'I don't see how I can do a sexy thing if I come on playing hopscotch and puffing and blowing like a whale. Truly.'

'Destiny : listen to what he wrote. Listen.

                                        "*I saw her once*
Hop forty paces through the public street;
And having lost her breath, she spoke, and panted,
       That she did make defect perfection,
          And, breathless, power breathe forth."

'That's why I've made her fall off her horse and come hopping up the lane.'

'Was he sort of kinky?'

'Certainly not,' Marcus interrupted.

'Well, I only wondered. Gloves and everything.'

'Listen, darling. Here you are. Laughing and out of breath——'

'And hopping. *Honestly!*'

'All *right*,' said Marcus. 'We know what you mean but listen. You're marvellous. Your colour's coming and going and your bosom's heaving. He has an entirely normal reaction, Destiny darling. You *send* him. You do see, don't you? *You* send *me*.'

'With my hopping?'

'*Yes*,' he said irritably. 'That and all the rest of it. Come on, darling, do. Make your entrance to me.'

'Yes, Destiny,' Peregrine said. 'Destiny, listen. You're in a velvet habit with your bosom exposed, a little plumed hat and soft little boots and you're lovely, lovely, lovely. And young Dr. Hall has gone out to help you and is supporting you. Charles—come and support her. Yes : like that. Leave her as free as possible. Now : the door opens and we see you. Fabulous. You're in a shaft of sunlight. And *he* sees you. Shakespeare does. And you speak. Right? Right, Destiny? You say——Go on, dear.'

'*Here I come upon your privacy, Master Shakespeare, hopping over your doorstep like a starling.*'

'Yes, and at once, at that very moment you know you've limed him.'

'Limed?'

'Caught.'

'Am I keen?'

'Yes. You're pleased. You know he's famous. And you want to show him off to W.H. You come forward, Marco, under compulsion, and offer your help. Staring at her. And you go to him, Destiny, and skip and half-fall and fetch up laughing and clinging to him. He's terribly, terribly still. Oh, *yes*, Marco, yes. Dead right. Wonderful. And Destiny, darling, that's *right*. You know? It's right. It's what we want.'

'Can I sit down or do I keep going indefinitely panting away on his chest?'

'Look into his face. Give him the whole job. Laugh. No, not that sort of laugh, dear. Not loud. Deep down in your throat !'

'More sexy?'

'Yes,' Peregrine said and ran his hands through his hair. '*That's right. More sexy.*'

'And then I sit down?'

'Yes. He helps you down. Centre. Hall pushes the chair forward. Charles?'

'Could it,' Marcus intervened, 'be left-of-centre, dear boy? I mean I only suggest it because it'll be easier for Dessy and I *think* it'll make a better picture,' Marcus said. 'I can then put her down. Like this.' He did so with infinite grace and himself occupied centre stage.

'I think I like it better the other way, Marco, darling. Could we try it the other way, Perry? This feels false, a bit, to me.'

They jockeyed about for star positions. Peregrine made the final decision in Knight's favour. It really was better that way. Gertrude came on and then Emily : very nice as Joan Hart, and finally Harry Grove, behaving himself and giving a bright, glancing indication of Mr. W. H. Peregrine began to feel that perhaps he had not written a bad play and that, given a bit of luck, he might, after all, hold the company together.

He was aware, in the back of his consciousness that some-one had come into the stalls. The actors were all on stage and he supposed it must be Winter Morris or perhaps Jeremy who often looked in, particularly when Destiny was rehearsing.

They ran the whole scene without interruption and followed it with an earlier one between Emily, Marcus and the in-effable Trevor in which the boy Hamnet, on his eleventh birth-day, received and wore his grandfather's present of a pair of embroidered cheverel gloves. Marcus and Peregrine had suc-ceeded in cowing the more offensive exhibitionisms of Trevor and the scene went quite well. They broke for luncheon. Pere-grine kept Harry Grove back and gave him a wigging which he took so cheerfully that it lost half its sting. He then left and Peregrine saw with concern that Destiny had waited for him. Where then was Marcus Knight and what had become of his proprietary interest in his leading lady? As if in explana-tion, Peregrine heard Destiny say : 'Darling, the King Dol-phin's got a pompous feast with someone at the Garrick. Where shall we go?'

The new curtain was half-lowered, the working lights went out, the stage-manager left and the stage-door banged dis-tantly.

Peregrine turned to go out by front-of-house.
He came face to face with Mr. Conducis.

II

It was exactly as if the clock had been set back a year and
three weeks and he again dripped fetid water along the aisle
of a bombed theatre. Mr. Conducis seemed to wear the same
impeccable clothes and to be seized with the same indefinable
oddness of behaviour. He even took the same involuntary step
backwards, almost as if Peregrine was going to accuse him of
something.

'I have watched your practice,' he said as if Peregrine was
learning the piano. 'If you have a moment to spare there is a
matter I want to discuss with you. Perhaps in your office?'

'Of course, sir,' Peregrine said. 'I'm sorry I didn't see you
had come in.'

Mr. Conducis paid no attention to this. He was looking,
without evidence of any kind of reaction, at the now re-
splendent auditorium : at the crimson curtain, the chandeliers,
the freshly-gilt scrollwork, the shrouded and expectant stalls.

'The restoration is satisfactory?' he asked.

'Entirely so. We shall be ready on time, sir.'

'Will you lead the way?'

Peregrine remembered that on their former encounter Mr.
Conducis had seemed to dislike being followed. He led the
way upstairs to the office, opened the door and found Winter
Morris in residence, dictating letters. Peregrine made a complicated but apparently eloquent face and Morris got to his
feet in a hurry.

Mr. Conducis walked in looking at nothing and nobody.

'This is our manager, sir. Mr. Winter Morris, Mr. Conducis.'

'Oh, yes. Good morning,' said Mr. Conducis. Without giving
an impression of discourtesy he turned away. 'Really, old boy,'
as Mr. Morris afterwards remarked. 'He might have been
giving me the chance to follow my own big nose instead of
backing out of The Presence.'

In a matter of seconds Mr. Morris and the secretary had gone to lunch.

'Will you sit down, sir?'

'No, thank you. I shall not be long. In reference to the glove and documents : I am told that their authenticity is established.'

'Yes.'

'You have based your piece upon these objects?'

'Yes.'

'I have gone into the matter of promotion with Greenslade and with two persons of my acquaintance who are conversant with this type of enterprise.' He mentioned two colossi of the theatre. 'And have given some thought to preliminary treatment. It occurs to me that, properly manipulated, the glove and its discovery and so on, might be introduced as a major theme in promotion.'

'Indeed it might,' Peregrine said fervently.

'You agree with me? I have thought that perhaps some consideration should be given to the possibility of timing the release of the glove-story with the opening of the theatre and of displaying the glove and documents, suitably protected and housed, in the foyer.'

Peregrine said with what he hoped was a show of dispassionate judgment that surely, as a piece of pre-production advertising, this gesture would be unique. Mr. Conducis looked quickly at him and away again. Peregrine asked him if he felt happy about the security of the treasure. Mr. Conducis replied with a short exegesis upon wall safes of a certain type in which, or so Peregrine confusedly gathered, he held a controlling interest.

'Your public relations and press executive,' Mr. Conducis stated in his dead fish voice, 'is a Mr. Conway Boome.'

'Yes. It's his own name,' Peregrine ventured wondering for a moment if he had caught a glint of something that might be sardonic humour but Mr. Conducis merely said : 'I daresay. I understand,' he added, 'that he is experienced in theatrical promotion but I have suggested to Greenslade that having regard for the somewhat unusual character of the type of material we propose to use, it might be as well if Mr. Boome

were to be associated with Maitland Advertising which is one
of my subsidiaries. He is agreeable.'

'I'll be bound he is,' Peregrine thought.

'I am also taking advice on the security aspect from an
acquaintance at Scotland Yard, a Superintendent Alleyn.'

'Oh, yes.'

'Yes. The matter of insurance is somewhat involved, the
commercial worth of the objects being impossible to define. I
am informed that as soon as their existence is made known there
is likely to be an unprecedented response. Particularly from the
United States of America.'

There followed a short silence.

'Mr. Conducis,' Peregrine said, 'I can't help asking you this.
I know it's no business of mine but I really can't help it Are
you—have you—I mean, would you feel at all concerned about
whether the letters and gloves stay in the country of their
owner or not?'

'In my country?' Mr. Conducis asked as if he wasn't sure
that he had one.

'I'm sorry—no. I meant the original owner.'

Peregrine hesitated for a moment and then found himself
embarked upon an excitable plea for the retention of the
document and gloves. He felt he was making no impression
whatever and wished he could stop. There was some indefinable and faintly disgusting taint in the situation.

With a closed face Mr. Conducis waited for Peregrine to
stop and then said: 'That is a sentimental approach to what
is at this juncture a matter for financial consideration. I cannot
speak under any other heading: historical, romantic, nation-
alistic or sentimental. I know,' Mr. Conducis predictably
added, 'nothing of such matters.'

He then startled Peregrine quite shockingly by saying with
an indefinable change in his voice: 'I dislike pale gloves.
Intensely.'

For one moment Peregrine thought he saw something like
anguish in this extraordinary man's face and at the next that
he had been mad to suppose anything of the sort. Mr. Conducis made a slight movement indicating the interview was

at an end. Peregrine opened the door, changed his mind and
shut it again.

'Sir,' he said. 'One other question. May I tell the company
about the letters and glove? The gloves that we use on the
stage will be made by the designer, Jeremy Jones—who is an
expert in such matters. If we are to show the original in the
front of house he should copy it as accurately as possible. He
should go to the museum and examine it. And he will be so
very much excited by the whole thing that I can't guarantee his
keeping quiet about it. In any case, sir, I myself spoke to him
about the glove on the day you showed it to me. You will remember you did not impose secrecy at that time. Since the
report came through I have not spoken of it to anyone except
Morris and Jones.'

Mr. Conducis said : 'A certain amount of leakage at this
stage is probably inevitable and if correctly handled may do
no harm. You may inform your company of all the circumstances. With a strong warning that the information is, for the
time being, confidential and with this proviso : I wish to
remain completely untroubled by the entire business. I realise
that my ownership may well become known : is known in fact,
already, to a certain number of people. This is unavoidable.
But under no circumstances will I give statements, submit to
interviews or be quoted. My staff will see to this at my end. I
hope you will observe the same care, here. Mr. Boome will be
instructed. Good morning. Will you——?'

He made that slight gesture for Peregrine to precede him.
Peregrine did so.

He went out on the circle landing and ran straight into
Harry Grove.

"Hall-lo, dear boy,' said Harry, beaming at him. 'I just
darted back to use the telephone. Destiny and I——' He
stopped short, bobbed playfully round Peregrine at Mr.
Conducis and said : '*Now*, see what I've done! A genius for
getting myself in wrong. My only talent.'

Mr. Conducis said : 'Good morning to you, Grove.' He
stood in the doorway looking straight in front of him.

'*And* to you, wonderful fairy godfather, patron, guiding

light and all those things.' Harry said. 'Have you come to see your latest offspring, your very own performing Dolphins?'

'Yes,' said Mr. Conducis.

'Look at dear Perry!' Harry said. 'He's stricken dumb at my misplaced familiarity. Aren't you, Perry?'

'Not for the first time,' Peregrine said and felt himself to be the victim of a situation he should have controlled.

'Well!' Harry said, glancing with evident amusement from one to the other of his hearers. 'I mustn't double-blot my copybook, must I? Nor must I keep lovely ladies waiting.' He turned to Mr. Conducis with an air of rueful deference. 'I do hope you'll be pleased with us, sir,' he said. 'It must be wonderful to be the sort of man who uses his power to rescue a drowning theatre instead of slapping it under. All the more wonderful since you have no personal interest in our disreputable trade, have you?'

'I have little or no knowledge of it.'

'No. Like vinegar, it doesn't readily mix with Oil,' Harry said. 'Or is it Shipping? I always forget. Doing any yachting lately? But I mustn't go on being a nuisance. Good-bye, sir. Do remember me to Mrs. G. See you later, Perry, dear boy.'

He ran downstairs and out by the main door.

Mr. Conducis said: 'I am late. Shall we——?' They went downstairs and crossed the foyer to the portico. There was the Daimler and, at its door, Peregrine's friend the chauffeur. It gave him quite a shock to see them again and he wondered for a dotty moment, if he would be hailed away once more to Drury Place.

'Good morning,' Mr. Conducis said again. He was driven away and Peregrine joined Jeremy Jones at their habitual chophouse on the Surrey Side.

III

He told the company and Jeremy Jones about the glove before afternoon rehearsal. They all made interested noises. Destiny

Meade became very excited and confused on learning that the
glove was 'historic' and persisted in thinking they would use it
as a prop in the production. Marcus Knight was clearly too
angry to pay more than token attention. He had seen Destiny
return, five minutes late and in hilarious company with W.
Hartly Grove. Gertrude Bracey was equally disgruntled by the
same phenomenon.

When Harry Grove heard about the glove he professed the
greatest interest and explained, in his skittish manner. 'Someone ought to tell Mrs. Constantia Guzman about this.'

'Who on earth,' Peregrine had asked, 'is Mrs. Constantia
Guzman?'

'Inquire of The King Dolphin,' Harry rejoined. He insisted
on referring to Marcus Knight in these terms to the latter's
evident annoyance. Peregrine saw Knight turn crimson to the
roots of his hair and thought it better to ignore Harry.

The two members of the company who were whole-heartedly
moved by Peregrine's announcement were Emily Dunne and
Charles Random and their reaction was entirely satisfactory.
Random kept saying: 'Not true! Well, of *course*. Now, we
know what inspired you. No—it's incredible. It's too much.'

He was agreeably incoherent.

Emily's cheeks were pink and her eyes bright and that too
was eminently satisfactory.

Winter Morris, who was invited to the meeting, was in
ecstasy.

'So what have we got?' he asked at large. 'We have got a
story to make the front pages wish they were double elephants.'

Master Trevor Vere was not present at this rehearsal.

Peregrine promised Jeremy that he would arrange for him to
see the glove as often as he wanted to, at the museum. Morris
was to get into touch with Mr. Greenslade about safe-housing
it in the theatre and the actors were warned about secrecy for
the time being although the undercover thought had clearly
been that a little leakage might be far from undesirable as long
as Mr. Conducis was not troubled by it.

Stimulated perhaps by the news of the glove the company
worked well that afternoon. Peregrine began to block the tricky

second act and became excited about the way Marcus Knight approached his part.

Marcus was an actor of whom it was impossible to say where hard-thinking and technique left off and the pulsing glow that actors call star-quality began. At earlier rehearsals he would do extraordinary things : shout, lay violent emphasis on oddly selected words, make strange, almost occult gestures and embarrass his fellow players by speaking with his eyes shut and his hands clasped in front of his mouth as if he prayed. Out of all this inwardness there would occasionally dart a flash of the really staggering element that had placed him, still a young man, so high in his chancy profession. When the period of incubation had gone by the whole performance would step forward into full light. 'And,' Peregrine thought, 'there's going to be much joy about this one.'

Act Two encompassed the giving of the dead child Hamnet's gloves on her demand to the Dark Lady : a black echo, this, of Bertrand and Bassanio's rings and of Berowne's speculation as to the whiteness of his wanton's hand. It continued with the entertainment of the poet by the infamously gloved lady and his emergence from 'the expense of spirit in a waste of shame.' It ended with his savage reading of the sonnet to her and to W. H. Marcus Knight did this superbly.

W. Hartly Grove lounged in a window seat as Mr. W. H. and, already mingling glances with Rosaline, played secretly with the gloved hand. The curtain came down on a sudden cascade of his laughter. Peregrine spared a moment to reflect that here, as not infrequently in the theatre, a situation in a play reflected in a cockeyed fashion, the emotional relationships between the actors themselves. He had a theory that, contrary to popular fancy, this kind of overlap between the reality of their personalities in and out of their roles was an artistic handicap. An actor, he considered, was embarrassed rather than released by unsublimated chunks of raw association. If Marcus Knight was enraged by the successful blandishments of Harry Grove upon Destiny Meade, this reaction would be liable to upset his balance and bedevil his performance as Shakespeare deceived by Rosaline with W. H.

And yet, apparently, it had not done so. They were all going great guns and Destiny, with only the most rudimentary understanding of the scene, distilled an erotic compulsion that would have peeled the gloves off the hands of the dead child as easily as she filched them from his supersensitive father. 'She really *is*,' Jeremy Jones had said, 'the original overproof *femme fatale*. It's just there. Whether she's a goose or a genius doesn't matter. There's something solemn about that sort of attraction.'

Peregrine had said: 'I wish you'd just try and think of her in twenty years' time with china-boys in her jaws and her chaps hitched up to her ears and her wee token brain shrunk to the size of a pea.'

'Rail on,' Jeremy had said. 'I am unmoved.'

'You don't suppose you'll have any luck?'

'That's right. I don't. She's busily engaged in shuffling off the great star and teaming up with the bounding Grove. Not a nook or cranny left for me.'

'Oh, dear, oh dear, oh dear,' Peregrine had remarked and they let it go at that.

On this particular evening Peregrine himself had at last succeeded, after several rather baffling refusals, in persuading Emily Dunne to come back to supper at the studio Jeremy, who supervised and took part in the construction and painting of his sets at a warehouse not far away, was to look in at The Dolphin and walk home with them over Blackfriars Bridge. It had appeared to Peregrine that this circumstance, when she heard of it, had been the cause of Emily's acceptance. Indeed, he heard her remark in answer to some question from Charles Random: 'I'm going to Jeremy's.' This annoyed Peregrine extremely.

Jeremy duly appeared five minutes before the rehearsal ended and sat in the front stalls. When they broke, Destiny beckoned to him and he went up to the stage through the pass-door. Peregrine saw her lay her hands on Jeremy's coat and talk into his eyes. He saw Jeremy flush up to the roots of his red hair and glance quickly at him. Then he saw Destiny link her arm in Jeremy's and lead him upstage, talking hard.

After a moment or two they parted and Jeremy returned to Peregrine.

'Look,' he said in stage Cockney, 'do me a favour. Be a pal.'

'What's all this?'

'Destiny's got a sudden party and she's asked me. Look, Perry, you don't mind if I go? The food's all right at the studio. You and Emily can do very nicely without me: damn' sight better than with.'

'She'll think you're bloody rude,' Peregrine said angrily, 'and she won't be far wrong, at that.'

'Not at all. She'll be enchanted. It's you she's coming to see.'

'I'm not so sure.'

'Properly speaking, you ought to be jolly grateful.'

'Emily'll think it's a put-up job.'

'So what? She'll be pleased as Punch. Look, Perry, I—I can't wait. Destiny's driving us all and she's ready to go. Look, I'll have a word with Emily.'

'You'd damn' well better though what in decency's name you can find to say!'

'It'll all be as right as a bank. I promise.'

'So *you* say.' Peregrine contemplated his friend whose freckled face was pink, excited and dreadfully vulnerable. 'All right,' he said. 'Make your excuses to Emily. Go to your party. I think you're heading for trouble but that's your business.'

'I only hope I'm heading for *something*,' Jeremy said. 'Fanks, mate. You're a chum.'

'I very much doubt it,' said Peregrine.

He stayed front-of-house and saw Jeremy talk to Emily on stage. Emily's back was towards him and he was unable to gauge her reaction but Jeremy was all smiles. Peregrine had been wondering what on earth he could say to her when it dawned upon him that, come hell or highwater, he could not equivocate with Emily.

Destiny was up there acting her boots off with Marcus, Harry Grove, and now Jeremy, for an audience. Marcus maintained a proprietary air to which she responded like a docile concubine, Peregrine thought. But he noticed that she managed quite often to glance at Harry with a slight widening of her

eyes and an air of decorum that was rather more provocative
than if she'd hung round his neck and said : 'Now.' She also
beamed upon poor Jeremy. They all talked excitedly, making
plans for their party. Soon they had gone away by the stage
door.

Emily was still on stage.

'Well,' Peregrine thought, 'here goes.'

He walked down the aisle and crossed to the pass-door in
the box on the prompt side. He never went backstage by this
route without a kind of aftertaste of his first visit to The
Dolphin. Always, behind the sound of his own footsteps on
the uncarpeted stairway, Peregrine caught an echo of Mr. Conducis coming invisibly to his rescue.

It was a slight shock now, therefore, to hear, as he shut the
pass-door behind him, actual footsteps beyond the turn in this
narrow, dark and winding stair.

'Hallo?' he said. 'Who's that?'

The steps halted.

'Coming up,' Peregrine said, not wanting to collide.

He went on up the little stairway and turned the corner.

The door leading to the stage opened slightly admitting a
blade of light. He saw that somebody moved uncertainly as
if in doubt whether to descend or not and he got the impression that whoever it was had actually been standing in the
dark behind the door.

Gertrude Bracey said, 'I was just coming down.'

She pushed open the door and went on-stage to make way for
him. As he came up with her, she put her hand on his arm.

'Aren't you going to Destiny's sinister little party?' she
asked.

'Not I,' he said.

'Unasked? Like me?'

'That's right,' he said lightly and wished she wouldn't stare
at him like that. She leant towards him.

'Do you know what I think of Mr. W. Hartly Grove?' she
asked quietly. Peregrine shook his head and she then told
him. Peregrine was used to uninhibited language in the theatre,
but Gertrude Bracey's eight words on Harry Grove made him
blink.

'Gertie, *dear*!'

'Oh, yes,' she said. 'Gertie, dear. And Gertie dear knows what she's talking about, don't you worry.'

She turned her back on him and walked away.

IV

'Emily,' Peregrine said as they climbed up Wharfingers Lane, 'I hope you don't mind it just being me. And I hope you don't think there's any skulduggery at work. Such as me getting rid of Jer in order to make a heavy pass at you. Not, mark you, that I wouldn't like to but that I really wouldn't have the nerve to try such an obvious ploy.'

'I should hope not,' said Emily with composure.

'Well, I wouldn't. I suppose you've seen how it is with Jeremy?'

'One could hardly miss it.'

'One couldn't, could one?' he agreed politely.

Suddenly for no particular reason they both burst out laughing and he took her arm.

'Imagine!' he said. 'Here we are on Bankside, not much more than a stone's throw from The Swan and The Rose and The Globe. Shakespeare must have come this way a thousand times after rehearsals had finished for the day. We're doing just what he did and I do wish, Emily, that we could take water for Blackfriars.'

'It's pleasant,' Emily said, 'to be in company that isn't self-conscious about him and doesn't mistake devotion for idolatry.'

'Well, he *is* unique, so what's the matter with being devoted? Have you observed, Emily, that talent only fluctuates about its own middle line whereas genius nearly always makes great walloping bloomers?'

'Like Agnes Pointing Upwards and bits of *Cymbeline*?'

'Yes. I think, perhaps, genius is nearly always slightly lacking in taste.'

'Anyway, without intellectual snobbery?'

'Oh that, certainly.'

'Are you pleased with rehearsals, so far?'

'On the whole.'

'I suppose it's always a bit of a shock bringing something you've written to the melting pot or forge or whatever the theatre is. Particularly when, as producer, you yourself *are* the melting pot.'

'Yes, it is. You see your darling child being processed, being filtered through the personalities of the actors and turning into something different on the way. And you've got to accept all that because a great many of the changes are for the good. I get the oddest sort of feeling sometimes, that, as producer, I've stepped outside myself as playwright. I begin to wonder if I ever knew what the play is about.'

'I can imagine.'

They walked on in companionship: two thinking ants moving eastwards against the evening out-swarm from the City. When they reached Blackfriars it had already grown quiet there and the little street where Jeremy and Peregrine lived was quite deserted. They climbed up to the studio and sat in the window drinking dry martinis and trying to see. The Dolphin on the far side of the river.

'We haven't talked about the letter and the glove,' Emily said. 'Why, I wonder, when it's such a tremendous thing. You must have felt like a high-pressure cooker with it all bottled up inside you.'

'Well, there was Jeremy to explode to. And of course the expert.'

'How strange it is,' Emily said. She knelt on the window-seat with her arms folded on the ledge and her chin on her arms. Her heart-shaped face looked very young. Peregrine knew that he must find out about her: about how she thought and what she liked and disliked and where she came from and whether she was or had been in love and if so what she did about it. 'How strange,' she repeated. 'To think of John Shakespeare over in Henley Street making them for his grandson. Would he make them himself or did he have a foreman-glover?'

'He made them himself. The note says "mayde by my father".'

'Is the writing all crabbed and squiggly like his signatures?'

'Yes. But not exactly like any of them. People's writing isn't always like their signatures. The handwriting experts have all found what they call "definitive" points of agreement.'

'*What* will happen to them, Perry? Will he sell to the highest bidder or will he have any ideas about keeping them here? Oh,' Emily cried, 'they *should* be kept here.'

'I tried to say as much but he shut up like a springtrap.'

'Jeremy,' Emily said, 'will probably go stark ravers if they're sold out of the country.'

'Jeremy?'

'Yes. He's got a manic thing about the draining away of national treasures, hasn't he? I wouldn't have been in the least surprised, would you, if it had turned out to be Jeremy who stole the Goya "Wellington." Simply to keep it in England, you know.'

Emily chuckled indulgently and Peregrine thought he detected the proprietary air of romance and was greatly put out. Emily went on and on about Jeremy Jones and his shop and his treasures and how moved and disturbed he was by the new resolution. 'Don't you feel he is perfectly capable,' she said, 'of bearding Mr. Conducis in his den and telling him he mustn't let them go?'

'I do hope you're exaggerating.'

'I really don't believe I am. He's a fanatic.'

'You know him very well, don't you?'

'Quite well. I help in their shop sometimes. They *are* experts, aren't they, on old costume? Of course Jeremy has to leave most of it to his partner because of work in the theatre but in between engagements he does quite a lot. I'm learning how to do all kinds of jobs from him like putting old tinsel on pictures and repairing bindings. He's got some wonderful prints and books.'

'I know,' Peregrine said rather shortly. 'I've been there.'

She turned her head and looked thoughtfully at him. 'He's madly excited about making the gloves for the show. He was saying just now he's got a pair of Jacobean gloves, quite small, and he thinks they might be suitable if he took the existing beadwork off and copied the embroidery off Hamnet's glove on to them.'

'I know, he told me.'

'He's letting me help with that, too.'

'Fun for you.'

'Yes. I like him very much. I do hope if he's madly in love with Destiny that it works out but I'm afraid I rather doubt it.'

'Why?'

'He's a darling but he hasn't got anything like enough of what it takes. Well, I wouldn't have thought so.'

'Really?' Peregrine quite shouted in an excess of relief. He began to talk very fast about the glove and the play and what they should have for dinner. He had been wildly extravagant and had bought all the things he himself liked best : smoked salmon with caviare folded inside, cold partridge and the ingredients for two kinds of salad. It was lucky that his choice seemed to coincide with Emily's. They had Bernkastler Docktor with the smoked salmon and it was so good they went on drinking it with the partridge. Because of Jeremy's defection there was rather a lot of everything and they ate and drank it all up.

When they had cleared away they returned to the window-seat and watched the Thames darken and the lights come up on Bankside. Peregrine began to think how much he wanted to make love to Emily. He watched her and talked less and less. Presently he closed his hand over hers. Emily turned her hand, gave his fingers a brief matter-of-fact squeeze and then withdrew.

'I'm having a lovely time,' she said, 'but I'm not going to stay very late. It takes ages to get back to Hampstead.'

'But I'll drive you. Jeremy hasn't taken the car. It lives in a little yard round the corner.'

'Well, that'll be grand. But I still won't stay very late.'

'I'd like you stay for ever and a day.'

'That sounds like a theme song from a rather twee musical.'

'Emily : have you got a young man?'

'No.'

'Do you have a waiting list, at all?'

'No, Peregrine.'

'No preferential booking?'

'I'm afraid not.'

'Are you ever so non-wanton?'

'Ever so.'

'Well,' he sighed, 'it's original, of course.'

'It's not meant to madden and inflame.'

'That was what I feared. Well, O.K. I'll turn up the lights and show you my photographs.'

'You jolly well do,' said Emily.

So they looked at Peregrine's and Jeremy's scrapbooks and talked interminable theatre shop and presently Emily stood up and said : now she must go.

Peregrine helped her into her coat with rather a perfunctory air and banged round the flat getting his own coat and shutting drawers.

When he came back and found Emily with her hands in her pockets looking out of the window he said loudly : 'All the same, it's scarcely fair to have cloudy hair and a husky voice and your sort of face and body and intelligence and not even *think* about being provocative.'

'I do apologise.'

'I suppose I can't just give you "a single famished kiss"?'

'All right,' said Emily. 'But not too famished.'

'*Emily!*' Peregrine muttered and became, to his astonishment, breathless.

When they arrived at her flat in Hampstead she thanked him again for her party and he kissed her again but lightly this time. 'For my own peace of mind,' he said. 'Dear Emily, good night.'

'Good night, dear Peregrine.'

'Do you know something?'

'What?'

'We open a fortnight to-night.'

V

BLISS FOR BARDOLITERS
STAGGERING DISCOVERY
ABSOLUTELY PRICELESS SAY EXPERTS

MYSTERY GLOVE
WHO FOUND IT?
DOLPHIN DISCOVERY

FIND OF FOUR CENTURIES
NO FAKING SAY EGG-HEADS
SHAKESPEARE'S DYING SON

IN HIS OWN WRITE
BARD'S HAND AND NO KIDDING
INSPIRES PLAYWRIGHT JAY

Important Discovery
Exhaustive tests have satisfied the most distinguished scholars
and experts of the authenticity——

Glove—Letter—Sensation
'It's the most exciting thing that has ever happened to me,'
says tall, gangling playwright, Peregrine Jay.

WHO OWNS THE DOLPHIN GLOVE?
WE GIVE YOU ONE GUESS
'NO COMMENT'—CONDUCIS

FABULOUS OFFER FROM U.S.A.

AMAZING DEVELOPMENTS
DOLPHIN GLOVE MYSTERY

Spokesman for Conducis says No Decision on Sale. May go to
States.

Coming Events
The restored Dolphin Theatre on Bankside will open on
Thursday with a new play : *The Glove*, written and directed
by Peregrine Jay and inspired, it is generally understood, by
the momentous discovery of——

Opening To-morrow

At The Dolphin. Bankside. Under Royal Patronage. *The Glove* by Peregrine Jay. The Dolphin Glove with Documents will be on view in the foyer. Completely sold out for the next four weeks. Waiting list now open.

VI

'You've been so very obliging,' Jeremy Jones said to the learned young assistant at the museum, 'letting us have access to the glove and take up so much of your time, that Miss Dunne suggested you might like to see the finished copies.'

'That's very nice of you. I shall be most interested.'

'They're only stage-props, you know,' Jeremy said, opening a cardboard box. 'But I've taken a little more trouble than usual because the front row of the stalls will be comparing them to the real thing.'

'*And* because it was a labour of love,' Emily said. 'Mostly that, Jeremy, now, wasn't it?'

'Well, perhaps. There you are.'

He turned back a piece of old silk and exposed the gloves lying neatly, side by side. The assistant bent over them. 'I should think the front row of the stalls will be perfectly satisfied,' he said. 'They are really *very* good copies. Accurate in the broad essentials and beautifully worked. Where did you get your materials?'

'From stock. A thread of silk here, a seed-pearl there. Most of it's false, of course. The sequins are Victorian, as you see.'

'They fill the bill quite well, however, at a distance. I hope you never feel tempted,' the assistant said with pedantic archness, 'to go in for antiquarian forgery, Mr. Jones. You'd be much too successful.'

'To me,' Jeremy said. 'It seems a singularly revolting form of chicanery.'

'Good. I understand that a car will be sent here to collect the glove to-morrow. I am to deliver it at the theatre and to see it safely housed. I believe you have designed the setting.

Perhaps you would call in here and we can go together. I would prefer to have someone with me. Unnecessarily particular, I dare say, but there's been so much publicity.'

'I will be delighted to come,' said Jeremy.

'There is to be an observer at the theatre I understand, to witness the procedure and inspect the safety precautions. Somebody from the police, I think it is.'

'So I hear,' said Jeremy. 'I'm glad to know they are being careful.'

VII

The malaise of First Night Nerves had gripped Peregrine, not tragically and aesthetically by the throat but, as is its habit, shamefully in the guts.

At half past six on Thursday morning, he caught sight of himself in the bathroom shaving-glass. He saw, with revulsion, a long, livid face, pinched up into untimely wrinkles and strange dun-coloured pouches. The stubbled jaw sagged and the lips were pallid. There was a general suggestion of repulsive pig-headedness and a terrible dearth of charm.

The final dress-rehearsal had ended five hours ago. In fourteen hours the curtain would rise and in twenty-four hours he would be quivering under the lash of the morning critics.

'O God, God, why, why have I done this fearful thing!'

Every prospect of the coming day and night was of an excursion with Torquemada : the hours when there was nothing to do were as baleful as those when he would be occupied. He would order flowers, send telegrams, receive telegrams, answer telephone calls He would prowl to and fro and up and down all alone in his lovely theatre, unable to rest, unable to think coherently and when he met anybody—Winty Morris or the stage director or the S.M. or some hellish gossip hound —he would be cool and detached. At intervals he would take great nauseating swigs from a bottle of viscous white medicine.

He tried going back to bed but hated it. After a time he got up, shaved his awful face, bathed, dressed, suddenly was invaded by a profound inertia and sleepiness, lay down and was instantly possessed of a compulsion to walk.

He rose, listened at Jeremy's door, heard him snore and stole downstairs. He let himself out into London.

Into the early morning sounds and sights of the river and of the lanes and steps and streets. The day was fresh and sunny and would presently be warm. He walked to the gap where he could look across the Thames to Southwark. The newly-painted stage-house and dome of The Dolphin showed up clearly now and the gilded flag-pole glittered so brightly it might have been illuminated.

As he stared at it a bundle ran up and opened out into their new flag: a black dolphin on a gold ground. Jobbins was on his mark in good time. Big Ben and all the clocks in the City struck eight and Peregrine's heart's blood rose and pounded in his ears. The glory of London was upon him. A kind of rarefied joy possessed him, a trembling anticipation of good fortune that he was scared to acknowledge.

He was piercingly happy. He loved all mankind with indiscriminate embracement and more particularly Emily Dunne. He ran back to the flat and sang *Rigoletto* on his way upstairs.

'You look,' Jeremy said, 'like the dog's dinner and you sound like nothing on earth. Can you be joyful?'

'I can and I am.'

'Long may it last.'

'Amen.'

He could eat no breakfast. Even black coffee disgusted him. He went over to the theatre at nine o'clock. Jeremy was to come in at ten with Emily and the assistant from the museum to see the installation of the glove and documents. He, too, crackled like a cat's fur with first night nerves.

When Peregrine arrived at The Dolphin it was alive with cleaners and florists' assistants. As he went upstairs he heard the telephone ring, stop and ring again. The bar was in a state of crates, cartons and men in shirtsleeves, and on the top landing itself two packing cases had been opened and their contents displayed: a pair of wrought-iron pedestals upon which were mounted two bronze dolphins, stylised and sleek.

They were a gift from Mr. Conducis who had no doubt commissioned Mr. Greenslade to go to 'the best man.' This he might be said to have done with the result that while the dolphins were entirely out of style with their company and setting they were good enough to hold their own without causing themselves or their surroundings to become ridiculous.

Peregrine suggested that they should be placed in the circle foyer. One on each side of the steps from the sunken landing.

He crossed the foyer and went into the office.

Winter Morris was behind his desk. He was not alone. A very tall man with an air of elegance and authority stood up as Peregrine entered.

'Oh, lord,' Peregrine thought. 'Another of the Conducis swells or is it somebody to check up on how we behave with the Royals? Or what?'

'Morning, Perry old boy,' said Morris. 'Glad you've come in. Mr. Peregrine Jay, Superintendent Alleyn.'

5 . CLIMAX

Alleyn was not altogether unused to the theatrical scene or to theatrical people. He had been concerned in four police investigations in which actors had played—and 'played' had been the operative word—leading roles. As a result of these cases he was sardonically regarded at the Yard as something of an expert on the species.

It was not entirely on this score, however, that he had been sent to The Dolphin. Some five years ago, Mr. Vassily Conducis had been burgled in Drury Place. Alleyn had been sent in and had made a smartish catch and recovered the entire haul within twenty-four hours. Mr. Conducis was away at the time but on his return had asked Alleyn to call, probably with the idea of making a tangible acknowledgement. Possibly Alleyn's manner had made him change his mind and substitute a number of singularly unsparkling congratulations delivered in a stifled tone from somewhere in the region of his epiglottis. Alleyn had left, uncharmed by Mr. Conducis.

Their next encounter was the result of a letter to Alleyn's Great White Chief signed by Mr. Conducis and requesting advice and protection for the Shakespeare documents and glove.

'He's asked for you, Rory,' the Great White Chief said. 'No regard for your rank and status, of course. Very cool. In other respects I suppose, you *are* the man for the job: what with your theatrical past and your dotage on the Bard. These damned objects seem to be worth the spoils of the Great Train Robbery. Tell him to buy his protection from a reputable firm and leave us alone, by Heaven.'

'I'd be delighted.'

'No, you wouldn't. You're hell bent on getting a look at the things.'

'I'm not hell bent on getting another look at Conducis.'

'No? What's wrong with him, apart from stinking of money?'

'Nothing, I daresay.'

'Well, you'd better find out when these things are going to be transferred and check up on the security. We don't want another bloody Goya and worse on our hands.'

So Alleyn went to The Dolphin at nine o'clock on the morning of the opening performance.

The housing for the glove and letters was in a cavity made in the auditorium well above the sunken landing which was, itself, three steps below the level of the circle foyer. In this wall was lodged a large steel safe, with convex plate-glass replacing the outward side. The door of the safe, opposite this window, was reached from the back of the circle and concealed by a panel in the wall. Between the window and the exterior face of the wall were sliding steel doors, opened electrically by a switch at the back of the cavity. Concealed lighting came up when the doors were opened. Thus the glove and letters would be exposed to patrons on the stairs, the landing and, more distantly, in the foyer.

The safe was a make well-enough known to Alleyn. It carried a five-figure lock. This combination could be chosen by the purchaser. It was sometimes based on a key word and a very simple code. For instance, the numbers from one to zero might be placed under the letters of the alphabet from A to J and again from K to T and again from U to Z. Each number had therefore two and in the case of 1-6, three corresponding letters. Thus, if the key word was 'night' the number of the combination would be 49780.

Jeremy had caused the steel safe to be lined with padded yellow silk. On its floor was a book-hinged unit covered with black velvet, it had a variable tilt, and was large enough to display the glove and two documents. He had made a beautifully lettered legend which had been framed and would be hung below the wall cavity. During performances the sliding doors would be retracted and the plate glass window exposed.

Alleyn made a very thorough inspection and found the precautions rather more efficient than might have been expected. There were not, at large, many criminal virtuosi of the combination lock who would be equal to this one. It would have to be a cracksman's job. An efficient burglar alarm had been installed and would go into action at the first attempt at entry into the theatre. Once the glove and documents were housed the safe would not be re-opened, the interior lighting and sliding doors in front of the glass panel being operated from a switch inside the wall cavity. He pointed out that one man on another man's shoulders could effect a smash, snatch and grab and asked about watchmen. He was told that for as long as the objects were in the theatre, there would be a man on the landing. Jobbins, late Phipps Bros., was revealed in a brand new uniform. He was to be on duty from four up to midnight when he would be relieved by a trained man from a security organisation. Jobbins would sleep on the premises in an unused dressing-room and could be roused in case of need. A second man already on duty would take over at 8 a.m. and remain in the foyer until Jobbins returned at four. The burglar alarm would be switched on by Jobbins after the show when he locked up for the night.

Alleyn had been fully informed of these arrangements when Peregrine walked into the office. As they shook hands he saw the pallor and the shadows under the eyes and thought : 'First night terrors, poor chap.'

'Mr. Alleyn's had a look at our security measures,' Morris said, 'and thinks they'll pass muster. He's going to wait and see the treasure safely stored.' His telephone rang. 'Excuse me.'

Alleyn said to Peregrine : 'You're all in the throes of every kind of preoccupation. Don't pay any attention to me. If I may : while I'm waiting I'll look at this enchanting theatre. What a superb job you've done.'

This was unlike Peregrine's idea of a plain-clothes police-man. Alleyn had reached the door before he said : 'I'll show you round, sir.'

'I wouldn't dream of it. If I may just wander. You're up to your neck, I'm sure.'

'On the contrary. Morris is, but my problem,' Peregrine said, 'is not having anything real to do. I'd like to show you The Dolphin.'

'Well, in that case——'

It was a comprehensive tour. Alleyn was so clearly interested and so surprisingly well-informed that Peregrine actually en-joyed himself. He found himself talking about the play and what he had tried to do with it and how it had been born of his first sight of Hamnet Shakespeare's glove.

Alleyn knew about the terms of the Will and about Joan Hart getting the wearing apparel. Indeed Peregrine would have betted Alleyn knew as much as he did about Shakespearian scholarship and was as familiar with the plays as he was him-self.

For his part, Alleyn liked this strained, intelligent and modest young man. He hoped Peregrine had written and pro-duced a good play. Alleyn asked one or two questions and since he was a trained investigator and was personally attracted by the matter in hand, Peregrine found himself talking about his work with an ease that he would never have thought pos-sible on a ten minutes' acquaintance. He began to speak quickly and excitedly, his words tumbling over each other. His love of The Dolphin welled up into his voice.

'Shall we go backstage?' he said. 'Or—wait a moment. I'll

take the Iron up and you can see Jeremy Jones's set for the first act.'

He left Alleyn in the stalls, went through the pass-door, and sent up the elegantly painted fireproof curtain. He then moved onstage and faced the house. He had run up the pass-door passage very quickly and his blood pounded in his ears. Nervous exhaustion, wasn't it called? He even felt a bit dizzy.

The cleaners upstairs had unshuttered a window and a shaft of sunlight struck down upon the stage. It was peopled by dancing motes.

'Is anything the matter?' an unusually deep voice asked quite close at hand. Alleyn had come down the centre aisle. Peregrine, dazzled, thought he was leaning on the rail of the orchestra well.

'No—I mean—no nothing. It's just that I was reminded of my first visit to The Dolphin.'

Was it because the reminder had been so abrupt or because over the last week Peregrine had eaten very little and slept hardly at all that he felt so monstrously unsure of himself. Alleyn wouldn't have thought it was possible for a young man to turn any whiter in the face than Peregrine already was but, somehow he now contrived to do so. He sat down on Jeremy's Elizabethan dower chest and wiped his hand across his mouth. When he looked up Alleyn stood in front of him. 'Just where the hole was,' Peregrine thought.

He said : 'Do you know, underneath your feet there's a little stone well with a door. It was there that the trap used to work. Up and down, you know, for Harlequin and Hamlet's Ghost and I dare say for a Lupino or a Lane of that vintage. Or perhaps both. Oh, dear.'

'Stay where you are for the moment. You've been overdoing things.'

'Do you think so? I don't know. But I tell you what. Through all the years after the bomb that well gradually filled with stinking water and then one morning I nearly drowned in it.'

Alleyn listened to Peregrine's voice going on and on and Peregrine listened to it, too, as if it belonged to someone else. He realised with complete detachment that for a year and three months some rather terrible notion about Mr. Conducis had been stuffed away at the back of the mind that was Peregrine. It had been and still was, undefined and unacknowledged but because he was so tired and ravaged by anxiety it had almost come out to declare itself. He was very relieved to hear himself telling this unusual policeman exactly what had happened that morning. When he had related everything down to the last detail he said: 'And it was all to be kept quiet, except for Jeremy Jones so now I've broken faith, I suppose, and I couldn't care, by and large, less. I feel better,' said Peregrine loudly.

'I must say you look several shades less green about the gills. You've half-killed yourself over this production, haven't you?'

'Well, one does, you know.'

'I'm sorry I dragged you up and down all those stairs. Where does that iron curtain work from? The prompt side. Oh, yes I see. Don't move. I'll do it. Dead against the union rules, I expect, but never mind.'

The fire curtain inched its way down. Alleyn glanced at his watch. Any time now the party from the museum should arrive.

He said: 'That was an extraordinary encounter, I must say. But out of it—presumably—has grown all this: the theatre— your play. And now: to-night.'

'And now to-night. Oh, God!'

'Would it be a good idea for you to go home and put your boots up for an hour or two?'

'No, thank you. I'm perfectly all right. Sorry to have behaved so oddly,' Peregrine said, rubbing his head. 'I simply have no notion why I bored you with my saga. You won't, I trust, tell Mr. Conducis.'

'I shall,' Alleyn said lightly, 'preserve an absolute silence.'

'I can't begin to explain what an odd man he is.'

'I have met Mr. Conducis.'

'Did you think him at all dotty? Or sinister? Or merely plutocratic?'

'I was quite unable to classify him.'

'When I asked him where he found the treasure he said: at sea. Just that: at sea. It sounded rum.'

'Not in the yacht *Kalliope* by any chance?'

'The yacht—*Kalliope*. Wait a moment—what is there about the yacht *Kalliope*?' Peregrine asked. He felt detached from his surroundings, garrulous and in an odd way rather comfortable but not quite sure that if he stood up he might not turn dizzy. 'The yacht *Kalliope*' he repeated.

'It was his private yacht and it was run down and split in two in a fog off Cape St. Vincent.'

'*Now* I remember. Good lord——'

A commotion of voices broke out in the entrance.

'I think,' Alleyn said, 'that the treasure has arrived. Will you stay here for a breather? Or come and receive it?'

'I'll come.'

When they reached the foyer, Emily and Jeremy Jones and the assistant from the museum had arrived. The assistant carried a metal case. Winter Morris had run downstairs to meet them. They all went up to the office and the whole affair became rather formal and portentous. The assistant was introduced to everybody. He laid his metal case on Peregrine's desk, unlocked and opened it and stood back.

'Perhaps,' he said, looking round the little group and settling on Peregrine, 'we should have formal possession taken. If you will just examine the contents and accept them as being in good order.'

'Jeremy's the expert,' Peregrine said. 'He must know every stitch and stain on the glove by this time, I should think.'

'Indeed, yes,' said the assistant warmly. 'Mr. Jones, then—will you?'

Jeremy said : 'I'd love to.'

He removed the little desk from the case and laid it on the desk.

Peregrine caught Alleyn's eye. 'Stained, as you see,' he murmured, 'with water. They say : sea-water.'

Jeremy opened the desk. His delicate, nicotine-stained fingers folded back the covering tissues and exposed the little wrinkled glove and two scraps of documents.

'There you are,' he said. 'Shall I?'

'Please do.'

With great delicacy he lifted them from their housing and laid them on the desk.

'And this,' said the assistant pleasantly, 'is when I bow myself out. Here is an official receipt, Mr. Morris, if you will be good enough to sign it.'

While Morris was doing this Peregrine said to Alleyn: 'Come and look.'

Alleyn moved forward. He noticed as he did so that Peregrine stationed himself beside Miss Emily Dunne, that there was a glint of fanaticism in the devouring stare that Jeremy Jones bent upon the glove, that Winter Morris expanded as if he had some proprietary rights over it and that Emily Dunne appeared to unfold a little at the approach of Peregrine. Alleyn then stooped over the notes and the glove and wished that he could have been alone. There could, at such a moment, be too much anticipation, too much pumping up of appropriate reactions. The emotion the relics were expected to arouse was delicate, chancy and tenuous. It was not much good thinking: 'But the Hand of Glory moved warmly across that paper and four centuries ago a small boy's sick fist filled out that glove and somewhere between then and now a lady called M.E. wrote a tidy little memorandum for posterity.' Alleyn found himself wishing very heartily that Peregrine's play would perform the miracle of awareness which would take the sense of death away from Shakespeare's note and young Hamnet's glove.

He looked up at Peregrine. 'Thank you for letting me come so close,' he said.

'You must see them safely stowed.'

'If I may.'

Winter Morris became expansive and a little fussy. Jeremy, after a hesitant glance, laid the treasure on Peregrine's blotter. There was a discussion with the museum man about temperature and fire risks and then a procession of sorts formed up and they all went into the back of the circle, Jeremy carrying the blotter.

'On your right,' Morris said unnecessarily.

The panel in the circle wall was open and so was the door of the safe. Jeremy drew out the black velvet easel-shaped unit, tenderly disposed the glove upon its sloping surface and flanked the glove with the two documents.

'I hope the nap of the velvet will hold them,' he said. 'I've tilted the surface like this to give a good view. Here goes.'

He gently pushed the unit into the safe.

'How do the front doors work?' he asked.

'On your left,' Morris fussed. 'On the inside surface of the wall. Shall I?'

'Please, Winty.'

Morris slipped his fingers between the safe and the circle wall. Concealed lighting appeared and with a very slight whisper the steel panels on the far side slid back.

'Now!' he said. 'Isn't that quite something?'

'We can't *see* from here, though, Winty,' Peregrine said. 'Let's go out and see.'

'I know,' Jeremy agreed. 'Look, would you all go out and tell me if it works or if the background ought to be more tilted? Sort of spread yourselves.'

' *"Some to kill cankers in the moss-rose buds"?'* Alleyn asked mildly.

Jeremy looked at him in a startled manner and then grinned.

'The superintendent,' he said, 'is making a nonsense of us. Emily, would you stay in the doorway, love, and be a liaison between me in the circle and the others outside?'

'Yes. All right.'

The men filed out. Morris crossed the circle foyer. Peregrine stood on the landing and the man from the museum a little below him. Alleyn strolled to the door, passed it and remained in the circle. He was conscious that none of these people except, of course, the museum man, was behaving in his or her customary manner but that each was screwed up to a degree of inward tension over which a stringent self-discipline was imposed. 'And for them,' he thought, 'this sort of thing occurs quite often, it's a regular occupational hazard. They are seasoned troops and about to go into action.'

'It should be more tilted, Jer,' Peregrine's voice was saying. 'And the things'll have to be higher up on the easel.'

The museum assistant, down on the first flight, said something nasal and indistinguishable.

'*What's* he talking about?' Jeremy demanded.

'He says it doesn't show much from down below but he supposes that is unavoidable,' said Emily.

'Wait a bit.' Jeremy reached inside the safe. 'More tilt,' he said. 'Oh, *blast*, it's collapsed.'

'Can I help?' Emily asked.

'Not really. Tell them to stay where they are.'

Alleyn walked over to the safe. Jeremy Jones was on his knees gingerly smoothing out the glove and the documents on the velvet surface. 'I'll have to use *beastly* polythene and I hoped not,' he said crossly. He laid a sheet of it over the treasures and fastened it with black velvet-covered drawing pins. Then he replaced the easel in the safe at an almost vertical angle. There was a general shout of approval from the observers.

'They say : much joy,' Emily told him.

'Shall I shut the doors and all?'

'Yes.'

'Twiddle the thing and all?'

'Winty says yes.'

Jeremy shut the steel door and span the lock.

'Now let's look.'

He and Emily went out.

Alleyn came from the shadows, opened the wall panel and looked at the safe. It was well and truly locked. He shut the panel and turned to find that at a distance of about thirty feet down the passageway leading to the boxes, a boy stood with his hands in his pockets, watching him : a small boy, he thought at first, of about twelve, dressed in over-smart clothes.

'Hallo,' Alleyn said. 'Where did you spring from?'

'That's my problem,' said the boy. '*Would* you mind.'

Alleyn walked across to him. He was a pretty boy with big eyes and an impertinent, rather vicious mouth. '*Would* you mind!' he said again. 'Who are you staring at? *If* it's not a rude question?'

The consonants and vowels were given full attention.

'At you,' Alleyn said.

Peregrine's voice outside on the landing asked : 'Where's Superintendent Alleyn?'

'Here!' Alleyn called. He turned to go.

'Aeoh, I *beg* pardon, I'm sure,' said Trevor Vere. 'You must be the bogey from the Yard. What could I have been thinking of! Manners.'

Alleyn went out to the front. He found that Marcus Knight and Destiny Meade had arrived and joined the company of viewers.

Above the sunken landing where the two flights of stairs came out was an illuminated peepshow. Yellow and black for the heraldic colours of a gentleman from Warwickshire, two scraps of faded writing and a small boy's glove.

Jeremy fetched his framed legend from the office and fixed it in position underneath.

'Exactly right,' said the man from the museum. 'I congratulate you, Mr. Jones. It couldn't be better displayed.'

He put his receipt in his breast pocket and took his leave of them.

'It's perfect, Jer,' said Peregrine.

Trevor Vere strolled across the landing and leant gracefully on the balustrade.

'I reckon,' he observed at large, 'any old duff could crack that peter with his eyes shut. Kid steaks.'

Peregrine said: 'What are you doing here, Trevor? You're not called.'

'I just looked in for my mail, Mr. Jay.'

'Why aren't you at school?'

'I took one of my turns last night, Mr. Jay. They quite understand at school.'

'You're not needed here. Much better go home and rest.'

'Yes, Mr. Jay.' A terribly winning smile illuminated Trevor's photogenic face. 'I wanted to wish you and the play and everybody the most fabulous luck. Mummy joins me.'

'Thank you. The time for that is later. Off you go.'

Trevor, still smiling, drifted downstairs.

'Dear little manikin,' Jeremy said with venom.

Emily said: 'Men and cameras, Winty, in the lane.'

'The Press, darling,' Morris said. 'Shots of people looking at the glove. Destiny and Marcus are going to make a picture.'

'It won't be all that easy to get a shot,' Knight pointed out, 'with the things skied up there.'

'Should we have them down again?'

'I trust,' Jeremy said suddenly, 'that somebody knows how to work the safe. I've locked it, you might remember.'

'Don't worry,' said little Morris whose reaction to opening nights took the form of getting slightly above himself. 'I know. It was all cooked up at the offices and Greenslade, of course, told me. Actually The Great Man himself suggested the type of code. It's all done on a *word*. You see? You think of a *word* of five letters——'

Down below the front doors had opened to admit a number of people and two cameras.

'——and each letter stands for a figure. Mr. Conducis said he thought easily the most appropriate word would be——'

'*Mr. Morris.*'

Winter Morris stopped short and swung round. Alleyn moved out on the landing.

'Tell me,' he said. 'How long has this safe been in position?'

'Some days. Three or four. Why?'

'Have you discussed the lock mechanism with your colleagues?'

'Well—I—well—I—only vaguely, you know, only vaguely.'

'Don't you think that it might be quite a good idea if you kept your five letter word to yourself?'

'Well, I—well we're all—well——'

'It really is the normal practice, you know.'

'Yes—but we're different. I mean—we're all——'

'Just to persuade you,' Alleyn said, and wrote on the back of an envelope. 'Is the combination one of these?'

Morris looked at the envelope.

'*Christ*,' he said.

Alleyn said: If I were you I'd get a less obvious code word and a new combination and keep them strictly under your Elizabethan bonnet. I seriously advise you to do this.' He took the envelope back, blacked out what he had written and put it in his breast pocket.

'You have visitors,' he said, amiably.

He waited while the pictures were taken and was not at all surprised when Trevor Vere reappeared, chatted shyly to the pressman whom he had instinctively recognised as the authority and ended up gravely contemplating the glove with Destiny Meade's arm about him and his cheek against hers while lamps flashed and cameras clicked.

The picture, which was much the best taken that morning, appeared with the caption : 'Child player, Trevor Vere, with Destiny Meade, and the Shakespeare glove. "It makes me feel kinda funny like I want to cry," says young Trevor.'

II

Peregrine answered half a dozen extremely intelligent questions and for the rest of his life would never know in what words. He bowed and stood back. He saw himself doing it in the glass behind the bar : a tall, lank, terrified young man in tails. The doors were swung open and he heard the house rise with a strange composite whispering sound.

Mr Conducis, who wore a number of orders, turned to him.

'I must wish you success,' he said.

'Sir—I can't thank you——'

'Not at all. I must follow.'

Mr. Conducis was to sit in the Royal box.

Peregrine made for the left hand doors into the circle.

'Every possible good luck,' a deep voice said.

He looked up and saw a grandee who turned out to be Superintendent Alleyn in a white tie with a lovely lady on his arm.

They had gone.

Peregrine heard the anthem through closed doors. He was the loneliest being on earth.

As the house settled he slipped into the circle and down to the box on the O.P. side. Jeremy was there.

'Here we go,' he said.

'Here we go.'

III

'Mr. Peregrine Jay successfully negotiates the tightrope between Tudor-type schmaltz and unconvincing modernisation. His dialogue has an honest sound and constantly surprises by its penetration. Sentimentality is nimbly avoided. The rancour of the insulted sensualist has never been more searchingly displayed since Sonnet CXXIX was written.'

'After all the gratuitous build-up and deeply suspect antics of the promotion boys I dreaded this exhibit at the newly tarted-up Dolphin. In the event it gave no offence. It pleased. It even stimulated. Who would have thought——'

'Marcus Knight performs the impossible. He makes a credible being of the Bard.'

'For once phenomenal advance-promotion has not foisted upon us an inferior product. This play may stand on its own merits.'

'Wot, no four letter words? No drag? No kinks? Right. But hold on, mate——''

'Peregrine Jay's sensitive, unfettered and almost clinical examination of Shakespeare is shattering in its dramatic intensity. Disturbing and delightful.'

'Without explicitly declaring itself, the play adds up to a searching attack upon British middle-class mores.'

'—Met in the foyer by Mr. Vassily Conducis and escorted to a box stunningly tricked out with lilies of the valley, she wore——'

'It will run.'

IV

Six months later Peregrine put a letter down on the breakfast table and looked across at Jeremy.

'This is it,' he said.

'What?'

'The decision. Conducis is going to sell out. To an American collector.'

'My God!'

'Greenslade, as usual, breaks the news. The negotiations have reached a point when he thinks it appropriate to advise me there is every possibility that they will go through.'

The unbecoming mauvish-pink that belongs to red hair and freckles suffused Jeremy's cheeks and mounted to his brow. 'I tell you what,' he said. 'This can't happen. This can't be allowed to happen. This man's a monster.'

'It appears that the B.M. and the V. and A. have shot their bolts. So has the British syndicate that was set up.'

Jeremy raised a cry of the passionately committed artist against the rest of the world. 'But *why*! He's lousy with money. He's got so much it must have stopped meaning anything. What'll he *do* with this lot? Look, suppose he gives it away? So what! Let him give William Shakespeare's handwriting and Hamnet Shakespeare's glove away. Let him give them to Stratford or the V. and A. Let him give them to the nation. Fine. He'll be made a bloody peer and good luck to him.'

'Let him do this and let him do that. He'll do what he's worked out for himself.'

'*You'll* have to see him, Perry. After all he's got a good thing out of you and The Dolphin. Capacity business for six months and booked out for weeks ahead. Small cast. Massive prestige. The lot.'

'And a company of Kilkenny cats as far as good relations are concerned.'

'What do you mean?'

'You know jolly well. Destiny waltzing over to Harry Grove. Gertrude and Marco reacting like furies.' Peregrine hesitated. 'And so on,' he said.

'You mean me lusting after Destiny and getting nowhere? Don't let it give you a moment's pause. I make no trouble among the giants, I assure you.'

'I'm sorry, Jer.'

'No, no. Forget it. Just you wade in to Conducis.'

'I can't.'

'For God's sake! Why?'

'Jer, I've told you. He gives me the jim-jams. I owe him nothing and I don't want to owe him anything. Still less do I want to go hat in hand asking for anything. *Anything.*'

'Why the hell not?'

'Because I might get it.'

'Well, if he's not an old queer, and you say you don't believe he is, what the hell? You feel like I do about the glove and the letter. You *say* you do. That they ought to be here among Shakespeare's people in his own city or country town—*here.* Well?'

'I can't go pleading again. I did try, remember, when he came to The Dolphin. I made a big song and dance and got slapped right down for my trouble. I won't do it again.'

Jeremy now lost his temper.

'Then, by God, I will,' he shouted.

'You won't get an interview.'

'I'll stage a sit-down on his steps.'

'Shall you carry a banner?'

'If necessary I'll carry a sledge hammer.'

This was so startlingly in accord with Emily's half-joking prediction that Peregrine said loudly: 'For the Lord's sake, pipe down. That's a damn' silly sort of thing to say and you know it.'

They had both lost their tempers and shouted foolishly at each other. An all-day and very superior help was now in their employment and they had to quieten down when she came in. They walked about their refurnished and admirably decorated studio, smoking their pipes and not looking at each other. Peregrine began to feel remorseful. He himself was so far in love with Emily Dunne and had been given such moderate encouragement that he sympathised with Jeremy in his bondage and yet thought what a disaster it was for him to succumb to Destiny. They were, in common with most men of their age, rather owlish in their affairs of the heart and a good deal less sophisticated than their conversation seemed to suggest.

Presently Jeremy halted in his walk and said:

'Hi.'

'Hi.'

'Look. I have been a morsel precipitate.'

Peregrine said : 'Not at all, Jer.'

'Yes. I don't really envisage a sit-down strike.'

'No?'

'No.' Jeremy looked fixedly at his friend. 'On the whole,' he said, and there was a curious undertone in his voice, 'I believe it would be a superfluous exercise.'

'You *do*! But—well really, I do *not* understand you.'

'Think no more of it.'

'Very well,' said the astonished Peregrine. 'I might as well mention that the things are to be removed from the safe on this day week and will be replaced by a blown-up photograph. Greenslade is sending two men from the office to take delivery.'

'Where are they to go?'

'He says for the time being to safe storage at his offices. They'll probably be sold by private treaty but if they are put up at Sotheby's the result will be the same. The customer's hell bent on getting them.'

Jeremy burst out laughing.

'I think you must be mad,' said Peregrine.

V

The night before the Shakespeare relics were to be removed from The Dolphin Theatre was warm and very still with a feeling of thunder in the air which, late in the evening, came to fulfilment. During the third act, at an uncannily appropriate moment a great clap and clatter broke out in the Heavens and directly over the theatre.

'Going too far with the thunder-sheet up there,' Morris said to Peregrine who was having a drink with him in the office.

There were several formidable outbreaks followed by the characteristic downpour. Peregrine went out to the circle foyer. Jobbins was at his post on the half-landing under the treasure.

Peregrine listened at the double doors into the circle and could just hear his own dialogue spoken by strange disembodied voices. He glanced at his watch. Half past ten. On time.

'Good night, Jobbins,' he said and went downstairs. Cars, already waiting in Wharfingers Lane, glistened in the downpour. He could hear the sound of water hitting water on the ebony night tide. The stalls attendant stood by to open the doors. Peregrine slipped in to the back of the house. There was the man of Stratford, his head bent over his sonnet : sitting in the bow window of a house in Warwickshire. The scratch of his quill on parchment could be clearly heard as the curtain came down.

Seven curtains and they could easily have taken more. One or two women in the back row were crying. They blew their noses, got rid of their handkerchiefs and clapped.

Peregrine went out quickly. The rain stopped as he ran down the side alleyway to the stage-door. A light cue had been missed and he wanted a word with the stage-director.

When he had had it he stood where he was and listened absently to the familiar sounds of voices and movement in the dressing-rooms and front-of-house. Because of the treasure a systematic search of the theatre was conducted after each performance and he had seen to it that this was thoroughly performed. He could hear the staff talking as they moved about the stalls and circle and spread their dust sheets. The assistant stage-manager organised the backstage procedure. When this was completed he and the stage-crew left. A trickle of backstage visitors came through and groped their alien way out. How incongruous they always seemed.

Destiny was entertaining in her dressing-room. He could hear Harry Grove's light impertinent laughter and the ejaculations of the guests. Gertrude Bracey and, a little later, Marcus Knight appeared, each of them looking furious. Peregrine advised them to go through the front of the house and thus avoid the puddles and overflowing gutters in the stage-door alleyway.

They edged through the pass-door and down the stairs into the stalls. There seemed to be a kind of wary alliance between them. Peregrine thought they probably went into little indignation huddles over Destiny and Harry Grove.

Charles Random, quiet and detached as usual, left by the stage-door and then Emily came out.

'Hallo,' she said, 'are you benighted?'

'I'm waiting for you. Would you come and have supper at that new bistro near the top of Wharfingers Lane? The Younger Dolphin it's artily called. It's got an extension licence till twelve for its little tiny opening thing and it's asked me to look in. Do come, Emily.'

'Thank you,' she said. 'I'd be proud.'

'How lovely!' Peregrine exclaimed, 'and it's stopped raining, I think. Wait a jiffy and I'll see.'

He ran to the stage-door. Water still dripped from the gutters in the alleyway but the stars shone overhead. Destiny and her smart friends came out, making a great to-do. When she saw Peregrine she stopped them all and introduced him. They said things like: 'Absolutely riveting' and 'Loved your play' and 'Heaven.' They made off, warning each other about the puddles. Harry Grove said: 'I'll go on, then, and fetch it, if you really want me to. See you later, angel.' 'Don't be too long, now,' Destiny called after him. Peregrine heard Harry's sports car start up.

Peregrine told the stage-door keeper he could shut up shop and go. He returned to Emily. As he walked towards the darkened set he was aware of a slight movement and thought it must have been the pass-door into front-of-house. As if somebody had just gone through and softly closed it. A backstage draught no doubt.

Emily was on the set. It was shut in by the fire-curtain and lit only by a dim infiltration from a working lamp back-stage: a dark, warm, still place.

'I always think it feels so strange,' she said, 'after we've left it to itself. As if it's got a life of its own. Waiting for us.'

'Another kind of reality?'

'Yes. A more impressive kind. You can almost imagine it breathes.'

A soughing movement of air up in the grille gave momentary confirmation of Emily's fancy.

'Come on,' Peregrine said. 'It's a fine starry night and no

distance at all to the top of Wharfingers Lane.' He had taken her arm and was guiding her to the pass-door when they both heard a thud.

They stood still and asked each other : 'What was that?'

'Front-of-house?' Emily said.

'Yes. Winty or someone, I suppose.'

'Wouldn't they all have gone?'

'I'd have thought so.'

'What *was* it? The noise?'

Peregrine said : 'It sounded like a seat flapping up.'

'Yes. It did sound like that.'

'Wait a bit.'

'Where are you going?' she said anxiously.

'Not far. Just to have a look.'

'All right.'

He opened the pass-door. The little twisting stair was in darkness but he had a torch in his pocket. Steps led down to the stalls box and up from where he stood, to the box in the circle. He went down and then out into the stalls. They were in darkness. He flapped a seat down and let it spring back. That was the sound.

Peregrine called : 'Hallo. Anyone there?' but his voice fell dead in an upholstered silence.

He flashed his torch across walls and shrouded seats. He walked up the new central aisle and into the foyer. It was deserted and dimly lit and the street doors were shut. Peregrine called up the stairs.

'Jobbins.'

'Eh?' Jobbins's voice said. 'That you, guv? Anything up?'

'I heard a seat flap. In front.'

'*Did*jer, guv?'

Jobbins appeared on the stairs. He wore an extremely loud brown, black and white checked overcoat, a woollen cap and carpet slippers.

'Good lord!' Peregrine ejaculated. 'Are you going to the Dogs or Ally Pally or what? Where's your brown bowler?'

'You again, guv?' Jobbins wheezed. 'I'd of 'eld back me quick change if I'd known. Pardon the dishy-bill. Present from a toff this 'ere coat is and very welcome. Gets chilly,' he said descending, 'between nah and the witching ar, when my relief comes in. What's this abaht a seat?'

Peregrine explained. To his astonishment Jobbins pushed the doors open, strode into the auditorium and uttered in a sort of hoarse bellow——

'Nah then. Out of it. Come on. You 'eard.'

Silence.

Then Emily's voice sounded worried and lonely: 'What goes on?' She had groped her way down into the house.

'It's all right,' Peregrine shouted. 'Won't be long.' And to Jobbins: 'What *does* go on? You sound as if you're used to this.'

'*Which* I am,' Jobbins sourly endorsed. 'It's that perishing child-wonder, that's what it is. 'E done it before and 'e'll do it again *and* once too often.'

'Done what?'

''Angs abaht. 'Is mum plays the steel guitar in a caff, see, acrost the river. She knocks off at eleven and 'er 'earts-delight sallies forth to greet 'er at the top of the lane. And 'e fills in the gap, buggering rhand the theyater trying to make out 'e's a robber or a spectrum. 'E knows full well I can't leave me post so 'e 'ides 'isself in various dark regions. '"Ands up," 'e yells. "Stick 'em up," 'e 'owls, and crawls under the seats making noises like 'e's bein' strangulated *which* 'e will be if ever I lay me 'ands on 'im. Innit marvellous?'

From somewhere backstage a single plangent sound rang out and faded. It was followed by an eldritch screech of laughter, a catcall and a loud slam.

'There 'e goes,' said Jobbins and flung an ejaculation of startling obscenity into the auditorium.

'I'll get that little bastard,' Peregrine said. He foolishly made a dash for the treble-locked doors into the portico.

'You'll never catch 'im, guv,' Jobbins said. His voice had almost vanished with excessive vocal exercise. 'E'll be 'alf-way up the lane and going strong. His mum meets 'im at the top when she's sober.'

'I'll have the hide off him to-morrow,' Peregrine said. 'All right, Jobbins. I'll see you're not pestered again. And anyway as far as the treasure is concerned this is your last watch.'

'That's right, sir. Positively the last appearance in this epoch-making role.'

'Good night again.'

'Good night, guv. Best of British luck.'

Peregrine went into the stalls. 'Emily!' he called. 'Where are you, my poor girl?'

'Here,' Emily said, coming up the aisle.

'Did you see the little swine?'

'No. I was in front. He came down from the circle. I could hear him on the steps.'

Peregrine looked at his watch. Five past eleven. He took her arm. 'Let's forget him,' he said, 'and sling our hooks. We've wasted ages. They shut at midnight. Come on.'

They slammed the stage-door behind them. The night was still fine and quite warm. They climbed Wharfingers Lane and went in under the illuminated sign of the new bistro: 'The Younger Dolphin.'

It was crowded, noisy and extremely dark. The two waiters were dressed as fishermen in tight jeans, striped jumpers and jelly-bag caps. A bas relief of a dolphin wearing a mortar-board was lit from below.

As their eyes adjusted to the gloom they saw that Destiny and her three audience friends were established at a table under the dolphin and had the air of slumming. Destiny waggled her fingers at them and made faces to indicate that she couldn't imagine why she was there.

They ate grilled sole, drank lager, danced together on a pocket-handkerchief and greatly enjoyed themselves. Presently Destiny and her friends left. As they passed Emily and Peregrine she said: 'Darlings! We thought we would but oh, no, no.' They went away talking loudly about what they would have to eat when they got to Destiny's flat in Chelsea. At ten to twelve Peregrine said: 'Emily: why are you so stand-offish in the elder Dolphin and so come-toish in the younger one?'

'Partly because of your prestige and anyway I'm not all that oncoming, even here.'

'Yes, you are. You are when we're dancing. Not at first but suddenly, about ten minutes ago.'

'I'm having fun and I'm obliged to you for providing it.'

'Do you at all fancy me?'

'Very much indeed.'

'Don't say it brightly like that : it's insufferable.'

'Sorry.'

'And what do you mean, my prestige. Are you afraid people like Gertie, for example, will say you're having an advantageous carry-on with the author-producer?'

'Yes, I am.'

'How bloody silly. "They say. What say they? Let them say".'

'That aphorism was coined by a murdering cad.'

'What of it? Emily : I find you more attractive than any of my former girls. Now, don't flush up and bridle. I know you're not my girl, in actual fact. Emily,' Peregrine shouted against a screaming crescendo from the saxophonist. 'Emily, listen to me. I believe I love you.'

The little band had crashed to its climax and was silent. Peregrine's declaration rang out as a solo performance.

'After that,' Emily said, 'I almost think we had better ask for the bill, don't you?'

Peregrine was so put out that he did so. They left The Younger Dolphin assuring the anxious proprietor that they would certainly return.

Their plan had been to stroll over to Blackfriars, pick up Peregrine and Jeremy's car and drive to Hampstead.

They walked out of The Younger Dolphin into a deluge.

Neither of them had a mackintosh or an umbrella. They huddled in the entrance and discussed the likelihood of raising a cab. Peregrine went back and telephoned a radio taxi number to be told nothing would be available for at least twenty minutes. When he rejoined Emily the rain had eased off a little.

'I tell you what,' he said. 'I've got a gamp and a mac in the office. Let's run down the hill, beat Jobbins up and collect them. Look, it's almost stopped.'

'Come on, then.'

'Mind you don't slip.'

Hand in hand they ran wildly and noisily down Wharfingers Lane. They reached the turning at the bottom, rounded the corner and pulled up outside The Dolphin. They laughed and were exhilarated.

'Listen!' Emily exclaimed, 'Peregrine, listen. Somebody else is running in the rain.'

'It's someone in the stage-door alley.'

'So it is.'

The other runner's footsteps rang out louder and louder on the wet cobblestones. He came out of the alley into the lane and his face was open-mouthed like a gargoyle.

He saw them and he flung himself upon Peregrine, pawed at his coat and jabbered into his face. It was the night-watchman who relieved Jobbins.

'For Gawsake!' he said. 'Oh, my Gawd, Mr. Jay, for Gawsake.'

'What the devil's the matter? *What is it? What's happened!*'

'Murder,' the man said, and his lips flabbered over the word. 'That's what's happened, Mr. Jay. Murder.'

6. DISASTER

While he let them in at the stage-door the man—he was called Hawkins—said over and over again in a shrill whine that it wasn't his fault if he was late getting down to the theatre. Nobody, he said, could blame him. He turned queer, as was well-known, at the sight of blood. It was as much as Peregrine could do to get the victim's name out of him. He had gone completely to pieces.

They went through the stage-door into the dark house, and up the aisle and so to the foyer. It was as if they had never left the theatre.

Peregrine said to Emily: 'Wait here. By the box-office. Don't come any farther.'

'I'll come if you want me.'

'O Gawd no. O Gawd no, Miss.'

'Stay here, Emily. Or wait in front. Yes. Just wait in front.' He opened the doors into the stalls and fastened them back. She went in. 'Now, Hawkins,' Peregrine said.

'You go, Mr. Jay. Up there. I don't 'ave to go. I can't do nothing. I'd vomit. Honest I would.'

Peregrine ran up the graceful stairway towards the sunken landing : under the treasure where both flights emerged. It was dark up there but he had a torch and used it. The beam shot out and found an object.

There, on its back in a loud overcoat and slippers lay the shell of Jobbins. The woollen cap had not fallen from the skull but had been stove into it. Out of what had been a face, broken like a crust now, and glistening red, one eye stared at nothing.

Beside this outrage lay a bronze dolphin, grinning away for all it was worth through a wet, unspeakable mask.

Everything round Peregrine seemed to shift a little as if his vision had swivelled like a movie camera. He saw, without comprehension, a square of reflected light on the far wall and its source above the landing. He saw, down below him, the top of Hawkins's head. He moved to the balustrade, held on to it and with difficulty controlled an upsurge of nausea. He fetched a voice out of himself.

'Have you rung the police?'

'I better had, didn't I? I better report, didn't I?' Hawkins gabbled without moving.

'Stay where you are. I'll do it.'

There was a general purposes telephone in the downstairs foyer outside the box-office. He ran down to it and, controlling his hand, dialled the so celebrated number. How instant and how cool the response.

'No possibility of survival, sir?'

'God, no. I told you——'

'Please leave everything as it is. You will be relieved in a few minutes. Which entrance is available? Thank you.'

Peregrine hung up. 'Hawkins,' he said. 'Go back to the stage-door and let the police in. Go on.'

'Yes. O.K. Yes, Mr. Jay.'

'Well, go *on*, damn you.'

Was there an independent switch anywhere in the foyer for front-of-house lighting or was it all controlled from backstage? Surely not. He couldn't remember. Ridiculous. Emily was out there in the darkened stalls. He went in and found her standing just inside the doors.

'Emily?'

'Yes. All right. Here I am.'

He felt her hands in his. 'This is a bad thing,' he said hurriedly. 'It's a very bad thing, Emily.'

'I heard what you said on the telephone.'

'They'll be here almost at once.'

'I see. Murder,' Emily said, trying the word.

'We can't be sure.'

They spoke aimlessly. Peregrine heard a high-pitched whine inside his own head and felt sickeningly cold. He wondered if he was going to faint and groped for Emily. They put their arms about each other. 'We must behave,' Peregrine said, 'in whatever way one is expected to behave. You know? Calm? Collected? All the things people like us are meant not to be.'

'That's right. Well, so we will.' He stooped his head to hers. 'Can this be you?' he said.

A sound crept into their silence: a breathy intermittent sound with infinitesimal interruptions that seemed to have some sort of vocal quality. They told each other to listen.

With a thick premonition of what was to come, Peregrine put Emily away from him.

He switched on his torch and followed its beam down the centre aisle. He was under the overhang of the dress-circle but moved on until its rim was above his head. It was here, in the centre aisle of the stalls and below the circle balustrade, that his torchlight came to rest on a small, breathing, faintly audible heap which, as he knelt beside it, revealed itself as an unconscious boy.

'Trevor,' Peregrine said. '*Trevor.*'

Emily behind him said, 'Has he been killed? Is he dying?'

'I don't know. What should we do? Ring for the ambulance? Ring the Yard again? Which?'

'Don't move him. I'll ring Ambulance.'

'Yes.'

'Listen. Sirens.'

'Police.'

Emily said : 'I'll ring, all the same,' and was gone.

There seemed to be no interval of time between this moment and the occupation of The Dolphin by uniformed policemen with heavy necks and shoulders and quiet voices. Peregrine met the sergeant.

'Are you in charge? There's something else since I telephoned. A boy. Hurt but alive. Will you look?'

The sergeant looked. He said : 'This might be serious. You haven't touched him, sir?'

'No. Emily—Miss Dunne who is with me—is ringing the ambulance.'

'Can we have some light?'

Peregrine, remembering at last where they were, put the houselights on. More police were coming in at the stage-door. He rejoined the sergeant. A constable was told to stay by the boy and report any change.

'I'll take a look at this body, if you please,' the sergeant said.

Emily was at the telephone in the foyer saying : 'It's very urgent. It's really urgent. Please.'

'If you don't mind, Miss,' said the sergeant and took the receiver. 'Police here,' he said and was authoritative. 'They'll be round in five minutes,' he said to Emily.

'Thank God.'

'Now then, Mr. Jay.' He'd got Peregrine's name as he came in.

'May I go back to the boy?' Emily asked. 'In case he regains consciousness and is frightened? I know him.'

'Good idea,' said the sergeant with a kind of routine heartiness. 'You just stay there with the boy, Miss——?'

'Dunne.'

'Miss Dunne. Members of the company here, would it be?'

'Yes,' Peregrine said. 'We were at the new restaurant in Wharfingers Lane and came back to shelter from the rain.'

'Is that so? I see. Well, Miss Dunne, you just stay with the boy and tell the ambulance all you know. Now, Mr. Jay.'

A return to the sunken landing was a monstrous thing to contemplate. Peregrine said : 'Yes. I'll show you. If you don't mind I won't——' and reminded himself of Hawkins. 'It's terrible,' he said. 'I'm sorry to balk. This way.'

'Up the stairs?' The sergeant asked conversationally, as if he inquired his way to the Usual Offices. 'Don't trouble to come up again, Mr. Jay. The less traffic, you know, the better we like it.'

'Yes. Of course. I forgot.'

'If you'll just wait down here.'

'Yes. Thank you.'

The sergeant was not long on the landing. Peregrine could not help looking up at him and saw that, like himself, the sergeant did not go beyond the top step. He returned and went to the telephone. As he passed Peregrine he said : 'Very nasty, sir, isn't it,' in a preoccupied voice.

Peregrine couldn't hear much of what the sergeant said into the telephone. 'Some kind of caretaker—Jobbins—and a young lad—looks like it. Very good, sir. Yes. Yes. Very good' : and then after a pause and in a mumble of words, one that came through very clearly.

'—robbery——'

Never in the wide world would Peregrine have believed it of himself that a shock, however acute or a sight however appalling, could have so bludgeoned his wits. There, there on the wall opposite the one in which the treasure was housed, shone the tell-tale square of reflected light and there above his head as he stood on the stairs had been the exposed casket—exposed and brightly lit when it should have been shut off and——

He gave a kind of stifled cry and started up the stairs.

'Just a moment, sir. If you please.'

'The glove,' Peregrine said. 'The letters and the glove. I must see. I must look.'

The sergeant was beside him. A great hand closed without undue force round his upper arm.

'All right, sir. All right. But you can't go up there yet, you know. You join your young lady and the sick kiddy. And if you're referring to the contents of that glassed-in cabinet up there, I can tell you right away. It's been opened from the back and they seem to have gone.'

Peregrine let out an incoherent cry and blundered into the stalls to tell Emily.

For him and for Emily the next half-hour was one of frustration, confusion and despair. They had to collect themselves and give statements to the sergeant who entered them at an even pace in his notebook. Peregrine talked about hours and duties and who ought to be informed and Mr. Greenslade and Mr. Conducis, and he stared at the sergeant's enormous forefinger, flattened across the image of a crown on a blue cover. Peregrine didn't know who Jobbins's next-of-kin might be. He said, as if that would help : 'He was a nice chap. He was a bit of a character. A nice chap.'

The theatre continually acquired more police : plain-clothes, unhurried men, the most authoritative of whom was referred to by the sergeant as the Div-Super and addressed as Mr. Gibson. Peregrine and Emily heard him taking a statement from Hawkins who cried very much and said it wasn't a fair go.

The ambulance came. Peregrine and Emily stood by while Trevor, the whites of his eyes showing under his heavy lashes and his breathing very heavy, was gently examined. A doctor appeared : the divisional surgeon, Peregrine heard someone say. Mr. Gibson asked him if there was any chance of a return to consciousness and he said something about Trevor being deeply concussed.

'He's got broken ribs and a broken right leg,' he said, 'and an unbroken bruise on his jaw. It's a wonder he's alive. We won't know about the extent of internal injuries until we've had a look-see,' said the divisional surgeon. 'Get him into St. Terence's at once.' He turned to Peregrine. 'Would you know the next-of-kin?'

Peregrine was about to say : 'Only too well' but checked himself. 'Yes,' he said, 'his mother.'

'Would you have the address?' asked Mr. Gibson. 'And the telephone number.'

'In the office. Upstairs. No, wait a moment. I've a cast list in my pocket-book. Here it is : Mrs. Blewitt.'

'Perhaps you'd be so kind as to ring her, Mr. Jay. She ought to be told at once. What's the matter, Mr. Jay?'

'She meets him, usually. At the top of the lane. I—Oh God, poor Jobbins told me that. I wonder what she did when Trevor didn't turn up. You'd have thought she'd have come to the theatre.'

'Can we get this boy away?' asked the divisional surgeon crisply.

'O.K., Doc. You better go with them,' Mr. Gibson said to the constable who had stayed by Trevor. 'Keep your ears open. Anything. Whisper. Anything. Don't let some starched battle-axe push you about. We want to know what hit him. Don't leave him, now.'

Mr. Gibson had a piece of chalk in his hand. He ran it round Trevor's little heap of a body, grinding it into the carpet. 'O.K.,' he said and Trevor was taken away.

The divisional surgeon said he'd take a look-see at the body and went off with the sergeant. Superintendent Gibson was about to accompany them when Peregrine and Emily, who had been in consultation, said: 'Er——' and he turned back.

'Yes, Mr. Jay? Miss Dunne? Was there something?'

'It's just,' Emily said, '—we wondered if you knew that Mr. Roderick Alleyn—I mean Superintendent Alleyn—supervised the installation of the things that were in the wall-safe. The things that have been stolen.'

'Rory *Alleyn*!' the superintendent ejaculated. 'Is that so? Now, why was that, I wonder?'

Peregrine explained. 'I think,' he said finally, 'that Mr. Vassily Conducis, who owns the things——'

'So I understand.'

'—asked Mr. Alleyn to do it as a special favour. Mr. Alleyn was very much interested in the things.'

'He would be. Well, thank you,' said Mr. Gibson rather heavily. 'And now, if you'd phone this Mrs. Blewitt. Lives in my division, I see. Close to our headquarters. If she can't get transport to the hospital tell her, if you please, that we'll lay something on. No, wait. On second thoughts, I'll send a policewoman round from the station if one's available. Less of a shock.'

'Shouldn't we ring her up—just to warn her someone's coming,' Emily asked. 'Should I offer to go?'

Mr. Gibson stared at her and said that he thought on the whole it would be better if Peregrine and Emily remained in the theatre a little longer but, yes, they could telephone to Mrs. Blewitt after he himself had made one or two little calls. He padded off—not fast, not slow—towards the foyer. Peregrine and Emily talked disjointedly. After some minutes they heard sounds of new arrivals by the main entrance and of Superintendent Gibson greeting them.

'None of this is real,' Emily said presently.

'Are you exhausted?'

'I don't think so.'

'I ought to tell Greenslade,' Peregrine ejaculated. 'He ought to be told, good God!'

'And Mr. Conducis? After all it's his affair.'

'Greenslade can tackle that one. Emily, are you in a muddle like me? I can't get on top of this. Jobbins. That appalling kid. Shakespeare's note and the glove. All broken or destroyed or stolen. Isn't it beastly, all of it? What *are* human beings? What's the thing that makes monsters of us all?'

'It's out of our country. We'll have to play it by ear.'

'No, but we *act* it. It's our raw material—— Murder. Violence. Theft. Sexual greed. They're commonplace to us. We do our Stanislavsky over them. We search out motives and associated experiences. We try to think our way into Macbeth or Othello or a witch-hunt or an Inquisitor or a killer-doctor at Auschwitch and sometimes we think we've succeeded. But confront us with the thing itself! It's as if a tractor had rolled over us. *We're* nothing. Superintendent Gibson is there instead to put it all on a sensible, factual basis.'

'Good luck to him,' said Emily rather desperately.

'Good luck? You think? All right, if you say so.'

'Perhaps I can now ring up Mrs. Blewitt.'

'I'll come with you.'

The foyer was brilliantly lit and there were voices and movement upstairs where Jobbins lay. Camera men's lamps flashed and grotesquely reminded Peregrine of the opening night of his play. Superintendent Gibson's voice and that of the divisional surgeon were clearly distinguishable. There was also a new rather comfortable voice. Downstairs, a constable stood in front of the main doors. Peregrine told him that Mr. Gibson had said they might use the telephone and the constable replied pleasantly that it would be quite all right he was sure.

Peregrine watched Emily dial the number and wait with the receiver to her ear. How pale she was. Her hair was the kind that goes into a mist after it has been out in the rain and her wide mouth drooped at the corners like a child's. He could hear the buzzer ringing, on and on. Emily had just shaken her head at him when the telephone quacked angrily. She spoke for some time, evidently to no avail and at last hung up.

'A man,' she said, 'A landlord, I should think. He was livid. He says Mrs. Blewitt went to a party after her show and didn't meet Trevor to-night. He says she's "flat out to it" and nothing would rouse her. So he hung up.'

'The policewoman will have to cope. I'd better rouse Greenslade, I suppose. He lives at some godawful place in the stockbrokers' belt. Here goes.'

Evidently Mr. and Mrs. Greenslade had a bedside telephone. She could be heard, querulous and half-asleep, in the background. Mr. Greenslade said: 'Shut up, darling. Very well, Jay, I'll come down. Does Alleyn know?'

'I—don't suppose so. I told the superintendent that Alleyn would be concerned.'

'He should have been told. Find out, will you? I'll come at once.'

'*Find out*,' Peregrine angrily repeated to Emily. 'I can't go telling the police who they ought to call in, blast it. How can I *find out* if Alleyn's been told?'

'Easily,' Emily rejoined with a flicker of a smile. 'Because, look.'

The constable had opened the pass-door in the main entrance and now admitted Superintendent Alleyn in the nearest he ever got to a filthy temper.

II

Alleyn had worked late and unfruitfully at the Yard in company with Inspector Fox. As he let himself into his own house he heard the telephone ring, swore loudly and got to it just as his wife, Troy, took the receiver off in their bedroom.

It was the Chief Commander who was his immediate senior at the Yard. Alleyn listened with disgust to his story. '—and so Fred Gibson thought that as you know Conducis and had a hand in the installation, he'd better call us. He just missed you at the Yard. All things considered I think you'd better take over, Rory. It's a big one. Murder. Double, if the boy dies. And robbery of these bloody, fabulous museum pieces.'

'Very good,' Alleyn said. 'All right. Yes.'

'Got your car out or garaged?'

'Thank you. Out.'

It was nothing new to turn round in his tracks after one gruelling day and work through till the next. He took five minutes to have a word with Troy and a rapid shave and was back in the car and heading for the Borough within half an hour of leaving the Yard. The rain had lifted but the empty streets glistened under their lamps.

He could have kicked himself from Whitehall to Bankside. Why, why, why hadn't he put his foot down about the safe and its silly window and bloody futile combination lock? Why hadn't he said that he would on no account recommend it? He reminded himself that he had given sundry warnings but snapped back at himself that he should have gone further. He should have telephoned Conducis and advised him not to go on with the public display of the Shakespeare treasures. He should have insisted on that ass of a business manager scrapping his imbecile code-word, penetrable in five minutes by a certified moron, and should have demanded a new combination. The fact that he had been given no authority to do so and had nevertheless urged precisely this action upon Mr. Winter Morris made no difference. He should have thrown his weight about.

And now some poor damned commissionaire had been

murdered. Also, quite probably, that unspeakably ghastly little boy who had cheeked him in The Dolphin. And Hamnet Shakespeare's glove and Hamnet's father's message had in-spired these atrocities and were gone. Really, Alleyn thought, as he drew up by the portico of The Dolphin Theatre, he hadn't been so disgruntled since he took a trip to Cape Town with a homicidal pervert.

Then he entered the theatre and came face-to-face with Peregrine and Emily and saw how white and desperate they looked and recognised the odd vagueness that so often over-comes people who have been suddenly confronted with a crime of violence. He swallowed his chagrin and summoned up the professionalism that he had once sourly defined as an in-finite capacity to notice less and less with more and more accuracy.

He said: 'This is no good at all, is it? What are you two doing here?'

'We got here,' Peregrine said, 'just after.'

'You look as if you'd better go and sit down somewhere. 'Morning, Fred,' Alleyn said, meeting Superintendent Gibson at the foot of the stair. 'What's first?' He looked towards the half-landing and without waiting for an answer walked upstairs followed by Gibson.

Among the group of men and cameras was an elderly thick-set man with a grizzled moustache and bright eyes.

'Hallo,' Alleyn said. 'You again.'

'That's right, Mr. Alleyn,' said Inspector Fox. 'Just beat you to it. I was still at the Yard when they rang up so the C.C. said I might as well join in. Don't quite know why and I daresay Fred doesn't either.'

'More the merrier,' Mr. Gibson rejoined gloomily. 'This looks like being an extra curly one.'

'Well,' Alleyn said. 'I'd better see.'

'We covered him,' Gibson said. 'With a dust sheet. It's about as bad as they come. Worst *I've* ever seen. Now!'

'Very nasty,' Fox said. He nodded to one of the men. 'O.K., Bailey.'

Detective-Sergeant Bailey, a finger-print expert, uncovered the body of Jobbins.

It was lying on its back with the glittering mask and single
eye appallingly exposed. The loudly checked coat was open
and dragged back into what must be a knotted lump under the
small of the back. Between the coat and the dirty white sweater
there was a rather stylish yellow scarf. The letter H had been
embroidered on it. It was blotted and smeared. The sweater
itself was soaked in patches of red and had ridden up over the
chest. There was something almost homely and normal in the
look of a tartan shirt running in sharp folds under the belted
trousers that were strained across the crutch by spreadeagled
legs.

Alleyn looked, waited an appreciable time and then said:
'Has he been photographed? Printed?'

'The lot,' somebody said.

'I want to take some measurements. Then he can be moved.
I see you've got a mortuary van outside. Get the men up.'
The sergeant moved to the stairhead. 'Just make sure those two
young people are out of the way,' Alleyn said.

He held out his hand and Fox gave him a steel spring-tape.
They measured the distance from that frightful head to the
three shallow steps that led up to the circle foyer and marked
the position of the body. When Jobbins was gone and the
divisional surgeon after him. Alleyn looked at the bronze
dolphin, glistening on the carpet.

'There's your weapon,' Gibson said unnecessarily.

The pedestal had been knocked over and lay across the
shallow steps at the left hand corner. The dolphin, detached, lay below it on the landing, close to a dark blot on the
crimson carpet where Jobbins's head had been. Its companion
piece still made an elegant arc on the top of its own pedestal
near the wall. They had stood to left and right at the head
of the stairs in the circle foyer. Four steps below the landing
lay a thick cup in a wet patch and below it another one and a
small tin tray.

'His post,' Alleyn said, 'was on this sunken landing under
———'

He looked up. There, still brilliantly lit, was the exposed
casket, empty.

'That's correct,' Gibson said. 'He was supposed to stay there until he was relieved by this chap Hawkins at midnight.'

'Where is this Hawkins?'

'Ah,' Gibson said disgustedly, 'Sobbing his little heart out in the gents' cloaks. He's gone to pieces.'

Fox said austerely : 'He seems to have acted very foolishly from the start. Comes in late. Walks up here. Sees deceased and goes yelling out of the building.'

'That's right,' Gibson agreed. 'And if he hadn't run into this Mr. Jay and his lady friend he might be running still and us none the wiser.'

'So it was Jay who rang police?' Alleyn interjected.

'That's correct.'

'What about their burglar alarm?'

'Off. The switch is back of the box-office.'

'I know. They showed me. What then, Fred?'

'The sergeant's sent in and gets support. I get the office and I come in and we set up a search. Thought our man might be hiding on the premises but not. Either got out of it before Hawkins arrived or slipped away while he was making an exhibition of himself. The pass-door in the main entrance was shut but not locked. It had *been* locked, they say, so it looked as if that was his way out.'

'And the boy?'

'Yes. Well, now. The boy. Mr. Jay says the boy's a bit of a young limb. Got into the habit of hanging round after the show and acting the goat. Jobbins complained of him making spook noises and that. He was at it before Mr. Jay and Miss Dunne left the theatre to go out to supper. Mr. Jay tried to find him but it was dark and he let out a cat-call or two and then they heard the stage-door slam and reckoned he'd gone. Not, as it turns out.'

'Evidently. I'll see Hawkins now, Fred.'

Hawkins was produced in the downstage foyer. He was a plain man made plainer by bloodshot eyes, a reddened nose and a loose mouth. He gazed lugubriously at Alleyn, spoke of shattered nerves and soon began to cry.

'Who's going to pitch into me next?' he asked. 'I ought to

be getting hospital attention, the shock I've had, and not subjected to treatment that'd bring about an inquiry if I made complaints. I ought to be home in bed getting looked after.'

'So you shall be,' Alleyn said. 'We'll send you home in style when you've just told me quietly what happened.'

'I have! I have told. I've told them others.'

'All right. I know you're feeling rotten and it's a damn' shame to keep you but you see you're the chap we're looking to for help.'

'Don't you use that yarn to me. I know what the police mean when they talk about help. Next thing it'll be the Usual Bloody Warning.'

'No, it won't. Look here—I'll say what I think happened and you jump on me if I'm wrong. All right?'

'How do I know if it's all right!'

'Nobody suspects you, you silly chap,' Fox said. 'How many more times!'

'Never mind,' Alleyn soothed. 'Now, listen, Hawkins. You came down to the theatre. When? About ten past twelve?'

Hawkins began a great outcry against buses and thunderstorms but was finally induced to say he heard the hour strike as he walked down the lane.

'And you came in by the stage-door. Who let you in?'

Nobody, it appeared. He had a key. He banged it shut and gave a whistle and shouted. Pretty loudly, Alleyn gathered, because Jobbins was always at his post on the half-landing, and he wanted to let him know he'd arrived. He came in, locked the door and shot the bolt. He supposed Jobbins was fed up with him for being late. This account was produced piecemeal and with many lamentable excursions. Hawkins now became extremely agitated and said what followed had probably made a wreck of him for the rest of his life. Alleyn displayed sympathy and interest, however, and was flattering in his encouragement. Hawkins gazed upon him with watering eyes and said that what followed was something chronic. He had seen no light in the property room so had switched his torch on and gone out to front-of-house. As soon as he got there he noticed a dim light in the circle. And there—it had given him a turn

—in the front row, looking down at him was Henry Jobbins in his flash new overcoat.

'You never told us this!' Gibson exclaimed.

'You never arst me.'

Fox and Gibson swore quietly together.

'Go on,' Alleyn said.

'I said: "That you, Hen?" and he says "Who d'yer think it is" and I said I was sorry I was late and should I make the tea and he said yes. So I went into the props room and made it.'

'How long would that take?'

'It's an old electric jug. Bit slow.'

'Yes? And then?'

'O Gawd. O Gawd.'

'I know. But go on.'

He had carried the two cups of tea through the house to the front foyer and up the stairs.

Here Hawkins broke down again in a big way but finally divulged that he had seen the body, dropped the tray, tried to claw his way out at front, run by the side aisle through the stalls and pass-door, out of the stage-door and down the alley where he ran into Peregrine and Emily. Alleyn got his address and sent him home.

'What a little beauty,' Fred Gibson said.

'You tell me,' Alleyn observed, 'that you've searched the theatre. What kind of search, Fred?'

'How d'you mean?'

'Well—obviously, as you say, for the killer. But have they looked for the stuff?'

'Stuff——?'

'For a glove, for instance, and two scraps of writing?'

There was a very short silence and then Gibson said: 'There hasn't really been time. We would, of course.'

Fox said: 'If he was surprised, you mean, and dropped them? Something of that nature?'

'It's a forlorn hope, no doubt,' Alleyn said. He looked at Sergeant Bailey and the camera man who was Sergeant Thompson: both of the Yard. 'Have you tackled this dolphin?'

'Just going to when you arrived, sir,' Thompson said.

'Take it as it lies before you touch it. It's in a ghastly state but there may be something. And the pedestal, of course. What's the thing weigh?'

He went to the top of the stairs, took the other dolphin from its base, balanced and hefted it. 'A tidy lump,' he said.

'Do you reckon it could have been used as a kind of club?' Fox asked.

'Only by a remarkably well-muscled-up specimen, Br'er Fox.' Alleyn replaced the dolphin and looked at it. 'Nice,' he said. 'He does that sort of thing beautifully.' He turned to Gibson. 'What about routine, Fred?'

'We're putting it round the divisions. Anybody seen in the precincts of The Dolphin or the Borough or farther out. Might be bloody, might be nervous. That's the story. I'd be just as glad to get back, Rory. We've got a busy night on in my Div as it happens. Bottle fight at the Cat and Crow with a punch-up and knives. Probable fatality and three break-and-enters. *And* a suspected arson. You're fully equipped, aren't you?'

'Yes. All right, Fred, cut away. I'll keep in touch.'

'Good night, then. Thanks.'

When Gibson had gone Alleyn said : 'We'll see where the boy was and then have a word with Peregrine Jay and Miss Dunne. How many chaps have you got here?' he asked the sergeant.

'Four at present, sir. One in the foyer, one at the stage-door, one with Hawkins and another just keeping an eye, like, on Mr. Jay and Miss Dunne.'

'Right. Leave the stage-door man and get the others going on a thorough search. Start in the circle. Where was this boy?'

'In the stalls, sir. Centre aisle and just under the edge of the circle.'

'Tell them not to touch the balustrade. Come on, Fox.'

When Alleyn and Fox went into the now fully lit stalls the first thing they noticed was a rather touching group made by Peregrine and Emily. They sat in the back row by the aisle. Peregrine's head had inclined to Emily's shoulder and her arm was about his neck. He was fast asleep. Emily stared at Alleyn who nodded. He and Fox walked down the aisle to the chalk outline of Trevor's body.

'And the doctor says a cut on the head, broken thigh and ribs, a bruise on the jaw and possible internal injuries?'

'That's correct,' Fox agreed.

Alleyn looked at the back of the aisle seat above the trace of the boy's head. 'See here, Fox.'

'Yes. Stain all right. Still damp, isn't it?'

'I think so. Yes.'

They both moved a step or two down the aisle and looked up at the circle. Three policemen and the sergeant with Thompson and Bailey were engaged in a methodical search.

'Bailey,' Alleyn said raising his voice very slightly.

'Sir?'

'Have a look at the balustrade above us here. Look at the pile in the velvet. Use your torch if necessary.'

There was a longish silence broken by Emily saying quietly: 'It's all right. Go to sleep again.'

Bailey moved to one side and looked down into the stalls. 'We've got something here, Mr. Alleyn,' he said. 'Two sets of tracks with the pile dragged slantways in a long diagonal line outwards towards the edge. Some of it removed. Looks like finger-nails. Trace of something that might be shoe-polish.'

'All right. Deal with it, you and Thompson.'

Fox said: 'Well, well: a fall, eh?'

'Looks that way, doesn't it? A fall from the circle about twenty feet. I suppose nobody looked at the boy's finger nails. Who found him?' Fox, with a jerk of his head indicated Peregrine and Emily. 'They'd been sent in here,' he said, 'to get them out of the way.'

'We'll talk to them now, Fox.'

Peregrine was awake. He and Emily sat hand-in-hand and looked more like displaced persons than anything else, an effect that was heightened by the blueness of Peregrine's jaws and the shadows under their eyes.

Alleyn said: 'I'm sorry you've been kept so long. It's been a beastly business for both of you. Now, I'm going to ask Mr. Fox to read over what you have already said to Mr. Gibson and his sergeant and you shall tell us if, on consideration, this is a fair statement.'

Fox did this and they nodded and said yes: that was it.

'Good,' Alleyn said. 'Then there's only one other question. Did either of you happen to notice Trevor Vere's fingernails?'

They stared at him and both repeated in pallid voices : 'His fingernails?'

'Yes. You found him and I think you, Miss Dunne, stayed with him until he was taken away.'

Emily rubbed her knuckles in her eyes. 'Oh dear,' she said, 'I *must* pull myself together. Yes. Yes, of course I did. I stayed with him.'

'Perhaps you held his hand as one does with a sick child?'

'It's hard to think of Trevor as a child,' Peregrine said. 'He was born elderly. Sorry.'

'But I did,' Emily exclaimed. 'You're right. I felt his pulse and then, you know, I just went on holding his hand.'

'Looking at it?'

'Not specially. Not *glaring* at it. Although——'

'Yes?'

'Well, I remember I did sort of look at it. I moved it between my own hands and I remember noticing how grubby it was which made it childish and—then—there was something——' She hesitated.

'Yes?'

'I thought he'd got rouge or carmine make-up under his nails and then I saw it wasn't grease. It was fluff.'

'I tell you what,' Alleyn said. 'We'll put you up for the Police Medal, you excellent girl. Fox : get on to St. Terence's Hospital and tell them it's as much as their life is worth to dig out that boy's nails. Tell our chap there he can clean them himself and put the harvest in an envelope and get a witness to it. Throw your bulk about. Get the top battle-axe and give her fits. Fly.'

Fox went off at a stately double.

'Now,' Alleyn said. 'You may go, both of you. Where do you live?'

They told him Blackfriars and Hampstead respectively.

'We could shake you down, Emily,' Peregrine said. 'Jeremy and I.'

'I'd like to go home, please, Perry. Could you call a taxi?'

'I think we can send you,' Alleyn said. 'I shan't need a car yet awhile and there's a gaggle of them out there.'

Peregrine said : 'I ought to wait for Greenslade, Emily.'

'Yes, of course you ought.'

'Well,' Alleyn said 'We'll bundle you off to Hampstead, Miss Dunne. Where's the sergeant?'

'Here, sir,' said the sergeant unexpectedly. He had come in from the foyer.

'What's the matter?' Alleyn asked. 'What've you got there?'

The sergeant's enormous hands were clapped together in front of him and arched a little as if they enclosed something that fluttered and might escape.

'Seventh row of the stalls, sir,' he said, 'centre aisle. On the floor about six foot from where the boy lay. There was a black velvet kind of easel affair and a sheet of polythene laying near them.'

He opened his palms like a book and disclosed a little wrinkled glove and two scraps of parchment.

'Would they be what was wanted?', asked the sergeant.

III

'To me,' said Mr. Greenslade with palpable self-restraint, 'there can be only one explanation, my dear Alleyn. The boy, who is, as Jay informs us, an unpleasant and mischievous boy, banged the door to suggest he'd gone but actually stayed behind and, having by some means learnt the number of the combination, robbed the safe of its contents. He was caught in the act by Jobbins who must have seen him from his post on the half-landing. As Jobbins made for him the boy, possibly by accident, overturned the pedestal Jobbins was felled by the Dolphin and the boy, terrified, ran into the circle and down the centre aisle. In his panic he ran too fast, stumbled across the balustrade, clutched at the velvet top and fell into the stalls. As he fell he let go the easel with the glove and papers and they dropped, as he did, into the aisle.'

Mr. Greenslade looking, in his unshaven state, strangely unlike himself, spread his hands and threw himself back in Winter Morris's office chair. Peregrine sat behind his own desk and Alleyn and Fox in two of the modish seats reserved for visitors. The time was twelve minutes past three and the air stale with the aftermath of managerial cigarettes and drinks.

'You say nothing,' Mr. Greenslade observed. 'You disagree?'

Alleyn said : 'As an open-and-shut theory it has its attractions. It's tidy. It's simple. It means that we all sit back and hope for the boy to recover consciousness and health so that we can send him up to the Juvenile Court for manslaughter.'

'What I can't quite see——' Peregrine began and then said, 'Sorry.'

'No. Go on,' Alleyn said.

'I can't see why the boy, having got the documents and glove, should come out to the circle foyer where he'd be sure to be seen by Jobbins on the half-landing. Why didn't he go down through the circle by the box, stairs, and pass-door to the stage and let himself out by the stage-door?'

'He might have wanted to show off He might have—— I am persuaded,' Mr. Greenslade said crossly, 'that your objections can be met.'

'There's another thing,' Peregrine said, 'and I should have thought of it before. At midnight, Jobbins had to make a routine report to police and fire-station. He'd do it from the open telephone in the downstairs foyer'

'Very well,' said Mr. Greenslade. 'That would give the boy his opportunity. What do you say, Alleyn?'

'As an investigating officer I'm supposed to say nothing,' Alleyn said lightly 'But since the people at the bistro up the lane and the wretched Hawkins all put Jay out of the picture as a suspect and you yourself appear to have been some thirty miles away——'

'Well, I must say!'

'——there's no reason why I shouldn't ask you to consider under what circumstances the boy, still clutching his booty, could have fallen from the circle with his face towards the balustrade and as he fell have clawed at the velvet top, palms down in such a posture that he's left nail-tracks almost parallel with the balustrade but slanting towards the outside There are also traces of boot polish that suggest one of his feet brushed back the pile at the same time. I cannot, myself, reconcile these traces with a nose-dive over the balustrade. I can relate them to a blow to the jaw, a fall across the balustrade, a lift, a sidelong drag and a drop. I also think Jay's objections are very well urged. There may be answers to them but at the moment I can't think of any. What's more, if the boy's the thief and killer, who unshot the bolts and unslipped the iron bar on the little pass-door in the main front entrance? Who left the key in the lock and banged the door shut from outside?'

'*Did* someone do this?'

'That's how things were when the police arrived.'

'I—I didn't notice I didn't notice that,' Peregrine said, putting his hand to his eyes. 'It was the shock, I suppose.'

'I expect it was.'

'Jobbins would have bolted the little door and dropped the bar when everyone had gone and I think he always hung the key in the corner beyond the box-office 'No,' Peregrine said slowly, 'I can't see the boy doing that thing with the door. It doesn't add up.'

'Not really, does it?' Alleyn said mildly.

'What action,' Mr. Greenslade asked, 'do you propose to take?'

'The usual routine and a very tedious affair it's likely to prove. There may be useful prints on the pedestal or the dolphin itself but I'm inclined to think that the best we can hope for there is negative evidence. There may be prints on the safe but so far Sergeant Bailey has found none. The injuries to the boy's face are interesting.'

'If he recovers consciousness,' Peregrine said, "he'll tell the whole story.'

'Not if he's responsible,' Mr. Greenslade said obstinately.

'Concussion,' Alleyn said, 'can be extremely tricky. In the meantime, of course, we'll have to find out about all the members of the company and the front-of-house staff and so on.'

'Find out?'

'Their movements for one thing. You may be able to help us here,' Alleyn said to Peregrine. 'It seems that apart from the boy, you and Miss Dunne were the last to leave the theatre. Unless, of course, somebody lay doggo until you'd gone. Which may well be the case. Can you tell us anything about how and when and by what door the other members of the cast went out?'

'I think I can,' Peregrine said. He was now invested with the kind of haggard vivacity that follows emotional exhaustion : a febrile alertness such as he had often felt after some hideously protracted dress-rehearsal. He described the precautions taken at the close of every performance to ensure that nobody was left on the premises. A thorough search of the house was made by backstage and front-of-house staff. He was certain it would have been quite impossible for anybody in the audience to hide anywhere in the theatre.

He related rapidly and accurately how the stage-crew left the theatre in a bunch and how Gertrude Bracey and Marcus Knight went out together through the auditorium to escape the wet. They had been followed by Charles Random, who was alone and used the stage-door and then by Emily who stayed offstage with Peregrine.

'And then,' Peregrine said, 'Destiny Meade and Harry Grove came out with a clutch of friends. They were evidently going on to a party. They went down the stage-door alley and I heard Harry call out that he'd fetch something or another and Destiny tell him not to be too long. And it was then—I'd come back from having a look at the weather—it was then that I fancied——' He stopped.

'Yes?'

'I thought that the pass-door from stage to front-of-house moved. It was out of the tail of my eye, sort of. If I'm right and I think I am, it must have been that wretched kid, I suppose.'

'But you never saw him?'

'Never. No. Only heard him.' And Peregrine described how he had gone out to the front and his subsequent interview with Jobbins. Alleyn took him over this again because, so he said,

ie wanted to make sure he'd got it right. 'You shaped up to
chasing the boy, did you? After you heard him catcall and slam
he stage-door?'

'Yes. But Jobbins pointed out he'd be well on his way.
So we said good night and——'

'Yes?'

'I've just remembered. Do you know what we said to each
other? I said : "This is your last watch" and he said : "That's
right. Positively the last appearance." Because the treasure was
to be taken away to-day, you see. And after that Jobbins
wouldn't have had to be glued to the half-landing.'

Greenslade and Fox made slight appropriate noises. Alleyn
waited for a moment and then said : 'And so you said good
night and you and Miss Dunne left? By the stage-door?'

'Yes.'

'Was it locked? Before you left?'

'No. Wait a moment, though. I think the Yale lock was
on but certainly not the bolts. Hawkins came in by the stage-
door. He had a key. He's a responsible man from a good firm
though you wouldn't think it from his behaviour to-night. He
let himself in and then shot the bolts.'

'Yes,' Alleyn said. 'We got that much out of him. Nothing
else you can tell us?'

Peregrine said : 'Not as far as I can think. But all the same
I've got a sort of notion that there's some damn' thing I've
forgotten. Some detail.'

'To do with what? Any idea?'

'To do with—I don't know. The boy, I think.'

'The boy?'

'I fancy I was thinking about a production of *The Cherry
Orchard*, but—no, it's gone and I daresay it's of no conse-
quence.'

Mr. Greenslade said : 'I know this is not your concern,
Alleyn, but I hope you don't mind my raising the point with
Jay. I should like to know what happens to the play. Does
the season continue? I am unfamiliar with theatrical practice.'

Peregrine said with some acidity : 'Theatrical practice doesn't
habitually cover the death by violence of one of its employees.'

'Quite.'

'But all the same,' Peregrine said, 'there *is* a certain attitude——'

'Quite. Yes. The—er—"the show",' quoted Mr. Greenslade self-consciously, ' "must go on".'

'I *think we should* go on. The boy's understudy's all right. To-morrow—no, to-day's Sunday, which gives us a chance to collect ourselves.' Peregrine fetched up short and turned to Alleyn. 'Unless,' he said, 'the police have any objection.'

'It's a bit difficult to say at this juncture, you know, but we should be well out of The Dolphin by Monday night. To-morrow night, in fact. You want an answer long before that, of course. I think I may suggest that you carry on as if for performance. If anything crops up to change the situation we shall let you know at once.'

With an air of shocked discovery Peregrine said: 'There's a great deal to be done. There's that—that—that—dreadful state of affairs on the half-landing.'

'I'm afraid we shall have to take up a section of the carpet. My chaps will do that. Can you get it replaced in time?'

'I suppose so,' Peregrine said, rubbing his hand across his face. 'Yes. Yes, we can do something about it.'

'We've removed the bronze dolphin.'

Peregrine told himself that he mustn't think about that. He must keep in the right gear and, Oh God, he mustn't be sick.

He muttered: 'Have you? I suppose so. Yes.'

Mr. Greenslade said: 'If there's nothing more one can do——' and stood up. 'One has to inform Mr. Conducis,' he sighed and was evidently struck by a deadly thought. 'The Press!' he cried. 'My God, the Press!'

'The Press,' Alleyn rejoined, 'is in full lurk outside the theatre. We have issued a statement to the effect that a night-watchman at The Dolphin has met with a fatal accident but that there is no further indication at the moment of how this came about.'

'*That* won't last long,' Mr. Greenslade grunted as he struggled into his overcoat. He gave Alleyn his telephone number, gloomily told Peregrine he supposed they would be in touch and took his leave.

'I shan't keep you any longer,' Alleyn said to Peregrine. 'But I shall want to talk to all the members of the cast and staff during the day. I see there's a list of addresses and telephone numbers here. If none of them objects I shall ask them to come here to The Dolphin, rather than call on them severally. It will save time.'

'Shall I tell them?'

'That's jolly helpful of you but I think it had better be official.'

'Oh. Oh, yes. Of course.'

'I expect you'll want to tell them what's happened and warn them they'll be needed but we'll organise the actual interviews. Eleven o'clock this morning, perhaps.'

'I must be with them,' Peregrine said. 'If you please.'

'Yes, of course,' Alleyn said. 'Good night.'

Peregrine thought absently that he had never seen a face so transformed by a far from excessive smile. Quite heartened by this phenomenon he held out his hand.

'Good night,' he said, 'there's one saving grace at least in all this horror.'

'Yes?'

'Oh, *yes*,' Peregrine said warmly and looked at a small glove and two scraps of writing that lay before Alleyn on Winter Morris's desk. 'You know,' he said, 'if they had been lost I really think I might have gone completely bonkers. You—you will take care of them?'

'Great care,' Alleyn said.

When Peregrine had gone Alleyn sat motionless and silent for so long that Fox was moved to clear his throat.

Alleyn bent over the treasure. He took a jeweller's eyeglass out of his pocket. He inserted a long index finger in the glove and turned back the gauntlet. He examined the letters H.S. and then the seams of the glove and then the work on the back.

'What's up, Mr. Alleyn?' Fox asked. 'Anything wrong?'

'Oh, my dear Br'er Fox, I'm afraid so. I'm afraid there's no saving grace in this catastrophe, after all, for Peregrine Jay.'

'I didn't knock you up when I came in,' Peregrine said. 'There seemed no point. It was getting light. I just thought I'd leave the note to wake me at seven. And oddly enough I did sleep. Heavily.'

Jeremy stood with his back to Peregrine, looking out of the bedroom window. 'Is that all?' he asked.

'All?'

'That happened?'

'I should have thought it was enough, my God!'

'I know,' Jeremy said without turning. 'I only meant: did you look at the glove?'

'I saw it, I told you. The sergeant brought it to Alleyn with the two documents and afterwards Alleyn laid them out on Winty's desk.'

'I wonder if it was damaged.'

'I don't think so. I didn't *examine* it. I wouldn't have been let. Fingerprints and all that. It seems they really do fuss away about fingerprints.'

'What'll they do with the things?'

'I don't know. Lock them up at the Yard, I imagine, until they've finished with them and then return them to Conducis.'

'To Conducis. Yes.'

'I must get up, Jer. I've got to ring Winty and the cast and the understudy and find out about the boy's condition. Look, you know the man who did the carpets. Could you ring him up at wherever he lives and tell him he simply must send men in, first thing to-morrow or if necessary to-night. To replace about two or three square yards of carpet on the half-landing. We'll pay overtime and time again and whatever.'

'The half-landing?'

Peregrine said very rapidly in a high-pitched voice: 'Yes.

The carpet. On the half-landing. It's got Jobbins's blood and brains all over it. The carpet.'

Jeremy turned grey and said : 'I'm sorry. I'll do that thing,' and walked out of the room.

When Peregrine had bathed and shaved he swallowed with loathing two raw eggs in Worcester Sauce and addressed himself to the telephone, a task made no easier by a twanging fault on his line. The time was twenty past seven.

On the South Bank in the borough of Southwark, Superintendent Alleyn, having left Inspector Fox to arrange the day's business, drove over Blackfriars Bridge to St. Terence's Hospital, and was conducted to a ward where Trevor Vere, screened from general view and deeply sighing, lay absorbed in the enigma of unconsciousness. At his bedside sat a uniformed constable whose helmet was under his chair and his notebook in his hand. Alleyn was escorted by the ward sister and a house-surgeon.

'As you see, he's deeply concussed,' said the house-surgeon. 'He fell on his feet and drove his spine into the base of his head and probably crashed the back of a seat. As far as we can tell there's no profound injury internally Right femur and two ribs broken. Extensive bruising. You may say he was bloody lucky. A twenty foot fall, I understand.'

'The bruise on his jaw?'

'That's a bit of a puzzle. It doesn't look like the back or arm of a seat. It's got all the characteristics of a nice hook to the jaw. I wouldn't care to say definitely, of course. Sir James has seen him.' (Sir James Curtis was the Home Office pathologist.) '*He* thinks it looks like a punch.'

'Ah. Yes, so he said. It's no use my asking, of course, when the boy may recover consciousness?'

'I'm afraid no use at all. Can't tell.'

'Or how much he will remember?'

'The usual thing is complete loss of memory for events occurring just before the accident.'

'Alas.'

'What? Oh, quite. You must find that sort of thing very frustrating.'

'Very. I wonder if it would be possible to take the boy's height and length of his arms, would it?'

'He can't be disturbed.'

'I know. But if he might be uncovered for a moment. It really is important.'

The young house-surgeon thought for a moment and then nodded to the sister who folded back the bedclothes.

'I'm very much obliged to you,' Alleyn said three minutes later and replaced the clothes.

'Well, if that's all——?'

'Yes. Thank you very much. I mustn't keep you. Thank you, Sister. I'll just have a word with the constable, here, before I go.'

The constable had withdrawn to the far side of the bed.

'You're the chap who came here with the ambulance, aren't you?' Alleyn asked.

'Yes, sir.'

'You should have been relieved. You heard about instructions from Mr. Fox concerning the boy's fingernails?'

'Yes, I did, sir, but only after he'd been cleaned up.'

Alleyn swore in a whisper.

'But I'd happened to notice——' The constable—wooden-faced—produced from a pocket in his tunic a folded paper. 'It was in the ambulance, sir. While they were putting a blanket over him. They were going to tuck his hands under and I noticed they were a bit dirty like a boy's often are but the fingernails had been manicured. Colourless varnish and all. And then I saw two were broken back and the others kind of choked up with red fluff and I cleaned them out with my penknife.' He modestly proffered his little folded paper.

'What's your name?' Alleyn asked.

'Grantley, sir.'

'Want to move out of the uniformed arm?'

'I'd like to.'

'Yes. Well, come and see me if you apply for a transfer.'

'Thank you, sir.'

Trevor Vere sighed lengthily in his breathing. Alleyn looked at the not-quite-closed eyes, the long lashes and the full mouth that had smirked so unpleasingly at him that morning in The

Dolphin. It was merely childish now. He touched the forehead which was cool and dampish.

'Where's his mother?' Alleyn asked.

'They say, on her way.'

'She's difficult, I'm told. Don't leave the boy before you're relieved. If he speaks: get it.'

'They say he's not likely to speak, sir.'

'I know. I know.'

A nurse approached with a covered object.

'All right,' Alleyn said, 'I'm off.'

He went to the Yard, treating himself to coffee and bacon and eggs on the way.

Fox, he was told, had come in. He arrived in Alleyn's office looking, as always, neat, reasonable, solid and extremely clean. He made a succinct report. Jobbins appeared to have no near relations but the landlady at The Wharfinger's Friend had heard him mention a cousin who was a lock-keeper near Marlow. The stage-crew and front-of-house people had been checked and were out of the picture. The routine search before locking up seemed to have been extremely thorough.

Bailey and Thompson had finished at the theatre where nothing of much significance had emerged. The dressing-rooms had yielded little beyond a note from Harry Grove that Destiny Meade had carelessly tucked into her make-up box.

'Very frank affair,' Mr. Fox said primly.

'Frank about what?'

'Sex.'

'Oh. No joy for us?'

'Not in the way you mean, Mr. Alleyn.'

'What about the boy's room?'

'He shares with Mr. Charles Random. A lot of horror comics including some of the American type that come within the meaning of the act respecting the importation of juvenile reading. One strip was about a well-developed female character called Slash who's really a vampire. She carves up Olympic athletes and leaves her mark on them—"Slash," in blood. It seems the lad was quite struck with this. He's scrawled "Slash" across the dressing-room looking-glass with red greasepaint and we found the same thing on the front-of-house lavatory mirrors and on the wall of one of the upstairs boxes. The one on the audience's left.'

'Poor little swine.'

'The landlady at The Wharfinger's Friend reckons he'll come to no good and blames the mother who plays the steel guitar at that strip-tease joint behind Magpie Alley. Half the time she doesn't pick the kid up after his show and he gets left, hanging round the place till all hours, Mrs. Jancy says.'

'Mrs——?'

'Jancy. The landlady. Nice woman. The Blewitts don't live far off as it happens. Somewhere behind Tabard Street at the back of the Borough.'

'Anything more?'

'Well—dabs. Nothing very startling. Bailey's been able to pick up some nice, clean, control specimens from the dressing-rooms. The top of the pedestal's a mess of the public's prints, half dusted off by the cleaners.'

'Nothing to the purpose?'

'Not really. And you would expect,' Fox said with his customary air of placid good-sense, 'if the boy acted vindictively, to find his dabs—two palms together where he pushed the thing over. Nothing of the kind, however, nice shiny surface and all. The carpet's hopeless, of course. Our chaps have taken up the soiled area. Is anything the matter, Mr. Alleyn?'

'Nothing, Br'er Fox, except the word "soiled"'

'It's not too *strong*,' Fox said, contemplating it with surprise.

'No. It's dreadfully moderate.'

'Well,' Fox said, after a moment's consideration, 'you have a feeling for words, of course.'

'Which gives me no excuse to talk like a pompous ass. Can you do some telephoning? And, by the way, have you had any breakfast? Don't tell me. The landlady of The Wharfinger's Friend stuffed you full of newlaid eggs.'

'Mrs. Jancy *was* obliging enough to make the offer.'

'In that case here is the cast and management list with telephone numbers. You take the first half and I'll do the rest. Ask them with all your celebrated tact to come to the theatre at eleven. I think we'll find that Peregrine Jay has already warned them.'

But Peregrine had not warned Jeremy because it had not occurred to him that Alleyn would want to see him. When the telephone rang it was Jeremy who answered it. Peregrine saw his face bleach. He thought : 'How extraordinary : I believe his pupils have contracted.' And he felt within himself a cold sliding sensation which he refused to acknowledge.

Jeremy said : 'Yes, of course. Yes,' and put the receiver down. 'It seems they want me to go to the theatre, too,' he said.

'I don't know why. You weren't there last night.'

'No. I was here. Working.'

'Perhaps they want you to check that the glove's all right.'

Jeremy made a slight movement, almost as if a nerve had been flicked. He pursed his lips and raised his sandy brows. 'Perhaps,' he said and returned to his work-table at the far end of the room.

Peregrine, with some difficulty, got Mrs. Blewitt on the telephone and was subjected to a tirade in which speculation and avid cupidity were but thinly disguised under a mask of sorrow. She suffered, unmistakably, from a formidable hangover. He arranged for a meeting, told her what the hospital had told him and assured her that everything possible would be done for the boy.

'Will they catch whoever done it?'

'It may have been an accident, Mrs. Blewitt.'

'If it was, the Management's responsible,' she said, 'and don't forget it.'

They rang off.

Peregrine turned to Jeremy who was bent over his table but did not seem to be working.

'Are you all right, Jer?'

'All right?'

'I thought you looked a bit poorly.'

'There's nothing the matter with me. You look pretty sickly, yourself.'

'I daresay I do.'

Peregrine waited for a moment and then said: 'When will you go to The Dolphin?'

'I'm commanded for eleven.'

'I thought I'd go over early. Alleyn will use our office and the company can sit about the circle foyer or go to their dressing-rooms.'

'They may be locked up,' Jeremy said.

'Who—the actors?'

'The dressing-rooms, half-wit.'

'I can't imagine why but you may be right. Routine's what they talk about, isn't it?'

Jeremy did not answer. Peregrine saw him wipe his hand across his mouth and briefly close his eyes. Then he stooped over his work: he was shaping a piece of balsa wood with a mounted razor blade. His hand jerked and the blade slipped. Peregrine let out an involuntary ejaculation. Jeremy swung round on his stool and faced him. 'Do me a profound kindness and get the hell out of it, will you, Perry?'

'All right. See you later.'

Peregrine, perturbed and greatly puzzled, went out into the week-end emptiness of Blackfriars. An unco-ordinated insistence of church bells jangled across the Sunday quietude.

He had nothing to do between now and eleven o'clock. 'One might go into a church,' he thought, but the idea dropped blankly on a field of inertia. 'I can't imagine why I feel like this,' he thought. 'I'm used to taking decisions, to keeping on top of a situation.' But there were no decisions to take and the situation was out of his control. He couldn't think of Superintendent Alleyn in terms of a recalcitrant actor.

He thought: 'I know what I'll do. I've got two hours. I'll walk, like a character in Fielding or in Dickens. I'll walk northwards, towards Hampstead and Emily. If I get blisters I'll take a bus or a tube and if there's not enough time left for that I'll take a taxi. And Emily and I will go down to The Dolphin together.'

Having come to this decision his spirits lifted. He crossed Blackfriars Bridge and made his way through Bloomsbury towards Marylebone and Maida Vale.

His thoughts were divided between Emily, The Dolphin, and Jeremy Jones.

II

Gertrude Bracey had a mannerism. She would glance pretty sharply at a vis-à-vis but only for a second and would then, with a brusque turn of the head, look away. The effect was disconcerting and suggested, not shiftiness so much as a profound distaste for her company. She smiled readily but with a derisive air and she had a sharp edge to her tongue. Alleyn who never relied upon first impressions, supposed her to be vindictive.

He found support for this opinion in the demeanour of her associates. They sat round the office in The Dolphin on that Sunday morning, with all the conditioned ease of their training but with restless eyes and overtones of discretion in their beautifully controlled voices. This air of guardedness was most noticeable, because it was least disguised, in Destiny Meade. Sleek with fur, not so much dressed as gloved, she sat back in her chair and looked from time to time at Harry Grove who, on the few occasions when he caught her eye, smiled brilliantly in return. When Alleyn began to question Miss Bracey, Destiny Meade and Harry Grove exchanged one of these glances: on her part with brows raised significantly and on his with an appearance of amusement and anticipation.

Marcus Knight looked as if someone had affronted him and also as if he was afraid Miss Bracey was about to go too far in some unspecified direction.

Charles Random watched her with an expression of nervous distaste and Emily Dunne with evident distress. Winter Morris seemed to be ravaged by anxiety and inward speculation. He looked restlessly at Miss Bracey as if she had interrupted him in some desperate calculation. Peregrine, sitting by Emily, stared at his own clasped hands and occasionally at her. He listened carefully to Alleyn's questions and Miss Bracey's replies. Jeremy Jones, a little removed from the others, sat bolt upright in his chair and stared at Alleyn.

The characteristic that all these people had in common was that of extreme pallor, guessed at in the women and self-evident in the men.

Alleyn had opened with a brief survey of the events in their succession, had checked the order in which the members of the company had left the theatre and was now engaged upon extracting confirmation of their movements from Gertrude Bracey with the reactions among his hearers that have been indicated.

'Miss Bracey, I think you and Mr. Knight left the theatre together. Is that right?' They both agreed.

'And you left by the auditorium, not by the stage-door?'

'At Perry's suggestion,' Marcus Knight said.

'To avoid the puddles,' Miss Bracey explained.

'And you went out together through the front doors?'

'No,' they said in unison and she added : 'Mr. Knight was calling on the Management.'

She didn't actually sniff over this statement but contrived to suggest that there was something to be sneered at in the circumstance.

'I looked in at the office,' Knight loftily said, 'on a matter of business.'

'This office? And to see Mr. Morris?'

'Yes,' Winter Morris said. Knight inclined his head in stately acquiescence.

'So you passed Jobbins on your way upstairs?'

'I——ah——yes. He was on the half-landing under the treasure.'

'I saw him up there,' Miss Bracey said.

'How was he dressed?'

As usual, they said, with evident surprise. In uniform.

'Miss Bracey, how did you leave?'

'By the pass-door in the main entrance. I let myself out and slammed it shut after me.'

'Locking it?'

'No.'

'Are you sure?'

'Yes. As a matter of fact I——I re-opened it.'

'Why?'

'I wanted to see the time,' she said awkwardly, 'by the clock in the foyer.'

'Jobbins,' Winter Morris said, 'barred and bolted this door after everyone had left.'

'When would that be?'

'Not more than ten minutes later. Marco—Mr. Knight—and I had a drink and left together. Jobbins came after us and I heard him drop the bar across and shoot the bolts. My God!' Morris suddenly exclaimed.

'Yes?'

'The alarm! The burglar alarm. He'd switch it on when he'd locked up. Why didn't it work?'

'Because somebody had switched it off.'

'My God!'

'May we return to Jobbins? How was he dressed when you left?'

Morris said with an air of patience under trying circumstances. 'I didn't see him as we came down. He may have been in the men's lavatory. I called out good night and he answered from up above. We stood for a moment in the portico and that's when I heard him bolt the door.'

'When you saw him, perhaps ten minutes later, Mr. Jay, he was wearing an overcoat and slippers?'

'Yes,' said Peregrine.

'Yes. Thank you. How do you get home, Miss Bracey?'

She had a mini-car, she said, which she parked in the converted bombsite between the pub and the theatre.

'Were there other cars parked in this area belonging to the theatre people?'

'Naturally,' she said again. 'Since I was the first to leave.'

'You noticed and recognised them?'

'Oh, *really*, I *suppose* I noticed them. There were a number of strange cars still there but—yes I saw—' she looked at Knight. Her manner suggested a grudging alliance, '—*your* car, Marcus.'

'What make of car is Mr. Knight's?'

'I've no idea. What is it, dear?'

'A Jag, dear,' said Knight.

'Any others?' Alleyn persisted.

'I *really* don't know. I think I noticed—yours, Charles,' she said, glancing at Random. 'Yes. I did, because it *is* rather conspicuous.'

'What is it?'

'I've no idea.'

'A very, very, old, old, old souped-up Morris sports,' said Random. 'Painted scarlet.'

'And Miss Meade's car?'

Destiny Meade opened her eyes very wide and raised her elegantly gloved and braceleted hands to her furs. She gently shook her head. The gesture suggested utter bewilderment. Before she could speak Gertrude Bracey gave her small, contemptuous laugh.

'Oh, *that*,' she said. 'Yes, indeed. Drawn up in glossy state under the portico. As for Royalty.'

She did not look at Destiny.

Harry Grove said: 'Destiny uses a hire-service, don't you, love?' His manner, gay and proprietary, had an immediate effect upon Marcus Knight and Gertrude Bracey who both stared lividly at nothing

'Any other cars, Miss Bracey? Mr. Morris's?'

'I don't remember. I didn't go peering about for cars. I don't notice them.'

'It was there,' Winter Morris said. 'Parked at the back and rather in the dark.'

'When you left, Mr. Morris, were there any other cars apart from your own and Mr. Knight's?'

'I really don't know. There might have been. Do you remember, Marco?'

'No,' he said, widely and vaguely. 'No, I don't remember. As you say: it was dark.'

'I had an idea I saw your mini, Gertie,' Morris said, 'but I suppose I couldn't have. You'd gone by then, of course.'

Gertrude Bracey darted a glance at Alleyn.

'I can't swear to all this sort of thing,' she said angrily. 'I—I didn't notice the cars and I had——' she stopped and made a sharp movement with her hands. 'I had other things to think of,' she said.

'I understand,' Alleyn said, 'that Miss Dunne and Mr. Jay didn't have cars at the theatre?'

'That's right,' Emily said. 'I haven't got one anyway.'

'I left mine at home,' said Peregrine.

'Where it remained?' Alleyn remarked, 'unless Mr. Jones took it out?'

'Which I didn't,' Jeremy said. 'I was at home, working, all the evening.'

'Alone?'

'Entirely.'

'As far as cars are concerned that leaves only Mr Grove. Did you by any chance notice Mr. Grove's car in the bombsite, Miss Bracey?'

'Oh, yes!' she said loudly and threw him one of her brief, disfavouring looks. 'I saw *that* one.'

'What is it?'

'A Panther '55,' she said instantly. 'An open sports car.'

'You know it quite well,' Alleyn lightly observed

'Know it? Oh, yes,' Gertrude Bracey repeated with a sharp cackle. 'I *know* it. Or you may say I used to.'

'You don't think well, perhaps, of Mr. Grove's Panther?'

'There's nothing the matter with the *car*.'

Harry Grove said: 'Darling, what an infallible ear you have for inflection. Did you go to R.A.D.A.?'

Destiny Meade let out half a cascade of her celebrated laughter and then appeared to swallow the remainder. Morris gave a repressed snort.

Marcus Knight said: 'This is the wrong occasion, in my opinion, for mistimed comedy.'

'Of course,' Grove said warmly. 'I do so agree. But when is the right occasion?'

'If I am to be publicly insulted——' Miss Bracey began on a high note. Peregrine cut in.

'Look,' he said. 'Shouldn't we all remember this is a police inquiry into something that may turn out to be murder?'

They gazed at him as if he'd committed a social enormity.

'Mr. Alleyn,' Peregrine went on, 'tells us he's decided to cover the first stages as a sort of company call: everybody who was in the theatre last night and left immediately, or not long before the event. That's right, isn't it?' he asked Alleyn.

'Certainly,' Alleyn agreed and reflected sourly that Peregrine, possibly with the best will in the world, had effectually choked what might have been a useful and revealing dust-up. He must make the best of it.

'This procedure,' he said, 'if satisfactorily conducted, should save a great deal of checking and counter-checking and reduce the amount of your time taken up by the police. The alternative is to ask you all to wait in the foyer while I see each of you separately.'

There was a brief pause broken by Winter Morris.

'Fair enough,' Morris said and there was a slight murmur of agreement from the company. 'Don't let's start throwing temperaments right and left, chaps,' Mr. Morris added. 'It's not the time for it.'

Alleyn could have kicked him. 'How right you are,' he said. 'Shall we press on? I'm sure you all see the point of this car business. It's essential that we make out when and in what order you left the theatre and whether any of you could have returned within the crucial time. Yes, Miss Meade?'

'I don't want to interrupt,' Destiny Meade said. She caught her underlip between her teeth and gazed helplessly at Alleyn. 'Only : I don't *quite* understand.'

'Please go on.'

'May I? Well, you see, it's just that everybody says Trevor, who is generally admitted to be rather a beastly little boy, stole the treasure and then killed poor Jobbins. I *do* admit he's got some rather awful ways with him and of course one never knows so one wonders why, that being the case, it matters where we all went or what sort of cars we went in.'

Alleyn said carefully that so far no hard and fast conclusion could be drawn and that he hoped they would all welcome the opportunity of proving that they were away from the theatre during the crucial period which was between 11 o'clock when Peregrine and Emily left the theatre and about five past twelve when Hawkins came running down the stage-door alleyway and told them of his discovery.

'So far,' Alleyn said, 'we've only got as far as learning that when Miss Bracey left the theatre the rest of you were still inside it.'

'Not I,' Jeremy said. 'I've told you, I think, that I was at home.'

'So you have,' Alleyn agreed. 'It would help if you could substantiate the statement. Did anyone ring you up, for instance?'

'If they did, I don't remember.'

'I see,' said Alleyn.

He plodded back through the order of departure until it was established beyond question, that Gertrude and Marcus had been followed by Charles Random who had driven to a pub on the South Bank where he was living for the duration of the play. He had been given his usual late supper. He was followed by Destiny Meade and her friends, all of whom left by the stage-door and spent about an hour at The Younger Dolphin and then drove to her flat in Cheyne Walk where they were joined, she said, by dozens of vague chums, and by Harry Grove who left the theatre at the same time as they did, fetched his guitar from his own flat in Canonbury and then joined them in Chelsea. It appeared that Harry Grove was celebrated for a song sequence in which, Destiny said, obviously quoting someone else, he sent the sacred cows up so high that they remained in orbit forevermore.

'Quite a loss to the nightclubs,' Marcus Knight said to no-body in particular. 'One wonders why the legitimate theatre should still attract.'

'I assure you, Marco dear,' Grove rejoined, 'only the Lord Chamberlain stands between me and untold affluence'

'Or you might call it dirt-pay,' said Knight. It was Miss Bracey's turn to laugh very musically.

'Did any of you,' Alleyn went on, 'at any time after the fall of curtain see or speak to Trevor Vere?'

'I did, of course,' Charles Random said. He had an impatient rather injured manner which it would have been going too far to call feminine. 'He dresses with me. And without wanting to appear utterly brutal I must say it would take nothing less than a twenty-foot drop into the stalls to stop him talking.'

'Does he write on the looking-glass?'

Random looked surprised, 'No,' he said. 'Write what? Graffiti?'

'Not precisely. The word "Slash." In red greasepaint.'

'He's always shrieking "Slash." Making a great mouthful of it. Something to do with his horror comics, one imagines.'

'Does he ever talk about the treasure?'

'Well, yes,' Random said uneasily. 'He flaunts away about how—well, about how any fool could pinch it and—and : no, it's of no importance.'

'Suppose we just hear about it?'

'He was simply putting on his act but he did say anyone with any sense could guess the combination of the lock.'

'Intimating that he had, in fact, guessed it?'

'Well—actually—yes.'

'And did he divulge what it was?'

Random was of a sanguine complexion. He now lost something of his colour. 'He did not,' Random said, 'and if he had, I should have paid no attention. I don't believe for a moment he knew the combination.'

'And *you* ought to know, dear, oughtn't you?' Destiny said with the gracious condescension of stardom to bit-part competence. 'Always doing those ghastly puzzles in your intellectual papers. *Right* up your alleyway.'

This observation brought about its own reaction of discomfort and silence.

Alleyn said to Winter Morris, 'I remember I suggested that you would be well-advised to make the five letter key-group rather less predictable. Was it in fact changed?'

Winter Morris raised his eyebrows, wagged his head and his hands and said : 'I was always going to. And then when we knew they were to go—— One of those things.' He covered his face for a moment. 'One of those things,' he repeated and everybody looked deeply uncomfortable.

Alleyn said : 'On that morning, beside yourself and the boy, there were present, I think, everybody who is here now except Miss Bracey, Mr. Random and Mr. Grove. Is that right, Miss Bracey?'

'Oh, yes,' she said with predictable acidity. 'It was a photograph call, I believe. I was *not* required.'

'It was just for two pictures, dear,' little Morris said. 'Destiny and Marco with the glove. You know?'

'Oh, quite. Quite.'

'And the kid turned up so they used him.'

'I seem to remember,' Harry Grove observed, 'that Trevor was quoted in the daily journals as saying that the glove made him feel kinda funny like he wanted to cry.'

'Am I wrong?' Marcus Knight suddenly demanded of no one in particular, 'in believing that this boy is in a critical condition and may die? Mr.—ah—Superintendent—ah—Alleyn?'

'He is still on the danger list,' Alleyn said.

'Thank you. Has anybody else got something funny to say about the boy?' Knight demanded. 'Or has the fount of comedy dried at its source?'

'If,' Grove rejoined, without rancour, 'you mean me, it's dry as a bone. No more jokes.'

Marcus Knight folded his arms.

Alleyn said: 'Miss Meade, Miss Dunne, Mr. Knight, Mr. Jay and Mr. Jones—and the boy of course—were all present when the matter of the lock was discussed. Not for the first time, I understand. The safe had been installed for some days and the locking system had been widely canvassed among you. You had heard from Mr. Morris that it carried a five-number combination and that this was based on a five letter key-word and a very commonplace code. Mr. Morris also said, before I stopped him, that an obvious key-word had been suggested by Mr. Conducis. Had any of you already speculated upon what this word might be? Or discussed the matter?'

There was a longish silence.

Destiny Meade said plaintively: 'Naturally we *discussed* it. The men seemed to know what it was all about. The alphabet and numbers and not enough numbers for all the letters or something. And anyway it wasn't as if any of us were going to *do* anything, was it? But everyone *thought*——'

'What everyone thought——' Marcus Knight began but she looked coldly upon him and said: 'Please don't butt in, Marco. You've got such a way of butting in. Do you mind?'

'By *God*!' he said with all the repose of an unexploded landmine.

'Everyone thought,' Destiny continued, gazing at Alleyn, 'that this obvious five-letter *word* would be "glove." But as far as *I* could see that didn't get one any nearer to a five-figure *number*.'

Harry Grove burst out laughing. 'Darling?' he said, 'I adore you better than life itself.' He picked up her gloved hand and kissed it, peeled back the gauntlet, kissed the inside of her wrist and then remarked to the company in general that he wouldn't exchange her for a wilderness of monkeys. Gertrude Bracey violently re-crossed her legs. Marcus Knight rose, turned his face to the wall and with frightful disengagement made as if to examine a framed drawing of The Dolphin in the days of Adolphus Ruby. A pulse beat rapidly under his empurpled cheek.

'Very well,' Alleyn said. 'You all thought that "glove" was a likely word and so indeed it was. Did anyone arrive at the code and produce the combination?'

'Dilly, dilly, dilly come and be killed,' cried Harry.

'Not at all,' Alleyn rejoined. 'Unless (the security aspect of this affair being evidently laughable), you formed yourselves into a syndicate for robbery. If anyone did arrive at the combination it seems highly unlikely that he or she kept it to himself. Yes, Mr. Random?'

Charles Random had made an indeterminate sound. He looked up quickly at Alleyn, hesitated and then said rapidly:

'As a matter of fact, I did. I've always been mildly interested in codes and I heard everybody muttering away about the lock on the safe and how the word might be "glove." I have to do a lot of waiting about in my dressing-room and thought I'd try to work it out. I thought it might be one of the sorts where you write down numerals from 1 to 0 in three rows one under another and put in succession under each row

the letters of the alphabet adding an extra A B C D to make up
the last line. Then you can read the numbers off from the
letters. Each number has three equivalent letters and A B C D
have each two equivalent numbers.'

'Quite so. And you got——? From the word "glove"?'

'72525 or, if the alphabet was written from right to left,
49696.'

'And if the alphabet ran from right to left and then, at K,
from left to right and finally at U, from right to left again?'

'42596 which seemed to me more likely as there are no
repeated figures.'

'Fancy you *remembering* them like that,' Destiny ejaculated
and appealed to the company. 'I mean—*isn't* it? I can't so
much as remember anyone's telephone number—scarcely even
my own.'

Winter Morris moved his hands, palms up and looked at
Alleyn.

'But, of course,' Random said, 'there are any number
of variants in this type of code. I might have been *all* wrong.'

'Tell me,' Alleyn said, 'are you and the boy on in the same
scenes? I seem to remember that you are.'

'Yes,' Peregrine and Random said together and Random
added : 'I didn't leave any notes about that Trevor could have
read. He tried to pump me. I thought it would be extremely
unwise to tell him.'

'Did you, in fact, tell anybody of your solutions?'

'No,' Random said, looking straight in front of him. 'I
discussed the code with nobody.' He looked at his fellow
players. 'You can all bear me out in this,' he said.

'Well, I must say!' Gertrude Bracey ejaculated and
laughed.

'A wise decision,' Alleyn murmured and Random glanced
at him. 'I wonder,' he said fretfully.

'I think there's something else you have to tell me, isn't
there?'

In the interval that followed Destiny said with an air of
discovery : 'No, but you must all admit it's terribly *clever* of
Charles.'

Random said : 'Perhaps it's unnecessary to point out that

if I had tried to steal the treasure I would certainly not have told you what I *have* told you; still less what I'm going to tell you.'

Another pause was broken by Inspector Fox who sat by the door and had contrived to be forgotten. 'Fair enough,' he said.

'Thank you,' said Random, startled.

'What *are* you going to tell me, Mr. Random?' Alleyn asked him.

'That, whatever the combination may be, Trevor didn't know it. He's not really as sharp as he sounds. It was all bluff. When he kept on about how easy it was I got irritated—I find him extremely tiresome, that boy—and I said I'd give him a pound if he could tell me and he did a sort of "Yah-yah-yah, I'm not going to be caught like that" act.' Random made a slight rather finicky movement of his shoulders and his voice became petulant. 'He'd been helping himself to my make-up and I was livid with him. It blew up into quite a thing and—well, it doesn't matter but in the end I shook him and he blurted out a number—55531. Then we were called for the opening.'

'When was this?'

'Before last night's show.' Random turned to Miss Bracey. 'Gertie dresses next door to me,' he said. 'I daresay she heard the ongoings.'

'I certainly *did. Not* very helpful when one is making one's preparation which I, at any rate, like to do.'

'Method in her madness. Or is it,' Harry Grove asked, 'madness in her Method?'

'That will do, Harry.'

'Dear Perry. Of course.'

'You told us a moment ago, Mr. Random,' Alleyn said, 'that the boy didn't reveal the number.'

'Nor did he. Not the correct number,' Random said quickly.

Destiny Meade said: 'Yes, but why were you so sure it was the wrong number?'

'It's The Dolphin telephone number, darling,' Grove said. 'WAT 55531. Remember?'

'Is it? Oh, yes. Of course it is.'

'First thing to enter his head in his fright, I suppose,' Random said.

'You really frightened him?' asked Alleyn.

'Yes, I did. Little horror. He'd have told me if he'd known.' Random added loudly : 'He didn't know the combination and he couldn't have opened the lock.'

'He was for ever badgering me to drop a hint,' Winter Morris said. 'Needless to say, I didn't.'

'Precisely,' said Random.

Peregrine said : 'I don't see how you can be so sure, Charlie. He might simply have been holding out on you.'

'If he knew the combination and meant to commit the theft,' Knight said, flinging himself down into his chair again, 'he certainly wouldn't tell you what it was.'

There was a general murmur of fervent agreement. 'And after all,' Harry Grove pointed out, 'you couldn't have been absolutely sure, could you, Charles, that you hit on the right number yourself or even the right type of code? Or could you?' He grinned at Random. 'Did you *try?*' he asked. 'Did you *prove* it, Charles? Did you have a little tinker? *Before* the treasure went in?'

For a moment Random looked as if he would like to hit him but he tucked in his lips, gave himself time and then spoke exclusively to Alleyn.

He said : 'I do *not* believe that Trevor opened the safe and consequently I'm absolutely certain he didn't kill Bert Jobbins.' He settled his shoulders and looked defiant.

Winter Morris said : 'I suppose you realise the implication of what you're saying, Charles?'

'I think so.'

'Then I must say you've an odd notion of loyalty to your colleagues.'

'It doesn't arise.'

'*Doesn't* it!' Morris cried and looked restively at Alleyn.

Alleyn made no answer to this. He sat with his long hands linked together on Peregrine's desk.

The superb voice of Marcus Knight broke the silence.

'I may be very dense,' he said, collecting his audience, 'but I cannot see where this pronouncement of Charles's leads us.

If, as the investigation seems to establish, the boy never left
the theatre and if the theatre was locked up and only Hawkins
had the key of the stage-door : then how the hell did a third
person get in?'

'Might he have been someone in the audience who stayed
behind?' Destiny asked, brightly. 'You know? Lurked?'

Peregrine said: 'The ushers, the commissionaire, Jobbins
and the A.S.M. did a thorough search front and back after
every performance.'

'Well, then, perhaps *Hawkins* is the murderer,' she said
exactly as if a mystery-story were under discussion. 'Has anyone thought of *that?*' she appealed to Alleyn, who thought
it better to disregard her.

'Well, *I* don't know,' Destiny rambled on. 'Who *could* it
be if it's not Trevor? That's what we've got to ask ourselves.
Perhaps, though I'm sure I can't think why, and say what you
like motive *is* important——' She broke off and made an
enchanting little grimace at Harry Grove. 'Now don't *you*
laugh,' she said. 'But for all that just *suppose.* Just suppose
—it was Mr. Conducis.'

'*My dear girl*——'

'*Destiny, honestly.*'

'*Oh, for God's sake, darling*——'

'I know it sounds silly,' Destiny said, 'but nobody seems to
have any other suggestion and after all he was *there.*'

III

The silence that followed Destiny's remark was so profound
that Alleyn heard Fox's pencil skate over a page in his notebook.

He said: 'You mean, Miss Meade, that Mr. Conducis was
in the audience? Not backstage?'

'That's right. In front. In the upstairs O.P. box. I noticed
him when I made my first entrance. I mentioned it to you,
Charles, didn't I, when you were holding me up. "There's
God" I said, "in the O.P. box".'

'Mr. Morris, did you know Mr. Conducis was in front?'

'No, I didn't. But he's got the O.P. box for ever,' Morris said. 'It's his whenever he likes to use it. He lends it to friends and for all I know occasionally slips in himself. He doesn't let us know if he's coming. He doesn't like a fuss.'

'Nobody saw him come or go?'

'Not that I know.'

Gertrude Bracey said loudly: 'I thought our mysterious Mr. W.H. was supposed to be particularly favoured by Our Patron. Quite a Shakespearian situation or so one hears. Perhaps he can shed light.'

'My dear Gertie,' Harry Grove said cheerfully, 'you really should try to keep a splenetic fancy within reasonable bounds. Miss Bracey,' he said, turning to Alleyn, 'refers, I *think*, to the undoubted fact that Mr. Conducis very kindly recommended me to the management. I did him a slight service once upon a time and he is obliging enough to *be* obliged. I had no idea he was in front, Gertie dear, until I heard you hissing away about it as you lay on The King Dolphin's bosom at the end of Act I.'

'Mr. Knight,' Alleyn asked, 'did you know Mr. Conducis was there?'

Knight looked straight in front of him and said with exaggerated clarity as if voicing an affront, 'It became evident.'

Destiny Meade, also looking neither to left or right and speaking clearly, remarked: 'The less said about *that* the better.'

'Undoubtedly,' Knight savagely agreed.

She laughed.

Winter Morris said: 'Yes, but——' and stopped short. 'It's nothing,' he said. 'As you were.'

'But in any case it can be of no conceivable significance,' Jeremy Jones said impatiently. He had been silent for so long that his intervention caused a minor stir.

Alleyn rose to his considerable height and moved out into the room. 'I think,' he said, 'that we've gone as far as we can, satisfactorily, in a joint discussion. I'm going to ask Inspector Fox to read over his notes. If there is anything any of you wishes to amend will you say so?'

Fox read his notes in a cosy voice and nobody objected to a

word of them. When he had finished Alleyn said to Peregrine : 'I daresay you'll want to make your own arrangements
with the company.'

'May I?.' said Peregrine. 'Thank you.'

Alleyn and Fox withdrew to the distant end of the office
and conferred together. The company, far from concerning
themselves with the proximity of the police, orientated as one
man upon Peregrine, who explained that Trevor Vere's understudy would carry on and that his scenes would be rehearsed
in the morning. 'Everybody concerned, please, at ten o'clock,'
Peregrine said. 'And look : about the Press. We've got to be
very careful with this one, haven't we, Winty?'

Winter Morris joined him, assuming at once his occupational manner of knowing how to be tactful with actors.
They didn't, any of them, did they, he asked, want the wrong
kind of stories to get into the Press. There was no doubt
they would be badgered. He himself had been rung up
repeatedly. The line was regret and no comment. 'You'd all
gone,' Morris said. 'You weren't there. You've heard about it,
of course, but you've no ideas.' Here everybody looked at
Destiny.

He continued in this vein and it became evident that this
able, essentially kind little man was at considerable pains to
stop short of the suggestion that, properly controlled, the
disaster, from a box-office angle, might turn out to be no
such thing. 'But we don't *need* it,' he said unguardedly and
embarrassed himself and most of his hearers. Harry Grove,
however, gave one of his little chuckles.

'Well, that's all perfectly splendid,' he said. 'Everybody
happy. We've no need of bloody murder to boost our doorsales and wee Trevor can recover his wits as slowly as he likes.
Grand.' He placed his arm about Destiny Meade who gave
him a mock-reproachful look, tapped his hand and freed herself. 'Darling, *do* be good,' she said. She moved away from
him, caught Gertrude Bracey's baleful eye and said with
extreme graciousness : 'Isn't he *too* frightful?' Miss Bracey
was speechless.

'I can see I've fallen under the imperial displeasure,' Grove murmured in a too-audible aside. 'The Great King Dolphin looks as if it's going to combust.'

Knight walked across the office and confronted Grove who was some three inches shorter than himself. Alleyn was uncannily reminded of a scene between them in Peregrine's play when the man of Stratford confronted the man of fashion while the Dark Lady, so very much more subtle than the actress who beautifully portrayed her, watched catlike in the shadow.

'You really are,' Marcus Knight announced, magnificently inflecting, 'the most objectionable person—I will not honour you by calling you an actor—with whom it has been my deep, deep misfortune to appear in any production.'

'Well,' Grove remarked with perfect good-humour, 'it's nice to head the dishonours list, isn't it? Not having prospects in the other direction. Unlike yourself, Mr. Knight. "Mr." "Knight",' he continued, beaming at Destiny. 'A contradiction in terms when one comes to think of it. Never mind: it simply *must* turn into Sir M. Knight (Knight) before many *more* New Years have passed.'

Peregrine said: 'I am sick of telling you to apologise, Harry, for grossly unprofessional behaviour and begin to think you must be an amateur, after all. Please wait outside in the foyer until Mr. Alleyn wants you. No. Not another word. Out.'

Harry looked at Destiny, made a rueful grimace and walked off.

Peregrine went to Alleyn: 'I'm sorry,' he muttered, 'about that little dust-up. We've finished. What would you like us to do?'

'I'd like the women and Random to take themselves off and the rest of the men to wait outside on the landing.'

'Me included?'

'If you don't mind.'

'Of course not.'

'As a sort of control.'

'In the chemical sense?'

'Well——'

'O.K.,' Peregrine said. 'What's the form?'

'Just that.' Alleyn returned to the group of players. 'If you wouldn't mind moving out to the circle foyer,' he said. 'Mr. Jay will explain the procedure.'

Peregrine marshalled them out.

They stood in a knot in front of the shuttered bar and they tried not to look down in the direction of the half-landing. The lowest of the three steps from the foyer to the half-landing and the area where Jobbins had lain, were stripped of carpet. The police had put down canvas sheeting. The steel doors of the wall safe above the landing were shut. Between the back of the landing and the wall, three steps led up to a narrow strip of floor connecting the two halves of the foyer, each with its own door into the circle.

Destiny Meade said: 'I'm not going down those stairs.'

'We can walk across the back to the other flight,' Emily suggested.

'I'd still have to set foot on the landing. I can't do it. Harry!' She turned with her air of expecting everyone to be where she required them and found that Harry Grove had not heard her. He stood with his hands in his pockets contemplating the shut door of the office.

Marcus Knight, flushed and angry, said: 'Perhaps you'd like me to take you down,' and laughed very unpleasantly.

She looked coolly at him. 'Sweet of you,' she said. 'I wouldn't dream of it,' and turned away to find herself face-to-face with Jeremy Jones. His freckled face was pink and anxious and his manner diffident. 'There's the circle,' he said, 'and the pass-door. Could I——?'

'Jeremy, *darling*. Yes—please, please. I know I'm a fool but—well, it's just how one's made, isn't it? *Thank* you, my angel.' She slipped her arm into his.

They went into the circle and could be heard moving round the back towards the prompt side box.

Charles Random said: 'Well, I'll be off,' hesitated for a moment, and then ran down the canvas-covered steps, turned on the landing and descended to the ground floor. Gertrude Bracey stood at the top near the remaining bronze dolphin. She looked at it and then at the mark in the carpet where its companion had stood. She compressed her lips, lifted her head and walked down with perfect deliberation.

All this was observed by Peregrine Jay.

He stopped Emily who had made as if to follow. 'Are you all right, Emily?'

'Yes. Quite all right. You?'

'All the better for seeing you. Shall we take lunch together? But I don't know how long I'll be. Were you thinking of lunch later on?'

'I can't say I'm wolfishly ravenous.'

'One must eat.'

Emily said: 'You can't possibly tell when you'll get off. The pub's no good and nor is The Younger Dolphin. They'll both be seething with curiosity and reporters. I'll buy some ham rolls and go down to the wharf below Phipps Passage. There's a bit of a wall one can sit on.'

'I'll join you if I can. Don't bolt your rolls and hurry away. It's a golden day on the river.'

'Look,' Emily said. 'What's Harry up to *now*!'

Harry was tapping on the office door. Apparently in answer to a summons he opened it and went in.

Emily left the theatre by the circle and pass-door. Peregrine joined a smouldering Marcus Knight and an anxious Winter Morris. Presently Jeremy returned, obviously flown with gratification.

On the far side of the office door Harry Grove confronted Alleyn.

His manner had quite changed. He was quiet and direct and spoke without affection.

'I daresay,' he said, 'I haven't commended myself to you as a maker of statements but a minute or two ago—after I had been sent out in disgrace, you know—I remembered something. It may have no bearing on the case whatever but I think perhaps I ought to leave it to you to decide.'

'That,' Alleyn said: 'by and large, is the general idea we like to establish.'

Harry smiled. 'Well then,' he said, 'here goes. It's rumoured that when the nightwatchman, whatever he's called—'

'Hawkins.'

'That when Hawkins found Jobbins and, I suppose, when you saw him, he was wearing a light overcoat.'

'Yes.'

'Was it a rather large brown and white check with an over-check of black?'

'It was.'

'Loudish, one might say?'

'One might, indeed.'

'Yes. Well, I gave him that coat on Friday evening.'

'Your name is still on the inside pocket tag.'

Harry's jaw dropped. 'The wind,' he said, 'to coin a phrase, has departed from my sails. I'd better chug off under my own steam. I'm sorry, Mr. Alleyn. Exit actor, looking crestfallen.'

'No, wait a bit, as you are here. I'd like to know what bearing you think this might have on the case. Sit down. Confide in us.'

'May I?' Harry said, surprised. 'Thank you, I'd like to.'

He sat down and looked fully at Alleyn. 'I don't always mean to behave as badly as in fact I do,' he said and went on quickly : 'About the coat. I don't think I attached any great importance to it. But just now you did rather seem to make a point of what he was wearing. I couldn't quite see what the point *was* but it seemed to me I'd better tell you that until Friday evening the coat had been mine.'

'Why on earth didn't you say so there and then?'

Harry flushed scarlet. His chin lifted and he spoke rapidly as if by compulsion. 'Everybody,' he said, 'was fabulously amusing about my coat. In the O.K. hearty, public-school manner, you know. Frightfully nice chaps. Jolly good show. I need not, of course, tell you that I am not even a product of one of our dear old minor public schools. Or, if it comes to that, of a dear old minor grammar school like the Great King Dolphin.'

'Knight?'

'That's right but it's slipped his memory.'

'You *do* dislike him, don't you?'

'Not half as heartily as he dislikes me,' Harry said and gave a short laugh. 'I know I sound disagreeable. You see before you, Superintendent, yet another slum kid with a chip like a Yule log on his shoulder. I take it out in clowning.'

'But,' Alleyn said mildly, 'is your profession absolutely riddled with old Etonians?'

Harry grinned. 'Well, no,' he said. 'But I assure you there are enough more striking and less illustrious O.B. ties to strangle all the extras in a battle scene for Armageddon. As a rank outsider I find the network nauseating. Sorry. No doubt you're a product yourself. Of Eton, I mean.'

'So you're a post-Angry at heart? Is that it?'

'Only sometimes. I compensate. They're afraid of my tongue or I like to think they are.'

He waited for a moment and then said: 'None of this, by the way and for what it's worth, applies to Peregrine Jay. I've no complaints about him: he has not roused my lower-middle-class rancour and I do not try to score off him. He's a gifted playwright, a good producer and a very decent citizen. Perry's all right.'

'Good. Let's get back to the others. They were arrogant about your coat, you considered?'

'The comedy line was relentlessly pursued. Charles affected to have the dazzles. Gertrude, dear girl, shuddered like a castanet. There were lots of asides. And even the lady of my heart professed distaste and begged me to shuffle off my chequered career-coat. So I did. Henry Jobbins was wheezing away at the stage-door saying his chubes were chronic and believe it or not I did a sort of your-need-is-greater-than-mine thing, which I could, of course, perfectly well afford. I took it off there and then and gave it to him. There was,' Harry said loudly, 'and is, absolutely no merit in this gesture. I simply off-loaded an irksome, vulgar, mistaken choice on somebody who happened to find it acceptable. He was a good bloke, was old Harry. A good bloke.'

'Did anyone know of this spontaneous gift?'

'No. Oh, I suppose the man that relieved him did. Hawkins. Henry Jobbins told me this chap had been struck all of a heap by the overcoat when he came in on Friday night.'

'But nobody else, you think, knew of the exchange?'

'I asked Jobbins not to say anything. I really could *not* have stomached the recrudescence of comedy that the incident would have evoked.' Harry looked sidelong at Alleyn. 'You're a dangerous man, Superintendent. You've missed your vocation. You'd have been a wow on the receiving side of the confessional grille.'

'No comment,' said Alleyn and they both laughed.

Alleyn said : 'Look here. Would anyone expect to find *you* in the realm of the front foyer after the show?'

'I suppose so,' he said. 'Immediately after. Winty Morris for one. I've been working in a TV show and there's been a lot of carry-on about calls. In the event of any last minute changes I arranged for them to ring this theatre and I've been looking in at the office after the show in case there was a message.'

'Yes, I see.'

'Last night, though, I didn't go round because the telly thing's finished. And anyway I was bound for Dessy Meade's party. She commanded me, as you've heard, to fetch my guitar and I lit off for Canonbury to get it.'

'Did you arrive at Miss Meade's flat in Cheyne Walk before or after she and her other guests did?'

'Almost a dead heat. I was parking when they arrived. They'd been to the little joint in Wharfinger's Lane, I understand.'

'Anyone hear or see you at your own flat in Canonbury?'

'The man in the flat overhead may have heard me. He complains that I wake him up every night. The telephone rang while I was in the loo. That would be round about eleven. Wrong number. I daresay it woke him, but I don't know. I was only there long enough to give myself a drink, have a wash, pick up the guitar and out.'

'What's this other flatter's name?'

Harry gave it. 'Well,' he said cheerfully, 'I hope I *did* wake him, poor bugger.'

'We'll find out, shall we? Fox?'

Mr. Fox telephoned Harry's neighbour explaining that he was a telephone operative checking a faulty line. He extracted the information that Harry's telephone had indeed rung just as the neighbour had turned his light off at eleven o'clock.

'Well, God bless him, anyway,' said Harry.

'To go back to your overcoat. Was there a yellow silk scarf in the pocket?'

'There was indeed. With an elegant "H" embroidered by a devoted if slightly witchlike and acquisitive hand. The initial was appropriate at least. Henry J. was as pleased as punch, poor old donkey.'

'You liked him very much, didn't you?'

'As I said, he was a good bloke. We used to have a pint at the pub and he'd talk about his days on the river. Oddly enough I think he rather liked me.'

'Why should that be so odd?'

'Oh,' Harry said. 'I'm hideously unpopular, you know. I really *am* disliked. I have a talent for arousing extremes of antipathy, I promise you. Even Mr. Conducis,' Harry said opening his eyes very wide, 'although he feels obliged to be helpful, quite hates my guts, I assure you.'

'Have you seen him lately?'

'Friday afternoon,' Harry said promptly.

'Really?'

'Yes. I call on him from time to time as a matter of duty. After all he got me this job. Did I mention that we are distantly related? Repeat: *distantly*.'

'No.'

'No. I don't mention it very much. Even I,' Harry said, 'draw the line somewhere, you know.'

8. SUNDAY AFTERNOON

'What did you think of that little party, Br'er Fox?'

'Odd chap, isn't he? Very different in his manner to when he was annoying his colleagues. One of these inferiority complexes, I suppose. You brought him out, of course.'

'Do you think he's dropped to the obvious speculation?'

'About the coat? I don't fancy he'd thought of that one, Mr. Alleyn, and if I've got you right I must say it strikes me as being very far-fetched. You might as well say—well,' Fox said in his scandalised manner, 'you might as well suspect I don't know who. Mr. Knight. The sharp-faced lady: Miss Bracey, or even Mr. Conducis.'

'Well, Fox, they all come into the field of vision, don't they? Overcoat or no overcoat.'

'That's so,' Fox heavily agreed. 'So they do. So they do.' He sighed and after a moment said majestically, 'D'you reckon he was trying to pull our legs?'

'I wouldn't put it past him. All the same there *is* a point, you know, Fox. The landing was very dim even when the safe was open and lit.'

'How *does* that interior lighting work? I haven't had a look, yet.'

'There's a switch inside the hole in the wall on the circle side. What the thief couldn't have realised is the fact that this switch works the sliding steel front door and that in its turn puts on the light.'

'Like a fridge.'

'Yes. What might have happened is something like this. The doors from the circle into the upper foyer were shut and the auditorium was in darkness. The thief lay doggo in the circle. He heard Jay and Miss Dunne go out and bang the stage-door. He waited until midnight and then crept up to the door nearest the hole in the wall and listened for Jobbins to put through his midnight report to Fire and Police. You've checked that he made this call. We're on firm ground there, at least.'

'And the chap at the Fire Station, which was the second of his two calls, reckons he broke off a bit abruptly.'

'Exactly. Now, if I'm right so far—and I know damn' well I'm going to speculate—our man would choose this moment to open the wall panel—it doesn't lock—and manipulate the combination. He's already cut the burglar alarm off at the main. He must have had a torch, but I wouldn't mind betting that by intention or accident he touched the inner switch button and without knowing he'd done so, rolled back the front door which in its turn, put on the interior lighting. If it was accidental he wouldn't realise what he'd done until he'd opened the back of the safe and removed the black velvet display stand with its contents and found himself looking through a peephole across the upper foyer and sunken landing.'

'With the square of light reflected on the opposite wall.'

'As bright as ninepence. Quite bright enough to attract Jobbins's attention.'

'Now it gets a bit dicey.'

'Don't I know it.'

'What happens? This chap reckons he'd better make a bolt for it. But why does he come out here to the foyer?' Fox placidly regarded his chief. 'This,' he continued, 'would be asking for it. This would be balmy. He knows Jobbins is somewhere out here.'

'I can only cook up one answer to that, Fox. He's got the loot. He intends to shut the safe, fore and aft and spin the lock. He means to remove the loot from the display stand but at this point he's interrupted. He hears a voice, a catcall, a movement. Something. He turns round to find young Trevor Vere watching him. He thinks Jobbins is down below at the telephone. He bolts through the door from the circle to this end of the foyer meaning to duck into the loo before Jobbins gets up. Jobbins would then go into the circle and find young Trevor and assume he was the culprit. But he's too late. Jobbins having seen the open safe comes thundering up from

below. He makes for this chap who gives him a violent shove
to the pedestal and the dolphin lays Jobbins flat. Trevor
comes out to the foyer and sees this. Our chap goes for him.
The boy runs back through the door and down the central
aisle with his pursuer hard on his heels. He's caught at the
foot of the steps. There's a struggle during which the boy
grabs at the display stand. The polythene cover is dislodged,
the treasure falls overboard with it. The boy is hit on the face.
He falls across the balustrade, face down, clinging to it. He's
picked up by the seat of his trousers, swung sideways and
heaved over, his nails dragging semi-diagonally across the
velvet pile as he goes. At this point Hawkins comes down the
stage-door alley.'

'You *are* having yourself a ball,' said Mr. Fox, who liked
occasionally to employ the contemporary idiom. 'How long
does all this take?'

'From the time he works the combination it *needn't* take
more than five minutes. If that. Might be less.'

'So the time's now—say—five past midnight.'

'Say between 12 and 12.10.'

'Yerse,' said Fox and a look of mild gratification settled
upon his respectable face. 'And at 12.5, or 10 or thereabouts,
Hawkins comes in by the stage-door, goes into the stalls and
has a little chat with the deceased who is looking over the
circle balustrade.'

'I see you are in merry pin,' Alleyn remarked. 'Hawkins, Mr.
Smartypants, has a little chat with somebody wearing Jobbins's
new coat which Hawkins is just able to recognise in the
scarcely lit circle. This is not, of necessity, Jobbins. So, you see,
Harry Grove had a point about the coat.'

'Now then, now then.'

'Going too far, you consider?'

'So do you, Mr. Alleyn.'

'Well, of course I do. All this is purest fantasy. If you can
think of a better one, have a go yourself.'

'If only,' Fox grumbled, 'that kid could recover his wits,
we'd all know where we were.'

'We might.'

'About this howd'yedo with the overcoat. Is your story something to this effect? The killer loses his loot, heaves the kid overboard and hears Hawkins at the stage-door. All right! He bolts back to the circle foyer. Why doesn't he do a bunk by the pass-door in the front entrance?'

'No time. He knows that in a matter of seconds Hawkins will come through the auditorium into the front foyer. Consider the door. A mortice lock with the key kept on a hook behind the office. Two dirty great bolts and an iron bar. No time.'

'So you're making out he grabs the coat off the body, puts it on, all mucky as it is with blood and Gawd knows what—'

'Only on the outside. And I fancy he took the scarf from the overcoat pocket and used it to protect his own clothes.'

'Ah. So you say he dolls himself up and goes back to the circle and tells Hawkins to make the tea?'

'In a croaking bronchial voice, we must suppose.'

'Then what? Humour me, Mr. Alleyn. Don't stop.'

'Hawkins goes off to the property room and makes the tea. This will take at least five minutes. Our customer returns to the body and re-dresses it in the coat and puts the scarf round the neck. You noticed how the coat was: bunched up and stuffed under the small of the back. It couldn't have got like that by him falling in it.'

'Damn, I missed that one. It's an easy one too.'

'Having done this he goes downstairs, gets the key, unlocks the pass-door in the front entrance, pulls the bolts, unslips the iron bar, lets himself out and slams the door. There's a good chance that Hawkins, busily boiling-up on the far side of the iron curtain won't hear it or, if he does, won't worry. He's a coolish customer, is our customer, but the arrival of Trevor and then Hawkins and still more the knowledge of what he has done—he didn't plan to murder—have rattled him. He can't do one thing.'

'Pick up the swag?'

'Just that. It's gone overboard with Trevor.'

'Maddening for him,' said Mr. Fox primly. He contemplated Alleyn for some seconds.

'Mind you,' he said, 'I'll give you this. If it *was* Jobbins and not a murderer rigged out in Jobbins's coat we're left with a crime that took place after Jobbins talked to Hawkins and before Hawkins came round with the tea and found the body.'

'And with a murderer who was close by during the conversation and managed to work the combination, open the safe, extract the loot, kill Jobbins, half kill Trevor, do his stuff with the door and sling his hook—all within the five minutes it took Hawkins to boil up.'

'Well,' Fox said after consideration, 'it's impossible, I'll say that for it. It's impossible. And what's *that* look mean, I wonder,' he added.

'Get young Jeremy Jones in and find out,' said Alleyn.

II

When Harry Grove came out of the office he was all smiles. 'I bet you lot wonder if I've been putting your pots on,' he said brightly. 'I haven't really. I mean not beyond mentioning that you all hate my guts which they could hardly avoid detecting, one would think.'

'They can't detect something that's non-existent,' Peregrine said crisply. 'I don't hate your silly guts, Harry. I think you're a bloody bore when you do your *enfant terrible* stuff. I think you can be quite idiotically mischievous and more than a little spiteful. But I don't hate your guts : I rather like you.'

'Perry : how splendidly detached! And Jeremy?'

Jeremy, looking as if he found the conversation unpalatable, said impatiently : 'Good God, what's it matter! What a lot of balls.'

'And Winty?' Harry said.

Morris looked very coolly at him. 'I should waste my time hating your guts?' He spread his hands. 'What nonsense,' he said. 'I am much too busy.'

'So, in the absence of Charlie and the girls, we find ourselves left with The King Dolphin.'

As soon as Harry had re-appeared Marcus Knight had moved to the far end of the circle foyer. He now turned and said with dignity : 'I absolutely refuse to have any part of this,' and ruined everything by shouting : 'And I will not suffer this senseless, this insolent, this insufferable name-coining.'

'Ping!' said Harry. 'Great strength rings the bell. I wonder if the Elegant Rozzer in there heard you. I must be off. Best of British luck——' he caught himself up on this familiar quotation from Jobbins and looked miserable. 'That,' he said, 'was *not* intentional,' and took himself off.

Marcus Knight at once went into what Peregrine had come to think of as his First Degree of temperament. It took the outward form of sweet reason. He spoke in a deathly quiet voice, used only restrained gestures and, although that nerve jumped up and down under his empurpled cheek, maintained a dreadful show of equanimity.

'This may not be, indeed emphatically is *not*, an appropriate moment to speculate upon the continued employment of this person. One has been given to understand that the policy is adopted at the instigation of The Management. I will be obliged, Winter, if at the first opportunity, you convey to The Management my intention, unless Hartly Grove is relieved of his part, of bringing my contract to its earliest possible conclusion. My agents will deal with the formalities.'

At this point, under normal circumstances he would undoubtedly have effected a smashing exit. He looked restlessly at the doors and stairways and, as an alternative, flung himself into one of the Victorian settees that Jeremy had caused to be placed about the circle foyer. Here he adopted a civilised and faintly Corinthian posture but looked, nevertheless, as if he would sizzle when touched.

'My dear, *dear* Perry and my dear Winty,' he said. 'Please do take this as definite. I am sorry, sorry, sorry that it should be so. But there it is.'

Perry and Morris exchanged wary glances. Jeremy, who had looked utterly miserable from the time he came in, sighed deeply.

Peregrine said, 'Marco, may we, of your charity, discuss this a little later? The horrible thing that happened last night is such a *black* problem for all of us. I concede everything you may say about Harry. He behaves atrociously and under normal circumstances would have been given his marching orders long

ago. If there's any more of this sort of thing I'll speak about
it to Greenslade and if he feels he can't take a hand I shall—
I'll go to Conducis himself and tell him I can no longer
stomach his protégé. But in the meantime—*please* be patient,
Marco.'

Marcus waved his hand. The gesture was beautiful and
ambiguous. It might have indicated dismissal, magniloquence
or implacable fury. He gazed at the ceiling, folded his arms
and crossed his legs.

Winter Morris stared at Peregrine and then cast up his
eyes and very, very slightly rolled his head.

Inspector Fox came out of the office and said that if Mr.
Jeremy Jones was free Superintendent Alleyn would be grateful if he could spare him a moment.

Peregrine, watching Jeremy go, suffered pangs of an undefined anxiety.

When Jeremy came into the office he found Alleyn seated
at Winter Morris's desk with his investigation kit open before
him and, alongside that, a copy of *The Times*. Jeremy stood
very still just inside the door. Alleyn asked him to sit down
and offered him a cigarette.

'I've changed to a pipe. Thank you, though.'

'So have I. Go ahead, if you want to.'

Jeremy pulled out his pipe and tobacco pouch. His hands
were steady but looked self-conscious.

'I've asked you to come in,' Alleyn said, 'on a notion that
may quite possibly turn out to be totally irrelevant. If so
you'll have to excuse me. You did the décor for this production, didn't you?'

'Yes.'

'If I may say so it seemed to me to be extraordinarily right.
It always fascinates me to see the tone and character of a
play reflected by its background without the background itself
becoming too insistent.'

'It often does.'

'Not in this instance, I thought. You and Jay share a flat,
don't you? I suppose you collaborated over the whole job?'

'Oh, yes,' Jeremy said and, as if aware of being unforth-
coming, he added : 'It worked all right.'

'They tell me you've got a piece of that nice shop in Walton Street and are an authority on historic costume.'

'That's putting it much too high.'

'Well, anyway, you designed the clothes and props for this show?'

'Yes.'

'The gloves, for instance,' Alleyn said and lifted his copy of *The Times* from the desk. The gloves used in the play lay neatly together on Winter Morris's blotting pad.

Jeremy said nothing.

'Wonderfully accurate copies. And, of course,' Alleyn went on, 'I saw you arranging the real glove and the documents on the velvet easel and putting them in the safe. That morning in the theatre some six months ago. I was there, you may remember.'

Jeremy half rose and then checked himself. 'That's right,' he said.

Alleyn lifted a tissue paper packet out of his open case, put it near to Jeremy on the desk and carefully folded back the wrapping. He exposed a small, wrinkled, stained, embroidered and tasselled glove.

'This would be it?' he asked.

'I—yes,' said Jeremy, as white as a sheet.

'The glove you arranged on its velvet background with the two documents and covered with a sheet of polythene fastened with velvet-covered drawing pins?'

'Yes.'

'And then from the panel opening in the circle wall, you put this whole arrangement into the cache that you yourself had lined so prettily with padded gold silk. You used the switch that operates the sliding steel door in the foyer wall. It opened and the interior lights went on behind the convex plateglass front of the cache. Then you shut the back door and span the combination lock. And Peregrine Jay, Winter Morris, Marcus Knight, young Trevor Vere, Miss Destiny Meade and Miss Emily Dunne, all stood about, at your suggestion, in the circle foyer or the sunken landing and they all greatly admired the arrangement. That right?'

'You were there, after all.'

'As I reminded you. I stayed in the circle, you know, and joined you when you were re-arranging the exhibits on their background.' He gave Jeremy a moment or two and, as he said nothing, continued.

'Last night the exhibits and their velvet background with their transparent cover were found in the centre aisle of the stalls, not far from where the boy lay. They had become detached from the black velvet display easel. I brought the glove in here and examined it very closely.'

'I know,' Jeremy said, 'what you are going to say.'

'I expect you do. To begin with I was a bit worried about the smell. I've got a keen nose for my job and I seemed to get something foreign to the odour of antiquity, if one may call it that. There was a faint whiff of fishglue and paint which suggested another sort of occupational smell, clinging perhaps to somebody's hands.'

Jeremy's fingers curled. The nails were coloured rather as Trevor's had been but not with velvet pile.

'So this morning I got my lens out and I went over the glove. I turned it inside out. Sacrilege, you may think. Undoubtedly, I thought, it really is a very old glove indeed and seems to have been worked over and redecorated at some time. And then, on the inside of the back where all the embroidery is—look, I'll show you.'

He manipulated the glove, delicately turning it back on itself.

'Can you see? It's been caught down by a stitch and firmly anchored and it's very fine indeed. A single hair, human and—quite distinctly—red.'

He let the glove fall on its tissue paper. 'This is a much better copy than the property ones and they're pretty good. It's a wonderful job and would convince anyone, I'd have thought, from the distance at which it was seen.' He looked up at Jeremy. 'Why did you do it?' asked Alleyn.

III

Jeremy sat with his forearms resting on his thighs and stared at his clasped hands. His carroty head was very conspicuous. Alleyn noticed that one or two hairs had fallen on the shoulders of his suède jerkin.

He said: 'I swear it's got nothing to do with Jobbins or the boy.'

'That, of course, is our chief concern at the moment.'

'May Perry come in, please?'

Alleyn thought that one over and then nodded to Fox who went out.

'I'd rather he heard now, than any other way,' Jeremy said. Peregrine came in, looked at Jeremy and went to him. 'What's up?' he said.

'I imagine I'm going to make a statement. I want you to hear it.'

'For God's sake, Jer, don't make a fool of yourself. A statement? What about? Why?'

He saw the crumpled glove lying on the desk and the two prop gloves where Alleyn had displayed them. 'What's all this?' he demanded. 'Who's been manhandling Hamnet's glove?'

'Nobody,' Jeremy said. 'It's not Hamnet's glove. It's a bloody good fake. I did it and I ought to know.' A long silence followed.

'You fool, Jer,' Peregrine said slowly. 'You unspeakable fool.'

'Do you want to tell us about it, Mr. Jones?'

'Yes. The whole thing. I'd better.'

'Inspector Fox will take notes and you will be asked to sign them. If in the course of your statement I think you are going to incriminate yourself to the point of an arrest I shall warn you of this.'

'Yes. All right.' Jeremy looked up at Peregrine. 'It's O.K.,' he said. 'I won't. And don't, for God's sake, gawp at me like that. Go and sit down somewhere. And listen.'

Peregrine sat on the edge of his own desk.

'It began,' Jeremy said, 'when I was going to the Vic and Alb to make drawings of the glove for the two props. Emily Dunne sometimes helps in the shop and she turned out a whole mass of old tatt we've accumulated to see what there

was in the way of material. We found that pair over there
and a lot of old embroidery silks and gold wire and some
fake jewellery that was near enough for the props. But in the
course of the hunt I came across'—he pointed—'that one. It's
genuine as far as age goes and within fifty years of the
original. A small woman's hand. It had the gauntlet and tassel
but the embroidery was entirely different. I—I suppose I got
sort of besotted on the real glove. I made a very, *very* elaborate drawing of it. Almost a *trompe l'oeil* job isn't it, Perry?
And all the time I was working on the props there was this
talk of Conducis selling the glove to a private collection in the
U.S.A.'

Jeremy now spoke rapidly and directly to Alleyn.

'I've got a maggot about historic treasures going out of
their native setting. I'd give back the Elgin Marbles to
Athens to-morrow if I could. I started on the copy; first of all
just for the hell of it. I even thought I might pull Peregrine's
leg with it when it was done or try it out on the expert at the
Vic and Alb. I was lucky in the hunt for silks and for gold
and silver wire and all. The real stuff. I did it almost under
your silly great beak, Perry. You nearly caught me at it lots
of times. I'd no intention, then, absolutely none, of trying
substitution.'

'What *did* you mean to do with it ultimately? Apart from
leg-pulling,' said Alleyn.

Jeremy blushed to the roots of his betraying hair. 'I rather
thought,' he said, 'of giving it to Destiny Meade.'

Peregrine made a slight moaning sound.

'And what made you change your mind?'

'As you've guessed, I imagine, it was on the morning the
original was brought here and they asked me to see it housed.
I'd brought my copy with me. I thought I might just try my
joke experiment. So I grabbed my chance and did a little
sleight-of-hand. It was terribly easy : nobody, not even you,
noticed. I was going to display the whole thing and if nobody
spotted the fake, take the original out of my pocket, do my
funny man ha-ha ever-been-had stuff, re-switch the gloves and
give Destiny the copy. I thought it'd be rather diverting to
have you and the expert and everybody doting and on-going

and the camera men milling round and Marcus striking wonderful attitudes : all at my fake. You know?'

Peregrine said : 'Very quaint and inventive. You ought to
go into business with Harry Grove.'

'Well, then I heard all the chat about whether the cache
was really safe and what you, Mr. Alleyn, said to Winty about
the lock and how you guessed the combination. I thought : but
this is terrifying. It's asking for trouble. There'll be another
Goya's "Duke" but this time it'll go for keeps. I felt sure
Winty wouldn't get round to changing the combination. And
then—absolutely on the spur of the moment—it was some
kind of compulsive behaviour I suppose—I decided not to tell
about my fake. I decided to leave it on show in the theatre and
to take charge of the original myself. It's in a safe-deposit
and very carefully packed. I promise you. I was going to
replace it as soon as the exhibits were to be removed. I knew
I'd be put in charge again and I could easily reverse the
former procedure and switch back the genuine article. And
then : then—there was the abominable bombshell.'

'And I suppose,' Peregrine observed, 'I now understand
your extraordinary behaviour on Friday.'

'You may suppose so. On Friday,' Jeremy turned to Alleyn.
'Peregrine informed me that Conducis *had* sold or as good as
sold, to a private collector in U.S.A.'

Jeremy got up and walked distractedly about the office.
Alleyn rested his chin in his hand, Fox looked over the top of
his spectacles and Peregrine ran his hands through his hair.

'You must have been out of your wits,' he said.

'Put it like that if you want to. You don't need to tell me
what I've done. Virtually, I've stolen the glove.'

'Virtually?' Alleyn repeated. 'There's no "virtually" about
it. That is precisely what you've done. If I understand you,
you now decided to keep the real glove and let the collector
spend a fortune on a fake.'

Jeremy threw up his hands : 'I don't know,' he said. 'I
hadn't decided anything.'

'You don't know what you proposed to do with young
Hamnet Shakespeare's glove?'

'Exactly. If this thing hadn't happened to Jobbins and the

boy and I'd been responsible for handing over the treasure : I *don't know*, now, what I'd have done. I'd have brought Hamnet's glove with me, I think. But whether I'd have replaced it—I expect I would but—I just *do not know*.'

'Did you seriously consider any other line of action? Suppose you hadn't replaced the real glove—what then? You'd have stuck to it? Hoarded it for the rest of your life?'

'NO!' Jeremy shouted. '*No!* Not that, I wouldn't have done that. I'd have waited to see what happened, I think, and then—and then . . .'

'You realise that if the purchaser had your copy, good as it is, examined by an expert it would be spotted in no time?'

Jeremy actually grinned. 'And I wonder what the Great God Conducis would have done about that one,' he said. 'Return the money or brazen it out that he sold in good faith on the highest authority?'

'What *you* would have done is more to the point.'

'I tell you I don't know. Would I let it ride? See what happened? Do a kidnap sort of thing perhaps? Phoney voice on the telephone saying if he swore to give it to the Nation it would be returned? Then Conducis could do what he liked about it.'

'Swear, collect and sell,' Peregrine said. 'You must be demented.'

'Where is this safe-deposit?' Alleyn asked. Jeremy told him. Not far from their flat in Blackfriars.

'Tell me,' Alleyn went on, 'how am I to know you've been speaking the truth? After all you've only handed us this rigmarole after I'd discovered the fake. How am I to know you didn't mean to flog the glove on the freak black market? Do you know there is such a market in historic treasures?'

Jeremy said loudly : 'Yes, I do. Perfectly well.'

'For God's sake, Jer, shut up. *Shut up.*'

'No, I won't. Why should I? I'm not the only one in the company to hear of Mrs. Constantia Guzman.'

'Mrs. Constantia Guzman?' Alleyn repeated.

'She's a slightly mad millionairess with a flair for antiquities.'

'Yes?'

'Yes. Harry Grove knows all about her. So,' added Jeremy defiantly, 'do Marco and Charlie Random.'

'What is the Guzman story?'

'According to Harry,' Jeremy began in a high voice and with what sounded like insecure irony, 'she entertained Marco very lavishly when he had that phenomenal season in New York three years ago. Harry was in the company. It appears that Mrs. Guzman, who is fifty-five, as ugly as sin and terrifying, fell madly in love with Marco. Literally—*madly* in love. She's got a famous collection of pictures and objets d'art. Well, she threw a fabulous party—fabulous even for her—and when it was all over she kept Marco back. As a sort of woo she took him into a private room and showed him a collection of treasures that she said nobody else has ever seen.' Jeremy stopped short. The corner of Alleyn's mouth twitched and his right eyebrow rose. Fox cleared his throat. Peregrine said wearily, 'Ah, my God.'

'I mean,' Jeremy said with dignity, 'precisely and literally what I say. Behind locked doors Mrs. Guzman showed to Marcus Knight jewels, snuff-boxes, rare books, Fabergé trinkets: all as hot as hell. Every one a historic collector's item. And the whole shooting-match, she confided, bought on a sort of underground international black market. Lots of them had at some time been stolen. She had agents all over Europe and the Far East. She kept all these things simply to gloat over in secret and she told Marco she had shown them to him because she wanted to feel she was in his power. And with that she set upon him in no mean style. She carried the weight and he made his escape, or so he says, by the narrowest of margins and in a cold sweat. He got on quite well with Harry in those days. One evening when he'd had one or two drinks, he told Harry all about this adventure.'

'And how did you hear of it?'

Peregrine ejaculated: 'I remember! When I told the company about the glove!'

'That's right. Harry said Mrs. Constantia Guzman ought to know of it. He said it with one of his glances—perhaps they should be called "mocking"—at Marcus who turned purple. Harry and Charlie Random and I had drinks in the pub that evening and he told us the Guzman yarn. I must say he was frightfully funny doing an imitation of Mrs. Guzman saying : "But I *vish* to be at your bercy. I log to be in your power. Ach, if you vould only betray be. Ach, but you have so beautiful a botty".'

Peregrine made an exasperated noise.

'Yes,' said Jeremy. 'Well-knowing your views on theatre gossip, I didn't relay the story to you.'

'Have other people in the company heard it?' Alleyn asked.

Jeremy said : 'Oh, yes. I imagine so.'

Peregrine said : 'No doubt Harry has told Destiny,' and Jeremy looked miserable. 'Yes,' he said. 'He did. At a party.'

Alleyn said : 'You will be required to go to your safe-deposit with two C.I.D. officers, uplift the glove and hand it over to them. You will be asked to sign a full statement as to your activities. Whether a charge will be laid I can't at the moment tell you. Your ongoings, in my opinion, fall little short of lunacy. Technically, on your own showing, you're a thief.'

Jeremy, now so white that his freckles looked like brown confetti, turned on Peregrine and stammered : 'I've been so bloody miserable. It was a kind of diversion. I've been so filthily unhappy.'

He made for the door. Fox, a big man who moved quickly, was there before him. 'Just a minute, sir, if you don't mind,' he said mildly.

Alleyn said : 'All right, Fox. Mr. Jones : will you go now to the safe-deposit? Two of our men will meet you there, take possession of the glove and ask you to return with them to the Yard. For the moment, that's all that'll happen. Good-day to you.'

Jeremy went out quickly. They heard him cross the foyer and run downstairs.

'Wait a moment, will you, Jay?' Alleyn said. 'Fox, lay that on, please.'

Fox went to the telephone and established a sub-fusc conversation with the Yard.

'That young booby's a close friend of yours, I gather,' Alleyn said.

'Yes, he is. Mr. Alleyn, I realise I've no hope of getting anywhere with this but if I may just say one thing——'

'Of course, why not?'

'Well,' Peregrine said, rather surprised, 'thank you. Well, it's two things, actually. First: from what Jeremy's told you, there isn't any motive whatever for him to burgle the safe last night. Is there?'

'If everything he has said is true—no. If he has only admitted what we were bound to find out and distorted the rest, it's not difficult to imagine a motive. Motives, however, are a secondary consideration in police work. At the moment, we want a workable assemblage of cogent facts. What's your second observation?'

'Not very compelling, I'm afraid, in the light of what you've just said. He is, as you've noticed, my closest friend and I must therefore be supposed to be prejudiced. But I do, all the same, want to put it on record that he's one of the most non-violent men you could wish to meet. Impulsive. Hot-tempered in a sort of sudden red-headed way. Vulnerable. But essentially gentle. Essentially incapable of the kind of thing that was perpetrated in this theatre last night. I *know* this of Jeremy, as well as I know it of myself. I'm sorry,' Peregrine said rather grandly. 'I realise that kind of reasoning won't make a dent in a police investigation. But if you like to question anyone else who's acquainted with the fool, I'm sure you'll get the same reaction.'

'Speaking as a brutal and hide-bound policeman,' Alleyn said cheerfully, 'I'm much obliged to you. It isn't always the disinterested witness who offers the soundest observations and I'm glad to have your account of Jeremy Jones.'

Peregrine stared at him. 'I beg your pardon,' he said.

'What for? Before we press on, though, I wonder if you'd feel inclined to comment on the Knight-Meade-Bracey-Grove situation. What's it all about? A character actress scorned and a leading gent slighted? A leading lady beguiled and a second juvenile in the ascendant? Or what?'

'I wonder you bother to ask me since you've got it off so pat,' said Peregrine tartly.

'And a brilliant young designer in thrall with no prospect of delight?'

'Yes. Very well.'

'All right,' Alleyn said. 'Let him be for the moment. Have you any idea who the U.S. customer for the treasure might be?'

'No. It wasn't for publication. Or so I understood from Greenslade.'

'Not Mrs. Constantia Guzman by any chance?'

'Good God, *I* don't know,' Peregrine said. 'I've no notion. Mr. Conducis may not so much as know her. Not that that would signify.'

'I think he does, however. She was one of his guests in the *Kalliope* at the time of the disaster. One of the few to escape if I remember rightly.'

'Wait a bit. There's something. Wait a bit.'

'With pleasure.'

'No, but it's just that I've remembered—it might not be of the smallest significance—but I *have* remembered one incident, during rehearsals when Conducis came in to tell me we could use the treasure for publicity. Harry walked in here while we were talking. He was as bright as a button, as usual, and not at all disconcerted. He greeted Mr. Conducis like a long lost uncle, asked him if he'd been yachting lately and said something like : remember him to Mrs. G. Of course there are a thousand and one Mrs. G.'s but when you mentioned the yacht——'

'Yes, indeed. How did Conducis take this?'

'Like he takes everything. Dead pan.'

'Any idea what the obligation was that Grove seems to have laid upon him?'

'Not a notion.'

'Blackmail by any chance, would you think?'

'Ah, *no*! And Conducis is *not* a queer in my opinion if that's what you're working up to. Nor, good lord, is Harry! And nor, I'm quite sure, is Harry a blackmailer. He's a rum

customer and he's a bloody nuisance in a company. Like a
wasp. But I don't believe he's a bad lot. Not really.'

'Why?'

Peregrine thought for a moment. 'I suppose,' he said at
last, with an air of surprise, 'that it must be because, to me, he
really *is* funny. When he plays up in the theatre I become
furious and go for him like a pick-pocket and then he says
something outrageous that catches me on the hop and makes
me want to laugh.' He looked from Alleyn to Fox. 'Has either
of you,' Peregrine asked, 'ever brought a clown like Harry to
book for murder?'

Alleyn and Fox appeared severally to take glimpses into
their professional pasts.

'I can't recall,' Fox said, cautiously, 'ever finding much
fun in a convicted homicide, can you, Mr. Alleyn?'

'Not really,' Alleyn agreed, 'but I hardly think the presence
or absence of the Comic Muse can be regarded as an acid test.'

Peregrine, for the first time, looked amused.

'Did you,' Alleyn said, 'know that Mr. Grove is distantly
related to Mr. Conducis?'

'I did NOT,' Peregrine shouted. 'Who told you this?'

'He did.'

'You amaze me. It must be a tarradiddle. Though, of course,'
Peregrine said, after a long pause, 'it would account for
everything. Or would <u>it</u>?'

'Everything?'

'The mailed fist of management. The recommendation for
him to be cast.'

'Ah, yes. What's Grove's background, by the way?'

'He refers to himself as an Old Borstalian but I don't for a
moment suppose it's true. He's a bit of an inverted snob, is
Harry.'

'Very much so, I'm sure.'

'I rather think he started in the R.A.F. and then drifted on
and off the boards until he got a big break in *Cellar Stairs*.
He was out of a shop, he once told me, for so long that he got
jobs as a lorry-driver, a steward and a waiter in a strip-tease
joint. He said he took more in tips than he ever made speaking
lines.'

'When was that?'

'Just before his break, he said. About six years ago. He signed off one job and before signing on for another took a trip round the agents and landed star-billing in *Cellar Stairs*. Such is theatre.'

'Yes, indeed.'

'Is that all?' Peregrine asked after a silence.

'I'm going to ask you to do something else for me. I know you've got the change of casting and internal affairs on your hands but as soon as you can manage it I wonder if you'd take an hour to think back over your encounters with Mr. Conducis and your adventures of last night, and note down everything you can remember. Everything. And any other item, by the way, that you may have overlooked in the excitement.'

'Do you really think Conducis has got anything to do with last night?'

'I've no idea. He occurs. He'll have to be found irrelevant before we may ignore him. Will you do this?'

'I must say it's distasteful.'

'So,' said Alleyn, 'is Jobbins's corpse.'

'Whatever happened,' Peregrine said, looking sick, 'and whoever overturned the bronze dolphin, I don't believe it was deliberate, cold-blooded murder. I believe he saw Jobbins coming at him and overturned the pedestal in a sort of blind attempt to stop him. That's what I think and my God,' Peregrine said, 'I must say I do *not* welcome an invitation to have any part in hunting him down : whoever it was, the boy or anyone else.'

'All right. And if it wasn't the boy, what *about* the boy? How do you fit him in as a useful buffer between your distaste and the protection of the common man? How do you think the boy came to be dropped over the circle? And believe me he was *dropped*. He escaped, by a-hundred-to-one chance, being spilt like an egg over the stalls. Yes,' Alleyn said, watching Peregrine, 'that's a remark in bad taste, isn't it? Murder's a crime in bad taste. You've seen it, now. You ought to know.' He waited for a moment and then said, 'That was cheating and I apologise.'

Peregrine said: 'You needn't be so bloody upright. It's nauseating.'

'All right. Go away and vomit. But if you have second thoughts, sit down and write out every damn' thing you remember of Conducis and all the rest of it. And now, if you want to go—go. Get the hell out of it.'

'Out of my own office, I'd have you remember. To kick my heels on the landing.'

Alleyn broke into laughter. 'You have me there,' he said. 'Never mind. It's better, believe me, than kicking them in a waiting-room at the Yard. But all right, we'll have another go. What can you tell me, if your stomach is equal to it, of the background of the other members of your company.' Alleyn raised a hand. 'I know you have a loyalty to them and I'm not asking you to abuse it. I do remind you, Jay, that suspicion about this crime will fall inside your guild, your mystery, if I may put it like that, and that there's going to be a great deal of talk and speculation. With the exception of yourself and Miss Dunne and Miss Meade, whose alibis seem to us to be satisfactory and possibly Harry Grove, there isn't one of the company, and I'm including Winter Morris and Jeremy Jones, who absolutely could *not* have killed Jobbins and attacked the boy.'

'I can't see how you make it out. They were all, except Trevor, seen to leave. *I* saw them go. The doors were locked and bolted and barred.'

'The stage-door was locked but not bolted and barred. Hawkins unlocked it with his own key. The small pass-door in the front was unlocked when Miss Bracey left and was not bolted and barred until after Morris and Knight left. They heard Jobbins drop the bar.'

'That cuts them out, then, surely.'

'Look,' Alleyn said. 'Put this situation to yourself and see how you like it. Jobbins is still alive. Somebody knocks on the pass-door in the front entrance. He goes down. A recognised voice asks him to open up—an actor has left his money in his dressing-room or some such story. Jobbins lets him in. The visitor goes backstage saying he'll let himself out at the stage-door. Jobbins takes up his post. At midnight he does his routine telephoning and the sequel follows.'

'How do you know all this?'

'God bless my soul, my dear chap, for a brilliant play-wright you've a quaint approach to logic. I *don't* know it. I merely advance it as a way in which your lock-up theory could be made to vanish. There is at least one other, even simpler solution which is probably the true one. The only point I'm trying to make is this. If you clamp down on telling me any-thing at all about any member of your company you may be very fastidious and loyal and you may be protecting the actual butcher but you're not exactly helping to clear the other six—seven if you count Conducis.'

Peregrine thought it over. 'I think,' he said at last, 'that's probably a lot of sophistical hooey but I get your point. But I ought to warn you, you've picked a dud for the job. I've got a notoriously bad memory. There are things,' Peregrine said slowly, 'at the back of my mind that have been worrying me ever since this catastrophe fell upon us. Do you think I can fetch them up? Not I.'

'What do you connect them with?'

'With noises made by Trevor, I think. And then, with Conducis. With that morning when he showed me the treasure. But of course *then* I was drunk so I'm unreliable in any case. However : tell me what you want to know and I'll see about answering.'

'Too kind,' said Alleyn dryly. 'Start with—anyone you like. Marcus Knight. What's his background apart from the Press hand-outs? I know all about his old man's stationer's shop in West Ham and how he rose to fame. Is it true he's temperamental?'

Peregrine looked relieved. 'If it's only *that* sort of thing! He's hell and well-known for it but he's such a superb actor we all do our best to lump the temperament. He's a jolly nice man really, I daresay, and collects stamps but he can't take the lightest criticism without going up like a rocket. An unfavour-able notice is death to him and he's as vain as a peacock. But people say he's a sweetie at bottom even if it's a fair way to bottom.'

Alleyn had strolled over to a display of photographs on the far wall: all the members of the cast in character with their signatures appended. Marcus Knight had been treated to a montage with his own image startlingly echoed by the 'Grafton Portrait' and the Droushout engraving. Peregrine joined him.

'Extraordinary,' Alleyn said. 'The likeness. What a piece of luck!' He turned to Peregrine and found him staring, not at the picture but at the signature.

'Bold!' Alleyn said dryly.

'Yes. But it's not that. There's something about it. Damn! I thought so before. Something I've forgotten.'

'You may yet remember. Leave it. Tell me: is the sort of ribbing Knight got from Grove just now their usual form? All the King Dolphin nonsense?'

'Pretty much. It goes on.'

'If he's as touchy as you say, why on earth hasn't Knight shaken the Dolphin dust off his boots? Why does he stand it for one second?'

'I think,' Peregrine said with great simplicity, 'he likes his part. I think that might be it.'

'My dear Jay, I really do apologise: Of course he does. It's no doubt the best role, outside Shakespeare, that he'll ever play.'

'Do you think so? Really?'

'Indeed I do.'

Peregrine suddenly looked deeply happy. 'Now, of course,' he said, 'I'm completely wooed.'

'What can it matter what I think! You must know how good your play is.'

'Yes, but I like to be told. From which,' Peregrine said, 'you may gather that I have a temperamental link with Marco Knight.'

'Were he and Destiny Meade lovers?'

'Oh yes. Going steady, it seemed, until Harry chucked poor Gertie and came rollicking in. We thought the casting was going to work out very cosily with Dessy and Marco as happy as Larry on the one hand and Gertie and Harry nicely fixed on the other. Maddening, this dodging round in a company. It

D.A.T.D.   G always makes trouble. And with Marco's capacity to cut up plug-ugly at the drop of a hat—anything might happen. We can only keep our fingers crossed.'

'Miss Meade is—she's—I imagine, not an intellectual type.'

'She's *so* stupid,' Peregrine said thoughtfully. 'But so, *so* stupid it's a kind of miracle. Darling Dessy. And yet,' he added, 'there's an element of cunning too. Certainly, there's an element of cunning.'

'What a problem for her director, in such a subtle role!'

'Not really. You just say: "Darling, you're sad. You're heartbroken. You can't bear it" and up come the welling tears. Or: "Darling, you've been clever, don't you see, you've been one too many for them" and she turns as shrewd as a marmoset. Or, simplest of all: "Darling, you're sending him in a big way," and as she never does anything else it works like a charm. *She does* the things: the audience *thinks* them.'

'Temperamental?'

'Only for form's sake when she fancies it's about time she showed up. She's quite good-natured.'

'Did she slap Knight back smartly or gradually?'

'Gradually. You could see it coming at rehearsals. In their love scenes. She began looking at her fingernails over his shoulder and pulling bits of mascara off her eye-lashes. And then she took to saying could they just walk it because she was rethinking her approach. She talks like that but of course she never has an approach. Only an instinct backed up by superb techniques and great dollops of star quality.'

'She divorced her second husband, I believe, and lives alone?'

'Well—— Yes. Officially.'

'Anything else about her?'

'She's a terrific gambler, is Dessy. On the share-market, with the bookies and anything on the side that offers. That's really what broke up the second marriage. He couldn't do with all the roulette-party and poker-dice carry-on.'

'Is she a successful gambler?'

'I daresay she herself scarcely knows, so vague are her ways.'

'And Miss Bracey?'

'That's a very different story. I don't know anything about Gertie's background but she really does bear out the Woman Scorned crack. She's—she's not all that charitably disposed at any time, perhaps, and this thing's stirred her up like a wasp's nest. She and Marco exhibit the heads-and-tails of despised love. Marco is a sort of walking example of outraged vanity and incredulous mortification. He can't believe it and yet there it is. Rather touchingly, *I* think, he doesn't until to-day seem to have taken against Dessy. But I've trembled lest he should suddenly rear back and have a wallop at Harry.'

'Hit him?'

'Yes. Bang-bang. Whereas, Gertie doesn't vent all she's got on her rival but hisses and stings away at the faithless one.'

'And so Miss Meade is let off lightly at both ends and Grove is the object of a dual resentment?'

'And that's throwing roses at it,' said Peregrine.

'Knight and Miss Bracey have a real, solid hatred for him? Is that putting it too high?'

'No, it's not but——' Peregrine said quickly: 'What is all this? What's it matter how Marco and Gertie feel about Harry?'

'Nothing at all, I daresay. What about Random? Any comment on character?'

'Charlie? No trouble to anyone. Not, as you may have discerned, a hundred per cent he-man, but what of that? He doesn't bring it into the theatre. It was quite all right to let him dress with the boy, for instance.'

'Hobbies?'

'Well, as you've heard: Ximenes-class crosswords. Ciphers. And old manuscripts. He's quite an antiquarian, I'm told, is Charles. Jer says he's one of those characters who possess an infallible nose for a rare item. He spends half his time among the sixpenny and shilling bins in Long Acre and the Charing Cross Road. Good, conscientious actor. Minor public school and drama academy.'

'Did all the members of the company know each other before this production?'

'Oh, yes. Except Emily. She's at the beginning,' Peregrine said tenderly, 'and doesn't know many people in the West End yet.'

'Tell me, are you familiar with Harry Grove's overcoats?'

'I caught sight of him going away the other night wearing a contraption that screamed its way up the lane like a fire engine and heard a lot of carry-on about it among the company.'

'What was it?'

'I wasn't close enough to——' Peregrine's voice faded. He gaped at Alleyn. 'Oh *no*!' he said. 'It can't be. It's not possible.'

'What?'

'On—on Henry Jobbins?'

'Grove gave his overcoat to Jobbins on Friday evening. He said nobody seemed to like it. Didn't you know?'

Peregrine shook his head.

'I can't imagine,' he said slowly, 'I simply can not imagine why I didn't recognise it on poor Jobbins. I actually cracked a joke about it and he said it was a present.'

'Perhaps the scarf made a difference.'

'Scarf? I don't think he had a scarf on?'

'Did he not? A bright yellow scarf?'

'Wait. Yes,' said Peregrine, looking sick, 'of course. I—I remember. Afterwards.'

'But not before? When you spoke to him?'

'I don't remember it then. It wasn't showing.'

'Please say nothing about the overcoat, Jay. It's of the first importance that you don't. Not even,' Alleyn said with a friendly air, 'to your Emily.'

'Very well. May I know why it matters so much?' Alleyn told him.

'Yes, I see. But it won't really get you much further, will it?'

'If nobody knows of the transfer——'

'Yes, of course. Stupid of me.'

'And that really is all. I'm sorry to have kept you such an unconscionable time.'

Peregrine went to the door, hesitated and turned back.

'I'll do my best,' he said, 'to write down my Conduciae or should it be Conducii?'

'Or Conduciosis? Never mind. I'm glad you've decided to help. Thank you. Could you let me have it as soon as it's ready?'

'Yes. All right. Where will you be?'

'Here for another hour I should think. And then wherever developments send me. We'll leave a p.c. on duty in the theatre. If I've gone he'll take a message. Do you really mind doing this?'

'No. Not if it's remotely useful.'

'There now!' said Alleyn. 'Good-bye for the moment, then. On your way out, would you ask Mr. Knight to come in?'

'Certainly. It's half past twelve,' Peregrine said. 'He'll have got a bit restive, I daresay.'

'Will he indeed?' said Alleyn. 'Send him in.'

9 . KNIGHT RAMPANT

Marcus Knight was not so much restive as portentous. He had the air of a man who is making enormous concessions. When Alleyn apologised for keeping him waiting so long, he waved his hand as if to say: 'Think no more of it. Nevertheless——'

'One can't tell,' Alleyn said, 'in our job, how long any given interview will last.'

'It didn't escape my notice,' Knight said, 'that you were honoured with an earlier visit.'

'From Hartly Grove? Yes. He had,' Alleyn said, 'thought of something.'

'He thinks of a number of things, most of them highly offensive.'

'Really? This was quite harmless. I wonder if you've noticed his overcoat.'

Mr. Knight had noticed Mr. Grove's overcoat and said so briefly and with immeasurable distaste. 'One is not surprised

however,' he said. 'One recognises the form. It is entirely con
sistent. My God, what a garment! How he dares!'

It became evident that he did not know that the coat has
been given to Jobbins.

Alleyn briefly re-checked Knight's movements. He had
driven his Jaguar from the theatre to his house in Mont-
pelier Square where he was given supper as usual by the
Italian couple who looked after him. He thought it was probably about ten past eleven when he got in. He did not go out
again but could not absolutely prove it.

Extreme, wholly male beauty is not a commonplace phenomenon. Marcus Knight possessed it to a generous degree. His
oval face, with its subtly turned planes, his delicate nose,
slightly tilted eyes and glossy hair might have been dreamed
up by an artist of the Renaissance or indeed by the unknown
painter of that unknown man whom many observers call the
Grafton Shakespeare. He had the bodily harmony that declares
itself through its covering and he moved like a panther. How
old was he? Middle thirties? Younger? Forty, perhaps? It
didn't matter.

Alleyn led him cautiously by way of his own exquisite performance to the work of his fellow players. He uncovered a
completely egotistic but shrewd appreciation of the play and a
raw patch of professional jealousy when the work of his associates, particularly of Harry Grove, came into question.
Grove's Mr. W.H., it seemed, was not a true reading. It was
showy. It was vulgar. It was even rather camp, said Marcus
Knight.

Alleyn spoke of the theft of the glove and documents.
Knight rejoiced that they had been recovered. He gazed with
passionate concern at Alleyn. Was it certain they were un-
injured? Was it quite, quite certain? Alleyn said it was and
began to talk of their unequalled worth. Knight nodded
several times very slowly in that larger-than-life manner that
Alleyn associated with persons of his profession. It was more
like a series of bows.

'Unique,' he said, on two mellifluous notes. 'U-nique!'

Alleyn wondered what he would say if he knew of Jeremy's
substitution.

'Well,' he said lightly. 'At least Mr. Conducis and the American purchaser can breathe again. I can't help wondering who she may be.'

'*She?*'

'Now, why did I say "she"?' Alleyn ejaculated. 'I suppose I must have been thinking of Mrs. Constantia Guzman?'

It was formidable to see how rapidly, with what virtuosity, Knight changed colour from deepest plum to parchment and back again. He drew his brows together. He retracted his upper lip. It crossed Alleyn's mind that it was a pity the role of William Shakespeare didn't offer an opportunity for a display of these physical demonstrations of fury.

'What,' he asked, rising and looming over Alleyn, 'has that person—Grove—said to you? I demand an answer. What has he said?'

'About Mrs. Constantia Guzman, do you mean? Nothing. Why?'

'You lie!'

'I don't, you know,' Alleyn said composedly. 'Grove didn't mention her to me. Really. She's an extremely well-known collector. What's the matter?'

Knight glowered at him in silence for some time. Fox cleared his throat.

'Do you swear,' Knight began in the lowest register of his voice, building up a crescendo as he went on. 'Do you swear the name of Guzman has not—ah—has not been—ah—mentioned to you in connection with My Own. Here in this room. To-day. Do you swear to this? Hah?'

'No, I don't do that, either. It has.'

'*All!*' he bellowed suddenly. '*The whole pack of them!* He's lunched and bloody dined on it. Don't attempt to contradict me. He's betrayed a deeply, *deeply* regretted confidence. A moment of weakness. On my part. Before I knew him for what he is: a false, *false* man.' He pointed at Alleyn. 'Has he —has he told—her. Miss Meade? Destiny? You need not answer. I see it in your face. He has.'

'I've not spoken with Miss Meade,' Alleyn said.

'They've laughed together,' he roared. 'At Me!'

'Perfectly maddening for you if they have,' Alleyn said,

'but, if you'll forgive me, it isn't as far as I know, entirely
relevant to the business under discussion.'

'Yes, it is,' Knight passionately contradicted, 'By God i
is and I'll tell you why. I've put a restraint upon myself.
have not allowed myself to speak about this man. I have been
scrupulous lest I should be thought biased. But now—*now*!
I tell you this and I speak from absolute conviction: if, a
you hold, that appalling boy is not guilty and recovers his
wits and if he was attacked by the man who killed Jobbins
and if he *remembers who attacked him*, it will be at W
Hartly Grove he points his finger. *Now!*'

Alleyn, who had seen this pronouncement blowing up for
the past five minutes, allowed himself as many seconds in
which to be dumbfounded and then asked Marcus if he had
any reasons, other, he hastily added, than those already ad-
duced, for making this statement about Harry Grove. Nothing
very specific emerged. There were dark and vague allusions to
reputation and an ambiguous past. As his temper abated, and
it did seem to abate gradually, Knight appeared to lose the
fine edge of his argument. He talked of Trevor Vere and said
he couldn't understand why Alleyn dismissed the possibility
of his having been caught out by Jobbins, overturned the
dolphin and then run so fast down the circle aisle that he
couldn't prevent himself diving over the balustrade. Alleyn
once again advanced the logical arguments against this theory.

'And there's no possibility of some member of the public
having hidden during performance?'

'Jay assures me not. A thorough routine search is made
and the staff on both sides of the curtain confirm this. This is
virtually a "new" theatre. There are no stacks of scenery or
properties or neglected hiding places.'

'You are saying,' said Knight, beginning portentously to
nod again, 'that this thing must have been done by One of
Us.'

'Thats' how it looks.'

'I am faced,' Knight said, 'with a frightful dilemma.' He
immediately became a man faced with a frightful dilemma
and looked quite haggard. 'Alleyn: what can one do? Idle

for me to pretend I don't feel as I do about this man. I *know* him to be a worthless, despicable person. I know him——'

'One moment. This is still Harry Grove?'

'Yes.' (Several nods.) 'Yes. I am aware that the personal injuries he has inflicted upon me must be thought to prejudice my opinion.'

'I assure you——'

'And *I* am assuring *you*—Oh with such deadly certainty—that there is only one among us who is capable of the crime.'

He gazed fixedly into Alleyn's face. 'I studied physiognomy,' he surprisingly said. 'When I was in New York'—for a moment he looked hideously put out but instantly recovered, 'I met a most distinguished authority—Earl P. Van Smidt—and I became seriously interested in the science. I have studied and observed and I have proved my conclusions. Over and again. I have completely satisfied myself—but com-pletely—that when you see a pair of unusually round eyes, rather wide apart, very light blue and without depth—look out. *Look out!*' he repeated and flung himself into the chair he had vacated.

'What for?' Alleyn inquired.

'Treachery. Shiftiness. Utter unscrupulousness. Complete lack of ethical values. I quote from Van Smidt.'

'Dear me.'

'As for Conducis! But no matter. No matter.'

'Do you discover the same traits in Mr. Conducis?'

'I—I—am not familiar with Mr. Conducis.'

'You have met him, surely?'

'Formal meeting. On the opening night.'

'But never before that?'

'I may have done so. Years ago. I prefer—' Knight said surprisingly, 'to forget the occurrence.' He swept it away.

'May I ask why?'

There was an appreciable pause before he said : 'I was once his guest, if you can call it that and I was subjected to an insolent disregard which I would have interpreted more readily if I had at that time been acquainted with Smidt. In my opinion,' Knight said, 'Smidt should be compulsory reading for all police forces. You don't mind my saying this?' he added in a casual, lordly manner.

'Indeed no.'

'Good. Want me any more, dear boy?' he asked, suddenly gracious.

'I think not. Unless—and believe me I wouldn't ask if the question was irrelevant to the case—unless you care to tell me if Mrs. Constantia Guzman really confided to you that she is a buyer of hot objets d'art on the intercontinental black market.'

It was no good. Back in a flash came the empurpled visage and the flashing eye. Back, too, came an unmistakable background of sheepishness and discomfort.

'No comment,' said Marcus Knight.

'No? Not even a tiny hint?'

'You are mad to expect it,' he said and with that they had to let him go.

II

'Well, Br'er Fox, we've caught a snarled up little job this time, haven't we?'

'We have that,' Fox agreed warmly. 'It'd be nice,' he added wistfully, 'if we could put it down to simple theft, discovery and violence.'

'It'd be lovely but we can't, you know. We can't. For one thing the theft of a famous object is always bedevilled by the circumstance of its being indisposable through the usual channels. No normal high-class fence, unless he's got very special contacts, is going to touch Shakespeare's note or his son's glove.'

'So for a start you've got either a crank who steals and gloats or a crank of the type of young Jones who steals to keep the swag in England or a thorough wised-up, high grade professional in touch with the top international racket. And at the receiving end somebody of the nature of this Mrs. Guzman who's a millionaire crank in her own right and doesn't care how she gets her stuff.'

'That's right. Or a kidnapper who holds the stuff for ransom. And you *might* have a non-professional thief who knows all about Mrs. G. and believes she'll play and he'll make a packet.'

'That seems to take in the entire boiling of this lot, seeing Mr. Grove's broadcast the Guzman-Knight anecdote for all it's worth. I tell you what, Mr. Alleyn; it wouldn't be the most astonishing event in my working life if Mr. Knight took to Mr. Grove. Mr. Grove's teasing ways seem to put him out to a remarkable degree, don't you think?'

'I think,' Alleyn said, 'we'd better, both of us, remind ourselves about actors.'

'You do? What about them?'

'One must always remember that they're trained to convey emotion. On or off the stage, they make the most of everything they feel. Now this means they express their feelings up to saturation point. When you and I and all the rest of the non-actors do our damndest to understate and be ironical about our emotional reflexes, the actor even when he underplays them, does so with such expertise that he convinces us laymen that he's *in extremis*. He isn't. He's only being professionally articulate about something that happens off-stage instead of in front of an official audience.'

'How does all this apply to Mr. Knight, then?'

'When he turns purple and roars anathemas against Grove it means, A, that he's hot-tempered, pathologically vain and going through a momentary hell and B, that he's letting you know up to the nth degree just *how* angry and dangerous he's feeling. It doesn't necessarily mean that once his present emotion has subsided he will do anything further about it, and nor does it mean that he's superficial or a hypocrite. It's his job to take the micky out of an audience and even in the throes of a completely genuine emotional crisis, he does just that thing if it's only an audience of one.'

'Is this what they call being an extrovert?'

'Yes, Br'er Fox, I expect it is. But the interesting thing about Knight, I thought, was that when it came to Conducis he turned uncommunicative and cagey.'

'Fancied himself slighted over something, it seemed. Do you reckon Knight believes all that about Grove? Being a homicidal type? All that stuff about pale eyes etcetera. Because,'

Fox said with great emphasis, 'it's all poppycock: there aren't any facial characteristics for murder. What's that you're always quoting about there being no art to find the mind's construction in the face? I reckon it's fair enough where homicide's concerned. Although,' Fox added opening his own eyes very wide, 'I always fancy there's a kind of look about sex offenders of a certain type. That I will allow.'

'Be that as it may it doesn't get us much farther along our present road. No news from the hospital?'

'No. They'd ring through at once if there was.'

'I know. I know.'

'What do we do about Mr. Jeremy Jones?'

'Oh, blast! What indeed! I think we take delivery of the glove and documents, give him hell and go no further. I'll talk to the A.C. about him and I rather *think* I'll have to tell Conducis as soon as possible. Who've we got left here? Only little Morris. Ask him into his own office, Br'er Fox. We needn't keep him long, I think.'

Winter Morris came in quoting Queen Mary. 'This,' he said wearily, 'is a pretty kettle of fish. This is a carry-on. I'm not complaining, mind, and I'm not blaming anybody but what, oh what, has set Marco off again? Sorry. Not your headache, old boy.'

Alleyn uttered consolatory phrases, sat him at his own desk, checked his alibi which was no better and no worse than anyone else's, in that after he left the theatre with Knight he drove to his house at Golder's Green where his wife and family were all in bed. When he wound up his watch he noticed it said ten to twelve. He had heard the Knight-Guzman story. 'I thought it bloody sad,' he said. 'Poor woman. Terrible, you know, the problem of the plain highly-sexed woman. Marco ought to have held his tongue. He ought never to have told Harry. Of course Harry made it sound a bit of a yell, but I didn't like Marco telling about it. I don't think that sort of thing's funny.'

'It does appear that on her own admission to Knight, she's a buyer on a colossal scale under the museum-piece counter.'

Winter Morris spread his hands. 'We all have our weak-

nesses,' he said. 'So she likes nice things and she can pay for
them. Marcus Knight should complain!'

'Well!' Alleyn ejaculated. 'That's one way of looking the
Big Black Market in the eyes I must say! Have you ever met
Mrs. Guzman, by the way?'

Winter Morris had rather white eyelids. They now dropped
a little. 'No,' he said, 'not in person. Her husband was a most
brilliant man. The equal and more of Conducis.'

'Self-made?'

'Shall we say self-created? It was a superb achievement.'

Alleyn looked his enjoyment of this phrase and Morris answered his look with a little sigh. 'Ah yes!' he said. 'These
colossi! How marvellous!'

'In your opinion,' Alleyn said, 'without prejudice and within
these four walls and all that : how many people in this theatre
know the combination of that lock?'

Morris blushed. 'Yes,' he said. 'Well. This is where I don't
exactly shine with a clear white radiance, isn't it? Well, as he's
told you, Charlie Random for one. Got it right, as you no
doubt observed. He says he didn't pass it on and personally I
believe that. He's a very quiet type, Charlie. Never opens up
about his own or anybody else's business. I'm sure he's dead
right about the boy not knowing the combination.'

'You are? Why?'

'Because as I said, the bloody kid was always pestering me
about it.'

'And so you would have been pretty sure, would you, that
only you yourself and Mr. Conducis knew the combination?'

'I don't say that,' Morris said unhappily. 'You see after that
morning they did all know about the five-letter word being an
obvious one and—and—well Dessy did say one day "Is it
'glove,' Winty? We all think it might be? Do you swear it's
not 'glove'." Well, you know Dessy. She'd woo the Grand
Master to let the goat out of the Lodge. I suppose I boggled a
bit and she laughed and kissed me. I know. I know. I ought to
have had it changed. I meant to. But—in the theatre we don't
go about wondering if someone in the company's a big-time
bandit.'

'No, of course you don't. Mr. Morris: thank you very much.
I think we can now return your office to you. It was more than
kind to suggest that we use it.'

'There hasn't been all that much for me to do. The Press
is our big worry but we're booked out solid for another four
months. Unless people get it into their heads to cancel we
should make out. You never know, though, which way a
thing like this will take the public.'

They left him in a state of controlled preoccupation.

The circle foyer was deserted, now. Alleyn paused for a
moment. He looked at the shuttered bar, at the three shallow
steps leading on three sides from the top down to the half-
landing and the two flights that curved down from there to the
main entrance; at the closed safe in the wall above the landing, the solitary bronze dolphin and the two doors into the
circle. Everything was quiet, a bit muffled and stuffily chilly.

He and Fox walked down the three canvas-covered steps
to the landing. A very slight sound caught Alleyn's ear. Instead of going on down he crossed to the front of the landing,
rested his hands on its elegant iron balustrade and looked into
the main entrance below.

His gaze lighted on the crown of a smart black hat and the
violently foreshortened figure of a thin woman.

For a second or two the figure made no move. Then the hat
tipped back and gave way to a face like a white disc, turned
up to his own.

'Do you want to see me, Miss Bracey?'

The face tipped backwards and forwards in assent. The lips
moved but if she spoke, her voice was inaudible.

Alleyn motioned to Fox to stay where he was and himself
went down the curving right hand stairway.

There she stood, motionless. The fat upside-down cupids
over the box-office and blandly helpful caryatids supporting
the landing, made an incongruous background for that spare
figure and yet, it crossed Alleyn's mind, her general appearance
was evocative, in a cockeyed way, of the period: of some
repressed female character from a Victorian play or novel.
Rosa Dartle, he thought, that was the sort of thing: Rosa
Dartle.

'What is it?' Alleyn asked. 'Are you unwell?'

She looked really ill. He wondered if he had imagined that she had swayed very slightly, and then pulled herself together.

'You must sit down,' he said. 'Let me help you.'

When he went up to her he smelt brandy and saw that her eyes were off-focus. She said nothing but let him propel her to Jeremy Jones's plushy settee alongside the wall. She sat bolt upright. One corner of her mouth drooped a little as if pulled down by an invisible hook. She groped in her handbag, fetched up a packet of cigarettes and fumbled one out. Alleyn lit it for her. She made a great business of this. She's had a lot more than's good for her, he thought and wondered where, on a Sunday afternoon, she'd get hold of it. Perhaps Fox's Mrs. Jancy at The Wharfinger's Friend had obliged.

'Now,' he said, 'what's the trouble?'

'Trouble? What trouble? I know trouble when I see it,' she said. 'I'm saturated in it.'

'Do you want to tell me about it?'

'Not a question of me telling you. It's what *he* told you. That's what matters.'

'Mr. Grove?'

'Mr. W. Hartly Grove. You know what? He's a monster. You know? Not a man but a monster. Cruel. My God,' she said and the corner of her mouth jerked again, 'how cruel that man can be!'

Looking at her Alleyn thought there was not much evidence of loving-kindness in her own demeanour.

'What,' she asked with laborious articulation, 'did he say about me? What did he say?'

'Miss Bracey, we didn't speak of you at all.'

'What *did* you speak about? Why did he stay behind to speak to you. He did, didn't he? Why?'

'He told me about his overcoat.'

She glowered at him and sucked at her cigarette as if it was a respirator. 'Did he tell you about his scarf?' she said.

'The yellow one with H. on it?'

She gave a sort of laugh. 'Embroidered,' she said. 'By his devoted Gerts. God, what a fool! And he goes on wearing it.

Slung round his neck like a halter and I wish it'd throttle him.'

She leant back, rested her head against the crimson plush and shut her eyes. Her left hand slid from her lap and the cigarette fell from her fingers. Alleyn picked it up and threw it into a nearby sandbox. 'Thanks,' she said without opening her eyes.

'Why did you stay behind? What do you want to tell me?'

'Stay behind? When?'

'Now.'

'*Then*, you mean.'

The clock above the box-office ticked. The theatre made a settling noise up in its ceiling. Miss Bracey sighed.

'Did you go back into the theatre?'

'Loo. Downstairs cloaks.'

'Why didn't you tell me this before?'

She said very distinctly : 'Because it didn't matter.'

'Or because it mattered too much?'

'*No.*'

'Did you see or hear anyone while you were in the downstairs foyer?'

'No. Yes, I did. I heard Winty and Marco in the office upstairs. They came out. And I left, then. I went away. Before they saw me.'

'Was there someone else you saw? Jobbins?'

'No,' she said at once.

'There was someone, wasn't there?'

'No. No. *No.*'

'Why does all this distress you so much?'

She opened her mouth and then covered it with her hand. She rose and swayed very slightly. As he put out a hand to steady her she broke from him and ran hazardously to the pass-door. It was unlocked. She pulled it open and left it so. Alleyn stood in the doorway and she backed away from him across the portico. When she realised he wasn't going to follow she flapped her hand in a lunatic fashion and ran towards the car park. He was in time to see her scramble into her mini-car. Someone was sitting in the passenger seat. He caught sight of Alleyn and turned away. It was Charles Random.

'Do you want her held?' Fox said at his elbow.

'No. What for? Let her go.'

III

'I *think* that's the lot,' Peregrine said. He laid down his pen, eased his fingers and looked up at Emily.

The bottom of Phipps Lane having turned out to be windy and rich in dubious smells, they had crossed the bridge and retired upon the flat. Emily got their lunch ready while Peregrine laboured to set down everything he could remember of his encounters with Mr. Conducis. Of Jeremy there was nothing to be seen.

Emily said : ' "What I did in the Hols. Keep it bright, brief and descriptive".'

'I seem to have done an unconscionable lot,' Peregrine rejoined. 'It's far from brief. Look.'

'No doubt Mr. Alleyn will mark it for you. "Quite G, but should take more pains with his writing." Are you sure you haven't forgotten the one apparently trifling clue round which the whole mystery revolves?'

'You're very joky, aren't you? I'm far from sure. The near-drowning incident's all complete, I think, but I'm not so sure about the visit to Drury Place. Of course, I was drunk by the time that was over. How *extraordinary* it was,' Peregrine said. 'Really, he *was* rum. Do you know, Emmy, darling, it seems to me now as if he acted throughout on some kind of compulsion. As if it had been he not I who was half-drowned and behaving (to mix my metaphor, you pedantic girl) like a duck that's had its head chopped off. *He* was obsessed while *I* was merely plastered. Or so it seems, now.'

'But what did he *do* that was so odd?'

'Do? He—well, there was an old menu card from the yacht *Kalliope*. It was in the desk and he snatched it up and burnt it.'

'I suppose if your yacht's wrecked under your feet you don't much enjoy being reminded of it.'

'No, but I got the impression it was something *on* the

card——' Peregrine went into a stare and after a long pause
said in a rather glazed manner, 'I think I've remembered.'

'What?'

'On the menu. Signatures: you know? And—Emmy, listen.'

Emily listened. 'Well,' she said. 'For what it's worth: put
it in.'

Peregrine put it in. 'There's one other thing,' he said. 'It's
about last night. I think it was when I was in front and you
had come through from backstage. There was the disturbance
by the boy—cat-calls and the door-slamming. Somewhere about
then, it was, that I remember thinking of *The Cherry Orchard*.
Not *consciously* but with one of those sort of momentary, back-
of-the-mind things.'

'*The Cherry Orchard*?'

'Yes, and Miss Joan Littlewood.'

'Funny mixture. She's never produced it, has she?'

'I don't think so. Oh, *damn*, I wish I could get it. Yes,'
Peregrine said excitedly. 'And with it there was a floating re-
membrance, I'm sure—of what? A quotation: "*Vanished with
a*—something *perfume and a*——" what I think it was
used somewhere by Walter de la Mare. It was hanging about
like the half-recollection of a dream when we walked up the
puddled alleyway and into Wharfingers Lane. Why? What
started it up?'

'It mightn't have anything to do with Trevor or Jobbins.'

'I know. But I've got this silly feeling it has.'

'Don't *try* to remember and then you may.'

'All right. Anyway the end of hols essay's ready for what
it's worth. I wonder if Alleyn's still at the theatre.'

'Ring up.'

'O.K. What's that parcel you've been carting about all day?'

'I'll show you when you've rung up.'

A policeman answered from The Dolphin and said that
Alleyn was at the Yard. Peregrine got through with startling
promptitude.

'I've done this thing,' he said. 'Would you like me to bring
it over to you?'

'I would indeed. Thank you, Jay. Remembered anything
new?'

'Not much, I'm afraid.' The telephone made its complicated angling sound.

'What?' Alleyn asked. 'What's that twanging? What did you say? Nothing new?'

'Yes!' Peregrine suddenly bawled into the receiver. 'Yes. You've done it. I'll put it in. Yes. Yes. Yes.'

'You sound like a pop singer. I'll be here for the next hour or so. Ask at the Yard entrance and they'll send you up. Bye.'

'You've remembered?' Emily cried. 'What is it? You've remembered.'

And when Peregrine told her, she remembered, too.

He re-opened his report and wrote feverishly. Emily unwrapped her parcel. When Peregrine had finished his additions and swung round in his chair he found, staring portentously at him, a water-colour drawing of a florid gentleman. His hair was curled into a cockscomb. His whiskers sprang from his jowls like steel wool and his prominent eyes proudly glared from beneath immensely luxuriant brows. He wore a frock coat with satin revers, a brilliant waistcoat, three alberts, a diamond tie-pin and any quantity of rings. His pantaloons were strapped under his varnished boots and beneath his elegantly arched arm, his lilac-gloved hand supported a topper with a curly brim. He stood with one leg straight and the other bent. He was superb.

And behind, lightly but unmistakably sketched in, was a familiar, an adorable façade.

'Emily? It isn't——? It must be——?'

'Look.'

Peregrine came closer. Yes, scribbled in faded pencil at the bottom of the work: 'Mr. Adolphus Ruby of The Dolphin Theatre. "Histrionic Portraits" series, 23 April 1855.'

'It's a present,' Emily said. 'It was meant, under less ghastly circs. to celebrate The Dolphin's first six months. I thought I'd get it suitably framed but then I decided to give it to you now to cheer you up a little.'

Peregrine began kissing her very industriously.

'Hi!' she said. 'Steady.'

'Where, you darling love, did you get it?'

'Charlie Random told me about it. He'd seen it on one o
his prowls in a print shop off Long Acre. Isn't he odd? H
didn't seem to want it himself. He goes in for nothing late
than 1815, he said. So, I got it.'

'It's not a print, by Heaven, it's an original. It's a Phi
original, Emmy. Oh, we shall frame it so beautifully an
hang it——' He stopped for a second. 'Hang it,' he said, 'i
the best possible place. Gosh, won't it send old Jer sky high !

'Where is he?'

Peregrine said : 'He had a thing to do. He ought to b
back by now. Emily, I couldn't have ever imagined myse
telling anybody what I'm going to tell you so it's a sort o
compliment. Do you know what Jer did?'

And he told Emily about Jeremy and the glove.

'He must have been demented,' she said flatly.

'I know. And what Alleyn's decided to do about him, wh
can tell? You don't sound as flabbergasted as I expected.'

'Don't I? No, well—I'm not altogether. When we wer
making the props Jeremy used to talk incessantly about th
glove. He's got a real fixation on the ownership business, hasn
he? It really is almost a kink, don't you feel? Harry was sayin
something the other day about after all the value of those kin
of jobs was purely artificial and fundamentally rather silly. I
he was trying to get a rise out of Jeremy, he certainly su
ceeded. Jeremy was livid. I thought there'd be a punch-u
before we were through. Perry, what's the matter? Have
been beastly?'

'No, no. Of course not.'

'I *have*,' she said contritely. 'He's your great friend and I'
been talking about him as if he's a specimen. I *am* sorry.'

'You needn't be. I know what he's like. Only I do *wish* I
hadn't done this.'

Peregrine walked over to the window and stared across th
river towards The Dolphin. Last night, he thought, on
sixteen hours ago, in that darkened house, a grotesque ove
coat had moved in and out of shadow. Last night—— H
looked down into the street below. There from the directic
of the bridge came a ginger head, thrust forward above hea

shoulders and adorned, like a classic ewer, with a pair of
outstanding ears.

'Here he comes,' Peregrine said. 'They haven't run him in as
yet, it seems.'

'I'll take myself off.'

'No, you don't. I've got to drop this stuff at the Yard. Come
with me. We'll take the car and I'll run you home.'

'Haven't you got things you ought to do? Telephonings and
fussings. What about Trevor?'

'I've done that. No change. Big trouble with Mum. Compensation. It's Greenslade and Winty's headache, thank God.
We want to do what's right and a tidy bit more but she's out
for the earth.'

'Oh, dear.'

'Here's Jer.'

He came in looking chilled and rather sickly. 'I'm sorry,'
he said. 'I didn't know you had—Oh hallo, Em.'

'Hallo, Jer.'

'I've told her,' Peregrine said.

'Thank you very much.'

'There's no need to take it grandly, is there?'

'Jeremy, you needn't mind my knowing. Truly.'

'I don't in the least mind,' he said in a high voice. 'No
doubt you'll both be surprised to learn I've been released with
a blackguarding that would scour the hide off an alligator.'

'Surprised and delighted,' Peregrine said. 'Where's the
loot?'

'At the Yard.'

Jeremy stood with his hands in his pockets as if waiting for
something irritating to occur.

'Do you want the car, Jer? I'm going to the Yard now,'
Peregrine said and explained why. Jeremy remarked that Peregrine was welcome to the car and added that he was evidently
quite the white-haired Trusty of the Establishment. He stood
in the middle of the room and watched them go.

'He *is* in a rage,' Emily said as they went to the car.

'I don't know what he's in but he's bloody lucky it's not the
lock-up. Come on.'

IV

Alleyn put down Peregrine's report and gave it a definitive slap. 'It's useful, Fox,' he said. 'You'd better read it.'

He dropped it on the desk before his colleague, filled his pipe and strolled over to the window. Like Peregrine Jay, an hour earlier, he looked down at the Thames and he thought how closely this case clung to the river as if it had been washed up by the incoming tide and left high-and-dry for their inspection. Henry Jobbins of Phipps Passage was a waterside character if ever there was one. Peregrine Jay and Jeremy Jones were not far east along the Embankment. Opposite them The Dolphin pushed up its stage-house and flagstaff with a traditional flourish on Bankside. Behind Tabard Lane in the Borough lurked Mrs. Blewitt while her terrible Trevor, still on the South Bank, languished in St. Terence's. And as if to top it off, he thought idly, here *we* are at the Yard, hard by the river.

'But with Conducis,' Alleyn muttered, 'we move West and, I suspect, a good deal farther away than Mayfair.'

He looked at Fox who, with eyebrows raised high above his spectacles in his stuffy reading expression, concerned himself with Peregrine's report.

The telephone rang and Fox reached for it. 'Super's room,' he said. 'Yes? I'll just see.'

He laid his great palm across the mouthpiece. 'It's Miss Destiny Meade,' he said, 'for you.'

'Is it, by gum! What's she up to, I wonder. All right. I'd better.'

'Look,' cried Destiny when he had answered. 'I know you're a kind, *kind* man.'

'Do you?' Alleyn said. 'How?'

'I have a sixth sense about people. Now, you won't laugh at me will you? Promise.'

'I've no inclination to do so, believe me.'

'And you won't slap me back. You'll come and have a delicious little dinky at six, or even earlier or whenever suits and tell me I'm being as stupid as an owl. Now, do, do, do, do, do. Please, please, please.'

'Miss Meade,' Alleyn said, 'it's extremely kind of you but I'm on duty and I'm afraid I can't.'

'On duty! But you've been on duty all *day*. That's worse than being an actor and you can't possibly mean it.'

'Have you thought of something that may concern this case?'

'It concerns ME,' she cried and he could imagine how widely her eyes opened at the telephone.

'Perhaps if you would just say what it is,' Alleyn suggested. He looked across at Fox who with his spectacles half-way down his nose, blankly contemplated his superior and listened at the other telephone. Alleyn crossed his eyes and protruded his tongue.

'—I can't really, not on the telephone. It's too complicated. Look—I'm *sure* you're up to your ears and not for the wide, wide would I——' The lovely voice moved unexpectedly into its higher and less mellifluous register. 'I'm nervous,' it said rapidly. 'I'm afraid. I'm terrified. I'm being threatened.' Alleyn heard a distant bang and a male voice. Destiny Meade whispered in his ear, '*Please come. Please come.*' Her receiver clicked and the dialling tone set in.

'Now who in Melpomene's dear name,' Alleyn said, 'does that lovely lady think she's leading down the garden path? Or is she? By gum, if she *is*,' he said, 'she's going to get such a rap on the temperament as hasn't come her way since she hit the headlines. When are we due with Conducis? Five o'clock. It's now half past two. Find us a car, Br'er Fox, we're off to Cheyne Walk.'

Fifteen minutes later they were shown into Miss Destiny Meade's drawing-room.

It was sumptuous to a degree and in maddeningly good taste: an affair of mushroom-coloured curtains, dashes of Schiaparelli pink, dull satin, Sèvres plaques and an unusual number of orchids. In the middle of it all was Destiny wearing a heavy sleeveless sheath with a mink collar: and not at all pleased to see Inspector Fox.

'Kind, kind,' she said, holding out her hand at her white

arm's length for Alleyn to do what he thought best wit
'Good afternoon,' she said to Mr. Fox.

'Now, Miss Meade,' Alleyn said briskly, 'what's the matter.
He reminded himself of a mature Hamlet.

'Please sit down. No, please. I've been so terribly distresse
and I need your advice so desperately.'

Alleyn sat, as she had indicated it, in a pink velvet bu*
toned chair. Mr. Fox took the least luxurious of the othe
chairs and Miss Meade herself sank upon a couch, tucked u
her feet which were beautiful and leant superbly over the ar
to gaze at Alleyn. Her hair, coloured raven black for th
Dark Lady, hung like a curtain over her right jaw and ha
her cheek. She raised a hand to it and then drew the han
away as if it had hurt her. Her left ear was exposed and en
bellished with a massive diamond pendant.

'This is so difficult,' she said.

'Perhaps we could fire point-blank.'

'Fire? Oh, I see. Yes. Yes, I must try, mustn't I?'

'If you please.'

Her eyes never left Alleyn's face. 'It's about——' she bega
and her voice resentfully indicated the presence of Mr. Fox
'It's about ME.'

'Yes?'

'Yes. I'm afraid I must be terribly frank. Or no. Why do
say that? To you of all people who, of course, understand—
she executed a circular movement of her arm—'everything.
know you do. I wouldn't have asked you if I hadn't know
And you see I have nowhere to turn.'

'Oh, surely!'

'No. I mean that,' she said with great intensity. 'I mean i
Nowhere. No one. It's all so utterly unexpected. Everythin
seemed to be going along quite naturally and taking the i
evitable course. Because—I know you'll agree with this—on
shouldn't—indeed one can't resist the inevitable. One is fate
and when this new thing came into our lives we both face
up to it, he and I, oh, over and over again. It's like,' sh
rather surprisingly added, 'Antony and Cleopatra. I forge
the exact line. I think, actually, that in the production it wa
cut but it puts the whole thing in a nutshell, and I told hi

so. Ah, Cleopatra,' she mused and such was her beauty and professional expertise that, there and then, lying (advantageously of course) on her sofa she became for a fleeting moment the Serpent of the old Nile. 'But now,' she added crossly as she indicated a box of cigarettes that was not quite within her reach, 'now, with him turning peculiar and violent like this I feel I simply don't *know* him. I can't cope. As I told you on the telephone, I'm terrified.'

When Alleyn leant forward to light her cigarette he fancied that he caught a glint of appraisal and of wariness but she blinked, moved her face nearer to his and gave him a look that was a masterpiece.

'Can you,' Alleyn said, 'perhaps come to the point and tell us precisely why and of whom you are frightened, Miss Meade?'

'Wouldn't one be? It was so utterly beyond the bounds of anything one could possibly anticipate. To come in almost without warning and I must tell you that of course he has his own key and by a hideous chance my married couple are out this afternoon. And then, after all that has passed between us to—to . . .'

She turned her head aside, swept back the heavy wing of her hair and superbly presented herself to Alleyn's gaze.

'Look,' she said.

Unmistakably someone had slapped Miss Meade very smartly indeed across the right-hand rearward aspect of her face. She had removed the diamond ear-ring on this side but its pendant had cut her skin behind the point of the jaw and the red beginnings of a bruise showed across the cheek.

'What do you think of that?' she said.

'Did Grove do this!' Alleyn ejaculated.

She stared at him. An indescribable look of—what? Pity? Contempt? Mere astonishment?—broke across her face. Her mouth twisted and she began to laugh.

'Oh, you poor darling,' said Destiny Meade. 'Harry? He wouldn't hurt a fly. No, no, no, my dear, this is Mr. Marcus Knight. His mark.'

Alleyn digested this information and Miss Meade watched him apparently with some relish.

'Do you mind telling me,' he said at length, 'why all this
blew up? I mean, *specifically* why. If, as I understand, you
have finally broken with Knight.'

'*I* had,' she said, 'but you see *he* hadn't. Which made
things so very tricky. And then he wouldn't give me back the
key. He has, now. He threw it at me,' she looked vaguely
round the drawing-room. 'It's somewhere about,' she said. 'It
might have gone anywhere or broken anything. He's so
egotistic.'

'What had precipitated this final explosion, do you think?'

'Well——' She dropped the raven wing over her cheek.
'This and that. Harry, of course, has driven him quite frantic.
It's very bad of Harry and I never cease telling him so. And
then it really was *too* unfortunate last night about the orchids.'

'The orchids?' Alleyn's gaze travelled to a magnificent stand
of them in a Venetian goblet.

'Yes, those,' she said. 'Vass had them sent round during
the show. I tucked his card in my décolletage like a sort of
Victorian courtesan, you know, and in the big love scene
Marco spotted it and whipped it out before I could do a
thing. It wouldn't have been so bad if they hadn't had that
flare-up in the yacht a thousand years ago. He hadn't realised
before that I knew Vass so well. Personally, I mean. Vassy
has got this thing about no publicity and of course I *respect* it.
I understand. We just see each other quietly from time to
time. He has a wonderful brain.'

' "Vassy"? "Vass"?'

'Vassily, really. I call him Vass. Mr. Conducis.'

10. MONDAY

As Fox and Alleyn left the flat in Cheyne Walk they encountered, in the downstairs entrance, a little old man in a fusty overcoat and decrepit bowler. He seemed to be consulting a large envelope.

'Excuse me, gentlemen,' he said, touching the brim of the bowler, 'but can you tell me if a lady be-the-namer Meade resides in these apartments? It seems to be the number but I can't discover a name board or indication of any sort.'

Fox told him and he was much obliged.

When they were in the street Alleyn said: 'Did you recognise him?'

'I had a sort of notion,' Fox said, 'that I ought to. Who is he? He looks like a bum.'

'Which is what he is. He's a Mr. Grimball who, twenty years ago and more was the man in possession at the Lampreys.'

'God bless my soul!' Fox said. 'Your memory!'

'Peregrine Jay did tell us that the Meade's a compulsive gambler, didn't he?'

'Well, I'll be blowed! Fancy that! On top of all the other lot—in Queer Street! Wonder if Mr. Conducis——'

Fox continued in a series of scandalised ejaculations.

'We're not due with Conducis for another hour and a half,' Alleyn said. 'Stop clucking and get into the car. We'll drive to the nearest box and ring the Yard in case there's anything.'

'About the boy?'

'Yes. Yes. About the boy. Come on.'

Fox returned from the telephone in measured haste.

'Hospital's just rung through,' he said. 'They think he's coming round.'

'Quick as we can,' Alleyn said to the driver and in fifteen minutes, with the sister and house-surgeon in attendance, they walked round the screens that hid Trevor's bed in the children's casualty ward at St. Terence's.

P.C. Grantley had returned to duty. When he saw Alleyn he hurriedly vacated his chair and Alleyn slipped into it.

'Anything?'

Grantley showed his note book.

'*It's a pretty glove,*' Alleyn read, '*but it doesn't warm my hand. Take it off.*'

'He said that?'

'Yes, sir. Nothing else, sir. Just that.'

'It's a quotation from his part.'

Trevor's eyes were closed and he breathed evenly. The sister brushed back his curls.

'He's asleep,' the doctor said. 'We must let him waken in his own time. He'll probably be normal when he does.'

'Except for the blackout period?'

'Quite.'

Ten minutes slipped by in near silence.

'Mum,' Trevor said. 'Hey, Mum.'

He opened his eyes and stared at Alleyn. 'What's up?' he asked and then saw Grantley's tunic. 'That's a rozzer,' he said. 'I haven't done a thing.'

'You're all right,' said the doctor. 'You had a nasty fall and we're looking after you.'

'Oh,' Trevor said profoundly and shut his eyes.

'Gawd, he's off again,' Grantley whispered distractedly. 'Innit marvellous.'

'Now then,' Fox said austerely.

'Pardon, Mr. Fox.'

Alleyn said 'May he be spoken to?'

'He shouldn't be worried. If it's important——'

'It could hardly be more so.'

'*Nosy Super,*' Trevor said and Alleyn turned back to find himself being stared at.

'That's right,' he said. 'We've met before.'

'Yeah. Where though?'

'In The Dolphin. Upstairs in the circle.'

'Yeah,' Trevor said, wanly tough. A look of doubt came

into his eyes. He frowned. 'In the cicle,' he repeated uneasily.

'Things happen up there in the circle, don't they?'

Complacently and still with that look of uncertainty : 'You can say that again,' said Trevor. 'All over the house.'

'*Slash?*'

'Yeah. *Slash,*' he agreed and grinned.

'You had old Jobbins guessing?'

'And that's no error.'

'What did you do?'

Trevor stretched his mouth and produced a wailing sound : '*Wheeeee.*'

'Make like spooks,' he said. 'See?'

'Anything else?'

There was a longish pause. Grantley lifted his head. Somewhere beyond the screens a trolley jingled down the ward.

'*Ping.*'

'That must have rocked them,' Alleyn said.

''Can say that again. What a turn-up! Oh, dear!'

'How did you do it? Just like that? With your mouth?'

The house-surgeon stirred restively. The sister gave a starched little cough.

'Do you *mind*?' Trevor said. 'My mum plays the old steely,' he added, and then, with a puzzled look : 'Hey! Was that when I got knocked out or something? Was it?'

'That was a bit later. You had a fall. Can you remember where you went after you banged the stage-door?'

'No,' he said impatiently. He sighed and shut his eyes. 'Do me a favour and pack it up, will you?' he said and went to sleep again.

'I'm afraid that's it,' said the house-surgeon.

Alleyn said : 'May I have a word with you?'

'Oh, certainly. Yes, of course. Carry on, Sister, will you? He's quite all right.'

Alleyn said : 'Stick it out, Grantley.'

The house-surgeon led him into an office at the entrance to the ward. He was a young man and, although he observed a markedly professional attitude, was clearly intrigued by the situation.

'Look here,' Alleyn said, 'I want you to give me your cold-blooded, considered opinion. You tell me the boy is unlikely to remember what happened just before he went over-board. I gather he may recall events up to within a few minutes of the fall?'

'He may, yes. The length of the "lost" period can vary.'

'Did you think he was on the edge of remembering a little further just now?'

'One can't say. One got the impression that he hadn't the energy to try and remember.'

'Do you think that if he were faced with the person whom he saw attacking the caretaker, he would recognise him and remember what he saw?'

'I don't know. I'm not a specialist in amnesia or the after effects of cranial injury. You should ask someone who is.' The doctor hesitated and then said slowly: 'You mean would the shock of seeing the assailant stimulate the boy's memory?'

'Not of the assault upon himself but of the earlier assault upon Jobbins which may be on the fringe of his recollection: which may lie just this side of the blackout.'

'I can't give you an answer to that one.'

'Will you move the boy into a separate room—say to-morrow—and allow him to see three—perhaps four visitors: one after another? For five minutes each.'

'No. I'm sorry. Not yet.'

'Look,' Alleyn said, 'can it really do any harm? *Really?*'

'I have not the authority.'

'Who has?'

The house-surgeon breathed an Olympian name.

'Is he in the hospital? Now?'

The house-surgeon looked at his watch. 'There's been a board meeting. He may be in his room.'

'I'll beard him there. Where is it?'

'Yes, but look here——'

'God bless my soul,' Alleyn ejaculated. 'I'll rant as well as he. Lead me to him.'

II

'Ten past four,' Alleyn said, checking with Big Ben. 'Let's do a bit of stocktaking.' They had returned to the car.

'You got it fixed up for this show with the boy, Mr. Alleyn?'

'Oh, yes. The great panjandrum turned out to be very mild and a former acquaintance. An instance, I'm afraid, of Harry Grove's detested old boymanship. I must say I see Harry's point. We went to the ward and he inspected young Trevor who was awake, as bright as a button, extremely full of himself and demanding a nice dinner. The expert decided in our favour. We may arrange the visits for to-morrow at noon. *Out* of visiting hours. We'll get Peregrine Jay to call the actors and fix up the timetable. I don't want us to come into it at this juncture. We'll just occur at the event. Jay is to tell them the truth : that the boy can't remember what happened and that it's hoped the encounters with the rest of the cast may set up some chain of association that could lead to a recovery of memory.'

'One of them won't fancy *that* idea.'

'No. But it wouldn't do to refuse.'

'The nerve might crack. There might be a bolt. With that sort of temperament,' Fox said. 'You can't tell what may happen. Still we're well provided.'

'If anybody's nerve cracks it won't be Miss Destiny Meade's. What did you make of that scene in her flat, Fox?'

'Well : to begin with, the lady was very much put out by my being there. In *my* view, Mr. Alleyn, she didn't fancy police protection within the meaning of the code to anything like the extent that she fancied it coming in a personal way from yourself. Talk about the go-ahead signal! It was hung out like the week's wash,' said Mr. Fox.

'Control yourself, Fox.'

'Now, on what she said we only missed Mr. Knight by seconds. She makes out he rang up and abused her to such an

extent that she decided to call you and that he walked in while
she was still talking to you.'

'Yes. And they went bang off into a roaring row which cul
minated in him handing her a tuppeny one to the jaw afte
which he flung out and we, within a couple of minutes, mince
in.'

'No thought in her mind, it appears,' Fox suggested, 'ol
ringing Mr. Grove up to come and protect her. Only you.'

'I daresay she's doing that very thing at this moment. I mus
say, I hope he knows how to cope with her.'

'Only one thing to do with that type of lady,' Fox said
'and I don't mean a tuppeny one on the jaw. He'll cope.'

'We'll be talking to Conducis in half an hour, Fox, and it'
going to be tricky.'

'I should damn' well think so,' Fox warmly agreed. 'Wha
with orchids and her just seeing him quietly from time to
time. Hi!' he ejaculated. 'Would Mr. Grove know about Mr
Conducis and would Mr. Conducis know about Mr. Grove?'

'Who is, remember, his distant relation. Search me, Fox
The thing at the moment seems to be that Knight knows abou
them both and acts accordingly. Big stuff.'

'How a gang like this hangs together beats me. You'
think the resignations'd be falling in like autumn leaves. Wha
they always tell you, I suppose,' Fox said. 'The Show Must G
On.'

'And it happens to be a highly successful show with fa
parts and much prestige. But I should think that even they
won't be able to sustain the racket indefinitely at this pitch.

'Why are we going to see Mr. Conducis, I ask myself. How
do we shape up to him? Does he matter, as far as the case i
concerned?'

'In so far as he was in the theatre and knows the combina
tion, yes.'

'I suppose so.'

'I thought him an exceedingly rum personage, Fox. A col
fish and yet a far from insensitive fish. No indication of any
background other than wealth or of any particular race. H
carries a British passport. He inherited one fortune and mad

lord knows how many more, each about a hundred per cent fatter than the last. He's spent most of his time abroad and a lot of it in the *Kalliope*, until she was cut in half in a heavy fog under his feet .That was six years ago. What did you make of Jay's account of the menu card?'

'Rather surprisng if he's right. Rather a coincidence, two of our names cropping up in that direction.'

'We can check the passenger list with the records. But it's not really a coincidence. People in Conducis's world tend to move about expensively in a tight group. There was, of course, an inquiry after the disaster and Conducis was reported to be unable to appear. He was in a nursing home on the Côte d'Azur suffering from exhaustion, exposure and severe shock.'

'Perhaps,' Mr. Fox speculated, 'it's left him a bit funny for keeps.'

'Perhaps. He certainly is a rum 'un and no mistake. Jay's account of his behaviour that morning—by *George*,' Alleyn said suddenly. 'Hell's boots and gaiters!'

'What's all this, now?' Fox asked placidly.

'So much hokum I daresay, but listen, all the same.'

Fox listened.

'Well,' he said. 'You always say don't conjecture but personally, Mr. Alleyn, when you get one of your hunches in this sort of way I reckon it's safe to go nap on it. Not that this one really gets us any nearer an arrest.'

'I wonder if you're right about that. I wonder.'

They talked for another five minutes, going over Peregrine's notes and then Alleyn looked at his watch and said they must be off. When they were half-way to Park Lane he said :

'You went over all the properties in the theatre, didn't you? No musical instruments?'

'None.'

'He might have had Will singing "Take, oh, take those lips away" to the Dark Lady. Accompanying himself on a lute. But he didn't.'

'Perhaps Mr. Knight can't sing.'

'You may be right at that.'

D.A.T.D.   H

They drove into Park Lane and turned into Drury Place.

'I'm going,' Alleyn said, 'to cling to Peregrine Jay's notes as Mr. Conducis was reported to have clung to his raft.'

'I still don't know *exactly* what line we take,' Fox objected.

'We let him dictate it,' Alleyn rejoined. 'At first. Come on.'

Mawson admitted them to that so arrogantly unobtrusive interior and a pale young man advanced to meet them. Alleyn remembered him from his former visit. The secretary.

'Mr. Alleyn. And—er?'

'Inspector Fox.'

'Yes. How do you do? Mr. Conducis is in the library. He's been very much distressed by this business. Awfully upset. Particularly about the boy. We've sent flowers and all that nonsense, of course, and we're in touch with the theatre people. Mr. Conducis is most anxious that everything possible should be done. Well—shall we? You'll find him, perhaps, rather nervous, Mr. Alleyn. He has been so very distressed.'

They walked soundlessly to the library door. A clock mellifluously struck six.

'Here is Superintendent Alleyn, sir, and Inspector Fox.'

'Yes. Thank you.'

Mr. Conducis was standing at the far end of the library. He had been looking out of the window, it seemed. In the evening light the long room resembled an interior by some defunct academician : Orchardson, perhaps, or The Hon. John Collier. The details were of an undated excellence but the general effect was strangely Edwardian and so was Mr. Conducis. He might have been a deliberately understated monument to Affluence.

As he moved towards them Alleyn wondered if Mr. Conducis was ill or if his pallor was brought about by some refraction of light from the apple-green walls. He wore a gardenia in his coat and an edge of crimson silk showed above his breast pocket.

'Good evening,' he said. 'I am pleased that you were able to come. Glad to see you again.'

He offered his hand. Large and white, it withdrew itself—it almost snatched itself away—from contact.

Mawson came in with a drinks tray, put it down, hovered, was glanced at and withdrew.

'You will have a drink,' Mr. Conducis stated.

'Thank you, but no,' Alleyn said. 'Not on duty, I'm afraid. This won't stop you from having one, of course.'

'I am an abstainer,' said Mr. Conducis. 'Shall we sit down?'

They did so. The crimson leather chairs received them like sultans.

Alleyn said : 'You sent word you wanted to see us, sir, but we would in any case have asked for an interview. Perhaps the best way of tackling this unhappy business will be for us to hear any questions that it may have occurred to you to ask. We will then, if you please, continue the conversation on what I can only call routine investigation lines.'

Mr. Conducis raised his clasped hands to his mouth and glanced briefly over them at Alleyn. He then lowered his gaze to his fingers. Alleyn thought : 'I suppose that's how he looks when he's manipulating his gargantuan undertakings.'

Mr. Conducis said : 'I am concerned with this affair. The theatre is my property and the enterprise is under my control. I have financed it. The glove and documents are mine. I trust, therefore, that I am entitled to a detailed statement upon the case as it appears to your department. Or rather, since you are in charge of the investigation, as it appears to you.'

This was said with an air of absolute authority. Alleyn was conscious, abruptly, of the extraordinary force that resided in Mr. Conducis.

He said very amiably : 'We are not authorised, I'm afraid, to make detailed statements on demand—not even to entrepreneurs of businesses and owners of property, especially where a fatality has occurred on that property and a crime of violence may be suspected. On the other hand, I will, as I have suggested, be glad to consider any questions you like to put to me.'

And he thought : 'He's like a lizard or a chameleon or whatever the animal is that blinks slowly. It's what people mean when they talk about hooded eyes.'

Mr. Conducis did not argue or protest. For all the reaction he gave, he might not have heard what Alleyn said.

'In your opinion,' he said, 'were the fatality and the injury to the boy caused by an act of violence?'

'Yes.'

'Both by the same hand?'

'Yes.'

'Have you formed an opinion on why it was done?'

'We have arrived at a working hypothesis.'

'What is it?'

'I can go so far as to say that I think both were defensive actions.'

'By a person caught in the act of robbery?'

'I believe so, yes.'

'Do you think you know who this person is?'

'I am almost sure that I do. I am not positive.'

'Who?'

'That,' Alleyn said, 'I am not at liberty to tell you. Yet.'

Mr. Conducis looked fully at him if the fact that those extraordinarily blank eyes were focused on his face could justify this assertion.

'You said you wished to see me. Why?'

'For several reasons. The first concerns your property : the glove and the documents. As you know they have been recovered but I think you should also know by what means.'

He told the story of Jeremy Jones and the substitution and he could have sworn that as he did so the sweet comfort of a reprieve flooded through Conducis. The thick white hands relaxed. He gave an almost inaudible but long sigh.

'Have you arrested him?'

'No. We have, of course, uplifted the glove. It is in a safe at the Yard with the documents.'

'I cannot believe, Superintendent Alleyn, that you give any credence to his story.'

'I am inclined to believe it.'

'Then in my opinion you are either incredibly stupid or needlessly evasive. In either case, incompetent.'

This attack surprised Alleyn. He had not expected this slow-blinking opponent to dart his tongue so soon. As if sensing his reaction Mr. Conducis recrossed his legs and said : 'I am too severe. I beg your pardon. Let me explain myself. Can you not see that Jones's story was an impromptu invention? He did not substitute the faked glove for the real glove six months ago. He substituted it last night and was discovered in the act. He killed Jobbins, was seen by the boy and tried to kill him. He left the copy behind, no doubt if he had not been interrupted he would have put it in the safe, and he took the real glove to the safe-deposit.'

'First packing it with most elaborate care in an insulated box with four wrappings, all sealed.'

'Done in the night. Before Jay got home.'

'We can check, you know, with the safe deposit people. He says he had a witness when he deposited the glove six months ago.'

'A witness to a dummy package, no doubt.'

'If you consider,' Alleyn said, 'I'm sure you will come to the conclusion that this theory won't answer. It really won't, you know.'

'Why not?'

'Do you want me to spell it out, sir? If, as he states, he transposed the gloves six months ago and intended to maintain the deception, he had no need to do anything further. If the theft was a last minute notion, he could perfectly well have effected the transposition to-day or to-morrow when he performed his authorised job of removing the treasure from the safe. There was no need for him to sneak back into the theatre at dead of night and risk discovery. Why on earth, six months ago, should he go through an elaborate hocus-pocus of renting a safe deposit and lodging a fake parcel in it?'

'He's a fanatic. He has written to me expostulating about the sale of the items to an American purchaser. He even tried, I am told, to secure an interview. My secretary can show you his letter. It is most extravagant.'

'I shall be interested to see it.'

A brief silence followed this exchange. Alleyn thought : 'He's formidable but he's not as tough as I expected. He's shaken.'

'Have you any other questions?' Alleyn asked.

He wondered if the long unheralded silence was one of Mr. Conducis's strategic weapons : whether it was or not, he now employed it and Alleyn with every appearance of tranquillity sat it out. The light had changed in the long green room and the sky outside the far windows had darkened. Beneath them, at the exquisite table, Peregrine Jay had first examined the documents and the glove. And against the left-hand wall under a picture—surely a Kandinsky—stood the bureau, an Oebeu or Rissones perhaps, from which Mr. Conducis had withdrawn his treasures. Fox, who in a distant chair had performed his little miracle of self-effacement, gave a slight cough.

Mr. Conducis said without moving, 'I would ask for information as to the continued running of the play and the situation of the players.'

'I understand the season will go on : we've taken no action that might prevent it.'

'You will do so if you arrest a member of the company.'

'He or she would be replaced by an understudy.'

'She,' Mr. Conducis said in a voice utterly devoid of inflection. 'That, of course, need not be considered.'

He waited but Alleyn thought it was his turn to initiate a silence and made no comment.

'Miss Destiny Meade has spoken to me,' Mr. Conducis said. 'She is very much distressed by the whole affair. She tells me you called upon her this afternoon and she finds herself, as a result, quite prostrated. Surely there is no need for her to be pestered like this.'

For a split second Alleyn wondered what on earth Mr. Conducis would think if he and Fox went into fits of laughter. He said : 'Miss Meade was extremely helpful and perfectly frank. I am sorry she found the exercise fatiguing.'

'I have no more to say,' Mr. Conducis said and stood up. So did Alleyn.

'I'm afraid that I have,' he said. 'I'm on duty, sir, and this *is* an investigation.'

'I have nothing to bring to it.'

'When we are convinced of that we will stop bothering

you. I'm sure you'd prefer us to deal with the whole matter here rather than at the Yard. Wouldn't you?'

Mr. Conducis went to the drinks tray and poured himself a glass of water. He took a minute gold case from a waistcoat pocket, shook a tablet on his palm, swallowed it and chased it down.

'Excuse me,' he said, 'it was time.'

'Ulcers?' wondered Alleyn.

Mr. Conducis returned and faced him. 'By all means,' he said. 'I am perfectly ready to help you and only regret that I am unlikely to be able to do so to any effect. I have, from the time I decided to promote The Dolphin undertaking, acted solely through my executives. Apart from an initial meeting and one brief discussion with Mr. Jay I have virtually no personal contact with members of the management and company.'

'With the exception, perhaps, of Miss Meade?'

'Quite so.'

'And Mr. Grove?'

'He was already known to me. I except him.'

'I understand you are related?'

'A distant connection.'

'So he said,' Alleyn lightly agreed. 'I understand,' he added, 'that you were formerly acquainted with Mr. Marcus Knight.'

'What makes you think so?'

'Peregrine Jay recognised his signature on the menu you destroyed in his presence.'

'Mr. Jay was not himself that morning.'

'Do you mean, sir, that he made a mistake and Knight was not a guest in the *Kalliope*?'

After a long pause Mr. Conducis said : 'He was a guest. He behaved badly. He took offence at an imagined slight. He left the yacht, at my suggestion, at Villefranche.'

'And so escaped the disaster?'

'Yes.'

Mr. Conducis had seated himself again : this time in an upright chair. He sat rigidly erect but as if conscious of this, crossed his legs and put his hands in his trouser pockets. Alleyn stood a short distance from him.

'I am going to ask you,' he said, 'to talk about something that may be painful to you. I want you to tell me about the night of the fancy dress dinner party on board the *Kalliope*.'

Alleyn had seen people sit with the particular kind of still-ness that now invested Mr. Conducis. They sat like that in the cells underneath the dock while they waited for the jury to come back. In the days of capital punishment, he had been told by a warder that they sat like that while they waited to hear if they were reprieved. He could see a very slight rhythmic movement of the crimson silk handkerchief and he could hear, ever so faintly, the breathing of Mr. Conducis.

'It was six years ago, wasn't it?' Alleyn said. 'And the dinner party took place on the night of the disaster?'

Mr. Conducis's eyes closed in a momentary assent but he did not speak.

'Was Mrs. Constantia Guzman one of your guests in the yacht?'

'Yes,' he said indifferently.

'You told Mr. Jay, I believe, that you bought the Shake-speare relics six years ago?'

'That is so.'

'Had you this treasure on board the yacht?'

'Why should you think so?'

'Because Jay found under the glove the menu for a dinner in the *Kalliope*—he thinks it was headed "Villefranche." Which you burnt in the fireplace over there.'

'The menu must have been dropped in the desk. It was an unpleasant reminder of a distressing voyage.'

'So the desk and its contents *were* in the yacht?'

'Yes.'

'May I ask why, sir?'

Mr. Conducis's lips moved, were compressed and moved again. 'I bought them,' he said, 'from——' He gave a grotes-que little cough, 'from a person in the yacht.'

'Who was this person, if you please?'

'I have forgotten.'

'Forgotten?'

'The name.'

'Was it Knight?'

'*No.*'

'There are maritime records. We shall be able to trace it. Will you go on, please?'

'He was a member of the ship's complement. He asked to see me and showed me the desk which he said he wanted to sell. I understand that it had been given him by the proprietress of a lodging-house. I thought the contents were almost certainly worthless, but I gave him what he asked for them.'

'Which was——?'

'Thirty pounds.'

'What became of this man?'

'Drowned,' said a voice from somewhere inside Mr. Conducis.

'How did it come about that the desk and its contents were saved?'

'I cannot conjecture by what fantastic process of thought you imagine any of this relates to your inquiry.'

'I hope to show that it does. I believe it does.'

'I had the desk on deck. I had shown the contents, as a matter of curiosity, to some of my guests.'

'Did Mrs. Guzman see it, perhaps?'

'Perhaps.'

'Was she interested?'

A look which Alleyn afterwards described as being profoundly professional drifted into Mr. Conducis's face.

He said, 'She is a collector.'

'Did she make an offer?'

'She did. I was not inclined to sell.'

Alleyn was visited by a strange notion.

'Tell me,' he said, 'were you both in fancy dress?'

Mr. Conducis looked at him with an air of wondering contempt. 'Mrs. Guzman,' he said, 'was in costume : Andalusian, I understand. I wore a domino over evening dress.'

'Gloved, either of you?'

'No!' he said loudly and added, 'We had been playing bridge.'

'Were any of the others gloved?'

'A ridiculous question. Some may have been.'

'Were the ship's company in fancy dress?'

'Certainly not!'

'The stewards?'

'As eighteenth century flunkeys.'

'Gloved?'

'I do not remember.'

'Why do you dislike pale gloves, Mr. Conducis?'

'I have no idea,' he said breathlessly, 'what you mean.'

'You told Peregrine Jay that you dislike them.'

'A personal prejudice. I cannot account for it.'

'Were there gloved hands that disturbed you on the night of the disaster? Mr. Conducis, are you ill?'

'I—no. No, I am well. You insist on questioning me about an episode which distressed me, which was painful, tragic an outrage to one's sensibilities.'

'I would avoid it if I could. I'm afraid I must go further Will you tell me exactly what happened at the moment of disaster: to you, I mean, and to whoever was near you then or later?'

For a moment Alleyn thought he was going to refuse. He wondered if there would be a sudden outbreak or whether Mr. Conducis would merely walk out of the room and leave them to take what action they chose. He did none of these things. He embarked upon a toneless, rapid recital of facts. Of the fact of fog, the sudden looming of the tanker, the breaking apart of the *Kalliope*. Of the fact of fire. Of oil on the water and of how he found himself looking down on the wooden raft from the swimming pool and of how the deck turned into a precipice and he slid from it and landed on the raft.

'Still with the little desk?'

Yes. Clutched under his left arm, it seemed, but with no consciousness of this. He had lain across the raft with the desk underneath him. It had bruised him very badly. He gripped a rope loop at the side with his right hand. Mrs. Guzman had appeared beside the raft and was clinging to one of the loops. Alleyn had a mental picture of an enormous nose,

n open mouth, a mantilla plastered over a big head and a
oundering mass of wet black lace and white flesh.

The recital stopped as abruptly as it had begun.

'That is all. We were picked up by the tanker.'

'Were there other people on the raft?'

'I believe so. My memory is not clear. I lost consciousness.'

'Men? Mrs. Guzman?'

'I believe so. I was told so.'

'Pretty hazardous, I should have thought. It wouldn't ac-
ommodate more than—how many?'

'I don't know. I don't know. I don't know.'

'Mr. Conducis, when you saw Peregrine Jay's gloved hands
linging to the edge of that hole in the stage at The Dolphin
nd heard him call out that he would drown if you didn't save
im—were you reminded——'

Mr. Conducis had risen and now began to move back-
vards, like an image in slow motion, towards the bureau.
'ox rose too and shifted in front of it. Mr. Conducis drew his
rimson silk handkerchief from his breast pocket and pressed
: against his mouth and above it his upper lip glistened. His
rows were defined by beaded margins and the dark skin of
is face was stretched too tight and had blanched over the
ones.

'Be quiet,' he said. 'No. Be quiet.'

Somebody had come into the house. A distant voice spoke
udly but indistinguishably.

The door opened and the visitor came in.

Mr. Conducis screamed: 'You've told them. You've be-
rayed me. I wish to Christ I'd killed you.'

Fox took him from behind. Almost at once he stopped
truggling.

III

revor, could be, as Alleyn put it, bent at the waist. He had
een so bent and was propped up in a sitting position in his
rivate room. A bed-tray on legs was arranged across his
tomach, ready for any offerings that might be forthcoming.

His condition had markedly improved and he was inclined though still feebly, to throw his weight about.

The private room was small but there was a hospital scree in one corner of it and behind the screen, secreted there befor Trevor was wheeled in, sat Inspector Fox, his large, decen feet concealed by Trevor's suitcase. Alleyn occupied the bed side chair.

On receiving assurances from Alleyn that the police wer not on his tracks Trevor repeated, with more fluency, h previous account of his antics in the deserted auditoriun but he would not or could not carry the recital beyond th point when he was in the circle and heard a distant tele phone ring. 'I don't remember another thing,' he said import antly. 'I've blacked out. I was concussed. The doc says I wa very badly concussed. Here! *Where* did I fall, Super? What the story?'

'You fell into the stalls.'

'*Would* you mind!'

'True.'

'Into the *stalls*! Cripes! *Why?*'

'That's what I want to find out.'

Trevor looked sideways. 'Did old Henry Jobbins lay int me?' he asked.

'No.'

'Or Chas Random?'

A knowledgeable look: a disfigured look of veiled grati fication, perhaps, appeared like a blemish on Trevor's page boy face. He giggled.

'He was wild with me, Chas was. Listen: Chas had it i for me, Super, really he did. I got that camp's goat, actually good and proper.'

Alleyn listened and absently noted how underlying cock ney seeped up through superimposed drama academy. Behin carefully turned vowel and consonant jibed a Southwar urchin. 'Goo' un' prop-*per*,' Trevor was really saying, how ever classy the delivery.

'Some of the company are coming in to see you,' Alley said. 'They may only stay for a minute or two but they' like to say hallo.'

'I'd be pleased,' Trevor graciously admitted. He was extremely complacent.

Alleyn watched him and talked to him for a little while longer and then, conscious of making a decision that might turn out most lamentably, he said:

'Look here, young Trevor, I'm going to ask you to help me in a very tricky and important business. If you don't like the suggestion you needn't have anything to do with it. On the other hand——'

He paused. Trevor gave him a sharp look.

'Nothing comes to the dumb,' he said.' What seems to be the trouble? Come on and give.'

Ten minutes later his visitors began to arrive, ushered in by Peregrine Jay. 'Just tell them,' Alleyn had said, 'that he'd like to see them for a few minutes and arrange the timetable. You can pen them up in the waiting-room at the end of the corridor.'

They brought presents.

Winter Morris came first with a box of crystallised fruit. He put it on the tray and then stood at the foot of the bed wearing his shepherd's plaid suit and his dark red tie. His hair, beautifully cut, waved above and behind the ears. He leaned his head to one side and looked at Trevor.

'Well, well, well,' he said. 'So the great star is receiving. How does it feel to be famous?'

Trevor was languid and gracious but before the prescribed five minutes had elapsed he mentioned that his agent would be waiting upon Mr. Morris with reference to the Management, as he put it, seeing him right.

'We don't,' Winter Morris said, eyeing him warily, 'need to worry just yet about that one. Do we?'

'I hope not, Mr. Morris,' Trevor said. He leant his head back against the pillows and closed his eyes. 'Funny how faint I appear to get,' he murmured. 'I hope it won't be kind of permanent. My doctors seem to take a grave view. Funny thing.'

Mr. Morris said, 'You played that line just like the end of Act I, but I mustn't tire you.'

He tiptoed elaborately away from the bed and as he passed Alleyn, let droop a heavy white eyelid.

Jeremy Jones had made a group of tiny effigies representing the characters in the play and had mounted them on a minuscule stage. 'Ever so quaint,' Trevor said. 'Ta, Mr. Jones. You *have* been busy. Put it on my tray, would you?'

Jeremy put his offering on the tray. Trevor gazed into his face as he did so. 'You *are* clever with your fingers,' he said. 'Aren't you, Mr. Jones?'

Jeremy looked suspiciously at him, turned scarlet and said to Alleyn : 'I mustn't stay too long.'

'Don't go,' said Trevor. 'Yet.'

Jeremy lingered, with one eye on Alleyn and awkwardly at a loss for anything to say. Peregrine tapped on the door, looked in, said : 'Oh, sorry,' when he saw his friend and retired.

'I want to see Mr. Jay,' Trevor said. 'Here! Call him back.'

Jeremy fetched Peregrine and seized the opportunity after a nod from Alleyn, to make his own escape. Peregrine, having already done his duty in that respect, brought no offering.

'Here!' Trevor said. 'What price that kid? My understudy. Is he going on to-night?'

'Yes. He's all right.' Peregrine said. 'Word perfect and going to give quite a nice show. You needn't worry.'

Trevor glowered at him. 'What about the billing, Mr. Jay? What about the programmes?'

'They've been slipped. "During your indisposition the part will be played——" You know?'

'Anything in the Press? They haven't brought me any papers,' the feeble voice grumbled. 'What's my agent doing? My mum says they don't want me to see the papers. Look, Mr. Jay——'

Alleyn said : 'You'll see the papers.'

Peregrine waited until Charles Random arrived. 'If you want me,' he then said to Alleyn, 'I'll be in the corridor.'

Random brought a number of dubious-looking comics. 'Knowing your taste in literature,' he said to Trevor. 'Not that I approve.'

Trevor indicated his tray. As Random approached him, he put on a sly look. 'Really,' he said, 'you shouldn't have troubled, Mr. Random.'

They stared at each other, their faces quite close together : Random's guarded, shuttered, wary and Trevor's faintly impertinent.

'You've got a bruise on your cheekbone,' Random said.

'That's nothing. You should see the rest.'

'Keep you quiet for a bit.'

'That's right.'

Random turned his head slowly and looked at Alleyn. 'Police taking a great interest, I see,' he said.

'Routine,' Alleyn rejoined. 'Merely routine.'

'At a high level.' Random drew back quickly from Trevor who giggled and opened his bundle of comics. 'Oh, fabulous,' he said. 'It's "Slash." *Z-z-z-z-yock!*' He became absorbed.

'That being that,' Random said, 'I shall bow myself off. Unless,' he added, 'the Superintendent is going to arrest me.'

Trevor, absorbed in his comic, said : 'You never know, do you? Cheerie-bye and ta.'

Random moved towards the door. 'Get better quick,' he murmured. Trevor looked up and winked. 'What do *you* think?' he said.

Random opened the door and disclosed Miss Bracey on the threshold.

They said : 'Oh, hallo, dear,' simultaneously and Random added : 'This gets more like a French farce every second. Everyone popping in and out. Wonderful timing.'

They both laughed with accomplishment and he went away.

Gertrude behaved as if she and Alleyn had never met. She said good-morning in a poised voice and clearly expected him to leave. He responded politely, indicated the bedside chair, called Trevor's attention to his visitor and himself withdrew to the window.

Miss Bracey said : 'You *have* been in the wars, dear, haven't you?' She advanced to the bedside and placed a small parcel on the table. Trevor lifted his face to hers, inviting an embrace. Their faces came together and parted and Miss Bracey sank into the chair.

'I mustn't stay too long : you're not to be tired,' she said. She was quite composed. Only that occasional drag at the corner of her mouth suggested to Alleyn that she had forti-

fied herself. She made the conventional inquiries as to
Trevor's progress and he responded with an enthusiastic
account of his condition. The worst case of concussion, he
said importantly, that they'd ever seen in the ward.

'Like what you read about,' he said. 'I was——'

He stopped short and for a moment looked puzzled. 'I was
having a bit of fun,' he began again. 'You know, Miss Bracey.
Just for giggles. I was having old Jobbins on.'

'Yes?' said Miss Bracey. 'That was naughty of you, dear,
wasn't it?'

'But,' Trevor said, frowning. 'You know. You were there.
Weren't you?' he added doubtfully.

She looked anywhere but at Alleyn. 'You're still confused,'
she said. 'You mustn't worry about it.'

'But weren't you, Miss Bracey? Down there? In front?
Weren't you?'

'I don't know when you mean, dear.'

'Neither do I. Not quite sure. But you were there.'

'I was in the downstairs foyer on Saturday night for a
minute or two,' she said loudly. 'As I told the superintendent.'

'Yeah, I know you were,' Trevor said. 'But where was I?'

'You didn't see me. You weren't there. Don't worry about
it.'

'I was. I was.'

'I'd better go,' she said and rose.

'No,' Trevor almost shouted. He brought his small fist
down in the bed tray and Jeremy's microcosms fell on their
faces. 'No! You've got to stay till I remember.'

'I think you should stay, Miss Bracey,' Alleyn said. 'Really.'

She backed away from the bed. Trevor gave a little cry.
'There!' he said, 'that's it. That's what you did. And you
were looking up—at him. Looking up and backing away and
kind of blubbing.'

'Trevor, be quiet. *Be quiet*. You don't know. You've forgotten.'

'Like what you're always doing, Miss Bracey. Chasing him.
That's right, isn't it, Miss Bracey? Tagging old Harry. You'd
come out of the downstairs lav. and you looked up and saw
him. And then the office door opened and it was Mr. Morris

and Mr. Knight and you done—you did a quick skarper, Miss
Bracey. And so did I! Back into the circle, smartly. I got it,
now,' Trevor said with infinite satisfaction. 'I got it.'

'How,' Alleyn said, 'did you know who he was? It must
have been dark up there.'

'Him? Harry? By his flash coat. Cripey, what a dazzler!'

'It's not true,' she gabbled and stumbled across the room.
She pawed at Alleyn's coat. 'It's not true. He doesn't know
what he's saying. It wasn't Harry. Don't listen. I swear it
wasn't Harry.'

'You're quite right,' Alleyn said. 'You thought it was
Harry Grove but it was Jobbins you saw on the landing.
Grove had given Jobbins his overcoat.'

Her hands continued for a second or two to scrabble at his
coat and then fell away. She looked into his face and her own
crumpled into a weeping mask.

Alleyn said: 'You've been having a bad time. An awful
time. But it *will* ease up. It won't always be as bad as this.'

'Let me go. Please let me go.'

'Yes,' he said. 'You may go now.'

And when she had gone, blowing her nose, squaring her
shoulders and making, instinctively he supposed, quite an
exit, he turned to Trevor and found him, with every sign of
gratification, deep in his comics.

'Do I have to see the others?' he asked. 'It's getting a bit of
a drag.'

'Are you tired?'

'No. I'm reading. His eye lit on Gertrude Bracey's parcel.
'Might as well look it over,' he said and unwrapped a tie.
'Where'd she dig that up?' he wondered and returned to his
comic.

'You are a young toad, aren't you?' Alleyn remarked. 'How
old are you, in heaven's name?'

'Eleven and three months,' Trevor said. He was helping
himself to a crystallised plum.

A slight rumpus broke out in the passage. Peregrine put his
head round the door. 'Marco and Harry are both here,' he
said and cast up his eyes.

When Alleyn joined him at the door he muttered: 'Marco

won't wait. He didn't want to come. And Harry says he got here first. He's up to his usual game,' Peregrine said, 'Knight-baiting.'

'Tell him to shut up and wait or I'll run him in.'

'I wish to heaven you would, at that.'

'Ask Knight to come along.'

'Yes. All right.'

'No sign of Conducis as yet?'

'No.'

When Marcus Knight came in he did not exhibit his usual signs of emotional disturbance: the flashing eye, the em-purpled cheek, the throbbing pulse and the ringing tone. On the contrary he was pale and as near to being subdued, Alleyn felt, as he could be. He laid his offering upon the now filled-to-capacity bed-tray. Fruit: in season and a gilded basket. He brusquely ran his fingers through Trevor's curls and Trevor immediately responded with a look that successfully combined Young Hamnet and Paul Dombey.

'Oh, Mr. Knight,' he said, 'you honestly shouldn't. You *are* kind. Grapes! How fab!'

A rather stilted bedside conversation followed during which Knight gave at least half his uneasy attention to Alleyn. Presently Trevor complained that he had slipped down in his bed and asked his illustrious guest to help him up. When Knight with an ill grace bent over him, Trevor gazed admiringly into his face and wreathed his arm round his neck. 'Just like the end of Act I come true,' he said, 'isn't it, Mr. Knight? I ought to be wearing the glove.'

Knight hurriedly extricated himself. A look of doubt crossed Trevor's face. '*The glove*,' he repeated. 'There's something about the real one—isn't there? Something?'

Knight looked a question at Alleyn who said: 'Trevor doesn't recall the latter part of his adventures in the theatre on Saturday night. I think Jay has explained that we hope one of you may help to restore his memory.'

'I *am* remembering more,' Trevor said importantly. 'I re-member hearing Mr. Knight in the office with Mr. Morris.'

Marcus Knight stiffened. 'I believe you are aware, Alleyn, that I left with Morris at about eleven.'

'He has told us so,' Alleyn said.

'Very well.' Knight stood over Trevor and imposed upon himself, evidently with difficulty, an air of sweet reasonableness. 'If,' he said, 'dear boy, you were spying about in front while I was with Mr. Morris in his office, and if you heard our voices, you doubtless also saw us leave the theatre.'

Trevor nodded.

'Precisely,' Knight said and spread his hands at Alleyn.

'*People come back*,' said the treble voice. Alleyn turned to find Trevor, the picture of puzzled innocence, frowning, his fingers at his lips.

'What the hell do you mean by that!' Knight ejaculated.

'It's part of what I can't remember. Somebody came back.'

'I really cannot imagine, Alleyn——' Knight began.

'*I—don't—think—I—want—to—remember.*'

'There you are, you see. This is infamous. The boy will be harmed. I absolutely refuse to take part in a dangerous and unwarranted experiment. Don't worry yourself, boy. You are perfectly right. Don't try to remember.'

'Why?'

'BECAUSE I TELL YOU,' Knight roared and strode to the door. Here he paused. 'I am an artist,' he said suddenly adopting a muted voice that was rather more awful than a piercing scream. 'In eight hours' time I appear before the public in a most exhausting role. Moreover I shall be saddled throughout a poignant, delicate and exacting scene with the incompetence of some revolting child-actor of whose excesses I am as yet ignorant. My nerves have been exacerbated. For the past forty-eight hours I have suffered the torments of hell. Slighted. Betrayed. Derided. Threatened. And now—this ludicrous, useless and impertinent summons by the police. Very well, Superintendent Alleyn. There shall be no more of it. I shall lodge a formal complaint. In the meantime—*Good-bye.*'

The door was opened with violence and shut—not slammed —with well-judged temperance.

'Lovely eggzit,' said Trevor yawning and reading his comic.

From outside in the corridor came the sound of applause, an oath, and rapidly retreating footsteps.

Alleyn reopened the door to disclose Harry Grove, gently

clapping his hands and Marcus Knight striding down the corridor.

Harry said, 'Isn't he *superb*? Honestly, you have to hand it to him.' He drew a parcel from his pocket. 'Baby roulette,' he said. 'Trevor can work out systems. Is it true that this is a sort of identification parade?'

'You could put it like that, I suppose,' Alleyn agreed.

'Do you mean,' Harry said, changing colour, 'that this unfortunate but nauseating little boy may suddenly point his finger at one of us and enunciate in ringing tones: "It all comes back to me. He dunnit".'

'That, roughly, is the idea.'

'Then I freely confess it terrifies me.'

'Come inside and get it over.'

'Very well. But I'd have you know that he's quite capable of putting on a false show of recovery smartly followed up by a still falser accusation. Particularly,' Harry said grimly, 'in my case when he knows the act would draw loud cheers and much laughter from all hands and the cook.'

'We'll have to risk it. In you go.'

Alleyn opened the door and followed Harry into the room.

Trevor had slithered down again in his bed and had dropped off into a convalescent cat-nap. Harry stopped short and stared at him.

'He looks, 'he whispered, 'as if he was quite a nice little boy, doesn't he? You'd say butter wouldn't melt. Is he really asleep or is it an act?'

'He dozes. If you just lean over him he'll wake.'

'It seems a damn' shame, I must say.'

'All the same I'll ask you to do it, if you will. There's a bruise on the cheekbone that mystifies us all. I wonder if you've any ideas. Have a look at it.'

A trolley jingled past the door and down the corridor. Outside on the river a barge hooted. Against the multiple shapeless voice of London, Big Ben struck one o'clock.

Harry put his parcel on the tray.

'Look at the bruise on his face. His hair's fallen across it. Move his hair back and look.'

Harry stooped over the boy and put out his left hand.

From behind the screen in the corner there rang out a single, plangent note. '*Twang.*'

Trevor opened his eyes, looked into Harry's face and screamed.

11. THE SHOW WILL GO ON

Harry Grove had given no trouble. When Trevor screamed he stepped back from him. He was sheet-white but he achieved a kind of smile.

'No doubt,' he had said to Alleyn, 'you will now issue the usual warning and invite me to accompany you to the nearest police station. May I suggest that Perry should be informed. He'll want to get hold of my understudy.'

And as this was the normal procedure it had been carried out.

So now, at Alleyn's suggestion they had returned, not to the Yard but to The Dolphin. Here for the first time Mr. Conducis kept company with the actors that he employed. They sat round the circle foyer while, down below, the public began to queue up for the early doors.

Peregrine had called Harry Grove's understudy and he and the new child actor were being rehearsed behind the fire curtain by the stage director.

'I think,' Alleyn said, 'it is only fair to give you all some explanation since each of you has to some extent been involved. These, as I believe, are the facts about Saturday night. I may say that Hartly Grove has admitted to them in substance.

'Grove left the theatre with Miss Meade and her party saying he would go to Canonbury and pick up his guitar. He had in fact brought his guitar to the theatre and had hidden it in a broom cupboard in the property room where it was found in the course of his illicit explorations, by Trevor. Grove got into his open sports car, drove round the block and parked the car in Phipps Passage. He re-entered the theatre by the pass-door while Mr. Morris and Mr. Knight were in the office. He may have been seen by Jobbins who would think nothing of it as Grove was in the habit of coming round for messages. He was not seen by Miss Bracey who mistook Jobbins for him because of the coat.

'Grove remained hidden throughout the rumpus about Trevor until, as he thought, the theatre was deserted except for Jobbins. At eleven o'clock he dialled his own number and let it ring just long enough for his wakeful neighbour to hear it and suppose it had been answered.

'It must have given him a shock when he heard Trevor, in the course of his fooling, pluck the guitar string. It was that scrap of evidence, by the way, when you remembered it, Jay, that set me wondering if Grove had left his instrument in the theatre and not gone to Canonbury. A moment later he heard the stage-door slam and thought, as Mr. Jay and Miss Dunne and Jobbins did, that Trevor had gone. But Trevor had sneaked back and was himself hiding and dodging about the auditorium. He saw Miss Bracey during his activities. Later, he tells us, he caught sight of Harry Grove and began to stalk him like one of his comic-strip heroes. We have the odd picture of Grove stealing to the broom-cupboard to collect his guitar, flitting like a shadow down a side passage, leaving the instrument ready to hand near the front foyer. Inadvertently, perhaps, causing it to emit that twanging sound.'

Peregrine gave a short ejaculation but when Alleyn looked at him said: 'No. Go on. Go on.'

'Having dumped the guitar Grove returns to the stairway from the stage to the circle, climbs it and waits for midnight in the upper box. And, throughout this performance, Trevor peeps, follows, listens, spies.

'At midnight Jobbins leaves his post under the treasure and goes downstairs to ring Police and Fire. Grove darts to the wall panel, opens it, uses his torch and manipulates the combination. There had been a lot of talk about the lock after the safe was installed and before the treasure was put into it. At that time it was not guarded and I think he may have done a bit of experimenting, after hours, on the possible "glove" combination.'

Winter Morris knocked on his forehead and groaned. Marcus Knight said: 'Oh God!'

'He opened the safe, removed the display-stand with its contents and I think only then realised he had engaged the switch that operates the front doors and the interior lighting. At that moment Trevor, who had stolen quite close (just as he did to me when I looked at the safe), said—it is his favourite noise at the moment—"z-z-z-z-yock. Slash."

'It must have given Grove a nightmarish jolt. He turned, saw the boy standing there in the darkened circle and bolted into the foyer clutching his loot. Only to find Jobbins rushing upstairs at him. He pushed the dolphin pedestal over and down. As Jobbins fell, Trevor came out of the circle and saw it all. Trevor is still not quite clear here but he thinks he screamed. He knows Grove made for him and he remembers plunging down the central steps in the circle. Grove caught him at the bottom. Trevor says—and this may be true—that he snatched the display-stand and threw it overboard before Grove could recover it. The last thing he remembers now, is Grove's face close to his own. It was the sight of it this morning, near to him, in association with the single twang effected by my colleague, Inspector Fox, who was modestly concealed behind a screen, that bridged the gap in Trevor's memory.'

' "*A faint perfume*",' Peregrine said loudly, ' "*and a most melodious twang*".'

'That's Aubrey, isn't it?' Alleyn asked. 'But shouldn't it be a *curious* perfume? Or not?'

Peregrine stared at him. 'It is,' he said, 'and it should. You're dead right and why the hell it's eluded me I cannot imagine. I heard it, you know, when Jobbins was hunting the boy.'

Emily said: 'And, of course, it's a single plangent note that brings down the curtain on *The Cherry Orchard*.'

'You see, Emily?' said Peregrine.

'I see,' she said.

'What the hell *is* all this?' Knight asked plaintively.

'I'll get on with it,' Alleyn said. 'After a brief struggle Grove, now desperate, rids himself of Trevor by precipitating him into the stalls. He hears Hawkins at the stage-door and once again bolts into the circle foyer. He knows Hawkins will come straight through to the front and he hasn't time to retrieve his guitar, get the key, unlock, unbolt and unbar the pass-door. There lies the body, dressed in his own outlandish coat. He strips off the coat, takes the scarf from the pocket to protect his own clothes and re-enters the darkened circle, to all intents and purposes, Jobbins. Hawkins, now in the stalls, sees him, addresses him as Jobbins, and is told to make the tea. He goes backstage. Grove has time, now, to bundle the body back into the coat, fetch his guitar and let himself out. He drives to Chelsea and gets there fully equipped to be the life and soul of Miss Meade's party.'

'And he *was*, you know,' Destiny said. 'He *was*.'

She clasped her hands, raised them to her face and began to weep. Knight gave an inarticulate cry and went to her.

'Never mind, my darling,' he said. 'Never mind. We must rise above. We must forget.'

Mr. Conducis cleared his throat. Destiny threw him a glance that was madly eloquent of some ineffable generalisation. He avoided it.

'The motive,' Alleyn said, 'was, of course, theft. Harry Grove knew a great deal about Mrs. Constantia Guzman. He knew that if the treasure was stolen she would give a fortune under the counter for it.'

Knight, who was kissing Destiny's hands, groaned slightly and shuddered.

'But I think he knew more about her than that,' Alleyn went on. 'She was a guest of Mr. Conducis's six years ago, in the *Kalliope* when the yacht was wrecked off Cape St. Vincent. At that time, six years ago, Grove was going through a bad patch and taking any jobs he could get. Lorry driving. Waiter in a strip-joint. And steward.'

He turned to Mr. Conducis. 'I was about to ask you yesterday when Grove himself interrupted us: was he a steward on board the *Kalliope*?'

Nobody looked at Mr. Conducis.

'Yes,' he said.

'How did that come about?'

'He brought himself to my notice. His father was a distant and unsatisfactory connection of mine. I considered this to be no reason for employing him but he satisfied me of his usefulness.'

'And he sold you the glove and documents?'

'Yes.'

'For thirty pounds?'

'I have already said so.'

Marcus Knight, whose manner towards Mr. Conducis had been an extraordinary blend of hauteur and embarrassment now said loudly : 'I don't believe it.'

'You don't believe what, Mr. Knight?' Alleyn asked.

'That he was aboard that—vessel.'

'You were scarcely there long enough to notice,' Mr. Conducis said coldly.

'I was there long enough——' Marcus began on a high note and dried. 'But no matter,' he said. 'No matter.'

Alleyn stood up and so did everybody else except Mr. Conducis.

'I won't keep you any longer,' Alleyn said. 'I would like to say how sorry I am that this has happened and how much I hope your play and your theatre will ride out the storm. I'm sure they will. I'm taking an unorthodox line when I tell you that Grove has said he will not contest the accusations of assault. He will, he states, admit to taking the treasure, overturning the bronze dolphin and struggling with the boy. He will plead that these were instinctive, self-protective actions committed without intention to kill. This defence, if adhered to, will mean a short trial with little evidence being called and I think, not a great deal of publicity.'

Little Morris said : 'Why's he taking that line? Why isn't he going all out for an acquittal?'

'I asked him that. He said he was suddenly sick of the whole thing. And he added,' Alleyn said with a curious twist in his voice, 'that he thought it would work out better that way for William Shakespeare, Mr. Peregrine Jay and The Dolphin.'

He saw then that the eyes of all the company had filled with tears.

When they had gone he turned back to Mr. Conducis.

'You said, sir, that you had something you wished to tell me.'

'I have something I wish to ask you. Has he said anything about me?'

'A little. He said you owed each other nothing.'

'I will pay for his defence. Let him know that.'

'Very well.'

'Anything else?'

'He said that as far as he is concerned—this was his phrase —he would keep the glove over his knuckles and I could tell you so. He asked me to give you this.'

Alleyn gave Mr. Conducis an envelope. He was about to put it in his pocket but changed his mind, opened it and read the short message it contained. He held out the paper to Alleyn.

'It seems,' Alleyn read, 'that we are both the victims of irresistible impulse. Which leads me to the ludicrous notion that you will, as they say, "understand." You needn't worry. I'm bored with it all and intend to drop it.'

Down below someone whistled, crossed the foyer and slammed the front doors. The Dolphin was very quiet.

'He clung to the raft,' said Mr. Conducis, 'and tried to climb aboard it. He would have overturned it. I smashed his knuckles with the writing-desk and thought I'd drowned him. His hands were gloved. They curled and opened and slid away in their own blood. Nobody saw. He has blackmailed me ever since.'

II

'They are not cancelling,' said Winter Morris, giving the box office plans a smart slap. 'And there's very little publicity. I can't understand it.'

'Could it be the hand of Conducis?'

'Could be, dear boy. Could be. Power,' said little Morris.

orrupts didn't somebody say? It may do: but it comes in
ndy, dear boy, it comes in handy.'

He ran upstairs to his office and could be heard singing.

'All the same,' Peregrine said to Emily, 'I hope it's *not*
e hand of Conducis. I hope it's The Dolphin. And us. You
ow,' he went on, 'I'm sure he stayed behind to unburden
mself to Alleyn.'

'What of?'

'Who can tell! I've got a feeling it was something to do
th his yacht. He's behaved so very oddly whenever it came
.'

'Perhaps,' Emily speculated idly, 'you reminded him of it.
at morning.'

'I? How?'

'Oh,' she said vaguely, 'people drowning, you know, or
arly drowning, or hanging on to bits of wreckage. Perhaps
was glad he rescued you. Or something.'

'You never know,' Peregrine said.

He put his arm round her and she leant against him. They
d become engaged and were happy.

They looked round them at the upsidedown cupids, the
yatids, the portrait of Mr. Adolphus Ruby now promin-
ly displayed and the graceful double flight of stairs. The
onze dolphins were gone and where the safe had been was a
ontage of the Grafton portrait overlaid by Kean, Garrick,
ddons, Irving and the present great Shakespearians all very
citingly treated by Jeremy Jones.

'If you belong to the theatre,' Peregrine said. 'You belong
erly.'

They went out to the portico.

Here they found an enormous Daimler and a chauffeur.
was like a recurrent symbol in a time play and for a moment
regrine felt as if Mr. Conducis had called again to take
n to Drury Place.

'Is that Dessy's car?' Emily said.

But it wasn't Destiny Meade in the back seat. It was an
ormous and definitely hideous lady flashing with dia-
onds, lapped in mink and topped with feathers.

She tapped on the glass and beckoned.

When Peregrine approached she let down the window an
in a deep voice, addressed him.

'You can perhaps assist me. I have this morning arrive
from America. I vish to inquire about the Shakespearia
Relics. I am Mrs. Constantia Guzman.'

Ngaio Marsh

'The finest writer in the English language of the pure, classical, puzzle whodunit. Among the Crime Queens, Ngaio Marsh stands out as an Empress.' *Sun.* 'Her work is as near flawless as makes no odds: character. plot, wit, good writing and sound technique.' *Sunday Times.* 'The brilliant Ngaio Marsh ranks with Agatha Christie and Dorothy Sayers.' *Times Literary Supplement*

Clutch of Constables

Colour Scheme

Death and the Dancing Footman

Death in Ecstasy

Died in the Wool

Hand in Glove

Scales of Justice

Tied Up in Tinsel

When in Rome

 Fontana Books

Agatha Christie

The most popular and prolific writer of detective fiction ever known, her intricately plotted whodunits are enjoyed by armchair crime-solvers everywhere.

Elephants Can
 Remember
Evil Under the Sun
Dumb Witness
Death Comes as the
 End
Peril at End House
Appointment with
 Death
The Murder of
 Roger Ackroyd
Hallowe'en Party

Murder on the
 Orient Express
The Sittaford
 Mystery
Destination
 Unknown
Endless Night
Five Little Pigs
Nemesis
Passenger to
 Frankfurt
The Clocks

and many others

Agatha Christie also writes novels of romance and suspense under the name

Mary Westmacott

Giant's Bread
Absent in the Spring

The Burden
The Rose and the Yew
 Tree

 Fontana Books

Rex Stout

'His stories of Nero Wolfe, that amiable epicure, always provide excitement, wit, unflagging interest and ingenuity.' *Books of Today*. 'If there is anyone in the civilised world who is not acquainted with Nero Wolfe, Mr. Stout's large, over-bearing investigator, here is the opportunity to plug a shameful gap . . .' *Evening Standard*. 'It is impossible for Rex Stout to be anything but supremely readable.' *Guardian*

Out Goes She

Death of a Doxy

The Final Deduction

The Mother Hunt

 Fontana Books

Fontana Books

Fontana is a leading paperback publisher of fiction and non-fiction, with authors ranging from Alistair MacLean, Agatha Christie and Desmond Bagley to Solzhenitsyn and Pasternak, from Gerald Durrell and Joy Adamson to the famous Modern Masters series.

In addition to a wide-ranging collection of internationally popular writers of fiction, Fontana also has an outstanding reputation for history, natural history, military history, psychology, psychiatry, politics, economics, religion and the social sciences.

All Fontana books are available at your bookshop or newsagent; or can be ordered direct. Just fill in the form and list the titles you want.